THE TREE OF KNOWLEDGE

THE LAST ARCHIVIST

THE TREE OF
KNOWLEDGE

BOOK THE FIRST

J.F. STREICH

NEW DEGREE PRESS

COPYRIGHT © 2020 J.F. STREICH

All rights reserved.

THE TREE OF KNOWLEDGE
The Last Archivist
Book the First

ISBN		
	978-1-64137-941-0	*Paperback*
	978-1-64137-746-1	*Kindle Ebook*
	978-1-64137-747-8	*Ebook*

For Mom, Dad, Matt, and Bryan.

CONTENTS

———

Life
is the jungle:
a cathedral feeling of wonder,
astonishment, and sublime devotion,
which fill and elevate the mind.

AUTHOR'S NOTE

"No man steps in the same river twice—for it is not the same river, and he is not the same man."
—HERACLITUS OF EPHESUS, 500 BC

Three days after taking the law school entrance exam, the hot sun hung low and my legs were numb. I'd been riding a temperamental palomino horse for hours through the sopping tobacco fields of Cuba's Viñales Valley when Norlys, my guide, stopped at the crest of a hill. In front of us lay a vast expanse of leafy green and terracotta. Norlys pulled the reins to face me and asked a simple question. *"¿Quieres saber que pasará ya*—do you want to know what happens now?"

My answer surprised both of us. "Not so much," I said and shrugged. That was the moment, staring into clouds of green and gold, I stopped worrying about the future. I finally put into practice the words I had read from those great men and women. I simply *was*. Several hours later, belly filled with *langostino cubano*, this book began.

I grew up half-blind, redheaded, and overweight in a split household where fantasy, science fiction, and sports were my escape from two recessions, insecurity, and a family history of brain illness. Lazy in one eye, clear in the other—the only life I knew was split. From the outside I appeared like an intelligent, sporty extrovert with many friends. On the inside I was a fraud with an arrogant, jaded outlook on life.

That's why I was a loner in college, a solo start-up founder thereafter, and why *The Tree of Knowledge* and I have an odd relationship. I wrote it in secret to escape my work, my anxiety, and the uncertain outside world.

The moment I stopped surviving and began fighting was the moment I picked up the pen. Art and writing have been around for as long as human beings, but not enough people talk about art and writing therapy.

The moment I began writing seriously was like walking into a room and turning on a light. Or pulling the rocks out from a dammed up river. How many times can you talk out the same problem before realizing it's not helping? Instead, I wrote myself a raft and floated down toward the sea.

Fortunately for me, this raft led me backpacking through Mexico, on twenty-five-mile hikes in the north of Spain, and road trips up, down, and across America.

Slowly, mile by mile, the ideas behind *The Tree of Knowledge* crystallized. I want to make a few things starkly clear. First, it does not matter your faith, profession, or skin color. Whether or not you are reading this book from Jordan, Jacksonville, or Japan, all human beings want the same things— freedom, loving connection, a sense of purpose—that we have for eighty thousand years.

The second is more controversial. During my travels, I noticed something similar about the environment. The hikes in San Sebastián were not so different than Monterey, California (nor was the wine). The sand on a beach in Greece felt like the pebbles in Narraganset. I made these travels expecting every experience to be different and came back scratching my head about how wrong I was.

And I came back with a blizzard of questions.

And I came back with a novel.

True courage, I've learned, comes from believing in yourself despite uncertainty. That is why I wrote this novel and why it takes place where it does. There is so much talk of "the end of the world," and among it, I am concerned about our beginning another. My hope is, through this story, people will realize everything is uncertain, and vying for power is both a coward's game and a fool's. I know because I was one.

The Buddhists say that "the world is like a burning house, constantly being torn down and rebuilt again." I quite like that. If it's all gone soon anyway, why not try what you love? That's why I ditched law school and began this novel—to stop fighting the flood. To dance with my secret mistress. To leave my contribution to Madame Culture. To plant the *Tree of Knowledge*.

I hope you enjoy.

~ JFS
Austin, Texas. 2020

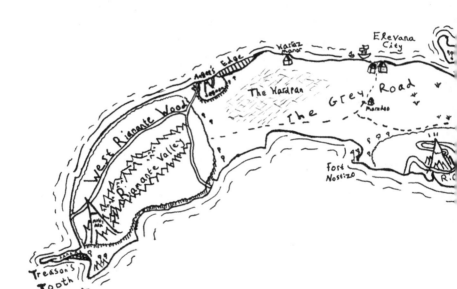

VÄNA

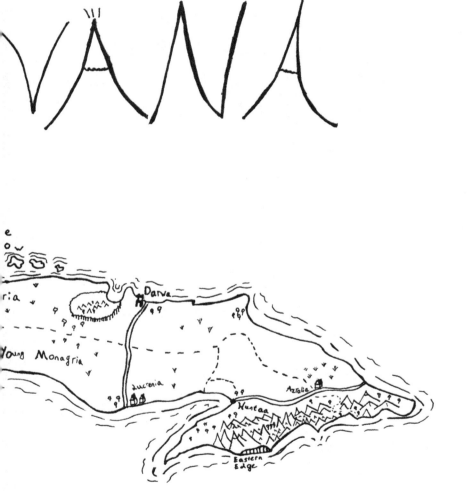

The World of
Aerth

KINGDOMS FALL

◇◇◇◇◇◇

The great city of Termara sizzled beneath a riot of sun. Burnt and smoldering, the world's greatest city hung with smoke, which gave way in shreds above ruined buildings. The raw, cloudless, blue sky stung Corie's eyes like salt water.

The Wraeth always came in summer, but Corie had never seen anything like this. Sweat clung to the fuzz of her hair and ran down the warp of her dress.

It must be a dream, she thought, *a painting, a photograph. The fire is not real. It must! It must!*

The top floor of Corie's home had a splendid view of towers jutting out from miles of unbroken stucco roofs. Beyond them lay the mountains.

Eleventy-four Hobbema Hill, her darling home, roasting. The young woman clung to the window with cherry fingers. She closed her eyes, panting. The sandstone shutters felt cool against her cheek. She hummed a song to herself, one her mother had sung to her, and recalled an early childhood memory.

She stood at the top window of Hobbema Hill. Her house was thin and soaring, twelve windows in its portico. Its foundation was lined with vines while the rest were splotched from sea breeze. Beneath the house on a hill grew sunflowers, ten feet tall. With the shutters pushed open, she could see a smattering of orange lichen rooftops. Puffins skimmed the battlements, and envelopes of vapor sheathed the steeple. Behind that, the ocean. Nearby, the Red Mountain.

A pillar crumbled down Hobbema Hill, shaking Corie's eyes open.

She rubbed disbelief from her eyes. The world was a burning house. She turned north toward the once-great sandstone city. Hot-air balloons polluted the air, hanging over the mountains, in them people fled into clouds of smoke.

Imprecise cries and horrible pleas emitted from newly minted widows and orphans. The few who remained had taken to the roofs to avoid the low-hanging smoke—pure, viscous, and inky. Wraethfire had poisoned the air.

A mewl, less distant, reminded her of a helpless fox pinned in a trap. Corie stood on a chair, looking out her lunette window. One shadowy creature glided, like a crow, toward a lone infant priman girl. Quick as steam, the creature disappeared behind ovens of fire.

Corie opened her lips and made to scream, but the heat burned her voice away.

Not to panic, Corie! Not to Panic. Panic is manic.

She rubbed her eyes. Sweat limped down her cheeks, evaporating before it hit the wooden floor.

Like the hiss of wind, the darkest figure stepped forward from a hill of fire. A Wraeth, cloaked but smoke-like, stood over the girl. The tips of his hair, white as sun, showed as he knelt beside her.

The little girl backed away, wailing for her mother.

With silent boots, the figure sashayed closer. A pillar crumpled from behind. The fire seemed to be as afraid of the Wraeth as the girl. It receded around them. In his hand was a weapon unlike any Corie had ever seen. The blade, a sable black crystal with pulsing purple veins, was so sharp it disappeared when viewed side-on. No priman could craft such a weapon.

Corie, a music instructor, had heard a sad song of it before, "Deathsword Sings Forever." She stepped away from the window, biting her lip. Then, a howl cracked the air from below.

The Wraeth swung his weapon with artistic madness. All of the sudden, the Deathsword was met by another, a challenger.

The Lady Belladonna!

Corie had never seen a warrior so gorgeous and strong and heroically armored.

The Wraeth threw the black blade in a sharp cut toward Belladonna's right knee, left knee, and right knee again, yet Belladonna avoided each one, dancing from side to side. She jabbed her longsword forward and purple sparks sizzled around the Wraeth's blade like boiling water as he parried her blow. Now off balance, Belladonna could not avoid a hard cut straight through the armor on her left side. She winced backward and the Wraeth gave her no time to recover.

He pressed closer to the backpedaling lady, and his every thrust seemed to be increasing in force. Belladonna kicked over a flaming, half-broken table and swung her blade at the Wraeth. More purple sparks flew as the crystal blade shimmied down Belladonna's blade closer and closer to her grip. The Wraeth pressed harder. They were now only a few feet from the whimpering child again. Lady Belladonna replied with a forceful lurch, sending the Wraeth back a few feet but also giving him momentum. He stepped up onto a pile of broken rubble and lifted his sword high over his head with two hands.

Corie squeezed her eyes closed. Behind her eyelids she saw smoke billowing into her home from the flames. Rubble hung where once were lush vines of kousa and magnolia. *Wake up, Corie,* she thought. *Please, wake up!*

Then a paralyzing clash of steel on crystal plowed through the air.

This was no dream.

Crumbling tent rocks, burning plateaus, death was everywhere. Somehow, the Red Mountain in the distance stood smaller than before and farther away. Corie squinted through the smoke.

All that remained of Lady Belladonna was her marvelous armor. The Wraeth stood over it, still as an ancient relic, but larger as if he had consumed her. Three others, slightly less magnificent, had joined him. He, the largest of the four, wore a diamond-shaped stone on his wrist, glowing a vicious blue. They took down their hoods. An inky cloud of oil swirled above their shoulders, suspended where a priman's head would be.

Firmly grounded in burning soot, the Wraeth clenched the pulsing Deathsword. With his other hand, he fingered the blue gem imperiously. Deep whistling came, not from his mouth, but from the aerth, like a whale song.

Water rushed across the plains in waves—not a flood or an effort to douse the fires. Unmistakably, as waves crashed around their knees, the sea had come to swallow them whole.

The Kingdom of Termara, once the world's greatest city, ended with its embers. Where Termara once struck the sky was now the ocean. What remained of the ruined city drifted like a sinking sailboat out to sea.

Two hours later, Corie was stowed aboard a fleeing balloon, like the others, floating away from her life. From below she heard a song, deep and harrowing, jutting through the air—"The Ode to Irkalla."

CHAPTER 1

THE RICHEST MAN
IN ELEVANA

"They came for me the day of graduation. The groundskeeper rolled by me at my favorite spot on the lawn. I should have noticed the way his eyes darted around, as if waiting for something to happen. Heavy footsteps echoed until they surrounded me," Aeron huffed. "I was only twelve years old, barely even graduated from Prep, but they sent five huge Paladins. Guards of Longleath—"

"Ye don't need to be schoolin' me on Paladin, boy," mumbled Lamark as he stoked the fire, which heated the aequipher in his shop.

Silence had never been so loud. For four days straight, after escaping that wretched prison, Aeron had stared at his family's Journal, the Mason Grimoire, admiring its longhand notes and stories, well-drawn sketches and cartoons, and smatters of blood and tea and water. He spoke to no one. He had lost his family, his future, even his name—everything save the Journal in his hand.

"The reason," Aeron scowled, "I mention it is because they weren't from the school. They were city Paladin, and high-ranking ones, I'd guess. Named no crime, but sure made a big mess of binding and dragging me into a building I'd never been inside before, and then we descended the stairs into a place with barely any light. The blossoms hadn't even begun to bud then. Now they're wilting from the heat, and I didn't see the sun until half a moon ago."

"Yer lucky," Lamark scoffed. "I once spent an entire year, during the sailing days, locked in the holding cell of a ship without even a candle. Thought I'd gone blind." He ran a hand through his receding hairline.

"Well, I did have a small candle, thanks to the strangest little man." Aeron scratched at the curls of his short black hair. One or two curls at the top had hints of flax.

"Eh?" Lamark grunted, folding his newsleaf in a stack. The paper held the crest of Elevana City, not Longleath, so the subtle pit in Aeron's belly relaxed. Far worse criminals were here than he.

Lamark rose from his seat and turned his back to Aeron. The shirt's salt stains stretched across his wide back that took up half the space behind the counter. Across the entire wall above him were bottles. Some were empty, some were filled with variously colored liquids or sands, and others held small gears, trinkets, and models. Up close there seemed to be no reason to the ordering, but as Lamark reached up and moved three uncorked bottles filled with a pungent orange spice to the center, Aeron could tell the Blue Bat had a method to its madness. Lamark knew what needed selling and what would garner the most profit.

When he turned back and leaned over the counter, Aeron resumed his story.

"Only a couple of days in, a dull pounding commenced from the opposite side of the wall. First it came softly and then louder until finally I smelled a cloud of dust as a knob of stone tumbled onto my mattress. Horrified, I backed away from the wall and strained my eyes outside the cell. No guards.

"Then another stone tumbled and a small man, about my size, flopped inside. When he hollered at the stone pressed in his back, I thought we were goners, but no one came. He grabbed me and I could tell how frail and gaunt he was, even before he pulled out matches from his robe to light a tiny candle.

"I remember wondering if I had lost my mind. I'd been refusing the food they were bringing until hearing my charge. I had no idea! Can you imagine being locked up and not knowing why?"

Lamark grinned as if it had happened to him many times when his hair had been more orange and less silver. The shop-keep spread his arms outward and pressed against the sink. Lamark's huge steps shook the bottles on the wall, and Aeron thought for a moment they would all come crashing down. An inch of Lamark's peach-colored belly poked out from beneath the soiled front of his shirt. He ran a hand through his hair, the man's most redeemable quality, and left it press-ing over his lips as though bored.

"But this man, wild-eyed and strange as he was—almost as if he'd come through that wall from five hundred years ago—knew more about me than I did. Down to every little detail, all the crummy things that had happened."

"Tell me, Aeron," asked Lamark, now more interested. "What be those 'crummy' things?"

The boy sealed his lips, and his throat choked closed. His scalp itched and he longed for a bath to scrape the dirt off his body. He knew what he must look like with his short curls a greasy mess of black. Aeron's sunken green eyes anchored his grim, soiled face. Ribs bulging behind his skin left him looking more emaciated than a stray dog. After a time he swallowed and went on.

"But he knew why I'd been put into prison. They thought I had—"

"Did ye?" broke in Lamark. "Did ye have a hand in killin' yer granddad and sister?"

The boy froze.

The shop fell silent as the seafloor. Lamark picked up a nail and the newsleaf from behind the counter and lifted the bar flap. Aeron remained while Lamark walked toward the door and passed an expensive couch on sale made of Indoshinese leather and a large glass-covered case of foreign weapons and armor.

He stopped at the door. Unfolding the newsleaf, a bright yellow paper fell face down to the floor. Lamark grumbled to himself. Too lazy to bend all the way, he lifted the leaf halfway with his toes and reached over to grab it. Lamark grabbed a small hammer from a side table next to the weapons case. He smoothed the paper against the door, pressed the sharp side of the nail to the top of the yellow sheet and pounded it three times into the wood.

When Lamark stepped to the side, the flier became visible and Aeron read it.

WANTED FOR MURDER, FRAUD, AND CONSPIRACY OF TREASON...

The face sketched beneath the words unhinged Aeron's jaw. Dark brown curls fell over a round forehead with slightly squinted eyes, a small nose, and thin lips like a slash in the face, all curled in a devious grin.

It was his own.

Lamark wore a devious grin. "I know ye, *Aeron Mason*. Maybe not so much as yer crazy friend, but I know things about ye."

"I don't know what you're talking about," Aeron lied, diverting his gaze. Lamark could have him arrested and tossed back in jail. Then he'd never clear his family name. Nor would he find the old man who'd told him about his fate as the last archivist and that he would someday save the largest, longest standing library on aerth—the Tree of Knowledge.

"Tell me the rest of yer story, the whole story, and I'll tell ye how well I knew yer old man."

"Loo? My father was a bucket of scum," Aeron spat. "I shouldn't be surprised you've met."

"Watch yerself talkin' to me, *boy*." The grim, black-eyed merchant scowled. He gave Aeron no chance to reply and bounded intimidatingly closer. "Me and my Waeve own every Blue Bat in Elevana. That's somethin' like fifty markets on one island. I traveled to each of the Four Corners and used what I learned to build that house my lady and I always wanted. If ye want to do business, ye best show some respect." Lamark's eyes glowed with menace and his breath stunk of sprig smoke. He spoke the Mother Tongue but in a broken way, and lazy.

"Fine," Aeron agreed, "but you're not the only man in Elevana who will pay well for these." He pulled a heartfruit from the sack. His hand, warmed by the heat of its outer layer, looked tiny behind the heart-sized gem. Inside, something swished and thumped infinitesimally, like a baby kicking.

"Half the bag has matured to stone, and we both know how much those are worth, but you're not giving me any reason to trust you," said Aeron. In truth the heartfruit held more value than ten chests of gold. Maybe even enough to entice a shopkeeper to let him go free.

"Do ye need a reason?" demanded Lamark in something of an annoyed manner. He passed back to the other side of the bar and dropped the bar flap.

"What I'm trying to figure out is why such a kind old man would send me to *you*."

The shopkeep opened one of the drawers and pulled out the biggest sprigar Aeron had ever seen, almost the size of a banana. Holding it between his thumb and forefinger, Lamark held the green paper sprigar into the flames, seeming not to feel the heat. The end ignited and Lamark shoved the dry side into his mouth and sucked, puckering his lips to get it burning.

The old man said I would find a friend at The Blue Bat... so far this one seems like a lazy sod who only helps himself.

Lamark blew a ring of smoke toward Aeron and leaned his huge head forward. Aeron coughed and lowered his green-eyed gaze, scanning the market's scuffed floorboards and spinning jennies while shifting side to side. Then he shifted his gaze out the window. The squinty morning had dissipated into a dark afternoon with skies cloudy like a nightmare. The haversack clung to Aeron's chest, sticky with humidity. He reached inside and pulled out one of the still edible heartfruit.

"You know where he is. Don't you? He trusts you, and this man did more than help me break out of prison. He taught me about things I never knew existed, assured me they will help me clear my name and my family's, and pointed me toward a shipping marinaer sailing for Elevana. But he had no way of knowing I would find the grove… I'm willing to trust you, Lamark, but I need you to tell me you know where he is."

"M'boy—" Lamark said shaking his head. "It sounds like yer friend is dead."

Aeron's thin lips split wide. He couldn't believe it. He refused to believe the only person who could help him had died—like the rest of them.

"I'm sorry, laddy," said Lamark, rummaging through a drawer.

"Well then," said Aeron, turning his back to the man, "I guess I'll be going." He gathered up the haversack.

"Ye might want to take a look at this message first…"

CHAPTER 2

THE GRAPPLE

◇◇◇◇◇◇

Lamark held up a rolled leaf of paper. When he unstrung it, Aeron recognized the thin, spidery script at once. It belonged to the old man.

"Had no idea what to make of it at the time."

Aeron leaned forward to grab the letter, but Lamark had quick hands and snatched it away.

"He meant it for me. Give it here." Still yet to have his teenage growth spurt, Aeron reached on his tip toes for the parchment but Lamark lifted it out of reach.

"No," he growled. "Rest of yer story first."

Aeron sighed and lowered his short arms. Hunger took over, and Aeron passed the heartfruit over to Lamark. The shopkeep held it up to his nose and sniffed at the fruity aroma. His eyes rolled back. Aeron cleared his throat and Lamark pulled open the brown latch above the aequipher's waterbox. Steam billowed up like smoke. He dropped the whole heartfruit inside and swiftly closed the cover.

The rest of Aeron's story seemed to fall apart almost as quickly. After escaping together, he'd hoped the old man would be his teacher through his teenage years, until he had skills enough to go out on his own. But here in Elevana, children his age were bought and sold. There were no orphanages, only child labor. If he were caught, it meant servitude for life.

"In the original plan, we followed the tunnel together. He must've been digging it for years, seeing how long it stretched, but on the day of—something happened. The time came and went and no sign of him. When I crawled to his cell, I saw the backs of three Paladin standing over his bed. Each wore one of those new masks, the ones made of recycled sprigleaves. I couldn't hear the whispers, but they hissed like bad news. Then they left in a storm, and the candle went with them.

"I dropped into the cell and rumbled around the pitch darkness until I found my way under the old man's bed frame. I waited for a few minutes in silence, too afraid the Paladin might be listening from the hall. I thought about going back for the original plan but then a low grumbling grew and scared me stiff as one of the men thrust the door off its track. Then the bed cart's wheels squealed and rolled. Uphill! I couldn't see behind the rumpled sheets, but I could feel it. My heart was exploding at that point. If they discovered me, I was done for and…"

Aeron paused and scratched his big ears. He pulled at the left one, which had been damaged by his drunken father at a young age, as if considering whether to trust the orangutan-like merchant.

"The Masons, our family line, would go extinct—dead in the pits. But they didn't! We paused and I heard grunting, which almost gave me an attack of the heart, but then I felt the cart get far lighter and we took off again.

"By the time I tasted fresh air and heard wind rustling leaves, my nails were bloody as a butcher's from the gnawing. We weren't outside for long before—" Aeron whistled and motioned his hand high to low in an arc. "My belly floated like butterflies and then—" he clapped, palm to fist. "*Bam!* Without those sheets I would've broke in two, but I wiggled out into that cold water, and found the surface.

"The cart was made of cheap wood, the kind they would rather toss than clean, I guess. No surprise. I clung to that split hunk of wood until it floated downstream to the city docks. And now, back to the plan, a ship was waiting there. Nothing huge, and older than you'd normally see in the Longleath Channel, which was why it hadn't left yet. If all had gone according to plan, we would've been cooked! But the marinaer had some kind of mechanical thing that pushed the shove time.

"Captain didn't say a word about the sopping hair or me being half-starkers. My way'd been paid."

"Hmm," began Lamark, "now 'ang on a moment. I remember… ye stumbled into this 'ere shop before close, near naked. And ye were asking fer…"

"The Merchant of Herraz."

Lamark turned away from Aeron. He rose from his seat and pulled the heartfruit from the aequifer's waterbox. It had split open in two clean halves. Lamark plated a half for Aeron. From his own, he cut off a sliver and set it aside.

"Nobody's called me that in 'alf a lifetime. That's when I met your father."

"When? You don't seem like the kind of guy who'd spend time in Longleath, no offense. How'd you—"

"Not in Longleath. Not since a long time ago. And not saying more until ye explain this…" He held up a piece of heartfruit between his huge fingers.

"I have to admit," Aeron said, taking a seat at one of the bamboo barstools. He licked his thumb and forefinger and then smoothed down his brown eyebrows. "All this talking's making be thirsty. And I've always wanted to taste hardwine."

Lamark looked cross but then scanned the wall of glass bottles with all sorts of fruits at their bottoms.

"I ain't goin' to tell you not to drink it, but I would be careful with the drinkin' till yer grown. Drink can do strange things to kids."

He poured a small glass for Aeron, who drank a bit and promptly coughed a fit.

"Woah," Aeron said and took a bite of the heartfruit. His round face made a twisted grin and his wide nose scrunched. "Weird."

Tasting the heartfruit, a rush of energy pulsed through him, as if a best friend had called to him from outside. Without a word, he swung the haversack's leather strap over one shoulder and jumped off the stool toward the exit.

The double doors swung closed behind him as he stepped into the strong, late afternoon sun. A palm tree had grown in a sideways J-shape to catch the light, and Aeron hopped up on it, Lamark following him as he went.

"The old man told me that if I showed the Merchant of Herraz this, you would help me right away," said Aeron, clutching the Mason Grimoire. "You didn't seem to care one bit, and I thought I had the wrong man. That botched everything, and I sort-of fell in a rotten way. And there's no kids here. Near everyone who's free is old, and they treated me like an urchin blatantly up to some skullduggery."

"Smart folk," Lamark sniggered.

"So I started west. That's where my granddad always talked about, but I was already half-starving before I got here. The walk, in that heat, with near nothing to eat? I know they say wild things live west of Elevana City, but…"

"Started seein' things, I reckon?"

"Not just seeing them, Lamark, but hearing them. This humming sound, like heat haze if you could hear it or hot metal vibrating. Maybe it's because of my bad ear? Ever since Loo shattered my eardrum with that note, I've heard strange things at strange times. I dunno, but there came a point where it was so loud and I was so delirious that I had to sit down in the shade of a big tree. When I woke up..."

Aeron felt around the lumps on the inside of the canvas haversack. He unstrung the drawstring that fed through a pair of grommets at the mouth of the pack.

"I'd never seen anything like it. I was sitting in a grove with the canopy above like a completely interwoven blanket of greenery. There were hundreds of them! Thousands! Speckling like a mad river of stars."

His fingers rubbed the ridges on the Mason Grimoire's leather spine.

"I was lucky that they had let me keep the Journal in prison, and that the pages don't mind water... because I never would've gotten these without it. I flicked through the pages to something from my great great great granddad and saw a diagram for a contraption he'd used to harvest honeycomb."

Aeron released the Journal and instead felt around the contents for one of the overripe heartfruit. Once a hearftfruit hardens it can no longer be eaten, but it can serve as fuel. Aeron pulled one from inside and held it up toward Lamark. It was the size of a small melon, and had nacarat colored skin.

"Ah Heartfruit..." Lamark said, stroking his chin. "Such a strange bounty. If ye leave 'em on the vine long enough, they'll 'arden into stone and ye feed 'em to trains, lorries, and buildings for power. If ye harvest 'em early on, a couple bites'll keep yer belly—well, a normal man's at least—quiet for days." Lamark scratched his chin, suddenly roaring with lust. "Back up a second lad. Did ye say *thousands?*"

But the stone in Aeron's hand had begun to pulse a cerulean blue on its ribbed outer lines, as if alive. Not with breath of its own, but Aeron's. Lamark flamed with curiosity.

"Usually they have a bit of a shine to them, like a lamp, but they've never done this before…"

Silent lightning streaked the air. The lanterns in and around the shop went out.

Aeron bit his lip on the side, exposing his nice white teeth. "My granddad used to say there comes a point when you must choose to trust or choose to be cheated. You may not trust me, but I'm going to trust you, Lamark."

Aeron tossed the strange heartfruit to Lamark. The man turned the stone over once and then twice. Distinct from the others, it was cut like a diamond and vaguely marble shaped. It was still goldish-orange like all heartfruit, but bluer and more translucent with a tiny heart of blue at the core. Lamark gave a throaty gasp.

"This—" the man said and pulled a pair of tiny spectacles from his pocket, inspecting it, "—is no heartfruit. Cedre be damned. Aeron. This be a Grapple. *The* Grapple. One of the rarest artifacts in all the world…" Lamark rolled the gem between his large thumb and forefinger.

"Listen good, Aeron. I've been to the Harroes and Indoshina and touched the four Corners of our four rifts. In all my travels, I've seen this come only to one man… never thought I'd see 'er again. And 'ere it is, in the 'aversack of a boy who can't even grow a beard," Lamark said and handed it back to Aeron, its brilliant shine waxing with the boy's touch. "That, Aeron, could rule the world… or end it."

He made true eye contact with the boy, and a hush filled the air as the Grapple mirrored the rhythm of Aeron's breath.

"I knew somethin' be different about ye, kid. Ye may have a friendly face and gotten along well in Longleath, but cripes, Mason, ye haven't the faintest idea what ye've gotten yourself into."

The merchant removed the crumpled leaf of paper he had retrieved inside and handed it to Aeron. Without reading it, Aeron tucked it into his haversack.

Dark clouds hurled in from the ocean.

"Drought's breaking," said Lamark, looking out over the horizon lost in thought. "Ye best be off."

Aeron nodded and brushed one of his dark curls from his forehead, emptying two thirds of his heartfruit into one of Lamark's old seafood crates.

"Ye know, Aeron," said Lamark, "this is worth enough to buy yer way out of trouble. And yer family."

Aeron shook his head. *And they'd tear me apart again once it's gone,* he thought.

"Keep it safe for me."

Lamark nodded. "Same to ye. Be careful. Elevana is a dangerous place fer the young."

The two stood together by the road, feeling the sky break into droplets, then needles, and finally, sheets.

"Aeron," Lamark called, his child-servant now standing beside him chewing on a small bit of heartfruit. "There's a storm risin'."

Aeron gestured all around him at the now-breaking storm.

Lamark shook his head. "No, boy! This be rain. A real one 'asn't come in yer lifetime. Best find yer friend before she breaks ye."

"Or," squeaked the young slave, "the Huntress do!"

CHAPTER 3

THE VOW

An abandoned bungalow, hidden beneath rows of palm trees and dune grass, stood behind a sandy meadow.

As the storm fizzled into a sprinkle, Aeron stuck his head out the door. Thousands of almost-washed-away footprints, his own, dotted the beach. Aeron sat back down in an old chair he had found.

Resting on the worktable, the Grapple's luster had faded from saffron to a subtle shade of orange, matching the Journal like a chameleon. Aeron stroked his family's name stamped on the inner folio.

Maybe life in Elevana is all I'm destined for.

A gust of wind whipped the cover open and Aeron placed the Grapple atop the blank page to weigh it down. Before, the page had been blank, but when the two connected a fleet of letters took wing across the page in the same mysterious, spidery script.

The mind roams to mystery when questions are afoot. But wisdom strikes when you surrender your trying to find it.

Hand shaking, he gripped the pen attached to the Journal's spine by a tassel. Tears threatening, his chest coiled like a snake, and he moved the Grapple from the page. The letters disappeared, and then Aeron wrote.

This Journal, passed from grandson to grandson, records the history of primen since its beginning. I, Aeron Mason, grandson of Mendel Mason, must now assume the role as archivist and knowingly take the vow:

With this hand I vow to write only truth, all truth, the only truth I know—my own.
With this hand I vow to read everything, so I can relay the great realities of history.
With this hand I vow to speak honestly and with good intention.
With this hand I vow to live like my forefathers, in the way of the Masons.
With this hand I vow to die, one final engagement with Aerth.
Now I am become the archivist, historian of world.
—Aeron Mason.

Aeron's fingers shifted to the next page as he wrote.

Not long ago, I escaped from prison with the help of the strangest old man. He taught me things I'd never been able to find in Longleath: the old language of Orangu, Epiphysics and its Aeros that hold great power. But that's not all. Apparently, I have been accused of having a hand in Granddad's death, and my sister's.

And now I cannot go home. Nor do I want to. I guess that makes me a fugitive by choice and by practice. That bald old man with huge hands and lips paid my way to Elevana, hawked a letter to me through the Merchant of Herraz, yet left no hints to the riddle.

"As it Soars, it Sears
The Skylo Sky-low:
be where you seek.
Grapple's Grapple,
The Inn is free
Beyond the brick blue teak."

Granddad Mendel used to say an archivist is rarely right, but he's never wrong. I hope that's true.

Until the next,
Aeron Mason

Aeron put the pen down and rubbed the bags beneath his eyes.

"There's only one place in all Elevana where skies hang low," Lamark had said. "Where wood and whisperin' wind and clouds dance together on the 'illtops. West Riamante. Be careful. There be dark things in West Elevana. And few men livin' in Riamante."

Then Lamark had leaned closer and the tree where they sat sagged. The memory of his hushed voice still gave Aeron chills.

"Legend be he owned the Map of the Reddheart. The scroll shows every 'eartfruit grove in Aerth, and more. Find that, and not a single man in Oriendo will question the Masons…

but beware, Aeron, they will come fer ye, there be no doubt. I fear maybe they already 'ave."

Lamark's final words echoed in Aeron's head.

The dim light from the Grapple partly lit the room. Every so often the Grapple skipped with Aeron's heart as he replayed the events of earlier in the day. He sat in meditation, trying to make sense of the message, with the seabreeze sliding in through the doorless opening.

It might be that the Map of the Reddheart would prove Granddad's story—that he's not a thief and found a heartfruit grove himself—but there must be another way to vindicate him and his family. One less dangerous.

CHAPTER 4

THE GREY ROAD

◇◇◇◇◇◇

"Treason's Tooth, West Elevana! Treason's Tooth, final stop!" the one-armed driver's voice echoed beneath cobalt-blue skies.

Ten primen packed into a mint-green lorry marked with an M-shaped hood ornament. The driver tightened the fuel cap and kicked at its whitewashed side beams as the final rider entered the lorry—a dark skinned girl with long, light brown hair and a low-pulled cap. She was close to Aeron's age and a rare sight. The girl struggled with a bag until the large, sweat-stained driver helped her sling it into cargo. Then, he pushed on a lever and the lorry crept slowly forward, moaning like a poisoned tree.

During those first hours, the seats were hot and did nothing to slake the heat, but the vehicle rumbled ahead through bends, twists, hills, and valleys. The cragged road jarred his head as he stared emptily out the window, imagining today in Longleath with its bustling streets, grumpy workers, and edgy students. He grinned, but a pothole reached up and cracked his head against the sideboard.

"Careful, *shijo,*" said the man beside him. He had nappy hair, a wide frame, and the knobbiest teeth Aeron had ever seen.

"Thanks," Aeron continued. "I recognize the accent. Where are you from?"

"Let's have a guess!" the man said and pursed his lips.

"Well, my granddad used to speak Eurovean occasionally. 'Shijo' means 'son,' I remember. So you are from there?"

Even in Longleath, Aeron had never met a priman of Eurovea. His professors at prep school argued that *real* civilization began in Eurovea, and those classic Eurovean primen rarely left their homeland.

"Well done, shijo," the man said. "I am impressed. And what brings you here? You are too young to come to Elevana." The man continued without giving Aeron a chance to respond. "I've heard whispers of a northerner, a boy, who has gone round making a fuss in our affairs. A boy with a bounty on his head in the north." The man's upturned expression, mousy but not insulting, had Aeron grinning. "Could that be you?"

Best not to give any hints, Aeron thought. *Lest he check the newspaper and see my face on the wanted boards.*

Aeron shook the joke away and turned back to the window as a green countryside rolled by with distant trees and hills, virulent with life.

The Eurovean sang quietly a child-like tune.

We wakes no more
Hearing the sound of the angelic trumpet;
Await, await the hostile quartet,
You and he browse the contents of her dismal tomb,
Ye understand her mythical womb,

The bodice sound, eternity echoes more.
So we passed onward o'er filthy mixtures
Of shadows and rain with footsteps slow,
Questing a little to future's glow.

The afternoon sun throbbed as the Eurovean nibbled on a square of dark icco bean with delight. He pressed one into Aeron's hands, and Aeron let its sweetness melt on his tongue.

"I have heard," said the Eurovean, "this boy carries with him an old treasure of some kind."

The prick of paranoia resonated on Aeron's skin, but the Eurovean cast a warm, friendly smile.

"Allay your fears, young friend!" the man said and clasped a hand to Aeron's shoulder. "Old me cannot read anyhow."

The balloon in Aeron's chest deflated. *He means the Journal, not the Grapple. Still, not good news.* Aeron thought for a minute and then unstrung his haversack and opened the mid-sized Journal with one hand to the messiest page.

"A bunch of scribbles and nonsense," said Aeron with a shrug. "Must be someone else."

"These hands cannot believe it," said the strange man. "I have not seen a book since the Great Wars!"

"Quiet!" Aeron whispered and stole a glance around the lorry. Luckily all, except for the driver, seemed to be sleeping.

"What beauty there must be in book magic!" the man said. "My homeland was built on them. Please, *shijo*, read old me something of your treasure."

Aeron paused, considering the wind. He flipped through the soft, sleepy pages and, against his better judgment, read aloud.

I stamp a perpetual journey, writing in
grassy leaves.
Traveling best through time and space—

Untrodden roads or none at all.
We are here to travel it for ourselves,
Perhaps waylaid since the day your leaf began,
Perhaps it sprays on water and land,
Dream by dream, those flattened reams
We find the weathered atoll.

Keep asking the greatest questions,
We hear them all the same.
As I face the ultimate gavel,
Two words come to mind:

Anudato Euthanasis,
Death is wicked. Death is great;
Too early to be never, too often to be late.
That Epiphysical lyric:
Two words to beat the darkest kiss.

Vido Mason—West Riamante

"Look out!" shouted the girl at the front.

Something round, black, and needled, large as a watermelon, lay squarely in the road.

The lorry driver swerved to avoid the baby boarcupus. The lorry's old, wooden wheels rocked violently to each side. Then, Aeron went weightless. A wheel had caught the blunt edge of a stone and the lorry, teetering like a domino, went skidding through a trestle of trees and into a deep, mud-filled gully.

Red with frustration, the driver turned around. "Anyone hurt?" he said.

"Only my chocolates!" the Eurovean hooted back, followed by ambiguous laughter.

"Good. Now look, *you*," said the driver, facing the girl with the cap seated behind him. "No more of that or you'll walk. And the same goes for everyone. This lorry hasn't failed me in thirty years. Let's keep it that way."

He spun forward and pressed down on the lever, but the lorry did not budge. The man punched at the handle once more, but only the sound of sputtering wheels was heard. Growling, he opened the door, stomped down the stairs, and squished his feet in a foot of mud.

"The mud." He scowled, grinding his teeth and shaking his head. "It's always something in these parts. Always."

He stroked the wheel with a finger.

"Buried in a foot of heavy mud," he complained. Each passenger filed out of the lorry, forming a small, tense crowd around him.

A middle-aged woman repacked their belongings. Three men argued like stubborn siblings. The Eurovean stood beside them, nibbling on some mint-leaves he had found by the road.

Away from the crowd, Aeron found a flat rock beneath a tree. The minutes crawled by, and his bad ear seemed duller than usual. He listened, as best he could, to the whistling treefrogs behind him and tasted the damp vegetal perfumes. He longed for the tall Mossy Mountain of West Riamante and was so lost in his thoughts he barely noticed the girl standing nearby.

"That smell," she said with a soft voice. "You cannot get that anywhere else. Can you?"

She stared straight upward at the leafy claws of the tree. Her face was dark skinned like the Euroveans but with a hint of sadness. Brown hair fell over her shoulders, covering the white lace on her chest which strung together a black tunic dress. Though wearing a black cap, her rounded eyebrows poked from beneath the bill, failing to hide an inquisitive set of almond-shaped brown eyes with double eyelids. Above average in height, the heavy haversack over her shoulders pulled from the back at the tunic, revealing an athletic build, which Aeron didn't blame her for trying to hide in Elevana.

Aeron sat up straighter and tightened his haversack.

Be careful, she has the fine clothes and boots of top grain leather with gold eyelets. Longleath is written all over her. But she's barely older than me, and everything about her screams, "Don't notice me." Why's someone like her in Elevana?

"What? Yeah. Well, no," he stammered. "It makes me think of my granddad's home."

"And where might that be?" asked the girl.

"South," he lied. "It's always green like this in Southern Rift, except in the Hinterlands."

"I know what you mean," she said and nodded, "though I haven't spent much time outside of Longleath in the last few years."

A spike of fear gripped Aeron. She was from Longleath. If she'd taken note of the wanted posters with his face on them, he'd be caught.

She began searching through her bag. "Hey, can I interest you in something to eat? I've still got some bread from my host in the city."

"I don't want to impose..." Aeron had enough heart-fruit to last weeks, and his years at prep school had made him suspicious.

She smiled, teeth bright like white chestnuts, holding half a loaf of sweet-smelling bread.

"It does smell good, though. Lemon?"

She nodded and sat beside him.

They chewed in a good thoughtful silence with no discomfort in it.

While they ate, he noticed her haversack had a slit down the middle. Without thinking, he tied the cloth crossways with a string he'd found at Lamark's.

"What's a girl from Longleath doing here in Elevana?" he asked casually.

"Well," she said with a thorn in her voice, "I had hoped you were the type to dispense with backstories. They only complicate things. But if you must know, I'm not *from* Longleath. I only live there, for the time being. My father and I have been traveling for all the years I can recall. Though I do love the place. Its wondrous power. Ceilinglessness. The way things grow—tangible and intangible. It's the place of dreams, they say."

"Spoken like a true Leath," said Aeron, tying a stitch.

"Where did *you* grow up, then?" said the girl.

"I told you already."

"Not much of a talker, are we?" she said. "No matter! I'll be quiet too once I hit Riamante—"

Aeron's sensitive ears pricked.

"You're going to West Riamante? I've heard it's dangerous there… especially during a storm."

"I am," she said, "and that's all nonsense anyway. There's no Huntress in Elevana anymore, nor Irkal nor anyone who'd hurt me."

"But you know they sell kids like us as slaves there. And you're so…"

"I'm so what?" she said, her black eyes squinting with distrust.

Beautiful. Brave. Trusting. "I would be careful. That's all."

"Look," said the girl, "they are going to turn around, head back for one of the towns we passed. But I have somewhere to be. I know it's not the safest place in the world, but it's not like it was. I'm going to keep following the Grey Road until it splits. If I need to, I'll outrun them.

"You can't outrun the weather," said Aeron as he turned her bag over to make one last knot.

"You and your storm! Look at the sun! It's overflowing."

He stood up from the rock and stretched his legs. The others' voices had grown into a racket.

"Why do you want to go there anyway?" asked Aeron.

"This feels like a lot of questions from someone whose name I don't even know. I might ask you the same question..."

He paused and pretended to readjust her bag.

She wrapped two long fingers around his wrist. A wisp of fear flitted across his face, and she let go.

"I'll be the mature one," she said. "My name is Paloma—no last names. And I don't want to know yours... unless..." she paused before continuing. "Unless you choose to come with me. I've never traveled alone before and, well, I can surely do it on my own, but... It'd be good for us kids to watch each other's backs."

Aeron paused to think. He had missed having other primen his age around; it might be better, so long as she didn't know his real name. Nor had he seen any recognition of his face.

"Hmm," said Aeron. "You never mentioned why you're going to Riamante?"

"Does it matter? If you are headed elsewhere, we'll be parting ways at the fork, and I'd rather you not know my reasons. It's only fair."

He remained silent, nervously refusing to meet her gaze.

"Fine, fine," she said. "I don't expect you're going to cause me trouble. Have you ever heard the Legend of the Four Great Rangers?"

Aeron nodded.

"I'm going to find one of them," said Paloma.

"But the Four Great Rangers is a—"

"Yes, I know," Paloma said and plucked at a low hanging leaf, "a myth. But, kid, I thought you, who believes in all the nonsense about Dark Aeros and the Huntress, might understand..."

"It's not a myth," Aeron shouted. "I know for a fact it's real—but the Four Great Rangers are dead."

"Not all of them."

Aeron chewed the side of his lip, not sure what to make of his strange new friend.

"It's going to take days to get to Riamante; do you have enough bread in there to last that long?"

"No," Paloma shrugged, "but I'm quite strong on the attack. Sport is sort of my thing. Anyway, I'll survive by eating fruit along the way."

"Not a good idea," said Aeron, thinking about his starved delirium. "I tried that and, well I wouldn't do that again." Aeron flashed with an idea. "But you could take the lorry..."

"Last time I checked it's stuck like wax."

A thin silence stretched between them, broken by Aeron, "Do you think you're going to find one of the Rangers?"

"Quite certain of it," she said.

He remembered one of his granddad's theater lines. *A life without trust is no life at all. But trust too much and you're bound to fall.*

"My name's Aeron."

They shook hands like two sailors meeting for the first time.

"Go have a listen at what they're saying," said Aeron. "I need a few minutes."

As she left, he began scribbling a list of items on a leaf of paper beside a light, circular sketch.

Several minutes later, she returned. "A dreadful group! You'd think they were kids the way they're bickering. Sounds like the group will head back to town before it gets dark and come back for the lorry tomorrow. Sounds like they already forgot about us."

"Even better. Let's keep it that way," he said, passing her the list.

"Roots from a fallen tree," she read aloud, "two composite stones, pith from a plant in bloom, two short beams of wood, one head of Darksprig. All of these exist in Elevana? Even... Darksprig?"

"Yes," he said, "I'm sure of it."

"How can you be so positive? You are from the Southern Rift. Unless you've—"

"I've been in there once before. It'd be quick during the day, but..." he gestured toward the sun, struggling to peek through the heavy forest canopy. "It's going to be dark as night in there soon.

"Look. I absolutely have to get further west than this tonight." Now word had spread of him in Elevana, so it was important to get as far from the city as he could.

"Can you handle it? I'll get started on this," he said and pointed at the sketch.

"Of course," said Paloma. A wisp of anger flitted across her face. "It'll be *easy.*"

She stepped forward toward the darkish forest.

"But only because I need to get west too. The Ranger is going to teach me how to become a Ranger Plus," she added, "I don't like the look in the driver's eye."

"Paloma," said Aeron rustling in his haversack. "You haven't been in there. It's... stay on the edges." He tossed her one of the normal heartfruit. It glowed like a lantern, as all heartfruit did, though far less than the Grapple.

"Where in Cedre's name did you get *that?*"

"In there," he lied.

Paloma's eyes narrowed. He nodded once and refocused on the sketch. She turned her back to him, and faced the forest. Holding the heartfruit ahead, she disappeared into a thunder of darkness.

CHAPTER 5

THE DEAD OF
THE WOOD

◇◇◇◇◇◇

All was quiet save for chittering crickets, hooting owls, and a chilly breeze. Leaves rustled as Paloma Murravillow walked beneath the forest canopy into a dim, dried out ravine.

A short way into the forest new grass bloomed, but the further she went the more the sunlight faded until the canopy was a dusk sky with glittering leaves above instead of stars. A vine, blooming white and blue flowers, crept up an old black jack oak, threatening to tear down what a seedling spent a hundred years building. Paloma yanked the flower off the vine for good measure and cleaved the excess. "Nasty bit o' weed you are," she said to a Prither Bloom—which served as the third item on the list. In such a lush forest, the wood too came easily—until the fifth and final item. The head of Darksprig.

A cute, short-haired rabbit twitched its nose in her direction. Two bearded reddish birds landed nearby to observe her as well. A choir of rocks tumbled from the subtle incline, indicating some larger animal nearby.

Odd, she thought, patting her cheeks. *It's as if they've never seen a priman before.*

Here and there, a shaft of sunlight sneaking between the canopy revealed blueish sap on the rocks, and she passed a patch of wild mushrooms. Then Paloma heard the thin crackling of fire. Somewhere in the distance must have been a wildfire. Every so often along the twisting, overgrown trail were more dabs of the blueish sap. It seemed to be getting thicker, and sometimes she would even see tiny spuds of sprig in them.

At a round widening in the path, a skitter of cold light caught Paloma's eye, but it disappeared behind a mountainous sprig tree. She went to step forward, but the crunch of loose aerth beneath her toes shocked her still. Aiming the heartfruit forward, she squinted over a deep, dark, delusory pit of detritus and rock. It must have been at least fifty feet deep. A single tree had fallen across it, stretching the length of the pit easily.

And even though it screamed out to her "trap!" like a parrot with a helpful tongue, Paloma set her bundle against a sad old bucket, which had been absorbed by the ground. On the other side stood the grandest of sprigtrees with enormous blue buds smelling of spring. Paloma had never seen anything so natural and sad. Its tall crown could not reach high enough for sunlight, and its branches rose at odd angles and twists.

"We Murravillows are fearless," she assured herself aloud, looking confidently over the drop. "No trick of the eye keeps us from what we want."

Heartfruit in hand, glowing as her only light source, she fastened on the chill, vibrating Darksprig blossoms and loped forward with the fluidity of a dancer after hours of practice.

One foot followed the other as Paloma primed her arms, pumping them forward step by step.

When she reached the other side, the forest tasted less like a pleasant grove and more like a home to the dead and dying. She held her breath behind the awful feeling of being watched. With a jump, Paloma tore the largest head she could from the Darksprig tree.

From up the ravine came a thin, wispy voice like the wind.

"I am glad to have found you," it spoke clearly as a man's voice, deep and clear with a tinge of hostility.

Paloma wheeled around. Orienting herself in the dim light, she held the heartfruit ahead of her, but only saw veils of biblical darkness.

"The Wraeth have reemerged," said the man with certainty. "Fear will keep primen from coming together against them. Fear of unity. Fear of losing the self. Fear of death."

He's talking to someone, Paloma thought. *They are above, somewhere higher in the ravine.*

All of the sudden, a smoky, icy cloud blanketed the ravine. Then, giving her a start, a flash of light ricocheted in every direction, and she dropped the heartfruit into the pit.

The cloud, she thought, *it feels... alive.*

Heavy footsteps from the direction of the voice pounded the ground.

"Who's there?" whispered Paloma, removing her cap.

The fog curled around her, leaving icy droplets of sweat on her skin.

Don't let it frighten you. Evil feeds on fear.

From high to the right, she heard crunching leaves beneath heavy feet. Suddenly, a shape moved through the mist. She could make out a figure, white but vague, flickering in and out behind gusts of smoke like a sputtering candle.

The hurried footsteps fell louder and the whitish creature swelled in size. It had giant arms and a thick torso but seemed to be faceless. The figure's movements, lithe and strong, contrasted its harsh exterior as if it were once a splendid being whose personality had been drained away.

Whether naked or clad from head to waist in a skin-tight, bone-white layer of spider silk, she did not wait to find out. Heart throbbing like drums of war, her leftmost toe edged over the pit. Instead of falling, she caught herself on the tree bridge and, without a thought, flew across it in long strides.

Near the edge of the bridge, she broke through the dark smoke, but she turned her head to catch a glimpse of what looked like a swirling galaxy of ink, colored by rippling eels of lightning above the horrid whitish man. Behind her, an icy breath rose from the pit.

A mirage-like image of a bloody, dying version of her father's face stabbed her mind.

No. It's an illusion! Father is safe.

Her foot connected with a knot and she tumbled forward, her long fingers swinging out desperately. They connected with something wooden and sturdy enough to hold her weight. She swung side to side like a frog until her foot caught the edge it needed. She gathered herself above the pit and huffed with relief. The Darksprig lay, slightly crushed but still intact, on the trail. Without a moment's hesitation, she gathered her bundle and broke into a run.

Ahead, a pin of purple and blue light shone the way forward. It must have been the sunset. She crashed away through the undergrowth, doing the best she could not to lose anything. Soon, natural light bled softly through the forest wall, but the image of her emaciated father had been burned into her eyes like a candle she'd stared at for too long.

This was the second time she had been given a pre-monition to her father's death, this time by some kind of Wraeth, and only one man alive could save him—the Last Great Ranger.

CHAPTER 6

IN THE RIAMANTE VALLEY

"You!" shouted the driver, wagging his chunky arm at Aeron. "You, Northerner. This is your fault! I knew I should not have let you and your young floozy on board. Foreigners always stir up trouble in these parts. The land *knows*." The driver lingered heavily on the word as if it were morning dew.

Dusk had risen fast. Each of them must have known if they did not leave soon, darkness would be about, and the Grey Road was no place to be at night.

"If the wheel is unmendable," said the Eurovean, "we should make for Marillo. The village is not close, but if we head back now, we will arrive before the inn runs out of wine!"

"Regardless," said another with a bright green jacket, "we should make for Marillo. It's a whole lot further to the next town."

As the crowd grumbled and prepared their bags to walk, Paloma crashed through the thicket beside Aeron. He jumped back, ready to run. In a haze of shock and relief, she dropped the bundle beside him and walked away without saying a word. None seemed to notice her.

"What happened?" asked Aeron.

Paloma did not reply. Even with her back facing him, hands on her hips, Aeron could sense something had happened.

"Paloma?"

"This horrible country!" She growled and heaved a rock into the forest. "All the dark places and lazy fools who live here!" Now she had their attention. A scowl burned across her cheeks.

"To the pits with this one," mewed a middle-aged woman carrying a straw bucket. The others seemed to agree, speaking quietly between themselves.

After a few moments, the Eurovean with bad teeth approached Aeron, staring at the ground as he walked.

"Mr. Sir," started the Eurovean in his formal Mother Tongue. "I am to inform you that your friend, the girl, is not welcome with the group, or on the lorry tomorrow."

"Just her?" said Aeron.

The man nodded. Aeron stole a glance at Paloma. Where they had veered boasted a breathtaking view, and she watched the sun's final droop behind the Mossy Mountains.

"You come with us now."

"That's okay," said Aeron. "I'm going to stay with her."

"Like a true blue jay!" said the Eurovean with a bow. Aeron smiled politely as the man continued. "Luck to you, *shijo* of the books."

Aeron watched him, sad to see the man go.

"I'm impressed," said Paloma, now sitting beside him. She ran three fingers through her brown hair. "Didn't think it would be so easy to get them away."

Aeron shrugged and knelt beside the items Paloma had collected.

"Are you all right?" he asked. "Seemed more than little shaken up."

"I'm fine," she said. "Just got a bit lost is all."

Aeron shrugged again. Even if she had lied, he didn't need any more nightmares.

"You see this?" he said, pointing to the sketch. "I'm going to use what you've brought to make a jack. Wedge this tightly as we can beneath the spokes and yank, again and again until the wheel budges free from the mud."

"Looks like one of the cranks they use on the newer lorries in Longleath."

"Yes," said Aeron. "But they've better materials and lighter lorries…"

It didn't take them long to put together the crank. He used the sappy Darksprig as a lubricant for the rocks, roots, and pith. By roping them together, plus a few pieces of wood, Aeron formed a diamond-shaped jack to lift the lorry from the mud.

By the time he finished the sky had gone dark and a damp, dank odor billowed from the forest.

They each carried a side of the jack and wedged the rectangular end into the mud so it barely fit beneath the belly of the lorry. Aeron stepped onto the platform and lurched on top of the lever. A whipcrack of wood near its breaking point resounded through the night. But no budge.

"Push harder!" Paloma shouted.

Aeron gave his mightiest hurl and the crank slipped out. He landed hand-to-knee in the mud. Paloma readjusted it and thrust one more time.

"Hey!" she said. "Get out of there, it's tipping…"

Aeron rolled onto the dirt in the nick of time. The wheel raised and crashed in the holes where his feet had been.

Ankle deep and covered in mud, Aeron turned to Paloma.

"I have an idea," said Aeron. "Give me that heartfruit?" He'd forgotten about it until then.

"Mmm," Paloma hesitated, "well, you see, that's why I was so worked up before. I know you must have spent a fortune on that, and I seem to have lost it."

Aeron cocked his head. He couldn't shake off the feeling that something was different about this girl. She'd lost a whole heartfruit and not thought twice about mentioning it, nor did she seem too apologetic—signs of a thief, a rich girl, or maybe both.

"What?" she asked.

"You have a quick tongue," said Aeron. "It worries me."

Aeron knew, somehow, what to do. He walked to the front of the lorry, haversack belted to his back, and called back to Paloma before entering.

"When I say so, give absolutely everything you can muster on the handle."

He pulled the drawstring on the haversack and shuffled through the remaining heartfruit until he felt the hardest, ripest, in the bundle—less a fruit than a large stone. He twisted the top off of the funnel shaped tube beside the steering wheel and dropped the heartfruit inside. The lorry purred, absorbing its fuel.

"Ready?" asked Aeron, pushing hard on the driver's lever. "*Heeaaave.*"

At first the lorry remained steady, but suddenly it lurched back and forth until finally rolling onward.

"Yes!" Aeron shouted. He ran alongside it, not daring to stop its forward motion for fear of getting stuck again. Instead, he knocked open the door. "You've got to—"

"Catch up?" said Paloma smiling as she leapt through the door.

"What'd you say you do again?" Aeron asked amazed as he reached for her hand.

She hauled him inside. "School at the Lyceum, and Cannaroo."

Cannaroo, Aeron's favorite sport, had been the only redeeming part of Longleath. After prep school, he would have been at Longleath Lyceum too and able to go to every Cannaroo match. The Lyceum's team was the best in Oriendo.

He slipped into the driver's seat and stared desperately at the foreign controls. This pedal for motion, that pedal for stop and a wheel turning the lorry in a direction, but that's all he could make out. Aeron eased on the speed as a corner approached. "Hang on, Paloma," said Aeron, stealing a glance at her. "Your bag..."

"It's fine. Only things. Things are replaceable." Paloma settled herself in the seat behind the driver's seat, her head peeking around Aeron's shoulder. "Hey," she said, "why do you look so tense?"

"I've, uh," Aeron stammered, "never driven one of these before."

Paloma rolled her eyes. "Move," she commanded, squeezing in the seat beside him. Aeron released the handle and let her take over. "Parents never taught you?"

"Haven't got any of those."

"Brother, sister?"

Aeron shook his head.

"In Longleath, the lorries drive themselves," said Paloma. "Can't imagine how you get around without a lorry in the Southern Rift—where you're *from*."

He couldn't tell whether she was calling his bluff or asking in earnest.

"We've other ways to get around."

Through the right window was an abandoned house with pink paint flaking from the walls. He feigned interest and changed the subject. "What do your folks do?"

Paloma's brow furled. "Remember what I said about backstories?"

The road became slightly bumpy but straightened out. Paloma's face was stone, but she must have been able to tell he wanted to know.

"Dad's a..." she paused, "businessman... Never met my mom. Dad doesn't say much about her, except that she left us in Eurovea after I was born. What'd yours do?" Her fake smile held something back, something lost and never found.

"Makes two of us. Never knew my mom either. But Granddad used to say Mom was the smartest woman he knew. That's saying something... my father was a fool, but he made music and people loved him for it—used to play in all the highest places you could imagine. He even played for the vizier of Longleath once or twice..."

"You mean," said Paloma, "Maya Mae Mattisun?"

"Is that her name?" Aeron lied. "I guess so—probably didn't know, or even care. He was a fool."

"My Uncle Oake always says fools change the world," said Paloma.

"You know," he trailed off, "you're not the first to tell me that..."

Paloma laughed. Laughter, he had learned from his grandfather, had a way of opening people up.

"And what are *you* then, Aeron?"

He shrugged. "Maybe we'll find out."

A silence, save for the purring lorry, filled the air. To their left lay the Dark Gilder Forest. To the right was a moonlit valley below a maze of stars. Paloma opened her mouth as if to speak, but the words must have slipped away.

"Sometimes I wish I had no family," Paloma finally said.

"No," said Aeron definitively. "You don't."

"You're right," Paloma agreed, readjusting her cap, "I don't know why I said that," She put both hands on the lorry. "Those are just thoughts and we can't control our thoughts."

"I think we can," said Aeron, "but not ones like that—the deeply buried ones."

"I like that," said Paloma.

"So—there's a Ranger in the Riamante Valley," said Aeron. "I hope you're ready. Come morning the Grey Road is going to split and you'll be on your own…"

"I think so," she said and pressed on the speed, but the lorry only continued its slow, steady pace.

"Are you sure you've done this before?" Aeron asked.

"Nope," said Paloma, shooting him a wry look. "Never driven in my life."

The lorry sputtered, lurched, and its even-keeled canter came to a halt.

Normally one heartfruit would be enough for days of driving, but this lorry had to be a hundred years old and chomped heartfruit like Lamark. He'd poured half his sack in and had no more heartfruit that would serve as fuel.

They had made good time. The lorry had first broken down right after the Grey Road split: West Riamante and the hardpan or Riamante and The Granaria. After salvaging the wheel and giving the lorry Heartfuel from real heartfruit, the vehicle carried them on the Grey Road near to the end of the hardpan.

"There," said Aeron. "Trees ahead. We must be closer to the Fork of Riamante than I'd expected."

Night pressed against the soft contours of Paloma's face. "Looks like morning came early…"

"Why don't we spend a few hours to rest here?" said Aeron.

"And let the athon come and trap us like goldfish? Or some band of Huntress come and sell us into the dirty child trade? No thanks, Mr. Aeron. I'll take my chances out *there*." She pointed vaguely into the darkness.

"Thought you said the Huntress were *gone*?" Aeron prodded.

"They are. That's why it's safe to go. Come on."

They clamored down the stairs and into the fresh air. The smell of dew mixed with the dark night caused a surge of blood from head to toe. He tapped his bad ear.

"Do you hear that?" he asked.

"Hear what?" she replied.

"Music," Aeron said. "Hope to Cedre you're not, but I think you might be wrong about the Huntress, Paloma."

Only the Huntress sang in Orangu.

CHAPTER 7

THE ODE TO TERMARA

Out on the Grey Road at midnight was nowhere for a young lady—or so Paloma had been told. If her family could see her now, they'd lock her in the city-baths for a week. Such a "beautiful girl," but never acting like it—always beating boys at sport rather than letting them chase her, painting murals at dawn, showing up to father's office late with paint splotched on her hands, fingers, and expensive shoes. "You're a mess," her nona would criticize, scratching at the wrinkles on her old arms. "No wonder the boys run away from you."

It was hard to believe they had only walked a few miles. When they left, the lorry was cracked and dusty with residue from the hardpan, Elevana's desert of scorched aerth.

Now they hiked single-file through woodland paths barely wide enough for one priman. For the most part, they kept quiet.

"It even smells different out here," she said as they walked an inconspicuous path along the Grey Road. "Like burning incense."

"I wish you would take this more seriously," said Aeron. She could feel his green eyes on her but did not look.

"I'm taking it quite seriously," Paloma spat and brushed aside a fern. "That doesn't mean I shouldn't enjoy myself too."

Suddenly, off in the distance, chiming bells broke the night.

Aeron froze. After a few paces, Paloma did too. She lifted a thigh-sized branch with yellowing leaves from the path.

"Shh," Aeron hissed and pushed a black curl from his face. "It's getting louder."

It was.

"Come on," said Paloma, charging through a flowering thicket of forest. "Let's see what they're up to…"

"Paloma…" Aeron replied, dodging one of the large tropical leaves, which sprung back toward him in her wake. "It could be followers of the Huntress. You know the remaining Huntress took exile here after the First Rift War and the Wraeth first appeared in Aerth.

"No," Paloma said with certainty and held back a needly branch so Aeron walked past unmolested. "You said it yourself. The Last Ranger came here to rid the place of them. And he never fails."

Aeron fell silent. His boyish round face fell into thought.

She swiped at the moths that flitted around her face. As they crossed a ridge, the songs of the night chimed in the wind. At last they came to a lookout over the valley.

"Mmm…" agreed Paloma. Churning water dripped from the lips of a stone fish. It drooled down in beads before filling a small concrete basin.

"Here," she said with dry lips. "Here's one of the old fountains. Let's have a drink. I'm parched."

Aeron agreed, holding the slat open with long fingers while she gulped icy water.

"Brilliant. Mountain runoff, always cold. Can't get any better."

"The Orangu were smarter than we think."

"Such a hard language," she said. "Are you sure it's Orangu?"

"I know so. Look there."

On the side of the fountain a large glyph had been etched into the stone in the shape of a curled foxtail or the bottom half of a bullseye.

"And the boy reads Orangu…" said Paloma. "I've a feeling that you're—"

"Shhh…" Aeron held a finger to his thin lips. From the distance they hear a sound, lyrical and sad but man-made all the same.

"Don't—" said Paloma, but he interrupted again.

"Music!" said Aeron. "I know that song… and it's in Orangu too."

Paloma tilted her head but heard only the voices of millions of insects, frogs, waving leaves and the hurrying stream.

"And you see that?" she said, gesturing over the bowl-shaped valley below them. "A light."

Aeron crouched low beneath a hedgerow. "You're right!"

They took off down the thinly wooded slope. Paloma led the way, like a lioness, leaping swiftly around boulders and tree stumps. They slipped between a row of ferns at the bottom of the hill and followed the path, which had once been a creek but was now no more than a tiny stream.

"It's getting close to dawn," said Aeron but Paloma barely heard him.

A wonderful odor had wafted past her nostrils—something warm and hearty being cooked. Finally, they might get supper after such a distressing day.

When the woody slope ended, the pair stood on a small crest outside a modest town, if it could be called a town. Between a row of silver trees and shining white grasses, the small moonlit glade held only two structures, both ancient. The water mill to the left had been abandoned years ago but the stone tavern beside held the muted sound of a party.

"We have to go in," Paloma commanded.

"Let's wait and watch a little first," said Aeron. "Maybe we'll catch someone in or out."

They should have guessed. Not a soul stirred for half an hour. Above them, an old and yellow owl flew off like an angel in the night.

"Perhaps we have a look at that?" Paloma pointed and made for the angora in the middle of the moon-drenched road.

The road had been recently paved and the stones shone brightly. If anyone watched, Paloma and Aeron would have been clear as day.

The statue had been cracked down its center—a priman woman, hoisting a lightning bolt into the sky. Her eyes were distinct yet beguiling.

The music rose and Paloma turned for the tavern.

"I hear it!" she said. "It is Orangu, oh haevens mercy! That song … it's 'The Ode to Termara.'"

Aeron's expression turned suddenly grave.

"What's wrong?" Paloma asked.

"My father—" Aeron said, "this was the song he played when…" He paused and pointed to his bad ear, the damaged one.

So his father had caused his impaired hearing?

They walked toward the tavern. It was brick and laden with red wooden paneling with leaves and moss spudded between the windows. Two oak barrels stood beside the door where the sound of a lute grew louder.

"Beautiful," said Aeron admiring the doorway. "Ancient, but they grow their buildings far better than we do. It's more… natural.

Life—an unmistakable sound. Through the window, a hearth flickered and a harmonium thronged in the night. The instruments yawning vibrations rippled through her jaw and teeth. Then the sound thinned and a raspier, truer, more melodious voice than she had ever heard tumbled from behind it.

"Father?" Aeron whispered in the silence between two notes.

His face was stricken with grief, confusion, and a tinge of malice. Aeron had said his father was dead. Fatigue must be getting to him.

She stepped away from the window. The night had grown cool and the warmth of the tavern was too much to resist. Paloma ran a finger over the grains of the wooden barrel and stepped toward the door. Aeron had a tear in his eye when she gripped and turned the handle. The door groaned like poisoned tree.

CHAPTER 8

THE PRIDE OF NEATH

◇◇◇◇◇◇

Paloma threw her head back like a dirty, old pirate. Draining the short glass dry, she thanked the older woman who had bought drinks for the two of them. Aeron, however, had fastened onto the man singing on stage.

Hours before, the heavy door had creaked and grinded as Paloma forced it open. Silence had spread across the tavern as Aeron and Paloma walked in. What a sight they must have been—two mud-soaked kids wandering in bashfully like escaped slaves.

As they entered, a crafty looking man with a white shirt and overalls strolled behind the bar to furnish Aeron and Paloma with cups of almond ale and roasted pinterseeds. Aeron assumed he owned the tavern by the way he referred to "The Sportsman" as his crown jewel.

Both Aeron and Paloma were young, but even normal primen chairs were half the size of those in the tavern. The people inside were huge. Neither he nor his companion came even to chest height to any of them, not even the chairs. Only one set of table and chairs were anywhere near their height and Aeron made his way to the normal-sized set to take a seat. Paloma followed.

Aeron did his best to ignore the dull murmuring that had spread throughout the tavern.

"I'd always wondered if pinterseeds were real…" commented Aeron as the music resumed.

"Real! It's just about the only thing we eat!" chirped a spritely older woman wearing the customary neath bandana leaf. She had blonde hair, tan skin, and was as tall as everyone else. "Bring out a round of shorts," she called to the owner. "On me."

"That is too kind of you," said Paloma. "To what do we owe this pleasure?"

"Well aren't you the most polite little priman?" said the woman and stood up. She was so tall her knees came even with the table.

"You are neath!" Aeron exclaimed, gaping.

"We are all neath in The Sportsman," she said.

Aeron scanned the room. All the men had tall, chiseled faces, perfect skin, and long hair. The women had similar faces, but even more beautiful, beneath short-cropped haircuts.

"Play your favorite, Yeats!" someone shouted from the corner. "For our young guests."

The drinks came out and Paloma drained the harsh liquor.

"Let's do another!" Paloma shouted. "Let's do another."

Aeron disguised his surprise with an absent smile. After a few sips, he could already feel the legendary strength of the neath wine.

The man on stage tipped his cap and strummed a neath longharp.

Arise now healthily, ahead forever—the
Marquis Innisfree.

*And a village of cabins to build there, of clay and
wattles made;
Nine bean-rows will we have there, a hive for the
honey bee,
And live alone in the bee-loud glade.
And we shall have some peace there, for peace comes
dropping slow,
Dropping from the veils of the morning to where the
cricket sings;
There midnight's all a glimmer, and noon a purple glow,
And evening full of the linnet's wings.
We will arise and go now, for always night and day
We hear lake water lapping with low sounds by the shore;
While you stand on the roadway, or on the
pavements grey,
We hear it in the deep heart's core.*

"Your friend drinks like a sailor," the woman with the
bandana said to Aeron. "And gambles like one too."

"Goodness!" Paloma's shout startled him. She and three
others stood over the table, rolling thorn dice. "Look at that
roll," she sang over the music.

"I can't hear the music." Aeron tapped Paloma and gestured toward the stage. "I'll be up front."

"Oh Aeron, don't you want to see me win?" she teased.

Aeron grinned. "Not one bit, but good luck," said Aeron.
He continued in a low voice. "Don't forget why we're here.
You've got to find the Ranger, and I think they can help me
find where an old friend lives. Remember, these are *neath*
men and women. If anyone will know about your Ranger,
it's them."

She raised her chin in a smug way that Aeron couldn't get a read on. The stool creaked as he rose and walked across the all-at-once sticky and slippery floor. He took a seat in the corner near a kind couple wearing the customary neath clothing—colorful, homemade, and elegantly designed. They had a baby with them whose eyes had already widened, as neath do in their first year.

The musician must have noticed Aeron because, after cheers from the crowd, he dropped his hat on the table and sat across from him.

"You look lost, son, in more ways than one," the musician said, pulling back his long hair. "I am Yeats… though on stage I am the Marquis of Innisfree."

"Aeron. You play well," he said, taking a sip of the harsh brown liquor. "Best I've seen in a while."

"Well I appreciate it, Aeron."

"Where'd you learn to play like that?"

"Well, after the fall of Termara, us neath-men grew afraid that our country would be next for the Wraeth. Nearly eight hundred years ago now. But I'm only three hundred and fifty. That was in my father's day."

"*Only* three hundred and fifty?" Aeron squeaked. "I'll be lucky to live out one hundred and twenty."

Yeats shrugged. "People seem to like us, the neath. Keep to ourselves. Make nice clothes and art. Grow good crops. Fast learners. Northern countries started opening doors to us, and I had big eyes, so Oriendo called my name. Used to mend instruments for some of the best in Longleath, but the big city tired me out. Elevana felt more like the neath I knew—plenty of trees, lots of animals, simple folk."

He considered asking if Yeats had known Loo Mason, a well-known bard known across the four rifts, but long years of tongue-biting practice at school paid off.

"You know," Yeats's voice had gone gravelly again. He washed it with a sip from his cup. "We haven't had a guest perform in quite a while. You primen and your large hands always impress me. Might you do us the honor?"

Aeron thought for a moment. Nothing would have made him happier, but it might have caused unwanted attention.

"Maybe another day…" he said.

"Funny," said Yeats. "There's one big gent, some kind of Ranger, who comes in every few years. Always says the same thing."

"Hellooo, hotcakes! That's me again," Paloma's shout bounced across the room. Aeron shook his head.

"Used to be more," Yeats went on, "but not many Rangers left—not in Elevana at least. Just the one here, probably because the Huntress are all gone. He comes in every now and again. And I'll tell you what." Yeats pointed to a brooding young guy in the corner with broad shoulders and a low farm hat. "See him?"

The boy had dark, ophidian eyes with a nose and lips that scrunched together in an unnatural way for a boy with such a large head and body. While Paloma rolled the thorndice, his wide fingers fumbled with a brown smoking leaf and some blue sprig buds on the table.

"He's not neath either…" said Aeron. "And looks like he's got a fix to make trouble if Paloma keeps winning at thorns, or he badly needs a sprigarette."

"True," said Yeats. "He is my farmhand. I have done my best since taking him in, but being raised by the Huntress leaves its mark. The other day I found three blue jays with broken necks near the barn. But he is strong and he only keeps growing."

"I've had it with this game," the young farmhand boomed, flaring at Paloma. "You're a dirty cheater!"

Aeron motioned to defend Paloma if need be, but Yeats pinched his sleeve. "Not so much older'n she is," said Yeats. "He's not mad. Don't want to see Throach mad. Only jealous. When the Ranger comes in… that's when I steer clear."

The man pulled his longharp off the stage and strummed the instrument absently. Aeron's eyelids grew heavy, and he rested his head in his hands.

Some hours passed and the tavern's dimness lifted behind floats of morning sun. A pool of saliva lay beside Aeron's cheek on the counter.

"Have a good rest?" asked Yeats. He must have fallen asleep. The crowd had dwindled to the staff, plus Yeats and his farmhand.

"She passed out 'round the same time you did," said Yeats, tipping his head to where Paloma lay on a honey-colored bench. "It's about noon, but your friend has been drinking neath wine. Won't be up for quite some time."

Aeron made to stand, but his feet could have been rolling pins.

"And you're not looking so great yourself. I've got an extra room on the ranch but, ah," he scrunched his lips and filled Aeron's cup from a ribbed reddish vase, "wish there were a better way, but I can't risk two runaways knowing where I live, so you'll have to drink this—or wear a blindfold."

"We're not," Aeron slurred, "runaways."

"Come on, kid. This ain't my first tumble."

Aeron pushed the drink away.

"Drink it, Aeron."

Had he told Yeats his name? He couldn't remember.

"The owner here is a huckster. He'll sell you two quick as a whip," he said and leaned closer over the round table. The back of his arm slid the short-glass closer to Aeron. Though Yeats wasn't the largest neath, it reminded Aeron of his powerlessness against them.

"I know you are searching for something, or someone. Drink it, and I will help you."

Aeron tightened the straps around his shoulders.

He felt something warm, the Grapple maybe, pressed against his lower back.

I need to find the man. He promised to show me things that would absolve Granddad and all the Masons.

Aeron held the roundish glass between his thumb and two forefingers. His ears buzzed as he spun it nervously on the table.

"Where in Riamante?" Aeron asked.

"West."

West. If the old man is in Elevana, he will be in the west.

Now was Aeron's turn to play pirate. He held the short-glass up and the reddish liquor stung his nostrils. Then, across the room, he and Yeats' dark-eyed farmhand with the sprigarette behind his ear made eye contact. A chill pinched his every vertebra. Aeron closed his eyes and drained the cup dry.

CHAPTER 9

A SILENT MUSICIAN

Paloma had never been so disoriented as waking the following morning. She looked around the strange room with a large window. At least an acre of farmland stretched to the east dotted with baby sprig trees, the kind people grind up and sell in pouches for smoking. They gave the space a strong natural odor. The bed beside her own had been tidied, but the sweating cup on the nightstand hinted that Aeron had spent the night there as well.

Beside Aeron's cup lay a paper kerchief with some writing on it. She read it, rubbing a bruise on her arm.

"The Pride of Neath—Cheers to having you at The Sportsman!"

With a vivid snap, the details cascaded back onto her like a dream. Paloma slid off the bed and out of the room. Closing the door silently, she toed the stairwell down into a kitchen lined with oak paneling and countertops. The chairs were welcoming but old and had round backs made of beech while the cabinets wore a fresh shade of mint paint. A bell-shaped vase with yellow begonias sat at the edge of the long counter.

She sighed a heavy, pleasant breath behind the smell of braided bread topped with two sunny-side eggs.

"Awake, are we?"

Startled, Paloma looked up. A man was standing at the stove three feet from her to the side of the stairwell. He had a hand on the drawstring of his straw hat and lowered it onto his back when Paloma entered. She recognized the pinched face, brooding eyes, and stubby receding hairline of the farmhand she'd beaten in thorndice. His attempt to smile was more fake than a bat pretending to be a bird. He fidgeted with three fingers at the knotted string around his neck. Though barely older than her, his neck was the size of her thigh. His ears were oddly low and one of them had a sprigarette behind it.

She feigned a smile and stepped away from him ever so slightly.

"Yes, felt better, but also felt quite the worse. Mind telling me how I got here…" said Paloma, "and where here is?"

He grinned but kept his attention on the crackling pan. "Sure. Are you hungry?"

"Famished." Paloma seated herself on a bamboo stool with more bravado than she felt.

She cut the toast, as had been taught, into small triangles. He watched with leering interest while slurping from a jar of juiced mango.

"You and your friend had quite the night. How you did it, I've no idea, but by the end of a few games of thorns, you'd won at least one drink from all of us."

"That explains the raging headache," she said, rubbing her forehead with two fingers. "What was your name again?"

He smiled with a dreadfully wide mouth. "Throach."

"And why am I here?"

He poured her a glass and slid it across the table. "My father, Yeats the singer," he said, "offered your friend the extra room."

"And where is my friend then?"

"Saw him, few hours ago, slip out the door, haversack strapped to his back. Looked like he thought no one would see him." Throach showed his sharp, devilish teeth. "But I'm always looking."

Paloma scarfed down her breakfast and stood up. "Thank you for the hospitality, sir, but I should be going."

"So soon?" he said. "West Riamante is a mysterious and dangerous place. Especially for a pretty girl like you."

Paloma nodded and made for the stairs. As she climbed, the nasty feeling of his gaze sent gooseflesh up her arms. She closed and bolted the door.

The creepy boy had been right. She could find no signs that Aeron had gone out to explore, intending to come back. Angry that Aeron would abandon her, she snatched a pillow and flung it hard against the wall. Something ceramic crashed to the floor behind her, a porcelain cat figurine.

"Are we all right, Ms. Paloma?" Throach called from below.

"All fine," her voice cracked a bit as she knelt and buffed the scratch on the cat's tail with her sleeve. Then she replaced it and straightened out the rest of the mantle. "Thanks for checking."

Having no belongings of her own left her feeling starkers in front of a crowd. What to do? She picked up a pen and the beer-soaked scrap of paper from the night before and traced the outline of The Sportsman until an idea sprang out.

"Sir," she called, cracking the door. "You wouldn't happen to have a pipe I could borrow. Would you?"

"Nay, I am no smoker," he called, still at the foot of the stairs. "But Father does. Would it make you happy if I fetch it?"

"Quite!"

Paloma waited for ten counts after hearing the downstairs screen door bang closed. Then she clicked open her door and hustled down the stairs. The kitchen had been cleaned to sparkle, the floors still wet from being mopped. She slipped past it right for the door. As she yanked on the handle, the farmhand's heavy fist slammed it closed from behind her.

She wheeled around.

"Why the rush, Ms. Paloma?" he asked and ran a finger up her spine. "Surely it's better to stay here. With us. We have citrus and pork and more smoke than you could dream of. And father's music."

His touch and dark expression spurred her heart to a gallop.

"Come," he said softly and touched the small of her back. "I want you to see the farm."

She stepped away, back toward the kitchen, and shook her head. No back door, Paloma noticed as she put distance between them. He moved closer.

"Let me show you," he said, planting his feet.

"I'd like to leave," she said. "If you wouldn't mind—"

"Oh, I would mind." Throach flashed his Huntress teeth with a sickening smile. Her belly revolted and threatened to send her breakfast back up.

He moved closer and made a second attempt, this time with force as his strong, callused hands brushed her already-bruised arm. She made quickly for the door, her feet sliding against the slick floor, but as she did Yeats entered the kitchen.

The old man's cheekbones flared, his gaze aimed like a burning arrow. Paloma's breath grew shallow for fear.

Is this how it ends? she thought.

"I told you," Yeats growled at Throach, "to stay in the field today."

"But, Father," said the young man, "it would have been rude for our guest to wake to an empty kitchen."

"Go," Yeats commanded. "Now. Go!"

When Throach didn't stir, Yeats took a strong, wide stance. A dense silence fell over the kitchen. All she could hear were their angry rasps of breath. After several moments, the farmhand made an aggressive reach in Paloma's direction.

Paloma rolled away, knocking over the stool deliberately in his path. The clean tiles, still slick from being mopped, made it hard to stop. Paloma continued to slide while the farmhand had caught himself on the counter. He unsheathed a knife from the cork block.

Blood trickled from his nose, and he let out a violent roar that spiraled through the kitchen.

"Move away, old man," he growled, his chest heaving. "Move away or I'll cut your throat. What a shame that would be. A silent musician." He turned to Paloma, who stood adjacent to Yeats.

"Come, Paloma," echoed the farmhand, "I'll show you the fields."

Yeats stepped forward, his chest soaring. He grabbed a large bottle and slung it forcefully against the wall. It shattered into a glass puzzle on the floor.

The younger man lunged forward, knife first. It missed, and the blade cracked clean into the wall six inches from the old man's head. Yeats had absorbed the blow well and knocked the knife away with the back of his hand. They rumbled around the kitchen, two boys fighting over a woman.

Broken glass stuck to their clothes as they rolled, exchanging punches.

Yeats made every strike count. He had the neath way of fighting. Paloma's Cannaroo coach in Longleath had been trained by the neath. The style was more of a float or a dance, avoiding the heavy punches as if thrown in slow motion.

After Yeats landed a jab between the farmhand's ribs, the younger man grunted and flailed out hard with his left arm. A hard slash of turquoise sea glass sliced through the air, landing beneath Yeats shoulder. Blood pooled fast on the floor.

The farmhand had fought like a Huntress would, and ran like one too. He stomped off in a half-lusty rage.

Paloma leapt forward, careful to avoid the glass, and shoved her hands over Yeats' wound. Blood was spilling fast.

She pulled open a nearby drawer and found a white rag. Paloma's hands pressed down hard, but the wound continued to leak. Unconscious, the man's face remained simple as when he had sung the night before.

For several minutes Paloma's tears dripped onto his stomach as she watched Yeats' lifeboat sink closer to death.

Then the heavy screen door banged closed.

CHAPTER 10

THE MARQUIS
OF INNISFREE

◇◇◇◇◇◇

Earlier that morning, Aeron had woken in a malaise, the taste of the fiery, cinnamon drink lingering on his tongue. Rolling out of bed, a large tree caught his attention some ways across the farm. Despite the ashen clouds, dawn had ignited the tree a whitish orange that called to Aeron.

Beside him, Paloma looked comfortable as her head rested in between two pillows. He would only be gone for an hour, so she wouldn't know he had left.

He passed down the stairs and through the empty kitchen. Atop the oak counter, Aeron saw a white leaf of paper with some messily scrawled words. Without reading, he tucked it in his pocket and made no noise passing out the door.

Where is Yeats? He said he would help me find the old man. I wonder if he knows the man's name...

Aeron sat on the top step of the porch and looked out on the wide-openness of Yeats' sprig plantation. Between a barn and a small island-copse were at least fifty rows of green-spudded bushes that resembled a cross between agave and aubergine. The naturally occurring sprig he had seen in the forest were thicker and had stickier buds.

A few animals roamed the field—a few cows, a goat, a handful of chickens—and all of them seemed to have free rein. He pulled the paper out of his pocket and flattened it out, but then a thin wisp of song drifted out from a short way across the farm. Yeats maybe? The tune hummed in his head more than rang in his ears, and it seemed to be coming from the trees rather than the barn or out in the field.

He jogged across a grassy green, which threaded between the rectangular plots of sprig. The smell of it still alive in the ground tasted so much more pleasant than it did dead in a smoke.

The tree lay behind a thick layer of brush. Aeron weaved through it, snagging his clothes at least a handful of times before arriving at the central clearing. He brushed aside an army of liana flowers curtaining from the tree that had called to him from the window: tall, lofty, and imposing.

He stepped closer. A point an inch below eye level in the tree's bark had manmade markings. He brushed his fingers against the soft carving; it felt like the marks on the Mason Grimoire, though these formed a wavelike glyph similar to that on the fountain from the day prior. None were written in Mother Tongue.

"Another Orangu rune," Aeron whispered.

In the mid-wood silence, the leaves seemed to whisper back. Then a loud thumping, too real to be an illusion, came crashing toward him. The road ran parallel to this tree, and Aeron whipped around to find the farmhand stomping past with a rioter's scowl.

He turned back to the tree. Though the old prisoner had taught Aeron the core of the Orangu language, he failed to recognize this symbol.

At once, he felt the need to return to the cabin. He sketched the two arched, rainbow shaped rune into the Journal and examined it for a moment. His ears perked as a cry came from the farmhouse. Paloma. As if avoiding a viper's fangs, he wheeled around, facing away from the tree, and burst into a sprint. A thorn caught his right sleeve and threw him off balance causing him to twist his foot on an exposed rock and stumble out from the hedgerow with a mouthful of torn leaves.

He circled a boulder and paused in front of the barn. The sky was clear, exactly as he had left it, but something in the air felt wrong. It was only then it occurred to him that leaving her alone in a strange house could be jarring. He needed to be there to explain things when she woke.

Aeron yanked on the pull straps of the haversack. He could feel the warmth as it sucked tighter against his back. He bolted forward, tucking the Journal into the inner breast pocket of his beige and green vest as he ran. Though small, Aeron had always been fast.

Feet barely touching the ground, he zigzagged down the rows of sprig and paused at the steps to the porch. The screen door made no sound on open, but it closed with a bang.

Paloma startled at the noise. She was pressing two hands down hard on Yeats's shoulder, bloody rag in hand.

"You!" she shouted, face beet red and flaring. "Look what you've done!"

Aeron fell silent, noticing the scent of citrus and blood that stung the air.

"We thought you had gone!" she said.

"I was just—"

"It doesn't matter," said Paloma, gesturing to the huge gash from Yeats' left shoulder down to the pit of his arm. "Here, quickly. Hold this down."

Yeats lay semi-conscious on the counter. The floor was lined with shards of broken turquoise glass and a sticky, reddish puddle. Though in a fugue, the man's breaths came in the sound of a broken tune. Suddenly, a thought pounced on Aeron.

"Innisfree…" he said, pressing the bloodied rag with all his strength. How had he not seen it before? The night Yeats had called himself "the Marquis of Innisfree."

"Arise now healthily, ahead forever—the Marquis Innisfree," Aeron sang the line. Then, he recalled two lines from Lamark's riddle.

"Grapple's Grapple, The Inn is free."

"Paloma," said Aeron. But she ignored him and continued rattling around the kitchen. "Paloma!"

"I'm looking for—" Paloma cried.

"I know what to do," said Aeron, carefully removing Yeats's necklace. He held it for a moment in his hand and stared at what looked like the ocean within. "Please fill up a pitcher of water from the well, and grab a new rag for the blood." He set down the pendant, which tinkled softly like a hummingbird. "Please."

Paloma's eyes throttled him like a girl in terrible pain but too proud to cry. Something dark must have happened.

"Get it yourself," she said and pressed down harder on the wound on Yeats's arm. Her hands were slick with red. "I'm keeping him alive."

"Palo," Aeron said and grabbed ahold of her, "he's dying. Please."

She must have seen the desperation in his eyes because she released the man's arm and turned for the door. Yeats's eyes flittered and then closed again. Aeron needed to study once more the page from his great-great-great-great grand-dad, the Epiphysicist Vido Mason. He reached into his breast pocket and pulled out the Mason Grimoire.

Death is wicked, death is great;
Too early to be never, too often to be late.
Remember them, those the words of
Epiphysical love. Anudato Euthanasis,
A lyric to save them all.

He dropped the haversack to the floor, away from the blood and glass. He unbelted it pulling the strings wide. A heat billowed from the bottom of the bag and thin shoots of light skirted from beneath a pile of heartfruit. He thrust his hand to the bottom. Though the Grapple was solid its skin was warm and soft, like silver. He gripped it and felt the slightest bit of give as he pulled it from the sack.

The Grapple pulsed with a mixture of nacarat, yellow, and hints of blue deep within. At the center, something barely visible swirled, like smoke.

"Who in Cedre's name—" Paloma began, eyes wide.

"Shhh," he comforted with the Grapple in one hand and the open Journal in the other.

"Yeats!" said Paloma, clapping her hands above him. "Mercy... stay with us, Yeats."

The sound of the neath man's unconscious humming meant he had not yet lost too much blood, Aeron guessed.

"Ah!" he shouted. The Journal remained open on the table and Aeron leaned back over the page once more. Each note in the Aero had to be sung right. He gulped a heaving breath, and the Grapple's blue ribs rippled. He closed his eyes, touched the Grapple to his temple, and called the words.

"Anudato euthanasis!"

As he sang them, Aeron pressed the Grapple gently into Yeats's shoulder. The bottles on the wall shook and clattered on the shelves.

"Anudato," Aeron shouted once more. A bottle crashed to the floor and splintered into shards. Then another and three, four.

"Euthanasis!" bottles rained to the floor. Aeron looked down at the bucket of water, now empty. The room felt dry as the desert sun.

For a moment nothing happened. Aeron closed his eyes like a boy afraid of failure. Teeth clenched, he waited for a sign. When he was about to open his eyes, a gasp stroked the air.

CHAPTER 11

PURADOR

"Holy Harroes," Yeats gasped. He sat up with a bit of a start and looked around the kitchen at the shattered dishes and bottles. Neath blood had a silver tint to it, and the pool of blood smeared on the floor had been spilt by him. He clenched Paloma's arm.

"Yeats!" said Paloma. "Oh, thank the haevens. I thought we had lost you." She wrapped her arms around him, bloodying herself all the more.

"Ah," grunted the man. "Easy there, miss."

Paloma pulled away and they both helped Yeats sit up on the table.

"I'll get you some water from the well," said Aeron.

"I'm sorry you had to deal with that, miss—"

The door banged closed.

"I've seen worse," said Paloma. "Thank you."

"No, my dear lady. Thank you. Only a matter of time before that happened. I'm glad you were here."

"Well," she said. "You'd be dead if it weren't for Aeron."

The door swung open and Aeron reemerged empty handed.

"Well," Aeron said with amazement, "the entire well's gone dry!"

"How could that be possible?" said Yeats.

"I, uh, well," Aeron stammered. "Let's say I used all your water."

Yeats looked less shocked than Paloma expected.

"I see," he said and made a momentous effort to move his injured side.

"Ahhgh." He grimaced, poking at the cut. "Looks like my longharp days may be gone. Arm is frozen stiff."

"Sorry," said Aeron, his eyes trailing the floor.

"Don't be," said Yeats, his voice eloquent and lingering. "I was always a singer anyway... like your father."

Aeron's face raised with alarm.

My father? Yeats knew Loo. But does he know I am wanted?

Aeron darted a look to Paloma.

Does she?

Yeats must have read the deer-eyed look on Aeron's face. "Think I wouldn't know the son of—"

"Don't!" Aeron shouted, unnerved.

"You mean," said Yeats, "she doesn't know?"

"What am I missing?" Paloma asked.

"I was your dad's luthier for a long time, Aeron. And I can spot kin from across a farm."

Aeron held his breath, hoping beyond hope that he could trust Yeats. That the neath-man hadn't turned him in to the authorities.

No one spoke for a whole minute.

"I know," said Paloma, "that we weren't going to do family names, but this is getting quite a bit odder than my liking."

"No names," Aeron burst out. Though Yeats knew who he was, Paloma still did not. Aeron intended to keep it that way. "But I have a question." Aeron flipped the Journal to the most recent page where he'd drawn the rune. "What do you make of this?"

"I see you've found the Tree of Innisfree," said Yeats, looking rather impressed. Yeats's breathing slowed and grew heavy. "It is Orangu, but I have never seen such a rune before." He made an arc-shape with the cup of his hand. "It could mean tornado, but it could also mean fire…"

"I'm looking for the map," said Aeron, stealing a glance at Paloma. If he could find the Reddheart's map, it would lead him straight to the old man.

"*The* map?" asked Yeats. "Or the man who owns it?"

Aeron's jaw fell open an inch. Like the Eurovean, Yeats seemed to know more than he let on.

First Lamark, now this Yeats? It seems like everyone here knows this old man, but not a soul knows how to find him.

"I do not know the old man, but I have heard that he lives in an enormous cave inside the mountain! Only one on this island can lead you to him," said Yeats. "Fortunately for you, I happen to know that man. Unfortunately for you, he does not like strangers. Especially ones from Oriendo."

"I knew you weren't from the Southern Rift," accused Paloma, her eyes narrow.

"Who?" Aeron asked Yeats.

"Manu Everett," Yeats replied. "The Wilder."

Paloma's jaw fell like a marionette, and Aeron was no less astonished.

"You mean…" said Aeron.

"The Last Great Ranger…" said Paloma.

Yeats nodded, but his eyes were heavier and growing more blank by the minute. He pointed to the wall behind Aeron. "Pass me that bottle, the dark blue one with the frosted glass."

Careful to avoid the shattered glass, Aeron crossed the kitchen to where the mid-sized bottle rested in a silver wall sconce. It was heavier than expected—either because of the glass or the liquid inside. Holding it by the neck, Aeron handed the bottle to Yeats.

Yeats wedged the bottle between his legs and flicked the metal swing-stopper open. He pulled out the cork, which fell to the counter.

Aeron's nostrils filled with a sweet but aerthy scent, somewhere between honey and nectar.

Paloma held one of the empty glasses on the table in front of him. Yeats gripped the bottle with his right hand, and it looked so much smaller compared to when Aeron had held it. But Yeats's strength was waning once again.

"Was it the Aero?" Aeron asked. "I must have sung it wrong."

"No, m'boy, you did wonderfully," said Yeats, shaking his head. He tipped the bottle to ninety degrees. A thin trickle of syrupy liquid fell slowly. "I was at death's door, and now I'm here. It was *him*." Yeats gestured out the door with his head.

He filled the cup no more than half an inch. The liquid was gold and had bluish flakes floating within.

Like the Grapple…

Yeats placed the bottle beside him on the wood and laid back again. He took up nearly entire the counter.

Eyes closed, he spoke quietly.

He's dying! I could have saved him, I know it.

Aeron turned back to the Journal and flipped through its old pages. There must be something else to do. Aeron needed Yeats to help him find the old man.

Yeats must have sensed Aeron's distress. "I saved the boy from the Huntress, and the Huntress worship one of Aerth's most vulgar flowers. Purple Rapien, it's called. A paralytic and powerful pain reliever. I feel it in me now. He must have used it on me."

His breaths grew shallow.

"Pour that in my mouth, slowly, when I lose—"

He laid motionless on the table. Paloma took two steps to her right to where Yeats's long face rested, peaceful as neath always appeared. His lips were open, the size of a grape, so she tipped the glass. The golden liquid fell in an unbroken trickle for a few seconds.

Nothing.

Paloma shook the cup and two final drops passed through his lips.

Yeats sprang up like a startled leopard. Gasping, his eyes grew wide, euphoric, and vigorous with life.

Aeron and Paloma backed away from the counter for fear of being accidentally struck.

A few seconds passed and Yeats returned from bliss to neutral.

"Yeats," Aeron said, "is that what I think it is?"

Yeats pinched the stopper back onto the top of the bottle. Immediately the room felt a tinge less bright.

Yeats nodded. "Purador."

"Purador is *not* real," said Paloma, "it's a faery tale."

Yeats lips pulled to a thin grin.

"Here," he said to Aeron, holding out the bottle. "This is for saving my life." Then he turned to face Paloma and bowed. "To both of you, for your troubles."

A dense, silent amazement cloaked the room. Paloma was right. Purador had appeared so many times in myths and old stories. "The Mead of Life," his great granddad called it…

Purador extends life, heals the sick, and gives strength to dying men. Apart from the Grapple, this bottle is more valuable than all the heartfruit I have.

"Take it," said Yeats. "But do not use it. The Ranger will be drawn to it. Otherwise, you will never find him."

"Yeats, this is," Aeron paused, "too much. This much purador would give you your arm back in a flash."

"No," said Yeats. "There is a great healer on the island. I have wanted an excuse to meet her. She will have another way."

Yeats eased down from the table and walked slowly toward the door. Paloma opened it for him and the three of them stepped out onto the deck.

"But I must ask one more favor."

"Anything," said Paloma.

"May I see it?" he asked Aeron. "The Grapple."

The boy nodded. He reached into his pocket and a leaf of paper fluttered free. Behind him, Paloma silently scooped it up and scanned the note.

The Praeth has returned. Send help.

She tucked the paper away as Aeron revealed the stone to Yeats.

"Incredible," Yeats repeated. "Absolutely incredible."

He hovered his hands over it like a warm fire. The Grapple's blue ripples seemed to respond as if alive.

"How did you know?" asked Paloma.

"I am a neath-man, after all," he said and winked, "I've been near death before, and I know what it feels like to have an Aero bring you back."

He cupped his good hand over his eyes to shield the sun. A warm breeze kicked pollen through the air.

"Now," he continued, "it is midday. You must be off if you are to reach the Gaelen's Gulch before sundown. I have a yearling horse you can take. I haven't ridden in quite some time, and with this arm…"

"Who is Gaelen?" Paloma asked.

"Gaelen is long gone, but her birds remain. That is how you will know." Yeats now faced them, his expression severe. "Listen now. Shortly after we left last night, I heard that a strange man, not neath, but Irkal, burst through The Sportsman's door asking about a wandering kid… I imagine that to be you."

CHAPTER 12

THE ATHON

◇◇◇◇◇◇

"Me?" Aeron asked in disbelief.

Walking along the dirt road on Yeats's ranch, a horse sputtered its lips. Paloma sped ahead of them and tried to peek inside, but the whitewashed barn door was locked.

I've been careful with who I trust, like Grandad always said. How do they know? And why me?

"All I'm after is righting what's been done to my family… what do they want with me?" Aeron continued. The dirt hardened as they approached the barn. "Plus, I haven't told a soul who I am—save you two and the Merchant of Herraz."

"Lamark?" said Yeats. "A huckster, for sure, but he would never deal with an Irkal."

"Then I have no idea."

"All the more reason you must find the Ranger."

Paloma turned and smiled. "Looks like you're going to West Riamante after all, Aeron."

He nodded, his heart heavy with the weight of the world. "Always was," but Paloma seemed keen on seeing the horse and did not hear him.

"Enough, children. You must be going before the blue jays have gone. They will lead you right to the gulch."

Yeats unlatched the door and presented a brown mare. She had streaks of white down her side and a leather nose bridle with reins attached. He held the reins out to Paloma. She took them in one hand as Yeats disappeared into the barn. Paloma pressed a hand to the horse's nose. The horse lifted a hoof and pressed it back down to the aerth. Paloma made a hushing noise to comfort her.

When Yeats reappeared, he carried a packsaddle with two seats. He swung it over the horse's back and belted the straps under her belly.

"Milvia has never had a priman rider. I imagine she'll enjoy less weight."

Paloma swung herself onto the saddle. "She is marvelous! Endless thank yous." She hooked her feet into the stirrups.

"No, thank you. Her mother is from Neath—she can run for hours with stopping. But the Oriendo in her needs watching. A bit... timid."

Aeron tightened the haversack with the purador and Grapple inside, but he needed a hand mounting. Yeats boosted the boy with his good arm. Even sitting on the horse, the neath man had to look down at him.

"I recommend you stow that on Milvia's pack," Yeats suggested.

"No," said Aeron. "I'll be keeping this close from now on."

"Very well," said Yeats with a bow.

"I hope to see you again, Yeats," said Aeron. "Next time."

"When you do, I expect a song. And I'll tell you more about my time in Longleath."

The three traded nods.

"Yah!" Paloma shouted with a kick that sent the horse bolting.

They galloped through the sound of chittering cicadas and clacking hooves as a flock of birds circled overhead.

Paloma felt like a heroine mounted atop such a healthy horse in such an ancient place.

Hugging the high ground, they snaked along the Grey Road. It was midday, and across the valley the forest was shrouded with sylvan luster.

Aeron looked skyward at the blue jays.

"The Eurovean had said the same thing," Aeron shouted over the noise. "Blue jays…"

"I don't know what to believe from you, Aeron, and what not to believe."

They rode for hours, winding ever deeper through the veins of the Gilder Forest. As they did, the land grew more and more coastal, the trees became taller, and the plants were more vibrant. The animals seemed bolder as well. During the hours they rode, the two primen had gained a following among the forest of hootia, parrox, and other animalia.

"This is incredible!" shouted Aeron, competing with the clamor of hooves.

"Just wait—" Paloma called over her shoulder, but her thoughts ran elsewhere. A short time later, she said, "I wonder why Yeats would put his farm so near the shadow of a mountain. A clever neath man would know better—unless the mountain had some other benefit…"

The rock itself was more than a hill but far less than a mountain, and it proved to be much larger than they expected as their journey continued into the valley.

As they galloped, Paloma rubbed at her lower back, but the river valley was too lush to care about her hurts. They curled around a leafy bend with a panorama of greens and yellows dotting the horizon.

"Ride hard," Yeats had said gravely. "Ride hard, around the mountain, until you find the gulch."

It had been several hours when Paloma felt Milvia's back go tense. She pulled the mount to a halt.

"Why have you stopped?" Aeron said. "Paloma, we're losing sight of the birds."

Ahead of them, the sun had fallen lower in the sky.

"She's been going for hours," said Paloma. "She needs a break. And look there." Paloma pointed to a family of blue jays chittering from a branch beside the path.

Beneath them was a heap of seaweed and vines. A balmy, briny scent licked the air, and the sound of all other wildlife had trailed off.

"Careful—" Aeron said as Paloma edged Milvia on. The mare's hooves made a squish against the wet aerth.

"Shh—do you feel that?"

There, directly in front of them, was a treacherous-looking gully. The bluff curved upward at its edge, and in between stood ten feet of damp, dark, fallen trees. The smell of rot permeated quite rudely.

Blocked by the mountain, the bluff had a damp and eerie darkness to it. Even the horde of blue jays above swarmed as a mindless bird might. A mixture of thoughts spooled through his mind.

Something happened here. I can feel it in the silence. There must be a reason no animals come near, and the birds seem trapped between this side of the Riamante and that side.

"This must be the gulch," she said. "On the other side we'll be in West Riamante and closer to the Ranger..."

"She's flighty," said Aeron. "Not good to mistrust an animal's instincts. We should cross the fault by foot."

"Nonsense," Paloma said and eased the horse down a low ramp of scree. The further down they went, the harder the horse resisted.

"Be easy, Milvia—" Aeron said, coaxing the horse.

"*Owww*, cut that out!" Paloma shouted.

The shriek startled the horse and she chipped forward, knocking a hoof against a stone. Aeron's weight teetered side to side.

"Oy!" Aeron cried. "Watch where you're going."

They sat mounted squarely in the fault's center in complete silence. The ditch smelled like ocean, wind, and danger.

Aeron, listening to the sound of echoes mating with silence, watched the evening star rising in the twilit sky.

"Look," said Aeron. "The walls between the roots have been scratched and burned raw..."

Milvia went rigid beneath them, and Paloma looked up, tracing the horse's gaze. Then she too became rock solid. An athon skulked toward them with merciless eyes, fearsome fangs, and a yellow streak from head to tail. Worse, the yellow streak meant this athon had been brought from far north, Irkalla, for tracking.

It had a blood-red mane with three eyes on each side of a strong brown snout. In body, athons were said to be somewhere in between wolves and tigers, but this one was huge and wore a saddle, as if to be ridden.

When Loo Mason became the first priman to perform in Irkalla, the vizier had given him a ceremonial dagger. Aeron remembered staring at it for long hours, admiring the strange runes etched onto the hilt. "The sharpest blade in the Northern Rift," its casing read.

Now staring into the jaws of that savage creature his mind returned to the dagger. The case had lied. These were the sharpest blades in Irkalla.

It all happened so fast. At the sight of those teeth, Milvia reared on two legs, sending both Aeron and Paloma vaulting through the air. The ground, soft and mulchy, seemed to have caught Paloma well enough.

But when a bed of rocks rushed up to greet Aeron, jabbing the contents of the haversack hard to his side, he heard a muffled crack beneath the right side of his chest.

Then he saw a harrowing streak of black and yellow as the athon leapt close enough to hear its breath. Propped on one side, Aeron closed his eyes and waited for pain. Instead, the sound of a falling boulder crushed the ground in front of him. He blinked. A boot adorned with two falcon feathers punched the aerth beneath a tree trunk of a leg with its calf rippling.

The athon growled, blinked three of its eyes, and backed away a step as if readying to pounce, but the boot did not move. The creature looked at the rock-solid face of the man now standing between predator and prey. Back arched and tail between its legs, the athon retreated until it scampered through the forest to the east from where it had come.

The man bent low. His face, mean-eyed and murderous, met with Aeron's.

This is it, Aeron thought.

The man scooped him up with one hand, as if he were a sack of potatoes. Struggling to breathe with jags of pain emanating from his right lung, Aeron wavered between consciousness and its dark underbelly.

This must be who Yeats meant.

"You," said the man to Paloma, his voice miles away, "Come with me or—"

As darkness collapsed over Aeron's senses he heard the man say, "He dies."

CHAPTER 13

A HOUSE DIVIDED

*I*t's dusk. Aeron is climbing his favorite tree, the oak in their side yard with the trunk as thick as a small lighthouse. It overlooks a busy street with two brick cafes, a mint green plant-shop, and a white stone official building. Many times, Aeron has watched his granddad enter into the building before he moved with Vella to the Northerlies.

Almost a year has passed since the news of Mendel Mason's "fraudulence." Though the papers have little proof, they had it on "high authority that the Masons had built their legacy on a series of thievery and lies."

A plain black nightjar alights on the branch beside him. Its flat head and red beak fringed with bristles are shocking because the bird has no eyes. For a minute, the bird's head stares at him, and Aeron finds it hard to look away.

Aeron shakes his head side to side. The nightjar's gaze tracks his moves with its whole head. He needs to see the end of the street, but it blocks him. He shimmies closer to the trunk, and the bird holds its wings out a bit wider to further block his view. Aeron finds the right twig and shoos, but the dark bird makes no movement.

Rather than go higher, he crawls further out on the branch. It's long and thick and has supported both he and his sister many times before. He grips a series of knots with each hand and crawls out. He stops at the midpoint, ten yards past the iron-wrung fence.

He's now past the fence of their yard. Granddad always said to never climb outside their yard, but today is a special occasion. His return.

A steady stream of lorries chugs up the hill and along the road by their house. He has been waiting patiently for Granddad's black lorry to appear.

The last time he saw his sister, Vella, was before the school year started, and granddad not since a visit during winter term. Now it's the end of spring term. Since graduation from Longleath Prep is in a few days, the dean has sent the kids home to stay with their families.

Down the road, a black lorry pokes out from over the blue gravel.

They're here!

He inches further out onto the tree and then comes to his senses. Granddad will be furious if he sees Aeron so far out on the tree. Aeron turns back.

The eyeless face is right. Aeron's hand slips and gravity yanks at him. Aeron reaches straight up and catches hold of a low hanging branch, steadying himself upright.

The bird bores into him with a cocked head. Aeron pretends to throw something at the bird. When it doesn't move, he scoots forward toward it.

"Move!" he hisses and swipes out. It does not react. Aeron swings again, this time harder. That seems to anger it. The bird lunges forward, red bill first. Startled, the call of gravity

returns. His hands reach skyward once more, but the leaves tear away from their twigs.

Tumbling off to the right side, he grasps for an offshoot branch and catches it. Holding with two hands, his arms and torso go taut while his legs dangle thirty feet above the hard-concrete sidewalk.

"Help!" he cries. "Someone help!"

"Look," a woman shouts from across the street.

A buzz of commotion gathers in the area. His fingers turn purple as he grasps the branch with desperate strength.

"Please! Someone!"

"Help comes!" cries a foreign woman with a singer's voice. "Help comes!"

His fingers begin to slip. He can feel splinters of wood gnarling them as he falls lower on the branch.

A cart of some kind rolls below and stops beneath him.

"Let go!" shouts a teenage boy. "You're safe now."

"Boy!" calls a different man. "Drop down now!"

Aeron closes his eyes and releases the branch. For a fraction of a second he falls, then his feet connect with the hood of a lorry. He somersaults forward and off the front where a host of arms catch him.

Cheers ripple out from the crowd and the nearby cafes. But they die quickly.

Aeron opens his eyes. It's one of the fruit-vending lorries that always sits on this street at the top of the hill.

"Grab it!" shouts a woman from behind. In the chaos, the vendor must not have locked the fruiter's wheels. They begin to turn, slowly at first. Two of the men reach out, but the lorry is too heavy and already in motion down the hill. Oranges, apples, crantleberries, feebee, and other fruits go flying in every direction.

Gasps spread across the crowd and followed by a terrible silence. There is only one lorry on the incline. Black. Old. Well-maintained. Granddad...

"Watch out!" someone calls from the crowd.

Aeron turns away. Up in the tree he sees the nightjar again, eyes still fixed on him, beak almost in a grin.

Its talons have turned crimson and the branch begins to smoke. They glow hotter and redder, like coals, until the branch catches fire.

The flames feast on the tree's woody fibers. They spread like paint in water, eating away at the tree's life-giving skin as a fast-spreading virus would. Soon, clouds of smoke wrap the oak's trunk.

A collision of wood and metal groans from below. There are screams, but all Aeron can hear are the words of this dying tree.

"You can still save me," it says beneath the dusk sky. The sound seems to be coming from the roots. No one else seems to hear it. "Find the Aero."

He had dreamt this memory before, but this time it was different. It was dusk, and every other time he watched the collision occur. This time, Aeron had seen the arsenious culprit. A nightjar. When questioned by the Paladin, he never had an answer why or how the fires had started. They wiped out everything on the hill, an entire neighborhood of Longleath. They had accused him of rigging the whole thing. "To be the last Mason," they said, "the sole heir to Mendel's hidden heartfruit." But it couldn't have been a bird?

A distant voice startled Aeron awake.

Paloma's voice still sounded far away. "Aeron's burning up, and trembling... I don't like it. He needs some of the purador."

Then came another voice, too far for Aeron to make out the words. Paloma spoke again, "Why not?" she growled.

"Too valuable? He's broken at least three ribs, probably punctured a lung. This is what it's…"

The other voice came clearer, closer, yet still indiscernible.

"How do you know yours will even work?" asked Paloma, lifting his head and pressing something warm to Aeron's lips.

The concoction tasted sappy, milky, and of soil.

Aeron's eyelids broke open with a start to see Paloma's warm, dark face in front of a cloudless blue sky. He made a heroic effort to rise. Too soon. Pain hurdled through his right side like daggers.

Paloma forced him to take another sip.

All the woozier, Aeron's limbs fell heavy as the sun dipped behind a cloud.

With exhausted thoughts, meddling like thieves in the night, Aeron drifted back into a dreamless sleep.

He awoke in the night, alone. Gentle heat billowed from a nearby fire crackling beneath a large tree, its crown aglow with orange flowers.

Flames nipped against his sensitive eyes. Trying to avoid reality, Aeron rolled to a side. A breathtaking mural arced the wall with mollusks, fish, frogs, snakes, mammals, and men. Then he saw a half-painted Wraeth.

"Paloma?" he asked. Or maybe whispered, with his voice so raspy and his good ear in the dirt, he couldn't tell.

Still no answer.

He rose, wobbling to and fro, to the sound of distant voices. The drink had dulled the pain and Aeron followed them as spring follows winter. Trims of moonlight peeked through the canopy, flecking the ground like a chessboard.

He stumbled as best he could down a slope. The voices grew and every so often Aeron would catch a word.

"*Kommorae.*" An Orangu word he couldn't recall.

Since entering the tavern, Aeron had lost all sense of time. It could have been one night or one hundred years, but his feet scuffled as a drunk would in search of lost friends.

"Athon wounds have a strange way about them," a man's voice explained. They seemed to be walking away. "He needs the right medicine to heal."

"You pretend like you *know*, but why should I trust you, Saunter?" asked Paloma.

"I have more experience with wounds than I should like," the man called Saunter replied. "With the eagle hunters, the Toltai, near Indoshina."

To Paloma, the man's way of speaking felt both eerie and familiar. It seemed native to Oriendo, but at the same time dark and jagged like the deep north. His leathery, rippled cheeks remained still and stoic, despite the boom in his voice.

"The purador will heal him on the spot," she said. "And I need to get west. Fast."

"So," he pointed out as if daring her. "Leave then."

They had begun to move faster now and, struggling to keep their pace, Aeron's wheezing grew. He pushed through curtains of tall grass in a hazy fugue.

But then came the man's voice, clear as a gong. "The only thing," Saunter said, "stopping me from taking this haversack, all the heartfruit and your purador is… curiosity."

"You wretch," Paloma scowled.

A large boulder blocked Aeron's way. From the other side came the sound of hands lapping in water. To the left, Aeron found a set of old trail stairs. His feet were anvils, but he made it to the top, feverish beads of sweat crawling down his cheeks, and rested on an outlook.

Paloma drank from a pool, still and dark, with a large tealeaf. The man, still hard to make out, took three huge, bearish gulps, and wiped his face.

"I'll feel a whole lot better when you two are both up and out of here."

"Likewise," Paloma barked.

Then there was silence, save for Saunter's thirsty sipping.

"Whoever is after your friend will shift their sights my way. Of course, even as an old grey beard, I could make quick work of them but... I'd rather be left alone with my moshrums." He paused for a moment and scratched his chin.

With beads of sweat crawling down Aeron's cheeks, he leaned over the slope to catch a closer glimpse. Instead, he tripped on a log and went crashing down the slope through the leaves.

Lying in a blanket of brush, he faded in and out of consciousness. But there seemed to be the faint sound of singing too. It reminded him of the day he'd come upon the heart-fruit grove.

After a few moments he rose, his hand pressed to his side, and peered through a pair of trees that had fused together and played vantage to a native's camp, lit by lantern and the moon.

The camp, though spartan, had a controlled insanity with all its various objects: shells from what must have been giant snails, ceramics that could have been from a different time, well-kept skulls and animal fossils.

"Maybe... I can point you in the right direction," said Saunter. "Then I won't feel guilty keeping one or two of these here heartfruit."

Then the aerth shook, as if the mountain behind them was angry.

"What was that?" she said from a knee.

"You picked the wrong time to come here," said the man, dusting off his jacket. "*The* storm approaches." He stood and looked up at the moon.

"I had no choice," hissed Paloma.

"We are our choices," said Saunter, "and *nothing* is easy to choose."

Aeron crept closer, and a branch cracked beneath his knee. He froze beside a blue lorry that smelled of fresh paint. For a breath, the conversation paused.

"I'm looking for someone," said Paloma. "On behalf of the vizier of Longleath."

"Orders from Vizier Mattisun?" asked the man, looking up from the pot. "You seem a little young."

"Well," Paloma admitted, "she didn't exactly send me. But my uncle happens to be a writer in the Council. He mentioned that she had put a reward out to whoever brings the Ranger back to Longleath."

The man rubbed steam from his eyes and face as he made to speak, but Paloma continued.

"And then I received a letter…"

The man's jacket rippled with movement. He turned away from her, fumbling through supplies on his workbench such as stones of opal, emerald, granite, homemade foraging tools, and farming weapons with white blades.

"It wasn't signed and, oh mercy," she sighed, speaking to his back. "I wasn't even sure it was meant for me. But I hadn't received a letter in ages! It looked like it had been written a hundred years ago, but I knew from the seal it was recent. They said that the Ranger had abandoned his post and gone missing somewhere in Western Elevana. I hadn't heard much about Elevana as they avoid teaching about it in schools because of how Elevanos treat children."

Saunter filled his wooden canteen with a large scoop of broth from the smaller pot. It stank of moshrum.

"Supposedly, he lives in West Riamante and has been spotted with a mint green lorry."

"Mint? Ugly color for a fugitive," he said and gestured behind him with his canteen hand to where his lorry sat cloaked by heavy hanging leaves. "I prefer blue."

Then came the sound of boiling water.

"Ahh," said Saunter. "Perfect timing. Moshrum is ready. And supper too. You should invite your friend to join us."

Paloma made for the hill.

"Girl," he said, "you are going the wrong way."

Part way up the slope, she turned back to face him, dark skin shimmering in the night as she furrowed her brow.

Holding Aeron's haversack in one hand, Saunter tapped a finger to his ear.

"He's behind my lorry. Fetch him, before he gets her bloody..." said Saunter.

As Paloma rushed across the camp, Aeron made to retreat back into the woods. Something about this man told Aeron that he wouldn't appreciate being spied on.

But such a rapid movement knocked Aeron off balance. Then came Saunter's voice once more.

"Maybe the little spy can convince me why I shouldn't sell you both," he said, "and keep this bottle of purador for my own."

CHAPTER 14

THE WRAETH PRINCE

◇◇◇◇◇◇

Heart-lamp in hand, Paloma crouched at Aeron's side. Though his wound looked better, the stitches along his ribs had split. The boy's glazed-over expression gave her the impression that the medicine had begun to wear off.

"Let's shut it about the purador," said Paloma, "and get him some more medicine."

"Fine, but I expect payment," said Saunter. He had two halves of a silver tribal feather in his hair at the back. His skin resembled the color of dried adobe and had gone leathery from time in the sun, and his thin lips and left eye were slightly off to the side of his wide nose. "Moshrums do not grow on—"

Paloma shot a glare and Saunter stopped short, glaring back with hazel brown eyes. He wore a red ribbon around his neck as well as a blue cord, but the blue cord was latched together with a small gold medallion. With a reluctant sigh, he took off his jacket and approached them, scooping up Aeron with two hands, this time more gently.

"Lay that out," he said, and Paloma spread the jacket on the ground. Saunter placed him on top of it.

"As I was saying," he continued, "Moshrum don't grow on—

"Eeeergh." Paloma raised a hand to her scrunched nose. "His wound stinks."

"It's cleaner than I expected," said Saunter, looking up at Paloma. "Good thing he had heartfruit in his blood already. Boy heals fast. Fill that horn by the sack to the brim; he needs to drink it all."

Paloma spooned the light brown liquid into the horn and raised the cup to her own lips. The smell of aerth, mint, and sweet icco filled her nostrils.

"Don't," Saunter commanded without looking up. "To the uninjured, moshrum can alight the senses. Sometimes to the point of insanity."

"You drink it all the time," said Paloma.

"Yes, and do I seem sane to you?" Saunter strung a new set of needles with suture-sprig.

Paloma lowered the horn and moved to Aeron. She lifted his head to a gentle tilt and held the concoction to his lips.

As Aeron drank, Paloma admired Saunter's khaki jacket, made from a material similar to Aeron's haversack. The jacket's trim coordinated a design with feathers and raised suede.

Something tells me this man knows about the Ranger, and maybe Aeron's old man too...

"Why don't the athon come here?" asked Paloma. "You don't have many defenses in place."

"Ha," Saunter said, shaking his head with a pompous grin. "You saw well enough how athon respond when they see me. Even ones sent by an Irkal."

"Do you not speak Mother Tongue?" Paloma hissed. "That doesn't answer my question."

"I should think," he said, lowering the needle toward Aeron, who now lay more calmly, "your concern would be the Irkal. They have your scent, it seems."

Paloma lifted the now-empty horn and placed it on the ground.

"Try to stay still," she said in her most soothing voice. "He is going to help you."

Aeron gave a subtle nod and Saunter went to work. Though his hands were large and calloused, Paloma was impressed by their nimbleness. The moshrum must be working or the needle point was sharp, for Aeron didn't move as Saunter stitched his wound.

"I don't know if they have my scent, his, or both. Haeven's mercy, I hope it's only one. One tracer athon is enough to worry about. Plus, the Huntress..."

"Gaaah," Aeron yelped.

Saunter's hands had skipped at the mention of the Huntress. Paloma coaxed Aeron back to stillness.

"There are no Huntress left," he said, wiping sweat away with the back of his free hand. "The Ranger made sure of that."

"So you know him?" Paloma asked, stiff as a bone.

For a moment, there was nothing but a thin silence. Saunter had finished the sixth stitch, halfway up the wound.

"Yes," Saunter finally replied and leaned back for a moment to take a sip from his horn.

"So can you help us find him? For that," Paloma said with excitement, "I'm sure Aeron would give you a heartfruit."

"Unfortunately," Saunter replied, "we are all after the same man."

Paloma's eyes narrowed. He must have read her suspicion.

"No more questions. Near the end is always the most dangerous. A mistake means less moshrum for me. After all, moshrums do not grow on—" he pulled away, twisting his face as though he had to sneeze.

Soon after Saunter had finished with Aeron's stitches, Aeron had fallen asleep on top of the Saunter's jacket, but he didn't seem to mind.

Paloma turned toward Saunter. They had each finished a bowl of his delectable stew.

"You did great, Saunter. Thank you," Paloma continued with tired eyes. "Now you should get some sleep. And in the morning, you can explain to Aeron and me how you found us in the first place… that should be an interesting story."

"I sleep little."

"Me as well."

Saunter laughed, but Paloma couldn't say why. Then he got up and, after refilling his horn with moshrum, entered his makeshift cabin.

Paloma passed the hours until dawn lying half asleep in a soft bed of grass. As the sun crawled into the sky, she was startled awake by the voice of a boy, distant at first. Then, as she rolled up, grass sticking to her cheek, she heard it louder.

"Hello, Paloma," said Aeron, propped up against Saunter's wooden throne. He held a bowl of stew in his lap.

"Glad to see some color back in those cheeks, Aeron."

"Well," Aeron cleared his throat, "the last thing I remember is Milvia's trembles, soaring through the air, and a streak of black and yellow fur. And now I wake up with a stitched side, next to a cold pot of stew." He paused and looked around. "This is how I'd imagined a Huntress to live."

Paloma surveyed the camp of several half-buried fire pits surrounded by plots of dead grass beside an old shanty.

Moshrums lay scattered in odd places, as did various weapons, seashells, and minerals.

Beside a smelting iron, the workbench held small blackish crystals and an ivory hilt. Three masks made of leather, green metal, and stone hung above the table along with feathers of owl, eagle, and one bird she did not recognize.

Could he be a Huntress?

"Aeron," she said, "we both need to find the Ranger. Right? This man—Saunter, he is called—is after the Ranger too and spoke as if they've met many times. You are right. I may have been too quick to trust him, but he did save your life after all."

Paloma's fear settled, recalling the man in action. Aeron finished his bowl and made to fill his horn with moshrum. Smelling the drink, his lips puckered with surprise.

"I'd love to hear what in god's name happened…"

Paloma grinned, breaking a twig to scratch at the ground. She spent the next minutes relating the last three days. First, she drew an athon with a streak on its back and then turned it into a large boot with feathers around the ankle. Finally she drew a small boy lying beside a camouflaged lorry.

"Keep going," Aeron said. "It comes back in pieces when you do."

"Somehow," she whispered, "he knew you were here the whole time and said nothing until I was about to get you from where we'd left you."

"Where you left me?"

"He said you would heal better up there. The air is thinner and there's this mural they say has regenerative powers."

"We have the purador," Aeron said and looked around for the haversack. Paloma had lain on it overnight, for safekeeping. She opened it up and shook her head.

"So that's what he wants then. The purador."

"For some reason," she said, "he refused to use it on you. Even a drop would be 'a waste.'"

"Do you remember what Yeats said?" Aeron asked. "Rangers can smell purador for miles…" With great difficulty, he gestured toward the haversack. "Reach in there and pass me the book inside."

She fished out the orange Journal and rolled over on one knee to reach him.

Mercy, I hope I put the bookmark back correctly.

He took it and flipped through the pages until landing on one of the older, flimsier leaves.

"Yes," he said, "as I thought." With a slight grimace, he held the page out so both of them could see. Paloma edged closer toward him on the ground.

A battle has existed since the beginning of time, old as the war between life and death. Huntress need it, Rangers want to keep them from it. Both have developed a knack for finding it.

"You said he too is searching for the Ranger," said Aeron. "He must know the Ranger will find it. When he does, this Saunter will claim we're runaway slaves trying to steal his fortune, or worse…" Aeron's eyes darted around the camp.

"I'm not so sure." Paloma wanted to believe that Saunter was no Huntress, but Aeron seemed so convinced. "You didn't see the way he stitched you up last night."

"Think about it," Aeron said taking a large sip from the horn.

"I *think* you should slow down with that drink."

Aeron ignored the remark. "Why was he there in the gulch at all? The timing is too—"

"It all began with the drought," Saunter's voice boomed from behind. Despite his tree-trunk legs, Saunter's feet had the silence of a thief's. He stepped between them and sat on a log across from Aeron. "As a younger man, every summer for twenty years I came back here, to Elevana, and I have never once seen even ten days go by without rain, let alone sixty. It has changed the shape of this land. I normally stay clear of the Gulch on the western side of Riamante, but I have had no choice.

"A friend and brother taught me to trust the signs. Birds that never leave were flying north, the tide was running high when it should be low, and even the neath have called off all weddings and their summer feast. He said that sixty nights with no rain means sixty-nights-worth will strike at once. And that is only the beginning."

"So you happened to be at the Gulch when the athon came?" asked Aeron. "How do we know you didn't send it in the first place?"

"It had a yellow streak, Aeron," said Paloma. "An Irkal sent it."

"That striped athon drew me there," Saunter said. "As your friend has told you, I have killed enough athon that they shrink at the sight of me. When this one ran through the ridge where I rested, and right past me, I chose to follow. There is always chaos behind roses. Maybe I would find luck."

"Boy, were you right," snorted Aeron. Paloma kicked him harder than she meant to and he yelped.

Saunter grinned for the first time. He had a unique face, but his grin reminded her of someone she knew, though *who* escaped her. Saunter rose and crouched between Aeron and the nearly empty pots. His expression turned sour.

"Skinny boy like you," said Saunter, "one would expect you to need less food and drink."

Side by side, she realized Aeron and Saunter may have been the two most dissimilar people on aerth. First, Saunter was at least three times Aeron's size. Aeron's emerald green eyes shined with youth while Saunter's hazel eyes were low and cynical. While Saunter's leathery face had three memorable almond-sized scars above his right cheek, Aeron's was simple and round and unblemished. Aeron always had a book in his hand, but Saunter had shown no signs of owning a single one.

"This storm," Aeron said with rivaling bitterness. "I've heard talk that it could lay waste to the island."

"The last *Draviño*," Saunter said, picking up the entire pot of stew. "Destroyed half the coast, and that was a small one. This is *Te Draviño*. They don't get any more dangerous." He opened his mouth wide and drained the remains directly from the iron.

"Maker," said Aeron thoughtfully. "In Orangu, *Draviño* means maker."

Saunter's eyebrows lifted as he turned to face Aeron.

"This one knows Orangu…" Saunter let the words hang in the air. "Interesting."

"Pardon my asking, Saunter," Paloma broke in, "but if this storm is how you say, will this little shack protect you?"

"No. I have another place. In the mountain."

"Is it safe to be on the side of a mountain when a hurricane hits?"

"Do you take me for a fool?" Saunter asked with an annoyed shake of his head. "Only a fool would do that. This place is *in* the mountain."

"*In* the mountain?" Aeron asked.

"I'm sorry," Paloma said. "I didn't know mountains had doors."

"No," he said, "but they do have keyholes."

"You're insa—"

"Shh," Paloma interrupted. "Let him finish."

"We head there," Saunter continued, pointing to the overgrown, upward sloping road. "And, yes, I say *we*. Unless you would rather end up dead."

A long silence. Paloma recalled the horse who must now be dead.

"Poor Milvia," said Paloma.

"Poor Milvia," Aeron agreed. "She'll be in my nightmares forev—"

"What is it, Aeron?"

"Last night, I had a dream about a nightjar. It was the day my family died and my granddad's house caught fire. A nightjar caused the whole thing. It had no eyes."

"Virusyrus," Saunter mumbled under his breath.

"What?" asked Paloma.

Without hesitation, Saunter rose and made for the workbench. He rummaged through it as if in dire need of something that had disappeared.

"Tell us what's going on, Saunter. What is Virusyrus?" asked Paloma.

"Viru, short for Virusyrus," said Saunter while stuffing a brass key and three stones—sapphire, opal, and emerald— into the bag along with an ominous-looking weapon. "Or as his followers call him, Praeth Viru."

Aeron reached once more for the haversack, this time able to grab it. *Good*, she thought, *his pain must be receding*. Aeron too groped through his belongings.

"We must go. We can take the lorry," said Saunter, turning to Aeron. "Son, can you move? You must keep quiet. Tracer athon can hear a boy scream from a dog's earshot. We now have two devils on our tails.

"The bird you saw, Aeron, in your dream, was Viru. Born in the Harroes, he is older than any man on aerth. Viru is the reason for the fall of Termara and, I expect, the eventual fall of Longleath too. I was orphaned in the Harroes. I'll never forget the oily smell, the rarity of sun, and the people—so white they look diseased.

"The storm, we can weather, but a run-in with the Wraeth Prince... None of us will survive."

CHAPTER 15

STEALING FIRE

By the time Paloma left the tree, the animals of evening sang songs while lightning bugs snow-flaked the air. Hat in hand, she toed her way down the mossy tree, over slick grasses, and down the rocky slope.

An owl's hooting announced her arrival at the clearing. In between tears and rage, Aeron looked up at her and scowled.

"I should have guessed!" he shouted. "Why else would you have joined up so quickly with a boy like me."

"I've no idea what you're talking about. Where's Saunter?" She looked around but the large man was gone.

"My haversack, the Grapple, the purador—he's stolen it all. I should've known he was a rotten old crook," Aeron said and tore a handful of leaves from the tree, "like you and all the others."

"Maybe I would care a bit more if you hadn't stolen it all," said Paloma, double-checking the lorry. As she closed the blue door, some paint chipped under her fingernails. Beneath it—green.

"Aeron—" Paloma said rubbing a knuckle to her bottom lip.

"No, Paloma!" Aeron fumed. "No clever words. You planned this. We'd stop and you'd lead me away so your friend could run off without me putting up a fight. I'd never expect *you*, the *beautiful* Paloma, to undermine me."

"Do you even listen to yourself?" she growled at his foolishness. "We spent the last three days nursing you like a little baby. Baaaby Aeron—you broke a couple ribs and didn't wake up for days. I've gotten crushed in Cannaroo and continued on that game. Why would we have wasted our time? Huh, Aeron? Why didn't we take your precious haversack, Journal and all?"

"I—" Aeron stammered, "I bet you thought I'd be desperate enough to lead you right to the grove so you two could plunder it like the stinking heathens you are."

"Aeron Mason, you little—" Paloma choked on her words, realizing her mistake. If he found out she had seen inside the Journal, she would have to admit it all—her snooping, her identity, their families' intertwined history.

"You—" he muttered. "This whole time, you knew… how?"

"Aeron—"

"No lies," he said and crossed his arms. "I want the truth."

"Fine," she sighed. A sudden tension coiled in her chest like a cobra. "It was an accident. The first night with Saunter I was at a loss of what to do. You were unconscious and he had helped, but I still felt uncomfortable around him. I thought it was the right thing to take inventory of your things—"

"You had an opportunity to snoop on me, so of course you *had* to take it."

"I did it," she said and gritted her teeth, "to make sure nothing would be stolen."

"Sure, Paloma," he shook his head. "That's why you opened my Journal and found my family name written all over it."

Do I tell him the rest? The secret history between our families that would most certainly make him hate me even more? No. It's like Father always said on the Cannaroo pitch. "Remember, Palo, deception is your weapon. But as our house motto goes, 'Patience is the shield.'" I will wait for a better time.

"No," said Paloma, eyes low. "That was my curiosity."

"Goodbye, Paloma *'Longleath'*—whoever you are," Aeron said and charged over to the lorry, mumbling beneath his breath. He began filling his canteen from Saunter's barrel of moshrum. "I'll be sure to tell the Ranger all about you. Good luck finding him on your own." Then, storming past Paloma, he scooped up the lone heartfruit and hissed. "If that's even what you're after."

She sat in silence for several minutes, cicadas and tree frogs singing around her. Though final light approached, only a few stars peeked through the clouds. For longer than she would like to admit, Paloma considered following Aeron down the mountain. Without Saunter, what good was climbing any higher?

Then, after she had replayed the day in her head once more, a thought collapsed on her.

Saunter must have gone up, she decided. If he went down, he would have taken the lorry. But how had he slipped past her unnoticed? Rather than ruminate any longer, Paloma lit one of the torches from the lorry's cargo. Beside it she noticed a strange-looking canister, like a large vial made of beechwood. She popped open the cork and a pungent, inky smell erupted in her nostrils. At once, she closed the vial and made the short walk over to the slope.

More foreboding and ominous in the low light, Paloma pushed aside a hanging wreath of wistaria. A family of moths crowded around the torch, and their company comforted her until a bat swooped low and stole three of them away.

The further she rose the thinner and more precarious the path became. Trees became scarce and moss grew on everything. Slick as ice, one misstep would have sent her tumbling down a lofty cliff. The going had become slow and every few yards meant some kind of scramble. In the dark, with a torch, she had difficulty using her hands and once nearly leaned all her weight on a loose stone.

When the scramble ended, heart thrashing, she sat in the middle of the path, head in her hands. She tasted the cold mountain air and tried to assure herself.

"Settle down, girl," she said. "You are the Orion, the scorer, on the top Cannaroo team in the Western Rift. This is nothing."

Then came the thought of her father. If he had seen her then, his face would have turned red. Only a fool climbs a mountain at night, he would have said, and Paloma had only the slightest idea where to head.

The keyhole in the mountain. His burrow must be close.

Then came an unexpected sound, something large and pounding with steps that echoed in a way that permeated the night. Paloma froze. Putting out the torch would leave her without light and without a weapon; instead, she stuck the torch into a snake's hole by her right foot and dashed to the side over a wall of stones. Beneath the path, she found a small inlet, perfect for one person to hide.

Paloma poked her head out. Up from a different side came a huge figure. As it approached the light, Paloma recognized the figure's khaki jacket. Saunter looked all around. He scooped up the torch and wheeled around.

"Where've you gone?" he whispered. "Fools. I've been looking for you…"

No haversack… could Aeron be the one playing games?

Saunter gazed over the edge of the path but was too large to go down there to see for himself. The next thing she knew, the torch shrank into the murky darkness.

Before losing sight of him, Paloma climbed back up to the path. Even in the low light, the next ascent seemed flatter and less precarious. She took off in a jog, twice rolling an ankle until coming close enough to hear the mountain's reaction to him with crunching grass, jostling rocks, and breaking twigs.

The man had slowed to a walk. Paloma heard him singing as if a young boy on a hike.

The woods,
Wherever yours may be,
Ever lovely, dark, and deep.
Environs complete
With painful love
of loveful pain.

His voice was old and worn but smooth and dark as velvet.

I'll never forget the first time I came
This owly man not mad nor sane
Alone with thoughts and books and candles.
Faster he glides,
Speeding through time,
Like a man in the clouds
With nothing but sandals.

With the elevation dizzying her, Paloma paused to catch her breath. She leaned against a stone. In the distance, Elevana City appeared like a lone star.

Oh haevens, why am I doing this? She squeezed her eyes shut. *To find the Ranger. To do something more than Cannaroo. To be someone more than my father's daughter.*

To ground herself, she paid close attention to Saunter's weathered but pleasant voice.

The burrow, the burrow, the keyhole in the mount
Visited by too many of Aerth's greatest to count.
But only the one who lives there
I trust him forever, even as I grow old:
Enchanting, longstanding, stranger than a white mare.

He moved again, this time slower, until they reached the end of the path. Paloma had been keeping a distance, but as the incline flattened, she tested going closer.

Torchlight bounced off a high and striking wall. They had come to a sweet-smelling, grassy flat buttressed by an unclimbable cliff.

Saunter waved the torch, lighting three lanterns—one on a wall, one on a tree, and the final one against a ruined set of stone stairs. *Some kind of ceremonial ground*, Paloma thought.

Manu the Wilder, the Woodland King,
Last of the Five Rangers, never learnt to sing
But, alas, I be the center of this world.
The Wilder, a conqueror,
Pries open the self,
Inside, the brightest of all pearls.

Considering the darkness of that night, the dell lit up well. Saunter had used the torch to light a fire in the middle of the clearing. He sat on the ground, leaned against a benchlike stone and took a large sip of moshrum.

Making sure to stay low and quiet, Paloma glided behind a run of brush. At this angle, Saunter was face up. The flame illumined his wrinkled forehead and half-drunk, sunken eyes. Next to him...

The haversack!

"If they climbed that high," Saunter said aloud, "I need do little. They will moth to the fire."

Saunter reached into the haversack and pulled out the blue bottle. He uncorked it and held the spout to his eye. For a second, Paloma wondered if he might down it all.

He recorked the bottle and closed his eyes. She waited and waited for him to fall asleep, but he never did. It felt like an eternity by the time he rolled over to one side, back facing her hiding place.

Making sure to stay on quiet grass, Paloma slid in the shadows across twenty yards of open space. If she made any noise, Saunter would catch her dry.

She reached the large stone, the backside of his resting place. His breath was deep and relaxed. Stealing the whole lot would be impossible, but the Grapple? That would be enough to get Aeron to trust her again.

As her hand fumbled through the bag, Saunter rose from the fetal position to a cross-legged seat. Paloma froze, blood throbbing in her skull.

After several moments, she peeked her head over the boulder. Saunter's eyes were closed and his hands rested on his knees, the purador beside him.

Holding her breath, a beacon of warmth drew her hand. Then she touched it.

At last!

Paloma's fingers locked around that strange, ribbed heart-fruit, which Aeron had used to save Yeats. Silent as night, she pulled it from the haversack.

She couldn't help but stare for a moment. Never had Paloma seen such an interesting artifact. Its marble-blue heart entranced her.

"Worth more than a thousand heartfruit," she recalled Aeron's words.

For a moment, Paloma considered making a play for the purador but resisted. *Patience wins out,* she thought.

Her footsteps seemed quieter than ever. The grass and rocks fell silent beneath her as she made for the path. Leaping over a low rock wall, her foot crunched through a dry, termite-ridden log. Then, she unleashed a doggish yelp that could have echoed for miles, but she didn't even hear her own voice cry out.

CHAPTER 16

THE KEYHOLE IN THE MOUNTAIN

◇◇◇◇◇◇

The wind tugged at Aeron's hair like an annoying sister.

Vella.

Guilt stamped his chest.

You should be alive, and I should be dead.

He sipped the near-empty canteen of moshrum.

You were always a better Mason.

The evening star had emerged faster than expected, and Aeron paused as a cloud covered the moon and full dark set in.

At first he had thought it wise to descend the mountain in search of Saunter. The trees grew taller and more numerous, the brushy walks grew wider, and the flowers smelled stronger.

Then the sound. When it came, he thought it a nightjar or some kind of insect; yet as he descended, the hum went from soft and sleepy to shrill and staggering, worsening to an excruciating point.

He fell to his knees on a steep rocky slope, wondering if it could be the moshrum. In want of flatter ground, he ascended, and as he did the song turned pleasant.

Could it be?

Aeron descended a few steps again, testing the theory. The scratchy hum returned. The shock knocked him off his feet. On his backside, he bear-crawled up the rocky slope. The harshness dissipated.

This must be some kind of Aero... has Saunter cursed me?

As Aeron sat to think for a moment, the shrill cry edged in again. His mind ran to Vella. Hearing her cry would be an impossible curse to bear. No, he decided, no Aero pushed at him from below. The pull came from above.

Wasting no time, Aeron pressed up the mountain, back from where he had come. He heard no rustling, no whistling birds, and no crickets tweeting. The only sound came softly, melodiously, like distant church bells from far above.

After several hours of hiking Aeron arrived at a sharp, precarious ledge that struck almost vertical and must have been no wider than a horse.

Draining the canteen dry, he wished he had remembered to refill it upon passing the lorry this time. Instead, for luck, he reached into his vest and kissed the Journal.

"Well," he said to no one. "This might the last of the archivists."

The first handhold, slick and mossy, sent through him a quiver of fear. Then he followed his feet, lighting on the second, third, and fourth boulders without slipping.

All of the sudden, a squall of wind tore against him from the side. Gripping the wall for dear life, pain searing through his side, two buttons flew from his vest at the neck. Aeron feared the worst. He'd rather die than survive as an Archivist with no Journal.

Nervous sweat rushed sidelong across his face as he gripped the final boulder. The wind swelled with rage, almost knocking Aeron to certain death. Cramped, his fingers screamed. He clung for life, and after the final few handholds, pulled himself onto flat ground.

He turned around to look over the view. Despite the darkness, Aeron saw a vast expanse of trees and mountains with a thin river snaking down between them. He was higher than the rest of the mountain peaks, and the way they threaded over one another reminded him of a quilt made from emerald greens, yellows, and snowy whites.

His breathing deepened but his head felt light and deprived of oxygen. Between the elevation and the moshrum, Aeron was too spent to move, so he propped himself on one knee.

He pushed both hands onto that knee and looked up. Something glowed faintly from a short distance up the slope. The humming returned as the glow came closer. Still lightheaded, he rose and waited for his knees to stop wobbling.

Step by step, he trudged up the slope, using his hands on exposed tree roots.

As he climbed, the shape increased in size from a pinhead to a plum. Then his knees collapsed. On hands and knees, his hands gripped the damp ground. If there was a creek nearby, he could not hear it beneath the humming.

He pressed hard against the loam and stood on his knees. Beneath the orb of light was a disembodied pair of legs. A girl's. He thought of his sister.

Vella? Is that you?

Falling back, haunches to heels, Aeron closed his eyes in a nasty confusion, the backs of his eyelids gyrating with color.

All of the sudden, the note ceased to hum. Hot as coals, hard ribs of carved stone brushed against his fingers.

No thought.

Complete absence of sound paired with the warm, but not harmful, touch of the stone pried open his eyes. Moonlight, finally freed from the dying clouds, struck the mountain a silver hue. He only knew one Aero, and it had failed him in the past. But Aeron had to try.

"*Anudato,*" he sang in a dull voice. The Grapple thrummed, glowing blue in Aeron's right hand, and hovered over his wound. Damp salt, as if he knelt in beach sand rather than mountain mud, stung his nostrils. "*Euthanasis.*"

No salt. No running water. No humidity. Every ounce of moisture, even that in the air, had been drained through the rivulets of the Grapple, now a muted shade of yellow, and into Aeron's side.

Dropping the Grapple into the grass, Aeron, now less disoriented, ran his fingers over the scar which had been flattened like a tattoo. The Grapple had healed him, as it had Yeats.

Lit by the stone and the moon, the area held a shade of saffron mixed with silver. Still examining himself, a girl's voice came, muffled but nearby.

"Vella?" he asked, raising his head.

"Vella?" Paloma crooked her head to the side. "Aeron, it's Paloma. What you just did…" she grasped for words. "Remarkable."

"So I'm awake? I thought the hallucinations had returned. I thought you—"

"Vella," said Paloma with repose. "Is that your sister?"

Aeron's gaze, brimming with tears that wanted nothing more than freedom, lowered to the side distrustfully. Her warm, curled finger, nudging his chin high, sent a ripple of gentility through his every vertebra.

"My name is Paloma. I was born in a small village on the border of Eurovea. I have never met my mother, but my father, founder of the Longleath Trading Company, on the other hand, is someone you may know."

"You are a Murravillow?"

Paloma nodded.

"And Beck Murravillow is your father?"

"Yes, Aeron." She rose, lending a hand to Aeron. "Can you walk? I don't like the looks of those new clouds. While we have it, we should use the moonlight."

Accepting her hand, soft yet strong and nimble, and though preparing for a rush of dizziness, Aeron found his head clear as could be at such elevation.

"Paloma," Aeron said while climbing a set of trail stairs. "Why in Cedre's name are you here? Your line, the Murravillows, may as well run Longleath! Why not go lie on a beach somewhere, or hire someone to teach you to range, or bring Paladin to guard you?"

"Riches are poison," she said. "I thought you of all people would understand."

Aeron's feet, one after another, pressed up the hill with less difficulty.

"So it's true then?" Paloma asked. "Vella was your sister, Loo your father, and the 'granddad' you so often mention is *Mendel Mason*, the *archivist*."

Aeron sighed.

"And that makes you..."

Though fixated ahead, where the path came to a final halt in front of a flat-faced rock, Aeron interrupted, "Their murderer."

"No," she said and pulled at his arm. Refusing to look her way and pretending to be concerned for the heavy wind, Aeron stopped at her touch. "An *archivist*."

"How did you get this?" Aeron asked, holding up the Grapple, all of the sudden suspicious.

"I—" she began, "procured it from our friend Saunter."

"*Procured*," Aeron mocked, "a fancy word for stealing. Why am I not surprised?"

"Aeron," she said with emotion. "What do you want from me? I've told you my name; I've told you I've come to find the Ranger. Yes, I peeked at your Journal. Yes, I stole the Grapple from Mr. Moshrum. But I put my life on the line right here, sneaking around that violent man, to keep it safe for *you*."

Aeron paused. "Why?"

Standing tall and confident, Paloma strode ahead toward where the road, wide and marred with footsteps, met the mossy wall. Paloma rested her hand beside an odd, wreath-like shape on the wall.

"This is it," Paloma said. "The keyhole in the mountain."

CHAPTER 17

THE SAGE

◇◇◇◇◇◇

"I need your help," said Paloma, removing her hand from the wall. The last shaft of moonlight, before the clouds rolled in, cast a light on Aeron.

After rescuing the Grapple from Saunter, Paloma had begun, in a mixture of curiosity and necessity, to think she may be well to stay and observe Saunter for a few minutes. The Grapple had emboldened her.

"I saw how he entered. See those vines up there," she pointed to a bush of purple flowers ten yards above the wreath. "They're false. It's a window."

"And how on aerth do you expect to get up there?"

"The same way he did," she said. "Which is where you come in. I tug on this lever, but nothing happens."

Holding the Grapple for light, Aeron approached where a flat stone jutted out so little he had to press his cheek against the wall to the right of the wreath.

"Show me."

Paloma brushed her hair out from her face in the whipping wind, took a deep breath with a hopeless sigh, and began.

Starting from where Saunter had, beside the embers, Paloma began taking long, awkward steps.

Yelling out each of them aloud over the howling wind, "One, two, three, four," she planted her feet hard into the soft aerth so they were covered in mud. "Five, six, seven." Her feet pawed forward with each step as she leaned into the gale-force weather until halting beside the lone torch fastened to the wall. The fire guttered and flamed against the torrent of rain that now beat down. She tugged on the lever and the stone near the wreath that Aeron examined jutted out, revealing some kind of graphic on the side.

"Do that again," said Aeron.

She tugged on the torch and let go. Water spilled over the edge as the torch dipped to an angle and then pulled back to hug the wall.

"It's Orangu…" he shouted over the wind, "and there's a symbol like the pagoda outside The Sportsman and at Yeats's."

Aeron pulled out the Journal from his vest with three fingers. Leafing through the pages while the wind did its best to close them, Aeron mumbled to himself until clarity came over his eyes. Then he called out the first word.

"Abandon," he said "Fear…" and paused on the page to read. "Or never shall you enter." Struggling to keep the Journal from blowing closed, Aeron swiped the stylus and attached it to the tassel across the page.

"I think the archiving can wait, Aeron." She brushed back the wreath to catch a better glimpse of Aeron. "We need—"

He turned the Journal to her. An otherwise blank page held the likeness of a crude but obvious moshrum with the words "Abandon fear or never shall ye awaken" beneath the drawing.

No sooner had he turned the page than Paloma felt the wreath tighten around her wrist. All of the sudden, her feet left the ground and she was sliding upward, through the moss, like a snake being tugged by the tail.

Then, even the dim moonlight disappeared. She found herself sliding down a cold, smooth slide until being coughed out into a dusty pile of moss.

Even in the city, she had never been comfortable with pure darkness. And that cave, dark as they came, sent pins across her skin. But at least she wasn't getting wet anymore. She wondered, stewing in fear, what she would do if Aeron remained stuck outside.

He's bright. A bit of a clutz, but he'll—

A soggy Aeron came tumbling down the chute, crashing into Paloma's ankles and cutting her thought at the knees. She fell right over him.

While he laughed in the dark, the Grapple came rolling down the tunnel.

"Shh!" Paloma hissed. "Our every sound will carry." Even that whisper seemed amplified.

Aeron took the lead, the Grapple revealing a single route forward.

Her hands grazed the walls, smooth and even as if carved by water, and Paloma followed Aeron downward. Every so often, she felt a gap in the stones. Each one breathed a tinge of heat over her hands. After one hundred paces the tunnel split five ways.

Aeron paused, holding the Grapple up to his ear, as if it were whispering to him. He continued through the second and, soon after, the tunnel split again. Again he chose the second path. This continued for quite some time, and as they went the cave became more geometric. Turns became sharper and handholds went from natural to manmade.

Then the tunnels stopped.

"We must be beneath the mountain by now," said Paloma.

Not yet.

They ended up on a circular platform that looked over a vast cavern. Far below, too far to see, a blueish hue lit the ground.

All of the sudden, the platform moved. The ground beneath them, a long pedestal, which must have been attached to some kind of pulley system, dropped lower while the enormous stone pillar across the way lifted high.

"Do you hear that?" Aeron whispered.

She shook her head, her heart drumming midnight rhythms. Paloma's fear scraped against the dark whetstone of uncertainty.

After a long, slow descent, the ground stopped moving.

An old man's voice came from below. "Wake up!" he snapped. "The door to hell is ajar, and death has slipped through."

Then came a familiar voice. "I hear you, my old Sage friend," Saunter's voice echoed from below. She leaned over the edge. The ground floor, still a bit below, had been lit by blue-flamed torches. "Tell me what to do."

She and Aeron exchanged a glance.

"This," said the old man, his final S hanging in the air, "is what I hoped you would already know."

"I am a new man—"

"Yes," said the other. "Lesser."

"No," Saunter rebuked. "Less foolish. I understand now, Master Skylo, that I am a child no longer."

"Understand! Ha!" snorted Skylo. "Would that you still were. Kids have no fear of their dreams."

"What do you want from me, Skylo? I have traveled the four rifts, saved children from the Huntress across the world, known women of every kind. I have lived my dreams."

"To wake up, fool. I want you to wake up!" said the man. "Even a dying man has dreams. Even a king has dreams. Even a sage has dreams."

"How would you know?" challenged Saunter. "You never leave this cave."

"Because I have been dying for five hundred years."

Five hundred years?

"I need you to wake up," Skylo continued. "To close the door, as the prophecy decried!"

"How many times have I told you," Saunter asked, "I am only half priman. Your prophecy is wrong, or you are."

Aeron tapped her wrist, and she leaned back from the ledge. He gestured behind them, where a tunnel lay, similar to the one before, hauntingly black.

"A wise man is willing to admit his mistakes," said the old man. "You are right. The prophecy is not about you, but you are in it."

Before entering the shaft, Aeron turned to backpedal, facing Paloma. He held the Grapple near his mouth and mouthed something to her. As he did, before she could make out the words, darkness reached out to grab him.

Then Aeron was gone.

CHAPTER 18

HYACINTH

◇◇◇◇◇◇

Aeron had never been cliff jumping before, but this, he imagined, would be how it felt. Fortunately for him, the slide let out to a bed of something soft and forgiving. He landed without a noise, Grapple still in hand.

"You know," came the old man's voice. "The war will be lost if the Great Tree is breached."

Aeron reoriented himself and waited several moments, but Paloma never came.

Where are you, Murravillow? Aeron thought, shining the Grapple up the chute from which he had fallen. *For both our sakes, I must hear this. It's less dark in here. She will find her way.*

He crept forward, following the old man's familiar voice and passing through a room scattered with thousands of huge books and tomes, hundreds of them lying open.

"Then the war is already over," said Saunter. "Because I am staying here."

"No!" Skylo's voice boomed louder than any old man's should. "You are going."

A chill went up Aeron's spine as he passed through a room with a small pool, water both falling and draining, that seemed to serve as a wash room.

Entering the final chamber, Aeron's nose curled behind a spicy, piquant aroma.

From his vantage, one flight above, Aeron had a clear view of the main parlor. The walls, lined every few steps with a blue torch, struck high until disappearing into the black abyss. Apart from an active smithing bench in the corner and two leafless trees, the ground floor contained little.

"There has been a sighting in the Western Rift, my friend, a Huntress priest in Orifornia. If the Wraeth find him, they will use it to divide primanity, and it will be the end of us all. You must go to Orifornia. We have no choice."

"Death," Saunter groaned, tossing a rock against the wall, "is other people. Here I have peace, and all the moshrum I need, even after the boy…"

"Boy?" the old man snapped. "What boy?"

"Athon came after a boy. Weak bones. I gave him moshrum and he—"

"He gave you that sack of heartfruit," said Skylo. "Tell me about this boy! What did he look like? Where has he gone?"

"I told them about *Te Draviño*. It must have scared them off," said Saunter.

"Them?"

"Aeron," Paloma hissed with angry eyes, emerging from the darkness of the wash room. Aeron pressed a finger to his lips.

"He had a friend. A girl, Paloma. From Longleath."

"And the boy!" said the man, frenetic. "The boy! What was his name!"

"Aeron."

Skylo ran a long, spidery hand over his bald head and, in one motion, slashed it forward, cracking Saunter on the cheek.

"I should—" Saunter curled a fist with dominion.

"Wake up! Wake up!" Skylo shouted. "That is the boy!"

"You mean…"

Paloma's jaw hung open. Aeron stumbled back on the landing.

"That's him, Paloma," Aeron whispered. "Lamark was wrong. The old man is not dead! The one who helped me escape Longleath is right there! He will know where the Ranger is. I am sure of it. We have to go down."

Palm pressed to Aeron's chest, Paloma shook her head, held up a finger, and turned back to the main flat.

"I will go, Master Skylo. My legacy is all I have. The Huntress religion is like a virus. I and I alone can stop the Huntress return. Mine is of failure," said Saunter in a low voice. "But I must tell you something first."

"Shhh," said Skylo. "I should like you to save it for when we are alone."

All of the sudden a flowerish, lightning-bug-sized shape of purple and blue flames burst outward to the size of a coconut.

Aeron shifted side to side, examining the strange floating object. Indigo and violet waves rippled out from the center. At its core was a dense clot of even tinier flowerish marbles— fractals, exactly the same as the larger. Each wave of flames tracked its origin to a single mini in the core. As if conscious, the shape followed him, watching.

"Welcome," Skylo's voice came from the flaming flower, "Paloma Murravillow."

"What are you?" she asked.

The shape did a pirouette in the air.

"This," Skylo whispered, again through the form, "is a flameflower. It is called 'Hyacinth.'"

Paloma reached out a hand. Vivid light danced on her skin.

"And you, Aeron Mason, my young prison mate. I worried you had forgotten our lessons."

Aeron leaned between the balustrade. It was strange seeing them side by side, Saunter and the old man. Then Skylo recited the poem Lamark had given him.

As it Soars, it Sears
The Skylo Sky-low:
be where you seek.
Grapple's Grapple,
The Inn is free
Beyond the brick blue teak.

"The poem from Herraz…" Aeron gasped. "Why did he tell me you were dead?" Aeron cried.

"Of course he did," Saunter snorted. "The Merchant of Herraz—who's real name is Lamark—bends the truth for sport."

With a flick of the wrist, Skylo's flameflower split in bee-sized flares up to the hundred candles, igniting a chandelier high above. Aeron tucked the Grapple away while he and Paloma descended the final slope to the main chamber.

"An honor to finally meet you, Ms. Murravillow," Skylo said.

Paloma kept her distance. "How is it," she said, "you know who I am?"

"Emmanwell, that old tosspot," Skylo gestured at Saunter, "has done a royal job at misleading you, it seems."

"Emmanwell?" Paloma said with a crook in her brow.

Thoughts cascaded through Aeron's mind. He put a hand to his chest, feeling the Mason Grimoire.

Emmanwell Everett, otherwise known as Manu, otherwise known as…

Howling with power that no man as old and wrinkled should be capable of, Skylo finished Aeron's thought.

"The Last Great Ranger!"

CHAPTER 19

THE AEROS OF AERTH

All the pieces came together in a flash. Paloma had noticed strange things around Saunter: the hidden green lorry paint, the purador obsession, and the way the athon had fled.

Emmanwell "Manu" Everett had gained fame across all of Aerth for two things—finding purador and killing Huntress priests. The man's strangeness now made sense to Paloma.

"Him?" said Aeron. "There must be a mistake! Saunter is a lazy lunk and a thief."

"Say what you will, boy," the Ranger said, looming large in the blue hue. "I, Manu Everett, care not."

He even talks like the faebles, thought Paloma.

"It all adds up, Aeron," said Paloma. "Rangers are drawn to purador. That's why he showed up out of thin air. And your stitches…"

"You let this fool work a wound?" Skylo said then turned to Manu. "You should have brought him to me at once."

"If I had been told he were *the* Mason, I would have," said Manu.

"You," Skylo said with a dangerous glare, "of all people, should have known."

"I apologize, Master Skylo. He is here now. All is safe."

"Right now, nothing is safe. *Te Draviño*—storm of all storms—is imminent, the Wraeth have reemerged, and, if what you say is true, the Wraeth Prince is after young Mason. Now, Aeron my boy, let's see if we can fix Manu's lousy stitching."

When Aeron removed his vest, the wrinkles on Skylo's forehead thickened.

"This is no handiwork..." He ran his long, bony fingers down Aeron's side where the wound had been. Manu leaned for a closer look. Skylo gazed off in thought, stroking his stalactite of a beard. He waved his forefingers and a host of fist-sized candle flames circled a slow orbit around his wrist. Then the plumes joined Hyacinth. As if it had a mind of its own, Hyacinth drifted toward Aeron, scanning his body as Skylo had.

"Yes," Skylo repeated, dragging out the word. "Yeesss..."

Hyacinth left Aeron's side, floating closer to the ground until alighting above his vest. Paloma felt its heat burning hotter on her legs.

"Heat," Skylo said, "radiates outward from a flame. But what is its opposite?"

"Reduction," Aeron answered, sounding sure of himself.

"No, Aeron. Reduction is just a word. But heat is a feeling, and the same can be said for hate, fear, love, even death. You may think the opposite of death is life, yet that is a mere thought. To understand something, you must feel it."

A light shimmered from inside Aeron's vest. He knelt and turned the pocket inside out, leaving the Grapple atop the pile. The way they pulsed, beat, and shimmered, he could have sworn they were in communication with each other.

"The Grapple," Skylo whispered with amazement. "Aeron, do you know what this means?"

Aeron said nothing.

"It means you are Sage, Aeron Mason," Skylo said and put a hand on his shoulder. "The Order of the Sage is old as Aerth itself."

"And," Manu added as he walked away toward the forge and workbench. "It means you have been summoned by the Tree of Knowledge."

"The Tree of Knowledge—you mean the Great Tree," asked Aeron, "which holds all the knowledge of Aerth?"

"That's a myth," said Paloma. "There are treescrapers in Longleath, not out in the wilderness."

"It is quite real. I have been there, and Manu has too, many times. There they have a wise Queen Vizier, Lera Strongheart. You will be in good hands."

"Or," said Paloma, "we could go back, the four of us, and present the Grapple to the Council of Longleath. They will use it for good."

The ding of metal came from the corner as Manu jabbed at something on the workbench.

"And what is good, Ms. Murravillow?"

"Good is prosperity and fairness and truth."

"And to you, Aeron?"

"Wisdom and honor," he said. "What my family has always stood for."

"Fine answers but both wrong."

Skylo clapped his hands together abruptly. He slid one forward so that his fingers were palm to tip. The flameflower returned to his open-faced hand, rolling over his knuckles.

"Good is a matter of perspective," he continued. "What's right in Irkalla may seem wrong to a priman. To be good is to listen to all three sides."

"Three?"

"Theirs, ours, and Aerth's," he explained. "I once knew a man who, like you, Aeron, began hearing the sounds of the Sage Order at a young age. When we arrived at the Great Tree, it sensed an inkling of evil and rejected us both. He blamed me, I blamed him, and we split ways. I, fascinated by the Aeros of Aerth and he, by growing cities with Epiphysics, we both sought a new way in."

Manu clang the hot metal again. He threw off his jacket and pounded the anvil hard. He might have been thick, but it was clear to Paloma why the Council wanted Manu in Longleath.

He would lead the Paladin and all guards of Longleath with valiance. But how to convince him?

"Alone, deep in the coldest part of the Southern Rift, I crashed through a false patch of snow into a hollow space of ice. Frigid and dying, *she* came to me. Hyacinth," he gestured toward the floating flames, "became my first teacher. My window to the Aeros."

"But," said Paloma, "Aeros are fables, faery tales. No one, even the gods, can control Aerth."

"True," Skylo began, "but we can *ask*. And, if we use her language, sometimes Aerth agrees."

"So, Aeros are a language then, and each Aero is like a word?"

"Yes and no." Skylo closed his eyes and leaned back in his chair. "The Aeros are both a language and an interleaving field of forces, which are created by and string together all beings—living and non."

Aeron scooped up the Grapple, and a ray of heat brushed her legs.

"The Sage look at it like a net," said Manu from the corner, wiping sweat from his brow. "They believe everything is its own knot. When many join with others, they form a mesh. As a collective, the net is mighty. Torn apart, it is a useless. A lump of knots."

Paloma nodded. "Then you, or this Lera Strongheart, can use Aeros to stop the storm you call *Te Draviño*, and kill the Wraeth."

"No," said Skylo. He leaned on his cane, an ebony stick with beautiful wintry carvings. With the fluidity of his movements, Paloma wondered if it was for show.

"Like me," he explained, "my friend found the Aeros, but he never returned to the Tree. He was seduced by another way, a dark way. And now I have been told that he has the Deathsword. With one jab into the Tree of Knowledge, the net is torn for good. Animals, plants, and ideas all will cease to exist. Only death outlives knowledge. Only the Wraeth and their Prince pose the greatest threat to us all."

"More than…" Paloma hesitated, "Viru?"

Making a diamond with his forefingers and thumbs, Skylo lowered his hand around Hyacinth. Inside its blueish flames flickered the shape of a figure Paloma had seen before in the dead of the wood.

"No, my dear," said Skylo. "They are one and the same. The man with the Deathsword *is* Viru."

CHAPTER 20

THE MAP OF DESIRE

"I think that's enough for today, Master Skylo," said Manu.

"I'm fine," Skylo hissed. "I could climb a mountain right now."

At the sight of Manu's face, Aeron tried and failed to stifle a laugh.

"Not you, old man," Manu sighed. "We've all had a long day."

"Right, right," said Skylo who rose and made for the slope. "Very well. I will be in my study. Help yourself to whatever you need." Gripping the balustrade, he ascended the slope, moving more slowly with each step. As he got higher, the wood-colored skin on his head shone. Then, he passed into the anteroom and, not long after, came the sound of music, an old harmgiano.

"That limp…" said Aeron. "He moves like he was born with it."

"You have seen buildings in your city," said Manu. "Grown from the aerth…"

"Hang on," said Paloma, "he *grew* that leg?"

"That is only the beginning of what Epiphysics can do," Manu said and doused the forge with water. "Here," he said, holding out a beautiful, scythe-like blade.

Paloma accepted, examining the hilt.

"Here, you are safe," said Manu, "but when we leave… things change during *Te Draviño*. It becomes every man for himself."

Manu ascended the same path as Skylo and, after disappearing for a moment, threw down an array of pillows and blankets.

"If the ground is too hard, lay down some moss. Best mattress I've had."

"Where are you going?"

"Tomorrow we leave. I must prepare."

"I can come with you," said Paloma.

"No," Manu replied. "You will slow me down."

"I'm faster than you, old man," said Paloma.

"Ha."

"I'm staying," Aeron yawned, "right here, thanks."

He took the cleanest pile of moss and spread a blanket over it. Glorious!

"I'm coming, Manu. Nothing you can say will stop me. Longleaf needs you."

"Words have never been my strong suit," said Manu, standing atop the landing. Then, he pulled on a long rope hanging from the ceiling. A tower of water, attached high on the walls above, poured into a series of vents and channels. Within seconds, the candelabra and every torch in the cavern went black.

Paloma growled.

"I'm going, Aeron. You get some sleep."

"Good luck," Aeron said, knowing better than to disagree with Paloma.

All the better. I always read faster when I'm alone.

Her footsteps grew quieter and more distant. From the hallway came the sound of something crashing on stone, a bowl or a pan, and then silence.

Lying down, Aeron pulled the covers over his head. Grapple in one hand and Journal in the other, he read the passage.

Dear sister,

It pains me to be so close yet so far. I care little that you are sick. Would that I were by your side, but father forbids it. I will write you here as much as he permits.

There is talk in town of two women, warring women whom have rooted out the remaining Irkals hiding in the Southern Rift. The large one, she is the famed "Lady Belladonna." The smaller, nimble, and lissome one calls herself "The Reddheart." Of her I have never heard.

Whispers have it that the Reddheart once spent much of her time with the Ranger called Manu, "The Wilder," Everett. Why she left him for Belladonna remains a mystery. All that is known of Reddheart is her skill with ink and quill.

I hope your eyes have not grown weary.

Please write me, Guinivere, if you can.

Delia Mason

Though his eyelids grew heavy, talk of Manu "The Wilder" pushed him onto the next page.

My beloved sister,

It means mountains to me to hear from you. I am feeling far better now, though my hands and feet are still icy white from plague.

Thank you for informing me of their arrival. Belladonna I have met before. Of the Reddheart I have heard only stories. It is said that she is working on something, a map of some kind. When I asked father, he said, "She is a Huntress witch." Men make me roll my eyes... What that means is that she is a Sage. It makes sense. Rangers

and Sages complete one another like salt and pepper. I have enclosed a letter here in the Journal for your friend, the Reddheart. Please deliver it in person. Use our name only if you must. You may read it if you wish. Write me again. I do love seeing your handwriting.

With endless love,

Guinivere Mason

As he turned the page, Aeron's eyes fell closed.

The smell of pinternut butter and toasted heartfruit pricked Aeron's nostrils. With a flutter, he yawned his body out wide and sat up. The light from the chandelier cast the cavern in a shade of white that made his eyes squint.

"You must tell me," said Skylo seated beside a lit aequipher with a book, a plate, and a cup of sprig tea, "how you managed to find so many heartfruit."

The haversack lay in an empty heap.

"You've cooked *all* seven?" said Aeron. "I was saving them for—"

"Lesson one—a raw heartfruit will last you a few days. A cooked heartfruit will stave off hunger for a week or more, my son." Skylo paused and sipped his cup of sprig tea. The old man exhaled smoked as if he were an old dragon. "Now do me a favor and run up to my study. There is a large leaf folded on the table. Bring that down as well as the book beside it."

As Aeron went up the slope, he paused to admire a drawing of an owl on the wall that reminded him of the one in his dream.

"Oh," Skylo called, "and the stone-tile weighing down the map. Bring that as well. Thank you, m'boy."

Aeron passed through the wash room and into the brown-hued study. The previous night, he had been too frightened to admire the space. Now, he struggled to grasp what lay before him. Immense books, the size of Aeron himself, lay open. Some even had smaller ones stacked on top. All had old leather spines and could have been hundreds of years old, though they'd been kept in excellent shape.

Scattered all about were inexplicable things. Chimes were made from rubies. A warrior's helmet had athon fangs where ears might go. Fossilized busts of animals hung on the walls. Even the oldest harmgiano Aeron had ever seen sat in the room.

I wonder if I still know it.

Aeron sat down on the stool. Surrounding him, in a one-hundred-and-eighty-degree arc, were two hundred and sixty-four keys. He ran his fingers along the soft ivory. First, he pressed a single key, and a high note tinkled the air. Then he found a chord, deeper and lasting. At last, he played a short morning melody. He dropped his hands to his lap, expecting the sound to reverberate. Instead, the harmgiano kept on playing. To Aeron's amazement, it repeated the melody again and again, occasionally making a change or two of its own.

Then, he backed away from the instrument and approached the table. On top of it lay a large yellow book called *A Storm of Aeros*. Beside that sat the yellow leaf Skylo had asked for. He tucked it inside and pinned the book to his left side.

"What a library," said Aeron as he passed down the slope. "And I thought I read big books…"

"You have only begun. Wait until you see the Great Tree and how it is run," said Skylo. "Now let's have a look."

Aeron passed the old man his book. Skylo opened it and secured the leaf from inside. It unfolded wider than Aeron had expected.

"Master Skylo," Aeron began timidly. "I've been wondering why we abandoned the plan in prison. You went through all that trouble."

"Planning is important, young Aeron, but adapting is key. I saw an opportunity in the guard on duty and took it. Now enough of that. What have you heard in your history lessons of a woman from one thousand years ago called the Reddheart?"

"Well," said Aeron. "She had a knack for the quill. A Sage and expert—" he froze. "Is that…"

"The Map of the Reddheart."

"Herraz mentioned that map. Said it would take me where I wanted to go."

"He spoke the truth in halves," said Skylo. "It does not *take* you to your deepest wishes, but it does show you where they are."

"As in…"

"What do you want most in this world, Aeron Mason?"

Aeron stopped to consider the question.

I must prove mine and my granddad's innocence to return the Mason legacy to its former glory.

"Redemption," Aeron said aloud.

Skylo's face filled with doubt and a slim grin.

"We shall see," he said and handed the map over to Aeron.

When Aeron unfolded the leaf, a heavy pencil sketch rather than a map filled the page. It showed him older and stronger, standing at the foot of a massive tree with the Grapple in hand. Soon, the sketch changed shape. The greys erased themselves and reformed into a more traditional map. On it, a winding line led up the Northerly River and through Orifornia to a dot that grew and shrank next to the ocean.

"As I suspected," said Skylo. "You are neither vain nor vengeful, my son. This is good. What you see is part one of your journey to the Aeros." He paused and broke off a piece of heartfruit, dipping it in the butter. "I would be curious to learn what our other friends want most."

"Yes," said Aeron, mid-chew. "Where've they gone?"

"Curious," said Skylo without looking up. "I thought maybe you knew. Nothing Manu said last night before you went to sleep? The storm is gathering power. I should think they would be quick."

Aeron froze as an invisible thread tightened around his lungs.

"After you went to your study last night, Manu made a comment about having to prepare for the storm. Paloma asked to go with him and he refused, but she went anyway…"

Skylo leaned back and the chair groaned. He muttered a word and Hyacinth flew away. It danced all about the room—up, down, far, near—before disappearing. The melody Aeron had played on the harmgiano fell away.

"Your granddad taught you that song."

"Yes," Aeron admitted. "How did you know?"

"Mendel Mason was a great man. Such a shame how it all ended."

"You knew him?"

"Oh yes, my dear Aeron. On our journey to Orifornia, I will tell you stories you will not believe."

"Journey?"

"You must get off Elevana, Aeron. If the eye of *Draviño* strikes, you will be stuck here for many, many months."

"But the mountain will keep us safe from the storm, Saunt—I mean Manu—said so."

"It would. But you want something else…" Skylo gestured to the map. "To travel and experience the Aeros of Aerth firsthand. Once the eye strikes, there is no going outdoors. It's a rare thing when the world requires you to seek out your desires."

"This is my first time away from Longleath," Aeron admitted. "What if Lera Strongheart turns me away."

"Tabula Rasa. So much better you will learn," Skylo added. "She would never disobey the wishes of the world."

"And what if the world is wrong?"

The old man smiled, wide and toothy. "Wake up, Aeron! The world is never wrong."

All of the sudden, Hyacinth popped into the room out of thin air like a hot kernel of corn. It floated a slow, grave circle around Skylo, and they seemed to be reading each other's thoughts.

"It is worse than I imagined," said Skylo.

"What's happened?"

"Your friend, Paloma, has kept something from you. From us all."

"What do you mean? What did Hyacinth say?"

"No time," Skylo replied. He rose from the table and dumped the cooked heartfruit into Aeron's haversack. "Come. We are leaving."

Skylo found Manu's jacket still hanging on a chair by the forge. He stuffed it in Aeron's sack.

"Now!" Skylo's voice cracked through the cave. Aeron had not moved. Startled, he beelined it across the parlor toward the old man.

"Wait!" piped Skylo, and Aeron skidded to a halt. "The Map. It is yours. Take it."

"Skylo!" said Aeron. "No, I can't. If someone catches me with the Grapple, Journal, and Map of the Reddheart…"

"You will go down as the greatest burglar of all time," joked Skylo. "Take it. I will explain later."

Aeron returned to the table at the center of the room, folded the map, and tucked it in his large breast pocket beside the Journal. For a moment, the stone tile seemed to shimmer on the table, as if responding to Aeron's touch.

"Keep quiet until we reach the boat," Skylo beckoned. "Since the Wraeths have returned, we can never know who is listening."

"Boat?" said Aeron. "Skylo, we're inside a mountain."

Skylo whispered an Aero. "*Anapsis.*" All light drained from the room save for an orb lighting the cave around them.

"Where are we going?" Aeron asked.

Skylo held a finger to his lips then mouthed one word. *Down.*

CHAPTER 21

THE RHYTHMS OF NATURE

Rain soaked Paloma to her bones. She stood beside the lorry, damp and dejected. Toppled plants, pools of water, dark skies—all signs pointing to a flood.

"What are we going to do?" she asked with despair.

"That tree is soft," Manu replied and pressed his hands against a huge rock nearby. "I will get this rock to tumble, and it will break her."

"I find it hard to believe that taking the lorry out in *Te Draviño* is safer than climbing back up to Skylo's burrow."

"Yes," he grunted while pushing, "I could have climbed. But you are too light. The wind would sweep you away. Like a feather."

The final words conjured a memory of her father.

"*You know,*" he would say before kissing her forehead and leaving to sleep for work. "*I do all this for you, Palo, my little feather.*"

She approached the boulder and jabbed her hands against the back of it hard. The first time they heaved, the boulder made no movement, and she slipped toward a mouthful of mud. The second time, Paloma grounded harder into her toes and…

"Let go!" Manu commanded.

The boulder moved ever so slightly. Paloma clenched a fist. Shaking her hand, she turned to curse the mountain, flinging the water from her arms. Then she heard a deep, rumbling crunch.

She wheeled around. The rock, a green barrel of moss, tore down the hill. Still picking up speed, it crushed a hole through the tree and continued down the road.

"Yes!" Paloma shouted.

"Shush now," Manu warned. "Until we know who is after you. Quiet."

"You think they would continue to chase through all this?"

He said nothing, but his expression conveyed a grave yes.

"Well," she said, assuring herself. "They're after a *boy*, anyway, not me."

Manu lifted one half of the trunk with heroic strength and pitched it widely enough for the lorry to pass through.

"That, I fear," he said while passing by her, "is no longer true."

What does that mean? I have nothing but my hat…

He approached the lorry and patted its hood. "There," he said, "will you work with us now?"

The lorry's engine purred.

"That's my girl," he said.

Paloma took one last look at the rugged greens of the Riamante Valley below.

"I thought—" she said closing the lorry door behind her and causing water to drizzle on the floor, "and I thought Longleath's driverless lorries were stubborn…"

Rain pelted so hard against the vehicle's rainlids that the lorry had to blink every few seconds.

"Where are we going anyway?" she continued. "I do think we'd be wise to shove off before getting stuck in the storm, on Elevana… say, when were you in Longleath last? You know, my father would love to meet you. And my Uncle Oake wrote a book about *The Whitethorne Accords*. I imagine he'd be elated to hear your story."

"Quiet," Manu said, leaning forward. Paloma had never driven in such poor visibility.

If this storm is one of a kind, many will die and much will be destroyed. I think something similar happened before the Whitethorne Accords—a Wraeth outbreak led to a storm and war. Manu the Wilder had been orphaned in Irkalla and, apparently, adopted by eagle hunters. He had no people of his own, so no surprise it was easy for him to be the judge at the accord to preach for cooperation. He learned to see through the priman propensity for self-preservation. Longleath will need him yet again if this Viru and the Wraeths continue to gain power.

The road fit Manu's lorry snugly. Branches yanked as they passed, and leaves came down in droves. The croak of flying bleefrogs peppered the air before a bolt of thunder.

Bulling over a patch of ferns, they turned a corner and a jarring, orange blaze struck through the rainy malaise.

"The forest!" Paloma shouted. "It's burning! In the rain! How is it burning?" A ray of thunder bit against the peak behind the flames, igniting a momentary scene of terrified birds and animals. Chains of desperation coiled inside her chest. "Can't we do something?"

"No," Manu shook his head. "Only fools try to control a storm. But it has dawned sooner than I had hoped."

"Everything and *everyone* is going to burn…"

"Yes," he said, "and we may too. A Ranger always knows when death is nearby."

"But think of your teacher. You won't even help the man who taught you to range and climb towers?"

"The rhythms of nature. We are each one string to be strummed."

"Evil men turn their backs on the teacher."

"We must reach the meeting place before dusk. Tracer athon run faster in the night. And in the rain," said Manu. "As far as my master… I expect they will beat us there."

An old man like Skylo out into this storm? Leaving Aeron alone in the cave? I have my doubts.

Crash after crash, nature torched its own beauty into splinters of ash.

"The ones after you will have been forced from their homes. They will be hungry and on the roam. We must reach shelter before dusk, or we will die."

The lorry passed through the final brush and out onto the Grey Road. Paloma wanted nothing more than to weep, but her pride prevented it. Instead, she followed the drops of rain that streamed across her window.

The late afternoon sky hung grey and foreboding. The lorry's rainlids blinked slower.

The Grey Road marked their leaving the Riamante Valley. On the other side, they caught a glimpse of the storm over a long straight of flatlands. Beside the road lay scatters of rubbish and windblown wood. No thunder struck, but the stark and powerful clouds reminded Paloma of a nightmare.

"Fire," Manu broke the silence. "Day one." True fear resonated in his voice. "*Te Draviño* has begun."

CHAPTER 22

THE FLUME

◇◇◇◇◇◇

"Aeron, m'boy!" Skylo shouted over his shoulder. "You sound like you're going to be sick."

As their log zoomed downward in the low light, Skylo turned around and gave Aeron's knee a squeeze.

"Enjoy it!" Skylo said, howling like a wolf.

Aeron's stomach dropped, curled and twisted.

"It's not every life you get to zoom down the veins of a mountain... Yarooo!"

"What..." Aeron's jaw slammed closed, "happened to being..." his head jerked sideways as they shot around a turn and into a slow part of the flume with a high ceiling, "quiet?"

Though far larger than the others, this room contained nothing but a central sandbar and a solitary elm tree.

"We keep quiet when the flameflower is elsewhere," said Skylo. "When she is here, I will know if anything or anyone is spying."

"Where did she go then?" asked Aeron. "While we were in the caves before this wretched log flume?"

They passed a bank covered with leafy plants and moss.

"Manu and Paloma," Skylo said, jabbing his cane against the bank for speed. "As I suspected, they were caught too low on the mountain when *Dravi̇ño* struck.

"You'd think a Ranger would know better…"

"Indeed," Skylo agreed. "He seems… distracted."

The old man turned to face Aeron behind him in the hollow. "Hang on tight now," he continued, clenching a fist of air.

Aeron's fingers curled tightly around Skylo's seat.

A stream of light peeked out from inside the haversack where the Grapple glowed hot against his leg. Ahead of them, blackness approached as if the tunnel halted all at once. Two male sculptured busts whispered to each other, watching Aeron and Skylo from a pedestal on their right. Their eyes watched his every move.

"Five, four…" counted Skylo. "Three." He held a fist over his head. Aeron and Skylo touched knuckles. "Two," Skylo re-gripped the wood. "Ooneee!"

The log roared down the flume, leaving Aeron with a feeling of total weightlessness. It would have been quite the rush had his stomach decided to join him.

At last, light burst them into a world of color, and Aeron tasted ocean air as a vast splash of water rained down on his forehead and lips.

"I've never been so glad to see grey skies and rain," Aeron shouted.

"Wooo," crooned Skylo. "I've been waiting a long time to use that way out again…"

Aeron turned back to examine the chute from outside. A large rock, controlled by some sort of Aero, closed over the secret exit. Above it, falls crashed against the shallow rocks that poked out from beneath foamy seas.

"It's dropped us in the channel that connects the ocean and the river," said Skylo. He pulled out two paddles from the inner sides of the log.

"Where could we possibly be going in a storm like this?" Aeron groaned over the wind. A mixture of rain and sea wind whipped against his cheeks.

"To an old running mate of Manu's, during his Ranging days," said Skylo. "Then, I will be paying a visit to a mutual friend of ours…"

"The Merchant of Herraz?" Aeron asked.

"I prefer to call him Lamark, but yes."

Skylo rowed in slow, steady movements. Aeron followed suit.

"You see that gap in the trees? Around the mountain to the right. That is the mouth of the Riamante River. It will take us down the valley and half-way to Elevana City." Skylo paused and looked at the foreboding clouds. "We must, Aeron, *must* make it before dusk."

"Why?" Aeron wondered. "Nobody will be out in this storm."

"Nobody *good* will be out," Skylo corrected. "But they say that during a thunderstorm a tracer athon can track you for miles. During the day Hyacinth will cover our tracks. Night is trickier."

Current pushing in their favor, the flume approached the mouth of the river. Between the brown current, the low-lying fog, and the swaying trees threatening to snap down at any moment, Aeron could have been peering into the soul of a Wraeth.

"A dark river in the middle of a storm…" Aeron called over Skylo's shoulder. "Sounds like a bad idea."

"With me," Skylo leaned back, grinning madly, "nothing is a bad idea."

CHAPTER 23

BILLBURRY'S HABERDASHERY

The lorry rolled to a complete stop.

"That," Paloma pointed to a shabby, weathered cabin, "is our shelter?"

It seems a cold shell compared to The Sportsman...

"Billburry's Haberdashery, yes," Manu said. "You keep quiet in there. A bondservant speaks when spoken to."

"And who, *master*, is this Billburry fellow? Why should we trust him?"

"Who says we should?" Manu replied, gazing out the window toward a rolling bale of hay. "And I am not your master." A frenetic herd of goats leapt a stone wall and ran past them. "I do not trust anyone. But he owes me. I saved him from losing his head to a party of pirates. He is a pain but consistent and always there when we needed a fast-talker. I have no trust for him, but I do understand him. He won't be a problem."

"Famous last words of an overconfident man," said Paloma with a shrug. "But you're the Ranger."

Manu swigged from his canteen.

"We must have made good time," Paloma continued. "From the looks of it, there's still a few minutes before dusk."

Almost the second they reached the Grey Road, all green had turned to clayish reds, sunburnt yellows, and terracotta. With the fires behind them, they headed east toward Elevana City and the Hardpan, which had long been too flat and rural to burn.

Paloma caught the homey whiff of supper. "Smell that?" she asked. "No idea what a haberdashery is, but that rings bells. Toasted ale and boiling veggies—reminds me of our cook in Longleath. He'd put out a glorious mountain of roast and potatoes for the entire neighborhood."

"Why did you leave then?" Manu asked, stone-faced.

"Mm, good question," Paloma said. Trying to play it off, she cracked open the lorry door. "Shall we go in?"

"After you tell me why."

Paloma closed the door and sighed as rain crashed against the tin roof.

"If you must know," she said, "my nona is old and sick. I heard that sprig from Elevana might do her good."

Manu said nothing, so she continued.

"And, I admit, I'm the Orion for Longleath's Cannaroo team. But we need a keeper. People say the best keepers are in Elevana."

Manu blinked.

How can I get this man to trust me?

"See," Manu said, "now I know the sound of you lying."

"But—"

"Look," Manu interrupted. A mannish figure in a large cloak dashed toward the haberdashery then as if from thin air behind the rains. The figure huddled on the deck for a minute and then knocked at the door.

"That is why we wait," said Manu, gesturing toward the man. "Good things come to those who pause."

"What are we waiting for anyway?"

"Others," said Manu.

"How are Skylo and Aeron getting here anyway? We had a lorry…"

Paloma fell silent and gave her eyes a rest. Manu had yet to turn off the lorry, and it purred gently.

Paloma must have fallen asleep, for she awoke at dusk. She rubbed her eyes open and gave a wide-arm stretch.

"Look there," said Manu, pointing toward a smaller cabin around the back. "The one we saw earlier has gone to the wash house. Now we go."

Manu opened the door and stepped out into the storm as Paloma did the same.

She heard the pop, pop, pop as hail the size of marbles clapped against the bill of her cap.

The rain had slowed, but the water had built up to ankle height, making it difficult to run. Mid-stride, she read the weathered maroon sign printed in flaked yellow letters.

BILLBURRY'S HABERDASHERY (AND MORE)

Water dumped from the gutters, and a heavy moat-like stream had formed around the building's foundation.

Behind her, Manu's heavy steps came thumping through the water. His boot skidded onto the patio and an oak barrel responded by tumbling from the stack. Manu fielded it like an athlete before it went rolling down the road.

Paloma grinned. "Looks like you've got the hands of a good keeper."

"I've always had tremendous hands," Manu said, setting the barrel down beside a wheelbarrow of something spoiled and molding. "Now remember," he continued in a low voice, "you are my slave. If Skylo and Aeron are inside, they are strangers to us."

Paloma nodded once.

Then Manu stomped his boot soles on the old wood floorboards, announcing their presence. Paloma did the same.

"Stop! Go away, whoever you are." Though muffled, the voice sounded high, hard, and male. "We got no more space for freeloaders!"

Manu pressed his arm against the bar of the door and swung it open.

At once, the smell of old linen and stale ale wafted over Paloma. Straight ahead stood a short, thin man with wiry eyebrows and an apron around his waist.

"Well I'll be an athon's uncle…" he said and wiped his hands, one of them missing a finger. "Manny! You big lunk, to what on aerth do I owe the pleasure?"

In the wide-open room, a series of sewing machines and half-used spools of yarn and thread layered three work tables. Although light came from the gas lamps, all six tables had a candle. A crummy book shelf with old and yellowing books nestled in the right corner beside a small hearth.

"Hello, old friend," said Manu.

Something is off in here. Manu must feel it too…

"Thirty years and that's all I get? Ain't nothing changed about you, Manny."

Manu feigned a grin as wide as he could muster.

Behind them both lay an overturned kitchen chair beside a sopping leather duffle and an abandoned chess board on a table in the center of the room. A black wooden bowl steamed on the table beside two brown mugs.

"My servant and I," said Manu, "were in Riamante picking moshrum for Lamark when the fires started before the storm. An inn would be too dangerous."

"Naturally," said Billburry, waving his hand with the missing finger toward his heart. "You came here, to the place of business of a faithful fellow Ranger."

Manu gave a half-nod and turned to Paloma.

"You go on upstairs now," he said and pointed to the lofted second floor.

Paloma bowed with her well-practiced "doe eyes" and skipped past the sewing tables to the opposite side of the room where the staircase began. The wall along the way sported a crowd of buttons, caps, furs, metals, and other random knick-knacks.

In the empty hayloft, she picked the smaller of two seats, turning it to face downstairs.

Billburry waved away from them toward another part of the haberdashery. The place had an open-floor setup with a stairwell and a loft. Various parts of the room had decorations like a home with various rooms. Billburry pointed the empty mug in his hand toward the kitchen corner, opposite the sewing benches. On the way to the kitchen, Billburry and Manu exchanged a few words, and Billburry handed Manu two wooden bowls. Then, they locked arms for a moment before Manu turned and climbed the stairs.

He climbed three at a time, and Paloma followed. Manu sat at a table far enough from the edge that they would not to be noticed, but still could see below. She removed her cap and wrung out some of the water, then set it on the side table. Manu placed the bowls on the table and the smell of a tomato-based soup with broccoli and a sunny-side egg floating on top barreled through her nose. They ate in silence.

"Manu," Paloma whispered after a time. "Skylo and Aeron—"

"Hush."

Her fingers choked the spoon. It took all her strength not to lash out at him.

The back door clanged closed followed by heavy footsteps.

"Please, ma'am," Billburry's voice came through loud and sharp, "leave your jacket and shoes. You are soaked as suds."

The figure's back came into view, still wearing cloak and boots.

"Now, ma'am" Billburry began, "I asked you nice, might I remind you that this is our home?"

Wide back, high burly shoulders, hood still pulled high, the woman planted herself into the nicer of the two chairs.

"Ma'am, that is my seat. Nobody sits in my seat but me. Not even Minnee."

"What's that, dear?" a shrill voice that must have been his wife came from the back room.

"Nothing, Minnee. Go back to your knitting."

The burly woman reached over to the table and turned it around so the black chess pieces were on her side. Then she pulled the wet duffel close.

"So that's how it's gonna be, eh? Fine. But before we pick up again, you tell me what the gods you are doing out in this storm."

The woman seemed to have said something, but Paloma couldn't hear her.

"I'm sorry, your accent is quite strange. A kid, you say?" Billburry echoed. "Your slave?"

Soundlessly, Manu put down the spoon. Paloma held her breath but still could not hear the strange woman's voice behind the wailing wind.

"What do you mean not privy to that information? I been generous enough to give shelter, at least till tomorrow. I'm an honest man. Used to be a Ranger, in fact. But those days are behind me. I likes to know, s'all."

"Quiet?" Billburry repeated incredulously. "How dare you! In my own home. With my own wife in the back." He turned and called over his shoulder. "Minnee, dear, our guest is telling *me* to be quiet."

"Sounds like a smart lass," piped the semi-distant female voice.

"Fine," said Billburry, rising from his chair. "I've got an old Aerostron from my ranging days. One of those magical music sets that play if you give 'em a bit of sugar water…" Grumbling, he disappeared from view toward the kitchen. "Better than silence."

Then a twangy tune came from the kitchen and Billburry returned to his seat by the chess board.

"I told him we are searching for a solo traveler. A boy, *alone,*" said Manu quietly to Paloma.

Paloma finished her bowl and went toward the edge of the hayloft.

The woman made a move on the chess board and leaned back, her arms wide on her hooded head.

Billburry returned and, seeing her move, let out a giddy holler. Billburry moved quickly and swiped his opponent's rook before leaning his chin on his hands.

Paloma came back to the table. Manu sat beneath a stuffed athon head on the wall.

Hideous. She now noticed the blood-red mane, many-eyed face, and strong brown snout. Doing her best to keep the devilish face out of her view, she leaned closed to Manu and whispered.

"She's foreign, for sure. Somewhere far."

"I had a hunch…" Manu said, reaching his long arm to stroke the animal's snout as he thought.

"Where are you thinking?"

"North, no doubt. Far, far north."

"Did he know anything about Skylo and Aeron?"

"No," Manu said. "And now that it is dark, they will not be coming here."

"So what do we do?"

"For now, we wait."

"So we are trapped here until this woman leaves?"

Manu shook his head. "There is more to this haberdashery than meets the eye."

CHAPTER 24

THE EGG IN YOUR PALM

◇◇◇◇◇◇

The heavy, burbling sound of rain on the river lessened. Gliding down with the now-slow current, Aeron and Skylo floated beneath an arching canopy of trees.

"You said someone followed you. Has your scent, yes?"

"Either mine," Aeron said, "or Paloma's—"

"Ehh?" Skylo shouted back. The rain fell loud upon the leaves. "Speak up, son."

They had been traveling down the river for several hours, but Skylo now dipped his paddle into the water to slow their pace.

"I started to say," Aeron continued, "I have no idea how they got my blood…" Aeron paused to think. He had fallen asleep on the lorry to West Riamante. But, unless the Eurovean put on a performance even granddad would find impressive, that was unlikely.

The neath? Or the farmhand…

"The only place I can think of is the tavern in Riamante."

"Which?" said Skylo.

"At the edge of the valley. The Sportsman, I think they called it."

"Ahh," Skylo sighed, deep in thought. "So you have met the neath. Tell me, Aeron, who performed that night?"

"The Marquis of Innisfree."

"Interesting," Skylo said, twisting his mouth as if he had an itch. "And how did you and Ms. Murravillow come to meet in the first place?"

"The lorry. That's when we met. Someone startled the driver and we swerved off the road into a foot of mud. After the others walked back for Marillo, I sprung the wheel free with a simple lever. We were the only two kids and—come to think of it—she was the one who startled the driver. I gave her a list of items. Nothing crazy. She went into the forest and came back with more than we needed."

The current had picked up a bit of speed again. Skylo lifted his left hand, with the flame flower in orbit, to his face. He squinted and lowered his eyelids. He examined it as if considering a terrible problem of Epiphysics.

"Yes," Skylo drew out the word, nodding.

"With a bit of leverage and a heartfruit, we got the lorry running until she ran out of steam."

"Yes…" Skylo said again.

"That's when the music started. And we followed it. Or I followed it and she followed me. We landed ourselves into that tavern. She got a bit too sauced off neath wine and I— long story short, we ended up in the home of the Marquis of Innisfree. But that was exactly where the poem Lamark gave me wanted us."

"Yes!" Skylo said with a wild grin.

"What's so funny?" Aeron asked.

"I wish you could see! Someday, perhaps you may…"

Skylo ran two fingers in the water beside the log. Then his voice came quietly and with a hint of song.

"*Anamastae.*"

Like a comet, Hyacinth fell out of orbit. It swelled, as if drinking the rain, and then collapsed to nothing.

"That!" Aeron shouted. "I want that! I want the Aeros! I want, like an archivist should, to be able to use my voice and my mind to do good. I want—"

"Listen to me now," Skylo said. "You may think otherwise, but your years have been lucky ones. You were born into an educated family, and you have avoided the terrible creatures that lurk in this world. You may not be rich, and you may not have traveled the world to see its sights and sounds and smell its fragrances, but you *are* wealthy. You *have* traveled."

Paloma's rich. She's seen the world. I have barely even been out of Longleath…

"Boats and trains and lorries are one way of traveling, but they leave you yearning for more. I have seen all four Corners of Aerth, and now all I want is to see the moon! You Aeron, have traveled on the bow of a far more potent vessel. Death. Death is the ultimate travel. Seeing it as a young boy is like being shown a glimpse at the secret of life. The true way."

"There is no true way," said Aeron, echoing one of his schoolmasters. "Everyone and everywhere is different."

"I used to believe such things. My school masters, those hundreds of years ago, stole the truth from me. It wasn't until the day I met my own master that I realized…" Skylo trailed off. From the river, he picked up a lily pad, which held a small stone.

"After we were turned away from the Tree," he said, turning the oval rock over between his thumb and forefinger, "I was lost. I went back home, to Termara—"

"*You* are from Termara?" Aeron gasped. "That makes you older than Longleath!"

"Indeed I am. And in Termara I learned my first Aero. My schoolmasters taught the same things yours did—arithmetic, language, and science. Mine too said that the Aeros and Epiphysics were a myth. Except for one. The old headmaster had been sacked and now ran a bookstore of no significance in the market. I went to him, seeking a book to distract me from the pain. It surprised me to see such a disappointing fellow. He even kept a sad old skyturtle as a pet.

"But the old headmaster listened to my story and said my problem, like most, had a simple solution. But before he told me, I needed to prove my worthiness. So he gave me an egg, like this stone. I could feel it held something living.

"'Walk this egg by every souk in the market,' he said, 'and to keep it from cracking, hold it in your palm. Return here when you have finished.'"

"Did you crack it?" Aeron broke in.

"I walked through that entire market, mobbed with life. Merchants hollered at me, kids knocked my shoulders as they wove in and out of crowds, women sang songs from makeshift stages, the changing scents of roasted nuts and sweet wine and fruit floated about, yet, I walked by every single one of them.

"When I returned, the old headmaster asked me how the wine was, and if I had seen what the merchants had on sale that day, and if any of the flowers looked worth buying.

"I hadn't seen a thing, I told him, except for my feet and the egg he gave me, which was still in excellent shape.

"He laughed at me so hard, I thought I might strike his skyturtle. I scooped up the egg and made the rounds once again. Darker now, the sky was smeared with crimson and orange. I saw all the beautiful women about and the men selling expensive tools or pieces of art. I even had a bit of wine, so I could report back.

"'Where's my egg?' he shouted at me as I walked through the door.

"I reached into my pocket and felt the cracks in it, so I told him I had lost it. I suspect he knew all along what happened, but he played along.

"'When you bring back my egg, I will tell you the secret way.'"

"Why? What's so special about an egg," Aeron asked.

"I never returned to him, and I think that was his intention. Still, that day I learned not one but three secrets."

Skylo paused. The rain had been drowned out by the sound of rushing waters, but he remained unfazed as he continued.

"Always be aware of Aerth's brilliant colors," he said as the rock floated an inch above his palm. "But remember to keep an eye on the egg in your hand." Skylo paused for a moment and they fell into silence.

Green trees swayed with violent, threatening waves. The Riamante Valley had flushed past as a wispy dream. Now out from the tunnel, rain dumped down in sheets on Skylo's bald head. Even so, the old man had the same smile.

"Would you like to hear the third secret, Aeron?"

"Yes, please," Aeron nodded.

"Never forget the Aero in your pocket."

Aeron thought for a moment and then reached into his haversack. He removed the Grapple, which beamed brighter than ever before, its light shattering on the hard grey waters and igniting a huge space on the river. Brow furled, he held it in the flat of his palm, as Skylo had. Staring into its frozen blue center, Aeron spoke quietly and with a hint of song.

"*Anamastae.*"

CHAPTER 25

THE IRKAL

◇◇◇◇◇

Below the hayloft, Billburry let out the most cackling of whines. The sound reverberated through the haberdashery, chilling Paloma to the bone.

"Minnee! You wench, get yourself out of bed and pour us another round."

Minnee said something, but the words were smothered by a crash of wind against the walls. Then, she came trundling out from the back room with four mugs. She "accidentally" knocked Billburry on the head with the edge of her tray as she passed and placed the cups on their table.

"Ooh, dearie," she said in a pleasant voice. "She has you beat!"

"Minnee. I love you. But shut it."

She knocked him again, this time grinning at the guest.

"I'm going to get a look at this person," whispered Paloma.

Manu tried to grab her, but Paloma slipped away. Near the stairwell, she stopped to contemplate the next move.

Down is a dreadful idea. Those stairs have "groaners" written all over them. No window up here. But how about...

She turned her gaze toward the pair of long wooden support beams, which extended out from the loft. Manu's tension screamed that it was a terrible idea. So she went ahead and did it anyway.

"Your move," said the hooded figure.

Paloma crept out on the cross beam, wide enough to support her two feet. One foot at a time she edged forward, stopping beneath a thick cobweb.

"Unfortunately," Billburry said, "you're right." He slid his piece with a satisfied look.

Where Paloma positioned herself, they would have to look straight up to see her.

The chair squealed as the figure leaned back with crossed arms.

"I've given up, but I'm not giving in," Billburry mocked. "*Your move.*"

When his opponent made the move to "castle," Billburry's eyes ignited with amusement.

"You fool!" He moved a different piece this time, the knight.

The figure reached up and, with two ringed fingers, removed its hood to reveal unmistakable bright, silvery-blond hair, a huge, harshly shaped round head, and a face paler than snow.

Paloma slapped a hand over her mouth to prevent herself from screaming. When she turned back toward Manu, she found him looking down from the rafter, unsurprised.

They are right. For some reason there are Irkal in Elevana. And I am crouching right above the one that's been looking for us…

"Say," said the Irkal with a voice like gravel. "Why four mugs? You expecting *guests*?"

Paloma had never seen an Irkal before, but she took this one for a female.

"Oh no," Billburry stammered, "my Minnee's extra thoughtful. Thought a tired lass like you might want extra."

An unnatural beat of silence skipped across the conversation.

"I see," said the Irkal. Still wearing a suede polishing glove, she rippled her pinky, ring, middle, and finally pointer finger's around Billburry's queen. "But if I should find that you're lying..."

Billburry's eyes darted, for an instant, up to the loft. The Irkal must have seen it, and she jerked over her right shoulder for a look. Leaping frantically out of sight to the opposite crossbeam, Paloma caught a face full of cobwebs.

"Then *my* guests," continued the Irkal, "will have your head as a nice mantle." She gripped the brown duffle and rose from her chair.

Something heavy and jagged is in there. I can see it in the leather. Like a weapon in pieces, or a sack of sharp glass.

The Irkal turned toward the wooden stairwell, crossed the room, and climbed the stairs two at a time.

"*Your* guests?" asked Billburry, nipping at her heels.

Manu pointed an emphatic finger at Paloma and then pointed toward the kitchen.

She swung down from the crossbeam and onto a bureau with uneven legs. It teetered side to side, but Paloma made herself small and steadied it. Then she jumped off, landing with a light-footed hustle into the "kitchen," which meant the corner with the sink and dirty dishes. Her scythe banged against her hip, so she unlatched the strap—just in case.

Minnee appeared from the back room. "Oh, Billburr—" she cut herself short.

Paloma backed into a wall cabinet with various bowls and plates. At least five dishes clamored to the floor.

"Darn it, Minnee!" Billburry hollered from above. "As if we ain't already got enough problems around here with *Draviño* comin' and all! Now quiet while I'm trying to show our guest the upstairs collection."

With no more chaos or rumbling, Billburry went back to entertaining the Irkal, waving solemnly at the athon's head on the wall.

Where could Manu have gone? He was right there a moment ago...

In the corner of the room was the jangling of metal and eye-catching movement. Minnee waved frantically for Paloma's attention, beckoning her like a kid dying to let out a secret that might save the day or at least give her a head-start.

"And if you look here," Billburry's voice came from above.

Paloma dashed over to where Minnee stood.

"In there, dear," she whispered, pointing to a barrel in the wall that said "Eurovean Dressing for Leather" beneath a string of unripe corn hanging from the ceiling.

Taken aback, Paloma knocked twice on the wood. Specks of dust puffed off the rim as its circular base swung wide open. And there was Manu's leathery face.

CHAPTER 26

INTO THE RAIN

The Grapple shook once, like a chick trying to hatch and take flight. Twice. But then came the nightmare. The log swooped fast and downward, and the stone popped out of Aeron's hand and into the foaming river.

"No!" Aeron shouted, probing at the rapids and nearly losing his hand on a jagged rock. "Skylo!" he shook the man. "What are we to do?"

"Nothing," the man growled while rowing both oars at once. "Now cut that out and help me row."

"The Grapple," Aeron cried, "it's gone!"

"The Grapple is never gone, Aeron Mason," howled Skylo. "Only resting!"

A thrash of water rocked their log boat, and Skylo steadied it with a dip of the oar.

"But you are a Sage, surely you can use an Aero to bring it back…"

"No," Skylo said. "Using one Aero to find another defies the Law of Nature. Doing so would be an act against the true way!"

"What do I do then?" Aeron asked desperately.

"Row!"

Aeron had been given a gift that appeared every thousand years, and he had lost it. Shame rained down on him twice as hard. All during the deaths in his family, the terrible years at prep, and his time in prison, Aeron had refused to cry. His dad always beat him when he cried. But he had never lost something that could silence footsteps and use water to heal wounds.

Rain slashed sideways against his face. He wept in silence, the storm mixing with tears.

The world whizzed by in jolts, rolls, and rumbles. Aeron turned over his left shoulder to see the Mossy Mountain struck high through the clouds.

The log lurched forward in a nosedive, and Aeron wheeled forward as Skylo reached the paddle backward over his head and thrust downward. An oar handle jabbed between Aeron's feet with such a surprising burst of force that his feet vibrated. The wood had sprung a tiny crack, but the log had leveled.

"The egg *and* the aerth," Skylo called over his shoulder. "Now focus."

Aeron knew what he meant. He gripped the paddle firmly between his fingers and rowed with all his might. At a turn, the log tilted and the Journal skimmed Aeron's leg from inside the haversack. It reminded him of something his granddad said on the way to his father's funeral that he hadn't understood until now.

Loss is the "L" in life. An archivist never loses. He wins more slowly.

Aeron tucked the haversack further beneath his legs and pushed away all the sad thoughts.

I have a map that takes me exactly to what I want most. I have a book that has all the histories and discoveries of the world. And I have a Sage who is a thousand years old keeping me safe. I have had it with thinking of myself as a terrible loser, the way Longleath does. I have to make sacrifices so I can learn the Aeros at the Tree of Knowledge. Manu the Wilder, the Last Great Ranger, started with less. Why can't I become even more? That's what I want. For people to sing songs of how Aeron Mason, the last archivist, rid the world of Wraeths.

While musing about these things, the river flattened. Yet still the rapids raged.

For a brief few moments, the sun came between a slit in the clouds, flooding the river with stunning rays that wavered on the water like flower pedals and Skylo's boyish figure with a glint of gallantry. A confusing excitement boiled up in Aeron. The whole world, for an instant—oar, leaves, rocks—was dazzling and dreamy and unstable.

"Prepare yourself!" Skylo called back.

Aeron leaned to one side for a better look. Flat ground and roiling waters meant one thing…

"A waterfall?" Aeron leaned forward for Skylo to hear.

"As I said," Skylo said, leaning back. The beard that had resembled a long pinecone earlier that morning stuck to his chin like a turkey's wattle. "Prepare yourself…"

Then Skylo sang.

That morning I dreamt a finest feast
Held asunder the Tree of True
She stamps the autumn airs with blue
Singing me great without a rue,
That morning! The Sky! Reveille! Release!
Shifting sides, my love is you!
Sing aloft the fields of clear water,
Watching the waves beneath the sea,
Drinking time at gradients of three,

Thinks her thoughts in fields of me
Oh Sorrow, she, that lost otter
A sallow terror; the feeling's nobody!

Darkly lover the at evil standstill
Aerthly chords, a pageant of delight,
Kept one small flower near for sight
Where dreams, a boy, to end the white,
Above the Aerthly sky a'trill
Where better to die than soundless flight!

Yar! Yar! No backs turned round,
Forgetting who lives and who has strayed;
Sighing vows for thought's invade
Left behind, that the gods displayed
A most glorious life to lead abound
Before I would find, the upturned spade!

They approached the final bend. On the other side of the rocks, the roiling sound of angry waters stirred.

Aerth and Sea and Sky and Storm
Western gullies, running stream,
In city's suffix people breathe them all
Aerth believes that time is worn
Orifornia, Orifornia, water, and steam
We find them running from haeven's fall!

Skylo's raspy voice, true and melodious, carried even after he had stopped singing. As the note finished echoing, Hyacinth warped into being and settled at the front of the log like a hood ornament.

As they rounded the corner, Skylo tucked his oar inside the log, and Aeron did the same.

For a moment his jaw unhinged with shock. Then, a thrust of force came from beneath their raft. As if a rock shot skyward from a geyser or a whale's spout, the log sailed through the air. Between the pounding of rain from above and the thrusting of water from below, Aeron's stomach lurched from the suspension. Between up and down, death and life melted into one. As he clenched his eyes, preparing for the end, Skylo squeezed tightly on Aeron's knee.

CHAPTER 27

THE AEROHIVE

◇◇◇◇◇◇

Paloma went reeling at Manu's disembodied head and hit a shelf above the sink. A jar of oranges teetered and went barreling for the ground. She caught it, as a good Cannaroo athlete should, an inch before shattering.

"Inside, dearie!" Minnee whispered. "They're coming."

Still cradling the jar, Paloma's horror dissipated. The barrel on the wall no longer held Manu's head, but his outstretched hand.

He's on the other side... it must be some kind of escape tunnel.

She passed him the oranges. His hand reacted with confusion. Paloma then hoisted herself up and went feet-first through the circular door. Paloma caught a foot on one of the metal bars leading below, where Manu now stood.

Paloma could smell the moisture from above in the tunnel. Though damp and brown, the passage seemed otherwise unaffected by the storm. Several huge, dusty bottles of wine lay in a row on one of the ledges, and bits of broken pottery and clay clumped near the wall. A wide network of roots spanned the tunnel's roof from end to end.

Before climbing down, Paloma turned back toward the haberdashery.

The door remained open, but Minnee's wide rump stood in front of it.

"Now what's all this *guest*, nonsense?" Billburry demanded. "I told you we ain't allowing any more freeloaders."

"My brother," said the Irkal woman, "and his friends should be arrivin' at any moment."

Minnee shifted her weight and Paloma caught a flash of the Irkal's face. White, baggy, uneven, tiny nose, huge jaws, and sharp eyes were all shrouded by long platinum-gold hair. Its dark eyes stared right at them.

Minnee backed against the wall, covering the barrel-door. Paloma squeezed the woman's hand for a second, as if to thank her, and then silently closed the door.

"Come," said Manu from a few paces down the hall. He held no torch, but the tunnel had been lit by primitive versions of lightseeds like they had in Longleath. These crystals still emanated light from the filament inside, but were smaller than the ones in the city and far older.

Paloma dropped down, landing like a dancer. Inside, Manu hunched over to accommodate the low roof.

"What is this place?" she asked.

"An old moshrum running channel. Been around since the first Wraeth invasion. After Termara, Wraeths came here looking for something. Elevana resisted and used tunnels to sneak around. This one transported moshrum."

Manu continued ahead and Paloma followed.

"I fear they are back again, in Elevana. For the same reason."

"Searching for something?"

"Yes." Manu paused. "Or someone."

Paloma pressed her hands against the sides of the tunnel. One of the crystal seeds sputtered dead at her touch. She touched another and it too went dead. The ease with which they went out sent a chilling thought through her.

Is this what the Wraeth will do to us?

"So you think the Irkal's guests were... Wraeths?"

Manu paused for a moment and continued ahead. "Wraeths, Irkals, athon, does it matter? Right now, *Te Draviño* is keeping us all safe. No man can outdo its power. And so the storm equalizes us all. But..."

Paloma waited for him to continued. When the silence continued, she spoke again.

"We've got to get off this island," she said. "All of us."

After a time, he responded. "You're not wrong."

He has his faults, but I can see why the Council reveres him. I can't remember the last time a grown man admitted I might be right.

"Hush now. I need to think."

The first tunnel had been a straight shot, but the going had been slow because of its small size. After the better part of an hour, they let out into a larger shaft with a gravel floor. This one could hold Manu, and their feet hastened.

"Carts," he broke the silence. "They would roll carts filled with moshrum through here, sometimes even have animals pull them."

"You seem to know a lot about this..."

"Elevana was one of my first rangings. Back then, the Huntress were the problem. The Wraeths had been forced back underground."

"Underground?"

"Yes," said Manu. "There is a country in the far north. Between Indoshina and Irkalla. It is called the Harroes."

"I *know* where the Harroes are," Paloma hissed.

"Somewhere inside the Harroes is a deep, dark place. No priman nor neath have ever seen it." He stopped for a moment and scooped up a corked bottle that lay on its side. He uncorked it and the heavy scent of moshrum emptied into the tunnel.

"The Aerohive," Manu gulped.

"The Aerohive?"

"Remember Skylo's story. He and Viru were turned away from the Tree. Skylo traveled. Viru went straight for the Aerohive. There he learned."

The lightseeds illuminating the way grew fewer and fainter. The ground trended upward as they walked.

"Manu," Paloma said and pulled at his arm. "I think…"

She brushed the wall with a hand. Soft and mossy.

"Out with it. A Ranger never hesitates."

"I think I saw him. Viru. In the dead of the wood."

Manu stopped, his sandy eyes piercing into her. He scrutinized her as if he could see the truth in her dark skin. Everything remained silent except for rain pounding somewhere nearby.

Manu nodded. "That you have…"

CHAPTER 28

GONE BUT NOT LOST

For an instant, Aeron felt like a crumpled leaf of paper. The world had imploded around him like a dying star. First thing he knew, they were being shot by an eruption of water in the air on their way to certain death. The next thing he knew, they were somewhere else—all in a flash.

Aeron's head swirled, and he opened his eyes to find grey clouds rolling behind the mountain.

"Skylo…" a pit of nausea turned over in Aeron's belly.

"That, Aeron, is what we call phantagration," said Skylo. "They will teach you at the Tree."

Mention of the Tree reminded Aeron of the lost Grapple, and his nausea transformed into pangs of guilt.

"But I've lost it," said Aeron, "the Grapple…"

"Gone," said Skylo pulling the oar out from inside the log, "but not lost."

Aeron scanned the space. On a normal day it may have been a nice place for a picnic, but today the clearing held three feet of water.

The river must have flooded over. That should slow down any athon still on the trace. But Manu and Paloma…

"Skylo," Aeron said. "Why can't you teach me the Aeros? And phantagration? Why do I have to go all the way to Orifornia? I'm ready. We could start right *now*."

"Oh, Aeron," said Skylo looking off in the distance. "Have you been sleeping all throughout these last few days? Those who seek the Aeros must first root out all desires and humbly accept their place where Knowledge was born, where lies a copy of every book ever written, including that one in your pocket. It is the seat of wisdom and virtue, and it is a place more valuable than all the gold and silver and honorable treasures of the world.

"To bring yourself to true happiness and peace, you must wake up. Most primen live their lives half-asleep. They live with some form of desire and hate and foolishness. The Aeros are for no such men.

"To walk safely through the maze of primen life, we must give ourselves up to the interconnection of all things. We must wake up, become aware of our thoughts, and live in the accordance with the secret way. Do you remember the secret way?"

They had rowed a short distance and docked at a small hillock. The water dwindled, and Skylo wedged his oar into the bank.

"Yes," said Aeron. "I think so."

"Good," said Skylo, stepping onto the rocks, "because you will need it. And sooner than I should like…"

Aeron swung his legs over the edge and strapped the haversack to his back. Then he rose to follow Skylo. The old man faced the eastern part of the hill. "See there, those four trees—the ones that lean into one another as a tent might, or the sticks of a campfire?"

Aeron nodded. Four tall birch trees poked out of the ground in a squarish shape. About ten feet above the ground was something pinkish.

"What's that in the middle?"

"That is where you shall stay tonight. It's a treehouse, of sorts. Inside is a woman called Pillee. A friend."

"What?" asked Aeron with surprise. "I thought we were meeting Manu and Paloma?"

"There has been a slight change of plans. I must continue on to Elevana City to call in a favor. We need a ship fast enough to get us to Orifornia before Bloom's Feast in Autumn. None are allowed into the Tree once its leaves begin changing color."

"So I'm going in... alone?"

"You have already called your first Aero, young Mason. Because of that, you will never be alone."

Skylo turned back toward the log and stepped inside.

"Skylo," said Aeron, "if you know phantagration, why did we have to go all this way? You should just go to the city that way. Or better yet we could go right to the Tree!"

"Spoken like a true archivist," Skylo wore a knowing grin. "Always trying to make the most out of things..." he picked up both oars. The flameflower seemed to have drooped in size and color. "Phantagrating is hard work. Hyacinth is tired. If we try again, I might kill her. Or she could kill me."

He pushed off the embankment in the direction of the rushing water.

"Farewell, Aeron!" he called. "Enjoy some of Pillee's sweetcakes for me."

Aeron reached around the Haversack to make sure he'd taken everything and then his breast pocket. Several heartfruit, the Journal, and...

The map!

Even as Skylo disappeared from sight, remembering the map passed a warming glimmer of hope from head to toe.

Gone but not lost.

As night fell, the winds picked up speed. Aeron charged toward the tree formation as best he could, determined to meet this Pillee. Then, once she had gone to bed, he could take a look at the Map of the Reddheart. Surely it would show him the Grapple.

The smell of fresh bread sent Aeron dreaming. His granddad's house in Longleath was right beside a bakery so famous that lines ran around the corners.

"Half-dozen for sale, half-dozen for the Masons," Aeron could still hear the baker's daughter call out to Granddad, who would try to decline. It never worked. Everyone felt like family around Mendel Mason.

To his left, the middle of the hill held nothing but green grass. But between those trees at the hill's end, Pillee's house bloomed with life—tomatoes, strawberries, and ten-foot sunflowers.

The house itself had been built in between the four trees. Tall and thin, Aeron counted seven stories—each with windows in odd and uneven places and each painted with a different fluorescent color. *Manu could never fit in there*, Aeron thought, wondering why they would choose the place.

Aeron's foot struck against something hard. He stumbled forward, catching himself on the rim of a long-dead tree stump. The fall had revealed a dangling sailor's ladder. In order to reach it, he stepped up onto the stump and gripped the lowest rung.

Though dark and windy, the storm had let up enough that Aeron could climb without much danger. After ten or so steps, he pulled himself, hands and knees, onto the wooden platform.

An old chipmunk-cheeked woman wearing an airy gown sat in a wicker rocking chair. Beside her was a plate of breads, cakes, and some reddish wine. The deck had the decorations of a home a few blocks from one of Elevana's beaches.

"Pillee?" Aeron said, approaching slowly. When she made no response, he edged closer. "Pillee, I am a friend of Skylo's."

She let out a grubby snore and smacked her lips.

She's asleep! Do I wake her? Might scare the life out of her if no one's told her I'm coming. I'll wait a few minutes. Maybe she will wake up. Or someone will come outside.

He helped himself to one of the yellow cakes and a cup of wine. The taste erupted in his mouth like a volcano of sweetness. He took a second and sat with his back against one of the support beams. With one foot dangling in the air, Aeron reached into his breast pocket.

He tucked the Reddheart Map back inside and opened the Journal.

Misfortune plumbs the abyss of primankind's mysteries, pressure cooks that misfortune, and oxygen vulcanizes it altogether. An old friend, perhaps I would call him my own teacher, once told me that. I used to think it most wretched that the only way to understand the Aeros is through loss. I failed my way through country after country in the Southern Rift before landing in Oriendo. If I had known I was planting seeds all across the world, I may have been less depressed about losing my wife and children. But then again, if I had known, I, Jameis Mason, may have never become the Duke of Constanto.

Before studying the Aeros, I felt death to be final. Now I see it as the beginning. And no Wraeth can take this away from us.

Everything and everyone dies. But the tales of the greatest forever survive.

So we must remember death—eumemento moros.

Jameis Durand Mason
Duke of Constanto

A deep pounding sound came from below. Though muffled, it carried a deep and violent drum to it. Aeron's pulse picked up speed. He put down the Journal and squinted in the low light, but it was too dark.

"Pillee," Aeron whispered. "Pillee, someone's here. Wake up."

She jerked her eyes open and mumbled but then fell back asleep.

"Hello?" Aeron called downward.

No response.

The pounding returned, harder and faster than before, as if an animal were trying to break free from its cage. Jags of fear cut up and down Aeron's arms and legs. He backed away from the ledge into a more shadowy area of the deck. Though they would be no use against an athon or a well-trained Irkal, Aeron grabbed a pair of bread knives.

Then he heard no more thumping. A door hinged behind a pair of muted whispers. Then, the familiar jangling of the wooden ladder. Finally, a dark hand swung onto the deck.

CHAPTER 29

IN THE SHELL

"**W**as beginning to think I'd never see you again, Mr. Mason," said Paloma.

Aeron stepped out of the shadows and into the orange lamp light. His sunken cheeks and low eyelids worried her.

"You look dreadful," Paloma continued and finished the cake on Aeron's plate. "But gods those are good. And where's your wily old friend?"

Still Aeron said nothing. Paloma poured herself a glass of wine to wash it down.

"What's wrong? I never remember you as one who minces words."

"I lost it, Paloma."

Mug to her lips, Paloma froze.

"The Grapple," Aeron said and shook his head with shame. "It's gone."

"What," Manu's voice came from behind her, "did you say?"

Aeron retreated a step. Manu's baritone voice must have surprised him. Too large for the house, Manu stood atop the false tree stump.

"It fell out of the raft," Aeron supplied, "into the river."

"Raft? River? Mercy... that explains the mangy-dog look."

"Do you realize," Manu said, running two hands over his scalp, "what this means?"

"Skylo said it will return," Aeron shot back. "He's sure of it."

"Of course he is. Always sure of everything. Yet the Wraeths have returned. You lot are being hunted. And now the most powerful artifact on Aerth is on the loose."

Aeron said nothing. Something—or rather someone—stirred to the right. The woman with puffy cheeks yawned and stretched out her thick hands.

"Halo, chill-dran," said the woman, unsurprised.

"Are you Pillee?" Paloma asked, "Minnee's mother?"

"Yes'm. And who are you?" Pillee replied in short stumpy words that matched her body.

"Friends of Skylo's," said Aeron.

"I no see Skylo… how you find me?"

"Hey, Pillee," Manu said.

"Oh no. Oh no, no no," said Pillee, shaking her head. "You no welcome here Ma-nu. You best no have that lor-ry."

"Good evening to you too, Pillee Hazel," said Manu.

"I no kidding, Ma-nu," she said gruffly. "Lorry disgusting. Ruin flowers. Chill-dran, keep your beast away from gar-den."

"There's no lorry, Ms. Pillee," Paloma assured her. "And we'll keep Manu away, no complaints there."

"I like you, girl. You know my Min-nee?"

"Yes," said Paloma. "We got into trouble, and she's the reason we're here."

"I fear," said Manu, "that Irkal is now the least of our worries."

"You quiet now, Ma-nu. Come, chill-dran, inside more cake for you." She rose from her white chair and left it rocking behind her as she went inside and then called back once more. "Remember, Manu. No lor-ry. No moshrum neith-er. Starflower no like it. Too greasy, too oily."

Paloma picked up the plates and glasses on the front porch. On the wall, decorations swung gently and a wind-chime tinkled. Beside Pillee's chair was a rocking bench whose chains had been strung with vines of white and red flowers.

"Storm lett-ing up," said Pillee. "For now."

Her voice came through the top of the open half-door. Paloma opened the bottom and entered behind her.

"But *Draviño* is supposed to go on for weeks..." Paloma said.

"Yes'm, girl, this how Dra-vin-yo go. Start bad, pause. Men are stupid, try to run a-way. Go running for ports. Then Dra-vin-yo get angry that men make same mistake!" Pillee shook her head.

A wisp of frantic voices came from outside.

"I'm sorry!" Aeron shouted at Manu from outside. Something hollow and wooden fell over on the deck. "But if you and Paloma had stayed in the burrow, we'd still be there right now." He swung open the door and went straight for a cushy, yellow pleated chair. He rested an arm on one of the sides and sank his chin into his hand in thought.

To her right, Paloma passed the ungodly steep staircase leading upstairs. She handed the dishes over to Pillee, whose round shape spanned the tiny kitchen.

"Here," whispered Pillee. She reached up on top of the cabinet where a glass covering held a few exquisite rose-shaped sweetcakes. "For friend."

Paloma smiled and nodded in thanks and then went around to sit on the mint-green couch in the middle of the room. She placed the tray nearest Aeron on the tea table.

"Miss Pillee," said Paloma over the sound of running water, "you talk about *Draviño* as if it is alive. Like it has thoughts and chooses how much damage to inflict."

Pillee turned off the water and wiped her hands on a pink towel. "Boy, who you?" Pillee ignored the question. "Too young to be out here. Both of you. But he smell like mosh-rum. Too young. Danger for chill-drun. Bad, now very bad time."

"That's Aeron," Paloma said. "But, ma'am, please, if I may, why is now so bad? *Draviño* of course but—"

"Storm least of your worr-ies. Bad primen here now. Worse com-ing."

"Who?" asked Aeron, uncrossing his arms.

"Drink," Pillee said, taking a seat in the largest armchair. "Drink and give cups to me."

After such a day, the wine was sweet and refreshing.

Aeron bit into one of the rose cakes. His eyes lit up and he finished it without stopping.

"Look chill-drun," said Pillee. She held out both mugs with one hand. "Wineleaf leave pictures. Tell fortune."

"*Runes?*" Aeron whispered. He leaned over and scrutinized the insides of the cups. "Paloma, it's like the one we saw in Riamante, and on the tree at Yeats farm."

Pillee placed the mugs on the coffee table.

Aeron pulled the Journal out from his breast pocket and flipped through it. Pillee hovered by while he unwound the pen from its tassel and sketched what he saw. Paloma rose and faced the window.

Even from the deck at night, Elevana remained immaculate. Sharp rays of moon lit up a valley of ripening fields and sylvan trees that nourished wildlife of all shapes and sizes as cicadas and nightjars sang loudly.

She turned and, without a stir from Pillee or Aeron, ascended the stairs until reaching the top floor. The wind had died down enough. She pressed open the latch and stood on the roof, square and damp and not much larger than her bed at home.

Paloma tilted her head back. Straight above, the clouds hung stark, heavy, and motionless, like frozen smoke. But toward the ocean…

Strange.

Miles away, stars shone through a break in the grey abyss. It wasn't a gap but a swirl, as if the clouds had taken the form of seashell or a maelstrom.

Through the *Draviño's* clear side of the curl of maelstrom, one constellation stuck out.

Pyxis. The compass.

"Paloma?" someone called from below.

"Hush," came Manu's deep voice from the ground.

Paloma leaned over the edge. Below seven stories of khaki and fuchsia and green, Manu laid with his arms cradling his head.

She took a final look at the strange break in the sky and stepped back through the hatch. Shells, flowers, paintings of water—every decoration up and down the staircase reminded her of it.

Between groans from the stairwell came Pillee's throaty voice.

"To-morrow, Ae-ron." Paloma stopped to listen. "Wear trust on sock. Irkal. Wraeth. Bad things. If no careful, the sea-shell…"

Paloma slipped into the room behind them. Aeron and Pillee sat on the couch facing the coffee table.

"What about a seashell?" Paloma said from behind them.

Aeron wheeled around. His eyes were red and puffy.

Weighed down by their two mugs, a large map stretched out on the table. It showed Elevana with a line sketched straight north toward the sea.

The Map of the Reddheart! Skylo must have given it to Aeron to help us off the island.

"Tomorrow is our last shot, Paloma," he said. "If we don't get the Grapple and get off this island… I think we might not survive the storm, let alone make it to the Tree before autumn."

"Don't say that," said Paloma.

"No, it's bad. See for yourself," he said and gestured in front of him.

She stood over the table. A thin layer of grey mist hovered on the map, as if someone had smudged the yellow paper with lead. Sea smoke.

The trees, mountains, and rivers—every element on the map was alive and moving. Paloma touched the snowcapped mountain, and coolness pricked her finger. Then she ran her hand through the clouds across the textured map.

"You see where the red line leads?" asked Aeron. "That's where I found the Grapple. That's where it must be. A straight shot north through the shell, into the desert hardpan, and back to the same grove where it all started. Without a lorry, we'll never make that in one day."

"Look, the storm is already receding," said Paloma. "The shell of the storm is getting wider and drifting our way." She pressed her hand flat against the map beneath the clouds. "I barely even feel any rain. I think we're going to have a clear day tomorrow. We can make it."

"Yes," Aeron agreed, "but that means so do *they*."

"But *they* don't have a map or Manu the Wilder," said Paloma. "This is going to work." She picked up one of the mugs. The rune inside stole her breath. A swirl, exactly like the one she had seen beneath the stars, was now twirling on the map.

"One way or another, Aeron," she said, "tomorrow, we go into the shell."

CHAPTER 30

THE WINFLOW

◇◇◇◇◇◇

On the outskirts of Elevana City, Lamark made the long walk home from the Blue Bat. Though *Draviño's* winds had died down, the rain pounded on him with full force. Trudging by an abandoned fruit vending cart, he examined it for any leftovers.

Why'd they 'ave to close the blast lorry lines? Lamark thought, heading back for the road.

He'd made the walk before, but never in ankle-deep water. And, for fear of looters at the store, he chose to take the boy's heartfruit home with him to weather the storm.

Carrying fifty heartfruit in a clunky sack over his shoulder, Lamark lumbered through the bright night. The road, waterlogged with dangling vines and grapes, resembled an empty wasteland. The short string of boarded-up homes and storefronts had lorries parked in odd places, as if their owners had to make a sudden escape.

Then the road forked in two and Lamark continued on the rightward road with trees and plants on either side. On this road nothing ever changed.

The forest gave a relative break from the rains and Lamark managed to pick up the pace until his breathing grew heavy and shallow. He stopped and leaned against a creaking birch tree.

Coulda run all this way... in the old days. But I'll take 'eavy pockets over sharp lungs any day.

The road let out close to Lamark's home, where he found the river had flooded over the banks up to the walls he had built when they first moved.

Not a good sign.

As he pressed down the final path, their house, a four-story mansion, came into view.

Thank gods for those Epiphysicists. Dravîño *began but our 'ome still growin' stronger 'n ever.*

The mumbling of voices came from the other side of the home by the beach. He placed the sack into one of the false boulders he'd traded for and followed the stone walkway around the side of the house. Inside only a few candles had been lit and none of the lamps. Between the dock and tulip garden, he slowed down to listen.

Skylo rose and leaned heavily on his walking stick. He stuck his hand out an open window to catch rain. The ground steamed in the grey sunlight with fuggy air and no wind at all.

"You were smart to put Manu with 'em. I know Lamark might disagree but... well nothing too bad seems to happen with him around."

Lamark recognized his wife Waeve's voice in an instant. They must have been standing above him on the veranda beneath the balcony. He stepped onto one of the pegs of the dock to catch a glimpse.

"Yes," said a man's voice, too quiet for Lamark to discern who, "but only a matter of time."

From the peg, he leapt forward onto the flat part of the rock wall that built up beneath the veranda. He landed with a smooth noiselessness.

Still the best climber in Elevana...

Lamark swung himself a few feet higher until he could look between the balusters. *Skylo! That dirty ole diviner... stirrin' up some sort of trouble, I'll bet.*

Skylo turned from the window. His walking stick, old and partly withered but made of the same woodstone they used to build Longleath, creaked beneath his weight. As he paced about, Skylo's eyes were more lurid than Lamark had ever seen.

"We need your help, Waeve. Your husband listens to no one but you. I have reason to believe there is still a great man buried inside him. Without his help..." Skylo sat down on a marble bench beside a bramble of berries. "Waeve, we need him, else Elevana may be the first to go."

"That's enough outta you," Lamark said, sweeping over the balustrade. "Waeve! What did I say 'bout strangers around right now?"

"Marky! Oh dear, I'm so sorry," Waeve said, hanging her head. "I know how much history you and Mr. Skylo have, and, well, I couldn't be rude!"

"Ahh," Lamark grumbled. "Could never be mad at ye," he reached an arm around Waeve and gave her a kiss. "And 'e could be a lot worse."

Lamark turned to Skylo. "What's business do ye 'ave with us?"

"I fear I come with sour news."

"Why don't that surprise me? Nothin' else coulda gotten ye out of yer mountain..."

Skylo plucked a handful of berries and let them rest in his lap.

"Oh, dearie, don't eat those," said Waeve. "We've got plenty to eat inside…"

Skylo popped two in his mouth anyway. "It seems *Draviño* is only the beginning of a long road of trouble in Elevana. I am leaving."

"Yer… *leaving*," Lamark continued with amazement. "When?"

"Tomorrow."

"Gods be crazed. Ye've been in Mossy Mountain for two hundred years. What gives? Agh, do I even want to know?"

"I'm afraid," said Skylo, "you have no choice."

"Manu?"

Skylo nodded.

Lamark squeezed Waeve's shoulder.

"'ow's about ye go inside and start up the aequipher? My belly could use a nice meal." He poked Waeve's plump mid-section and winked. "And yers could too."

"Of course, dearie," she said and kissed Lamark on the cheek. "Make sure he doesn't eat too many of those. They've got Purple Rapien in them. He'll go all wonky!"

After Waeve went inside, Lamark seated himself on the cushioned chair across from Skylo and kicked off his wet boots.

"Why do I feel like this 'as somethin' to do with the boy?" asked Lamark. "Does 'e know who the boy is?"

"Viru knows the boy's a Mason."

"Gods. What a mess yer draggin' me into."

"So you will help?"

"Depends. Don't go askin' me to go dyin' for some sad Mason. Or even Manny… I love the man like a brother but my Waevy and our stores are all that matters."

"Fine," said Skylo admiring one of the berries. "You keep the rest of Aeron's heartfruit, and there will be even more if you help him."

"Now yer talking."

"Tell me," said Skylo. "Has anyone strange come into the Blue Bat since Aeron left?"

"A coupla lunks from Longleath. Travelers, they said. A strange courtesan lady from far east—the Central Rift. And…"

Skylo's ears wiggled and he looked up from the berries in his lap.

"There was one. A strange one who struck me an edge the moment he walked through the door. Shiver up and down my spine, like 'e brought winter with 'im. Bigger than me, I'll admit it, with colorless hands and black wrappings all over his face. Cloak open, 'ood pulled down, dressed rick but with a dash of danger. Them eyes, can't even describe—'ideous, dark, but vivid. Like that."

Lamark pointed to the moon in the sky. It had peeked through one of the rings of the shell.

"Viru…" Skylo bit off and then tempered himself. "So it is true then. I am sorry, Lamark."

"Sorry?"

"That man was, to me, like Manu was to you—a brother. But he lost the way and never turned back."

"Ye never mentioned 'im to me before…"

"That's because," Skylo sighed, "I hoped he might never return. But I think I know what is happening. Tell me, Lamark. He came a few days after Aeron left you. Did he not?"

"That 'e did."

"The Grapple. When the Grapple enters the world, so does he. Straight from the Aerohive.

"So 'e wants to find yer boy then?"

"Yes," said Skylo. "But for you what's worse lies in his wake."

"Great," Lamark groaned.

"Praeth Viru, Prince of Wraeths. Behind him follows a trail of Wraeths... first he turns countries into islands, and then he destroys them. At the end, he turns them into hives."

"Yer tellin' me," Lamark narrowed his eyes, "the beast that wants to send ruin to our Aerth was right in front of me, and I didn't even know it?"

Skylo gave a pair of slow nods.

"Fer the love of all that is good 'n' decent... we're doomed."

"No," said Skylo, "I think we have a chance, but it has to be tomorrow."

Lamark rose and pressed his face against the window. The Aerostron glowed part-way, and Waeve danced around the kitchen while setting the table.

"If you want to enjoy this life you've built with her," said Skylo, "it's the only way."

Lamark sighed, turned back to Skylo, and leaned the back of his head against the window.

"Tell me what you need."

"What has been made of your ship?" asked Skylo.

"Look fer yerself," said Lamark, pointing out past the dock to the ocean to where the lithe beauty rested in shards of moonlight.

"And she is still the fastest ship in Elevana?"

"*Winflow* is no ship. She's got *marinaer blood in 'er. And not only Elevana. She's the fastest in the world.*"

"Then she'll do."

I never said ye could 'ave 'er, old man...

"But there's something else."

"What else could ye possibly need?"

A pink lightning bug alighted on Skylo's hand. He watched it the way a man looks at his smiling child.

Skylo leaned on his walking stick and walked behind Lamark's chair, leaning a spidery hand on his shoulder.

Then he whispered.

"You."

CHAPTER 31

THE MEAD OF LIFE

Back in Pillee's living room, Paloma stood with her hands on her head.

"We have to get off this island," she said with more fear than Aeron had seen from her. She paced the room, once exiting onto the deck.

"Tell him what you've seen," Manu's voice came from the open half-door.

She returned back inside, sat in a chair opposite Aeron, and took a deep breath. "I think it's worse than some thieves after us, Aeron," she paused. "I thought I came here for one reason, but now I see there's something much bigger at play."

"They're after me, Paloma," said Aeron. "Not you. You can still leave. You've got so much to lose, but I have nothing. Go home and tip off the council. They will thank you."

Pillee yawned and stretched herself flat on the couch.

"No, Aeron," Paloma shook her head. "Listen, for once. Earlier today Manu and I had a run-in with an Irkal. And tracer athon, like the one that hunted us down, come from Irkalla. We think she and whoever else she's with have been after us."

"You're sure there are others?" asked Aeron.

"Yes," Paloma nodded, "she made a point of mentioning her guests to Manu's friend. We both heard it. You and I know that no sane priman works with Irkals. She must have meant…"

"You think… it's a Wraeth? No," Aeron continued, shaking his head. "There would be signs—"

"No, Aeron," Paloma stood up and paced once more. "Remember when we first met and I helped you fix the lorry? I saw something there, deep in the wood. It's hard to describe. Perfect in its hideousness, colorless, talking to itself as if it had multiple heads. I saw a terrible, bloodied version of my father in the smoke. It was more than a Wraeth, Aeron."

She leaned close to look out the dirty window.

"You think you saw… Viru? And he let you get away?"

Maybe she's less bright than I thought…

"Aeron, stop!" said Paloma, wheeling back to him. "You can be so thick. It all adds up: the athon, the Irkal, the Grapple, even *Draviño* itself. Something bigger is going on here. You're just too stubborn to see it."

Aeron paused and reached for the last rose cake. Paloma approached the table too.

"It makes sense," she continued. "Why, all of the sudden, does the council call on an old Ranger? They must see the signs too and be desperate."

Aeron stood from the couch. All at once, the room became too small. Journal in hand, Aeron pushed the bottom door open and stepped out into the open air. He took a deep breath and leaned against one of the wooden columns on the deck. By some strange refraction among the *Draviño* clouds above, the night had been cast a bright shade of silver.

"If this is all true," said Aeron, "the Council must be told."

"Yes," said Paloma. "You are right. We will send a hawk at once to my father and uncle. They will relay the message."

Aeron shook his head. "They listen to warnings more believable than this and do nothing."

"But not letters from the Murravillows…"

"No, Paloma," said Manu, still lying on the tree stump below. "Even if the letter reached the right people, it's only words. They need to feel the danger."

"So what do we do?" she asked.

"*You* have to go," said Aeron.

Taken aback, Paloma responded at once. "Even if I wanted to, you heard Pillee. It's near impossible to get off the island right now."

"I will take you," said Manu. "Tomorrow. Indeed, once the shell passes, every ship that tries to flee will sink. But the shell will last until tomorrow eve."

"Perfect," said Paloma, "so we'll all go. We follow the map, get your Grapple back, and catch the first marinaer to ferry us out of here.

"No, Paloma." Aeron flung his hand from the beam with frustration. "Now you aren't getting it. They still hate me in Longleath. I'm going to the Tree of Knowledge. I have to find it, and Skylo is going to help. It's the only chance I have to learn the Aeros and join the Sage."

"Fine," Paloma butted in once more, "we'll split at port then. You go west, and I continue north."

Aeron opened his mouth but closed it before vocalizing his hurtful thoughts. He took deep breaths in and out for four counts, as Granddad had taught him.

"Go look at the map," he said and sat on the bench swing. Paloma went inside. "You see where the red line has a little yellow pin in it?"

"Yes."

"Now look where that is compared to the seaport."

Aeron wrapped three fingers around the support chain. Then Paloma reemerged.

"Due west," she said with sullen cheeks. "We'd never make it before nightfall, even with a horse or a lorry."

Aeron nodded.

"Skylo said something about calling in a favor," he recollected. "I wager he's arranging a place for us to shelter and then head north after the storm."

"And you, Manu, will you go back after?" Paloma asked, leaning over the railing. "It sounds like the Tree needs its protector now. Who knows how long *Draviño* will keep Skylo and Aeron inside. You could come north... a fast train that could take you west."

Manu sat up. One of the feathered designs on his jacket came loose and fell to the ground.

"I will do my part," said Manu. "As will you."

"How conveniently vague of you..." Paloma sneered, fingering a sketch of Pillee and Minnee from years ago.

"All I can worry about is myself. How I will be remembered. We all have our own legacy. I will flap my wings. The wind will carry me forward."

Paloma sat on the bench beside Aeron. It swung as if trying to coax them to sleep.

"How are you so calm about all of this, Manu?" asked Paloma "We've lost the Grapple, no offense, Aeron, and terrible, terrible people are after us."

"I always try to relax the night before a ranging."

Paloma's feet kicked aimlessly.

"Mercy," she said, "I should think the Wraeth Prince would have bigger problems than two kids. What could he want from us?"

Aeron jerked backward as something blue and gold clanged hard on the deck.

"Of course…" Paloma cried. "The purador! They could smell that all the way from the Harroes…"

A flurry of sense returned to Aeron. He opened the Journal to a passage he'd read the week before.

Purador, otherwise known as *The Mead of Life*, is known for its ability to stop the aging process and keep one's body and mind growing indefinitely. As the wives' tale goes, a glass a day keeps the hangman away.

"That is what he wants," said Manu. "To take every heart-fruit on Aerth and turn it into purador. So he can live forever, as Prince of the Wraeths."

A deep, penetrating silence colored the eerie grey night.

"Now get some rest, children. Tomorrow we face *Draviño's* best."

CHAPTER 32

A PROVEN FOOL

◇◇◇◇◇◇

Paloma woke with a crick in her neck.

Ooof. Must've fallen asleep on the swing.

A thin film of sweat covered her arms and upper lip. She flung back the scratchy blanket that had been thrown over her and sat up to look out into the morning.

At the edge of the deck, Aeron leaned against one of the stanchions with his head down in the Journal. The stark, bright morning illumined nearby trees and distant flats with hot, white light. Even the thin slice of ocean beneath the horizon shone bright and blue.

"Thought you never sleep?" said Aeron, holding the stylus between mid and fore-finger.

Paloma smiled with closed lips. "So this is the shell," she said. "It feels like a cruel joke—a day like this stuck between yesterday's chaos and whatever lies ahead." She rose, shaking her head, and stretched her body out long. "Where's Manu?"

Aeron shrugged. "Gone when I woke up. Pillee says he went to the hawkery."

"Good morning, chill-dran," she turned to Paloma. "Ma-nu gone hours now. Be back any minute. You two have break-fast."

Pillee waddled over to a large glass hanging from the roof that looked like two bowls melded together, rim to rim, to make a full sphere—like a fishbowl. One-third full with what could have been liquid gold.

"Azralian honey, better hot," said Pillee in her pidgin Mother Tongue. "Sweet like dreams."

She reached up and unhooked the glass by the wire handle. Aeron cleared a place on the table and Pillee put the bowl down onto a stone trivet. Then, she twisted off the top and a blissful breakfast aroma broke into her nostrils behind the satisfying sizzle of fresh bacon.

"One would think we should be going…" said Paloma, sitting back on the bench swing.

Aeron had gone back to writing at the end of the deck. A few moments later, Pillee returned with a tray of toast cut into various shapes, bacon, and a bed of sweet roasted almonds and pecans.

Aeron put the Journal to rest in his pocket and came to sit cross-legged beside the faded driftwood table with a glass top.

"Aeron," said Paloma, "our window is closing. We only have one day."

"I know," he replied, smoothing a bulb of honey onto a leaf-shaped piece of toast. "Every day I wonder more and more about the Last Great Ranger…"

"No, you're right," said Paloma. "He knows what he's doing. He must have a reason."

"She right. Ma-nu seem cra-zy," came Pillee's husky voice from inside, "but always have rea-son. May-be he send letter for help?"

"Or—" said Aeron while crunching into a slice of bread with almonds and honey evenly spread. Then Aeron paused and craned his neck over his right shoulder.

As if on cue, the leaves below rustled and a pair of small magnolia trees bent to either side. Manu, soiled and drenched with sweat, stepped between them, thinly avoiding one of the melon cacti growing near Pillee's garden.

Paloma bit into the best piece of bacon she'd ever tasted. It was smoky, crisp, and fatless, yet still tender and soft.

"We're leaving," Manu said with a tinge of hurry.

"Chill-dran need break-fast, Manu. You could use bath…" Pillee rose and gathered a bucket of water from the vat at the end of the deck above Aeron's haversack.

"No time," Manu said, climbing halfway up the largest of the four trees. He brought with him a terrible odor of sweat that had no business near Pillee's sweet little home.

Head and torso at deck height, he reached his free hand over the table and picked up the tray. He held it still for a moment while Paloma snatched a square of bacon-wrapped cheese and Aeron a handful of almonds. Then, the spread went sliding down into his mouth.

"I've sent messages north, east, and west," he said between chews.

He replaced the tray and gripped the glass of honey.

"Wait!" Aeron shouted, trying to warn him, but Manu seemed to have no nerves in his hands. He didn't seem to notice the hot glass in his hand.

"There is an abandoned church midway between here and the coast. We must reach it before the hot hour. Skylo should be there."

Still in the sun, he raised the bowl to his mouth and let the warm honey flow between his lips.

"The hot hour?" Paloma wondered, having never heard of it.

"Shell is hott-est day of year," said Pillee, tottering with the bucket over to the table. "After-noon du-ring shell is like being bare-foot on sand. Hard-pan is desert."

Without warning, she turned and thrust the water bucket toward Manu.

In the half-second of space between the bucket and Manu's face, the water turned to spray.

Even with extra sun coverings from Pillee, acorns of sweat formed on Paloma's neck. She wiped them away and felt the sensation of burnt skin.

I never burn…

"Manu," Aeron said from several yards behind. "This is…" he sounded dry and out of breath.

"We are nearly there," said Manu, stopping beside a yucca tree. Aeron snuck into its slight shade while Manu unstrung Aeron's haversack and passed him a skin of water. Then he slung it back over his shoulder with one hand. "You hold onto that. We are nearly there."

He pointed deeper into the hardpan where a smudged dot of brown lay behind miles of heat haze.

"What is it?" Paloma asked, pulling the bill of her cap low. Now far from both the forest and the ocean, the ground had grown barren in a sad shade of orange. Whatever the place was, she knew it would take at least another hour on foot.

"An old Orangu church," said Manu. "Taken by the Huntress."

"You've been there before," said Paloma. "Haven't you?"

Manu said nothing.

"What's that sound?" Aeron asked, eyes closed.

"I don't hear anything," said Paloma.

Paloma turned around. They had descended a slow, rolling hill that led down through the center of the hardpan. It was nothing but dirt and rocks beneath a vast and cloudless sky.

"It's getting louder."

Still, Paloma heard nothing.

"He's losing it," said Paloma to Manu. "We have to get him indoors."

"I think," Manu shook his head, "he may be right." Manu knelt and touched a finger to the ground. Dust spewed in every direction as a lorry came burning over the hill. Its stark blue paint clashed against the dull ground in the sharp sun.

"Manu," said Paloma, jaw agape, "your lorry…"

"Aeron. Get up," he said and took a deep breath, puffing himself up large. "Paloma, remember, you are my bondservant. Aeron, nephew. And you have both been here less than a week."

They stood in a row as the lorry slowed in front of them, its red glare blinding. Paloma squinted as the driver's door swung open. The man's head, of similar size to Manu's though fleshier and rounder, popped above it. When it did, the lorry lifted significantly having been released from his weight.

"Well," croaked the man, looking over the open door. "Are ye fixing to fry or do ye want a ride?"

"Lamark!" Aeron cried with joy. "Never thought I could be so happy to see you."

"What? You know him?" asked Paloma, but Aeron had already dashed toward the lorry.

"If I were you," Manu said quietly as they approached "I'd keep my family name to myself."

"Looky who we 'ave 'ere," said Lamark.

Paloma followed Aeron to the open door in the back, opposite Lamark. She gripped the lorry's frame and stepped up onto the sideboard. Aeron slid across the bench to the seat behind the driver.

"Been a while, eh? How come ye never came to see me?" asked Lamark from outside. "When ye got to Elevana."

"We will talk when this is over," said Manu as he stepped onto the sideboard. The lorry dipped heavily to the right. Lamark stepped up and swung a stumpy leg into the driver seat. With the two large men on either side, the lorry evened out beneath their weight.

"Stayin' out there on the runner?" asked Lamark.

Manu crouched over to see inside the lorry. He had both feet on the sideboard and a hand gripped to the roof of the vehicle. "Yes. I need to see the land. Now go."

Lamark's shaggy orange hair shook as he nodded and pressed the lever with his left hand.

"How is she on fuel?" asked Manu as they lurched into motion. Lamark let his right hand dangle out the window.

"Fine," said Lamark, giving the door a pat. The lorry gave a responsive purr. "Let 'er 'ave two of the 'eartfruit the boy left behind. One to mend from the storm ye left 'er in, and another fer fuel." Lamark turned to Aeron. "'ope ye don't mind, boy."

"Lamark," said Aeron, "right now you could tell me that you ate the lot and I would be fine with it."

"Aeron," said Lamark, grinning. "I lost the whole lot. Sorry. Ye'll be gettin' none of 'em back."

Aeron smiled and took off the bandana Pillee had given him.

As the lorry rolled on, Lamark turned his attention to Paloma.

"So who's yer pretty friend?" asked Lamark.

Paloma spat out the open window.

"With a hard side. I like it."

"Lamark," said Manu, bending low. Paloma had a hunch he had heard and meant to redirect the conversation. "How is Waeve? Is she safe at home?"

"Yar," said Lamark, "she's got nothin' to worry about. Brought all her plants 'ome and we've enough food to last a year… she even 'ad a little visit from your Master Skylo."

"You saw him!" Aeron broke in. "So he made it down the river? Where is he?"

"Said he had further business. Asked 'im why not do 'is little jump-through-space trick and meet us 'ere but… sounds like ye had a little situation of yer own? Cause 'is little floatin' star buddy looked mighty tired and used up."

"What's he talking about?" asked Paloma.

"Phantagration," said Aeron, "turns out Skylo can sort-of—"

"Man can jump from place to place in an instant!" Lamark broke in. "But it takes a toll on that thing…"

"Hyacinth," said Aeron.

The clay rushed by on either side as the lorry drove deeper into the desert. The grass turned from short and green to dead and hard yellow before dying out entirely. The rocks became larger and more jagged. Every so often, they passed a carcass being gnawed at by a coyote or kit fox.

"Slow down," Manu said and knocked a fist against the roof. Then he crouched low so they could hear him. "Look to the sky above the church. There's a bird circling."

"Skylo there?" suggested Lamark.

"Or someone else…" said Aeron.

"No," Paloma said, squinting her eyes. "That's no regular bird. It's huge and strange colors…"

Lamark eased the lorry up next to the decaying building. Before it stopped, Manu leapt off and approached the seedy church door. He pressed a hand against the door and pushed it open part way. He poked his head in and peered in either direction before slipping inside.

It was smaller than a shop or tavern. He reemerged a few moments later and nodded. Then he looked straight up to the sky and shielded his eyes.

"Boy," said Lamark, "go'n open the shed so we can 'ide Manny's awful-colored lorry." He rubbed behind the wheel and spoke to the vehicle. "No offense. Not yer fault." The lorry purred simply, as if to say, "None taken."

Aeron swung open the door and dashed over to the shed. He yanked hard at the rusted latch until it jolted open and he could push on each of the rolling doors. They slid open with a noisy groan.

"So," said Lamark as he edged the lorry into the saw-dust-smelling shed, "'ow'd they get ye into this mess, miss…"

Paloma resented his rotten tone.

"Paloma," she said. "And I got myself into this mess, thank you kindly."

Aeron closed the barn door behind them and everything went black.

"My 'ighest congratulations, Miss Paloma," he jeered. "Yer a proven fool."

CHAPTER 33

THE FENIX

In the low light of the barn, Lamark stepped out of the lorry and found Paloma stricken with a look like she had witnessed a religious sacrifice. She backed away, her lip quivering. Pouring from the uppermost part of the shed, a single window printed a squarish sheer of white sun on the ground near Lamark's feet.

Gods' grief, am I that 'orrible a sight?

He rolled his eyes. "I'm less than the prettiest bear in the family, but according to old Skylo we're in for a whole lot worse before day's end."

Lamark stepped through the sunlight toward the side door on the right. Its wood had so much splintering that pins of light scattered at random across the middle. He turned back around to find a silver blade shimmering in the light three inches from his face. Lamark jerked back against the wall, bumping over a dusty watering can with his rump. It clanked on the ground and broke in two rusty halves.

"Settle yerself, miss," he said to Paloma. *That scythe's Manny's handiwork. I'm sure of it. She could gut me dry.* "I'm 'ere to 'elp ye. Good luck against the Irkals without the only one of ye who's killed 'em before."

"How do I know you're not full of it?" she said poking the scythe closer. "Manu told us that Skylo would be here. What've you done with him? What do you want from us?"

"A bit cynical fer a girl yer age. Aren't ye?" he replied. "I'll prove it to ye."

The girl said nothing but gestured for him to continue. In that space of silence, the swoosh of wings came from outside.

"Can ye 'ear that?"

Distracted and straining to hear, she twisted her head to the side. Lamark smacked away the blade with the back of his hand and disarmed her. Anger streaked across her eyes.

"Come see fer yerself," said Lamark. He pushed open the door and walked out of the barn, leaving Paloma's scythe against the frame in a sign of solidarity.

Color and light rushed in so fast Lamark cringed. When his eyes adjusted, a huge red and blue bird—bigger even than Manu and Lamark—had swung to a perch atop the roof, talons stretched on either side of the ridge. It alighted with a dignified grace, shimmering like a crystal held to the sun.

A large scroll rolled down the roof and over the eaves of the church. The large leaf of paper fell to the ground near Aeron's feet. He bent, unstrung it, and read aloud.

"*Poxuna serpo*," said Aeron.

"That's it?" Paloma asked as she crossed the dusty driveway, scythe still in hand.

Course that's it. Everyone in all four rifts 'as 'eard these words—the motto of The Irkal King.

"House Hadrian," said Aeron. "More haste, less speed… Oddly relevant. But who would send this? And… the fenix?"

"Fate be with us," said Lamark, "I think ye 'ave friends in the west. Ye might be lookin' at the last fenix on Aerth… and they sent it for you."

"But why?" Paloma asked.

Lamark crossed his arms, one hand stroking the scruff on his meaty chin. He could only think of one reason the letter would have so little of use.

"Gimme that," Lamark said and made to snatch the scroll from him. The fenix gave a serpentine hiss and Lamark backed away. "Fine. Well if ye ask me, it's a warning. That we're dealin' with Irkals who're after ye. And not Irkal bandits—ones with pure evil in their blood. Afraid o' nothin' except for the neath-men.

"Manny," said Lamark, "yer half neath. What do ye make of this?"

No reply. He looked around the grubby side yard of dead bushes and a barren garden bed. "Manny?"

"Inside," said Paloma, standing by the door to the church, which hung by a single hinge.

The fenix leaned forward, pointing its immense beak between Aeron and the door. One of its eyes was the size of his head.

"Keep yer distance," Lamark warned. "Fenix can be less friendly than the stories say."

The bird whipped its head in Lamark's direction, and Lamark scampered backward. Then, the bird returned to Aeron, who now stood beside Paloma. It turned its head side to side, seeming to contemplate them both. Then it looked out over the hardpan.

Aeron reached his hand out toward the bird's black beak. Once the fenix realized he intended to touch it, the regal bird recoiled and took off with a flap of its wings. Both Aeron and Paloma doubled backward from its bouldering force.

On the ascent, the largest feather Lamark had ever seen waved back and forth through the air to the hard clay aerth near the door. Paloma picked it up between her first three fingers and thumb. In the hot sun, it glistened the color of red wine lees.

Wide eyed, she turned to Lamark, and he gestured his head inside. The two children went into the church and Lamark followed, bolting the door thereafter.

Right away, he parked himself beneath the remnants of an old wedding arch in the first big chair he saw.

The smell danced between old incense and sawdust.

"Always 'ated the Huntress smell. Purple Rapien," said Lamark. "Brings back dark memories from the north. Such a shame."

Manu had his back to the rest of them as he hunched on one knee beside a dusty mat made of straw.

The wedding arch had been put in front of the pulpit, which looked out over the rest of the tall room. The whole place had an old sea-greenish hue, like washed-out drift-wood. Paloma crossed the aisle, tiptoeing over a dusty carpet and around the wooden supports that had fallen from above. They now lay atop spudding weeds, which poked through cracks in the floor, and beneath a strangely shaped statue hanging twisted on the wall.

Nearby, the only unbroken window cast a purplish hue in the farthest part of the church where she stood by Manu.

"Manu?" she said, putting a hand to the shoulder of the still-crouched man.

He paused for a beat, then turned back to face them. Though the vagueness of tears remained in his eyes, Manu had swelled himself back to his normal air of confidence.

"I'm fine," he said, the way a stubborn man always does. "Aeron, lay your map out on the table."

Aeron cleared the dust and a singular leather-bound book from the ruined desk. The boy reached inside his vest pocket and pulled out a large leaf of paper. Unfolding it with care, he spread out the map.

"Looks like ye found yer friend, *and* the Reddheart Map, after all," said Lamark. "Well played, kid."

Manu found an intact barrel in one of the corners, pulled it over to the desk, and sat himself on the header.

With great effort, Lamark rose from his seat, and the four of them crowded around the map.

"We're here" said Aeron, pointing to a place toward the southern edge of the hardpan, Elevana's only bit of desert. "There's nothing showing now. Does that mean the Grapple is gone?"

"'ang on, boy," Lamark choked. "Ye lost yer treasure? What kinda fool loses the most valuable—"

Manu's eyes darted up to Lamark unhappily.

Lamark shut his mouth and started over. "So ye know where it is then. The map'll tell you that."

"Yes," said Aeron, "but the red line and the yellow pin are gone."

"Manu," said Paloma skeptically, "where is Skylo? He would know what to do."

"In truth," said Manu, "I've no idea. But no surprise. That man comes and goes like the tide. You are alone now, Aeron. As am I. That is life."

"Left us with a pretty crummy replacement," Paloma grumbled and cast a look to Lamark.

"Mind yer tongue, miss," Lamark growled.

"No," said Aeron. "He wouldn't. And even if he is gone, he would say we're not alone. We're never alone in this world.

You have me. I have you. I have my Journal. We have this map. He would say to trust it."

"Why's it gone all screwy then?" asked Lamark

"Maybe," said Paloma "there's something about the shell of the storm—messing with the map's Aeros?"

"Hmm," Aeron stepped back from the map and scratched his head. "It makes sense. And maybe that's why he's gone— the shell having some effect on his flameflower."

"Show me where," said Manu.

"It was around here," said Aeron, pointing to the strip of land north of the hardpan, near Angel's Lagoon.

"So you think it's back in the same grove?" asked Paloma.

"Now we're talkin'," said Lamark, dreaming about an entire grove of heartfruit trees.

"That's a harsh part of the island," said Manu. "I have never been there. I will admit it."

Aeron returned to the desk, holding the feather by the silvery quill with all five fingers. He rubbed it to his chin while thinking, and then set it down on the map.

"And where do the Irkals come in?" asked Paloma. "None of this explains the fenix."

"I told ye," said Lamark, "it's a warning. Now that Skylo's gone and ye lost yer Sage, only one thing can save ye." He picked up one of the small stones still on the table and put it where Aeron held his finger. "The 'eartfruit. All men can be bought."

There was a long pause. Lamark moved away from the desk toward one of the broken windows, waving away cobwebs as he went. He coughed on a swirl of dust and leaned his arms wide against the window's old worn frame.

Between the shell's thin and swirling clouds, the sun struck high slightly after midday. Both Aeron and Skylo had promised Lamark that he could keep Aeron's heartfruit for his own if he went along with this—enough to last he and Waeve the rest of their days—but an entire grove of heartfruit?

We'll be the richest man and lady in the world.

"Hey," said Aeron from behind. "Look at this…"

While the others paced about the large church, Aeron had remained at the desk. He held the silky feather in his hand, hovering it over the scroll left by the fenix.

Lamark kicked aside splinters of wood as he crossed the room. When he arrived at the desk, the scroll had changed.

Transfixed on the paper, Aeron pressed the tip down on the scroll, and a shadowy hint of color cropped up on the page.

"I put it down on the table next to the feather," said Aeron, "and this light shadow of color came on the edge of the scroll, like shining a lamplight in the dark. I moved the quill closer and it became deeper. And now…"

Centered around the finger-sized tip, the line, color, and shadow materialized on the paper, drawing itself.

"I can feel it in the quill… like blood is rushing through," said Aeron holding it still. "It's almost like the page was dry, and then it took a big gasp for breath and bloomed with color. The painting was hidden and needed the quill to bring it to life."

"Don't go sellin' yerself a dog." said Lamark. "Just a clever trick. No more to it."

"No," said Paloma, now standing over Aeron's shoulder. "I can see where it's going. The picture is the hardpan. It's drawing us, where we are right now, and…"

"And what?" asked Manu, having now come over to the table.

"*Them.*"

CHAPTER 34

WHERE BATTLES
ARE WON

Paloma could not believe her eyes. Color seemed to ripple out from the feather like a rock dropped into a pond. With every second, the painting became more and more detailed until it could have been a window on the church. Four mounted figures were front and center above the hardpan.

"And who might *them* be, miss?" asked Lamark.

"The enemy," said Manu, crossing the room toward the desk. "The ones who are after us."

"Who?" asked Aeron, now spinning one of the heartfruit nervously in his hand.

"See for yourself," he said, gesturing toward the painting.

While not an artist, Paloma could draw with natural ability and insight. She took note of every line, every stroke of detail being drawn out of the portrait by the fenix feather. The painting became clearer.

The sky was high and pasty and smeared by distant clouds. The horizon told a story of impending pain worse than broken bones.

The sea was a thin rail of ice, reflecting the haevens above. Slim and minimal in the distance, the horizon's slight V-shape gave the water an air of hatred, as if it had grown angry with the great gods whose tears filled it up day after day and decided to retaliate with pouted tides.

The hardpan consisted of four miles of rusty, unbroken, sun-stroked flats whose clays contrasted the rest of Elevana's lushness such that it could have been the raw under-side of a scab, which had never hardened. Its starkness made her wonder about who was in charge of life on this exile's land— primen or the island?

"Gods be cursed," said Lamark. "You know who that is?"

He saw five riders, one of their horses rearing. On the right end was the burly woman with blonde tipped hair from Billbury's, now sporting an Irkallan short sword. Its sheath kissed the hind quarters of a dark brown horse with golden blinders.

The youngest of them sat atop an equally strapping oak-brown horse with white hooves and a gaudy purplish saddle to the Irkal's right. Though a burly young man, the rider's eyebrows, nose, and lips came tightly together on his face to form a murderous triangle of angst behind a style of sungoggles she had seen somewhere in history but had forgotten.

The next man, between his rearing athon and regal pose, looked as if he could crush an ox, uproot a tree, and land the winning strike of Cannaroo all in one breath. His skin, tight and rippling, shone so black it could give fear to midnight itself. But it must not be Viru! Viru was Wraeth and as old as Skylo. This man was young and poised enough to conquer the world.

The fourth priman had on one of the sunburnt jackets of Western Oriendo with matching hat and seemed to be talking despite the stalk of hickory in the side of his mouth, which accented a devilish smirk. The horse beneath him, a priggish animal with a chestnut coat and grey spots, drooped its head despite the kicks from the man above whose spurs dug into her side.

The final rider, an Irkal, could have been a copy of the first—staunch, riding an identical horse, clad in the Irkal black and yellow, even the same mutinous eyes. This one, however, had his hair pulled back into a bun like a platinum-gold pimple.

"So what are they telling us then, Manu?" asked Aeron.

Manu picked up the heartfruit and tossed it up and down a few times.

"To use everything we've got," he said with a sullen expression.

"Ah, cripes," said Lamark, as if reading Manu's mind. "I'm sorry, Manny."

"Sorry for what?" asked Paloma. The painting had stopped filling in and she let the feather fall down to the side on the desk.

Manu placed the heartfruit down to the left on the lower third of the image. Paloma reached out and lifted it up to find a nightmarish version of Manu's lorry, as if some kind of demon had been let loose within the mint green shell and made a foul mess.

"The plan is simple," he continued, "whether it works or not, we shall see."

"So this is our plan…" Paloma said and stepped away from the desk. "Waste time until we hear the sound of hooves and kindly go out to greet them?"

Manu and Lamark exchanged a harried glance.

"So you agree then," Paloma continued. "We have a lorry. Let's ride it into—"

"Into where?" Manu interrupted. "I am to take you east to the seaport. Aeron's map points west to the grove. We cannot be in two places at once and cannot do both before sundown."

"You should go," said Aeron, only now looking up from the painting. "You need to tell your vizier of what's to come or millions of primen will die."

A whisper of silence filled the broken church. Paloma felt a presence in the place, as if the preachers had gone but their prayers had remained.

"Aeron," she said with a choked throat and turned away. "There's something I have to—"

"Hang on a second…" Aeron said with a glimmer of hope in his voice. He slid the painting over so both it and the map lay said by side. "Look!" he shouted, pointing to the top left corner of the painting beneath the horizon where the hardpan jutted higher into a cliff or bluff.

Paloma swallowed her words and turned back for the table. A pair of pygmy scorpidions crawled over the edge of the map's underside, as if they too were curious. She batted them away with an old candle and they whistled like canaries.

"Here," said Aeron, "do you recognize that symbol?" He pointed with his free hand to the point on the map north of where the Grapple should be.

"They're the same." Paloma said, her eyes tracing a swirl that reminded her of how the clouds had looked the night before on Pillee's roof. "Identical spirals on the map, on the portrait, in the sky…" she paused for a moment. "What does it mean?"

"There's one more," said Aeron reaching into his vest pocket. He pulled on the tassel and opened the Journal to the place he had marked. At the top of the page sat a rainbow-like glyph. At the bottom, the half-curled fox-tail from the fountain near the neath tavern where they had met Yeats.

Aeron folded the leaf to kiss the top and bottom together and there it was again. The swirl.

"It's the Tree." Manu's voice struck the room. "The people inside are speaking to us."

"Too bad they couldn't leave yer fenix to play," said Lamark. "That'd scare 'em off right and good. Instead, we've gotto leave Manny's lorry out for slaughter. Poor bloke."

"Plans are where battles are won," said Manu.

"Cripes," said Lamark, "where ye lose 'em too." The room fell silent for a moment and then Lamark leaned over the desk with two wide arms. "All right, brother. Let's hear what ye got."

Manu moved closer to the table.

Paloma leaned over the painting. Goosebumps tickled her arms. She couldn't pull her eyes away from the man with the Western hat, soiled canvas trousers, and a soulless look in his eye. His lips were pulled so wide she could almost hear his voice.

"Well I'll be double-dog-damned…" said the wiry man, a hickory stick bouncing on his lips by the word. "Never anticipated colliding with you again, Mister Merchant of Herraz, a.k.a. Lamark Bronta."

"Can't say it's a pleasure to see ye again either, Rowecinder," replied Lamark.

"I'm using my forename now—Boone," the thin man said with a wink and old-world cowboy-cap-tilt to Paloma. "Boone

Rowecinder." How perfectly his snaky, grizzly movements matched his tongue and sent her shuttering. He scratched furiously, like some kind of animal, against his scaly shoulder pads until his cheek turned a beety shade of red.

Five mounted men, at least two of them armed, are all exactly as the painting showed. Even the sky is the same and that stupid stick of hickory. Mercy, I hope they don't find Manu before we are ready.

"Last I'd heard," said Boone, his voice hoarse and wild, "you and an unfortunate female had hidden yourselves on a beach in the yonder east, heh heh…" he gestured toward Aeron and Paloma. "And who might we have here?"

Paloma opened her mouth, but Lamark interrupted.

"These be my niece and nephew," Lamark said. "Wife asked that I get 'em off the island before *Draviño.*"

Paloma pulled her hat lower over her eyes. Drops of sweat evaporated mid-fall.

Then they heard a deafening moment of windy silence chased by Boone's shrill, explosive laughter. He held his cap over his heart with the non-rein hand. His chestnut horse lifted its head a few inches; she had sad eyes with grey spots spattered down her neck, and she held the posture of exhaustion.

"You mean to tell me," hooted the man, "that these two and your enormous rump share the same blood? Take off that there cap, girl, need a better look. We mean ya no harm. Oriendo's honor."

"You are from Oriendo?" Paloma asked but regretted it immediately. Her high-born accent had surely betrayed her.

"Ahhh…" Boone sighed. Squinting at Paloma, his cheeks jutted beneath tightly wrapped skin. "You're one of them voluptuous ladies of Longleath. I used to frequent quite a few clubs there, back when I was working with Mendel Mason, and before it became the pitiful place of today... city could use someone like me to fix it up. Reckon I'll be back there soon."

So it's true then? I had thought the story had been planted in some shallow political scheme from my father's aides... but maybe Aeron's granddad had skeletons in his desk

The man in black to Boone's left shifted his cowled head. His slow, measured movements told stories of a man with sharp intuition and a mind that missed less than an archer shooting needled arrows at point-blank range. If Paloma's voice had not betrayed her to the foolish Boone, this one would have seen right through her. But he remained silent.

By the position of the low-hanging coal in the sky they had less than two hours before her marinaer ship departed from Elevana. Lamark's breath grew loud.

"If ye don't mind," Lamark said. "I 'ave to be g'tting' the kids to that there port, so we'll be goin' now. Good luck this Drav—"

"Not so fast there, Lamark," Boone said and rifled a bit of phlegm to the ground. "You take me for an unsuspecting fool? Tell me and my boys—"

The Irkal woman to his left coughed.

"Tell me and my *gang* why you happened to stop here at the Huntress church when time is so short... overcome with a streak of piety? And a mighty big weapon there on your back for such a harmless mission."

"We're in the shell of *Te Draviño*, Boone," said Lamark. "Never know when scum like yerself goin' to show up."

Boone spit the hickory stick onto the ground.

A mixed flock of birds swooped low above the hardpan. The wind had risen to a breeze, and the distant sound of snarled barking came with it.

"That would be my athon," said the Irkal woman.

"Ah," Boone grinned, "what excellent timing! You see, Marky, word has it that a boy has been runnin' around Elevana with something we desire—several things, in truth. Now you wouldn't know anything about that…"

Aeron shook his head.

"You, nephew, come here and let my associate have a look at you," said Boone, who seemed to have enough words for the entire lot. He rode in front of the line to address the other four at once. "In the meantime, you, goggles," he said to the young man mounted directly beneath the sun, "go and search the lorry."

"I would prefer the church, sir," said the young man. He urged the horse beside Boone's and Paloma recognized him at once as the farmhand who had attacked her.

Throach!

Icy skirts of terror leaked down her spine at the sight of Yeats's belligerent farmhand.

"The Huntress were my parents' people," he said.

"Exactly why I'm keeping you away, Throach" said Boone. "Take the lorry."

"Fine," said Throach. "And how will I know if I've found it?"

"I expect," said Boone casting a glance at the dark rider, "you'll know."

Throach nodded and whipped on the reins. The young man's horse crossed the bit of hardpan between them and the lorry in a handful of gallops.

They had positioned the lorry precisely as the painting showed it—fifty yards in the direction of the shore.

"Now which of you has the gall to check the church?"

"I," said the Irkal man, "will do it."

"Get on it then, Griz."

Griz yanked at the bun in his hair. Mats of whitish gold came toppling over his shoulders. He whipped his head back, whistled, and pressed forward on his horse's brown neck. They took off toward the church, less than a Cannaroo pitch away. The Irkal crossed the distance in a few seconds and disappeared through the half-broken door.

"Ye might want to send both yer Irkal-dogs for that one, Boone," Lamark said, gesturing to the church behind them with his head.

Boone's eyes narrowed. "And why's that?"

"Bad luck to enter a 'untress church alone. 'e might never return."

"Goth," said the hyena-like Boone. "Go and keep your brother company."

Mounted on an athon, the black rider was too cunning to fall for Lamark's baiting comment.

These must be athon from Irkalla. They are massive! Only a Wraeth could mount such an animal...

He turned and grabbed Boone by the elbow and shook his head in an imperious manner. They exchanged a few heated words before Boone ripped his arm away from the man's touch.

As Goth unsheathed her Irkallan short sword, Boone broke in.

"On second thought, Goth," he said, "you stay here with us."

Though his eyes were invisible beneath the cowl, Paloma could sense the dark man's eyes glowering toward the church.

His fingers tightened around the hilt by his hip, as if expecting the trap.

In the distance, the clouds of *Te Draviño* crept closer, surrounding them like rings of forest fire. Paloma drew in a deep breath, knowing chaos would soon begin.

The sun raced toward the horizon, bringing unwelcome shades of grey. A virga fell in the distance, and its rain evaporated before hitting the ground. Yet the air smelled like an ocean.

Lamark broadened himself, scratching a lone finger at the sweat beading down his scalp. "Come now, Boone. They be kids. They don't know where ye come from, 'n' why yer doin' what yer doin'. For the love of war, the woman you lost, and all the questions ye've swallowed, ye know in the bones of yer mind that me 'n' my kin be far from yer enemy."

"Oh, Marky," Boone said and echoed his name twice more. "I didn't recognize ya have such powers of persuasion. I relent. I relent. You go on your merry way!"

The distant snarling came again, no longer so distant.

"Goth's athon will have a rip-roaring time cutting you three down. Especially your fat—"

"Sir!" Throach called from inside the lorry. Strewn beside it on the ground were a leather belt, two mugs, a candle, a toolbox, and other assorted belongings. "Think I've found something…"

"What've you got?"

Throach poked his head up to be seen through the rear of the lorry. His eyes looked stranger than before, as if he had lost control, and he threw Aeron's haversack out the window. "It's got heartfruit inside… and then there's this." Throach thrust a hand out the window, clutching a black canister made of beechwood. "I know it. I know it. I recognize the weight," he said hurriedly and uncorked it. "Feels like there could be—"

"*Stop!*" hollered Boone. His high voice thrummed the aerth like hyena laughter.

But it was too late. Throach had removed the cork. From inside the lorry came a loud thwack like two huge hands clapping, followed by a sneeze of oozy-black liquid, which poured its way around the lorry and out each window. Shortly thereafter they heard Throach's jagged screams.

When Manu had uncorked the canister earlier and a blackish jellyfish-looking mass flopped onto the table, Paloma had her doubts that a sedimoctid could create such an explosion. Now, a brackish cloud hovered in and around the lorry where hot, black muck had been strewn with great enough force to knock Throach unconscious and paint a mad mural of moonless midnight on the hardpan.

The poisonous, oniony smell of cooking flesh stung Paloma's eyes and nostrils.

"What in the gods!" shrieked Boone, turning to face them. At first his eyes were hot and harrowing, but they soon grew wide and filled with fear.

Then Paloma spun around at the sound of galloping hooves.

CHAPTER 35

CHAOS WASHED ASHORE

Aeron peered over his shoulder. Bright over the burning hardpan, Manu appeared exactly as described in the old tales—proud, surly, and heroic with his feathered jacket rippling in the wind. He rode Griz's horse. With his left hand he clutched its reins, and his right held Paloma's scythe high, silver blade refracting in the sky.

"You fools!" Boone's voice quivered with fear. "Give us the key, now," his command landed empty as a spoiled child's. "I said, now!" With a flash of leather, Boone's coat gave way to two cross-bows held akimbo and pointed at Aeron and Lamark.

"Ye best point those elsewhere," said Lamark, reaching over his shoulder for a five-foot bone warclub whose bludgeon resembled the tusk of a mammoth.

Boone pressed each of the crossbow's hammers with his thumbs and the bolts on his crossbow whistled like canaries as they tightened backward.

The man in black trotted next to Boone, his back facing Aeron and the others. He said nothing, but they made eye contact and Boone gave a reluctant tilt of his head as if to say, "Fine, be my guest."

"Goth," Boone scowled, "it appears our incoming friend has killed your twin. I should hope you and your athon would cause havoc in the name of your brother."

At once, Goth charged past them toward Manu. Manu put his heels into his mount and pushed harder. They met a good fifty yards away from the rest. Her first cut was low, and Manu deflected it off his scythe. Goth was quicker than expected and almost caught Manu in the thigh, but he managed to parry and swing the blade back around to smash through Goth's shield. Slashes of wood exploded in all directions, and the shield cracked widthwise behind a rugged snap. She tossed it to the left.

Goth's short sword slashed at Manu's right side, left side, and then right again but all she accomplished was screaming steel against his deflections. Manu resorted to surprise. He jabbed at her head with the blunt end after deflecting her last strike. Goth almost fell from her mount but was saved by the horse staggering backward.

Manu raised the scythe for a final, spine-splitting cut to unburden the Irkal's body of her hideous head, but Goth broke into a gallop back toward the rest. Manu made the swing anyway, tearing through the air like a lunatic eager to rid the world of phantoms.

Aeron felt a rush of warm air as Goth whipped past them to Boone's side. She did not turn to face the others but instead let out a shrill whistle in the direction of a high-piled ramble of boulders to her far right. Though still quite far away, the movements of seven large athon were unmistakable.

Now, Manu fell in line with the rest of them.

"Manu the Wilder!" shouted Boone, still pointing one of his crossbows at Aeron. The bolts appeared to be wriggling inside, like live insects.

The man in black swung his right leg behind him and rolled off the mount. He landed like a cat on the hardpan and clawed for his sword. Manu too dismounted from his horse.

"Who are you?" Manu asked him.

The man made no reply but pulled out his sword, which to Aeron's surprise was nothing more than a bladeless hilt made of silver. But then the man reached into a brown duffle strapped to the back of his horse and yanked out two long shards of a sable black crystal, which were at least as long as Aeron. With one gloved hand, he clenched their teeth together at the break points. The puzzle fit snugly. His other hand, ungloved and white as marble, held the hilt. He took a wide stance and pressed the broken blade to the hilt.

At first nothing happened, but then Aeron saw it.

A blackish, silvery flameflower similar to Hyacinth snuck out from the man's sleeve, confirming Aeron's worst fear. This was Viru, the Wraeth Prince.

"It is time to add a new story to the Legend of the Last Great Ranger," said Manu and kissed his blade.

As the flameflower orbited Viru's hands, it weaved figure eights across his knuckles and wrists. In the flameflower's wake, a trail of blueish silver electricity remained like a spool of thread. Aeron traced the flares and shoots of the flameflower as the object moved. It resembled Hyacinth in so many ways except darker and more dangerous; it seemed to distort the few inches of space surrounding its center like a bent mirror or a black hole. Because of this illusion, Viru's hands and the sword appeared to bend and contort at the hilt as if made of rubber. The flameflower dove inside the sword, and the electric spool of thread melted within the weapon.

Viru held a huge sword with two hands beneath a huge blade. The blade was made of sharp black crystal that had veins pulsing as if filled with purple blood. The blood glistened with the incandescence of glowworms. He jabbed it into the ground and cupped his hands over the blunt end, which was now even with his heart.

Aeron threw his hands to his head. At once, a mixture of music and noise cascaded upon him. He clenched his eyes. In one ear he heard the same metallic screeching that had come while climbing the mountain in search of the Grapple. In the other he heard the tenderest, sweetest music—neath music.

When Aeron opened his eyes, Viru was pulling the sword free from the hardpan. He took an intimidating step toward Manu.

When Manu showed no fear, Viru charged with the grace of a gazelle. His movements were younger, faster, and more fluid than Aeron had ever seen. Aeron felt a misplaced sense of adoration for the man. He would never be as huge as Lamark nor as strong as Manu, but Aeron knew he could fight this way—like a dancer. He hated himself for such a thought.

Manu moved fast enough for Viru's first lunge and his scythe leapt up to meet the cold black sword. Fat sparkles of purple popped from the sword like sputtering wood, and the blades sang to each other. At once, Viru made another slash, this time with two hands. Manu shuffled to the side and clay went flying from where Viru's blade clashed against a clay rock.

Viru sent sharp and fluid cuts aimed at Manu's shoulders and legs to the left, right, and left again, but each one Manu deflected. As he swung, Viru's sword drew phantoms of violet and silver in the early evening air. Every single move the Wraeth Prince made, Manu dodged until it seemed as though he had been caged by those same phantoms.

"Now!" Lamark screamed, twisting for his hammer. A horde of athon were cantering toward them, only seconds away. No surprise, athon of Irkalla were the only kind large enough to ride.

Paloma broke for the lorry, and the athon closed in from both sides. She dove into the inky mess for shelter from their jaws.

As instructed, Aeron stayed still while Lamark smashed one of them down with a terrible crunch. Having regained her courage, Goth charged at Lamark. She was too fast for him, and her slicing, weaving movements left cuts on his arms as well as the hammer on the ground.

The Wraeth Prince gave Manu no moment of reprieve. He pushed harder on the backpedaling Ranger, dark arms never ceasing to move for even a moment. The weapons crashed and leapt away and crashed again. Sparks of metal chipped from Manu's scythe as Viru's blows came ever closer to landing. Manu moved leftward but was blocked by an athletic sidestep from Viru, driving him in the opposite direction toward Aeron and the now-weaponless Lamark. Manu defended every slash, but the scythe seemed to be weakening at the point of balance. A hopeful glance toward the ramble of boulders left him momentarily distracted, and Viru landed a blow to Manu's left bicep.

"Stop!" Paloma shouted from the lorry. She had pushed the still unconscious farmhand's ink-covered body through the broken window onto the ground, but the athon showed little interest.

Boone, who had stayed still until then, turned one of his crossbows toward her and loosed the bolt. It sailed hard and straight, hacking into the door beside Paloma's hand. He pointed the second her way and closed one eye.

"Nooooo!" Aeron shouted as Boone tightened around the crossbow's action. With a jolt, Boone whipped the crossbow toward Aeron who closed his eyes, expecting pain.

As he waited to die, the sound of trotting horses mixed with the familiar sweetness of music found his good ear.

And we shall have some peace there, for peace comes
dropping slow,
Dropping from the veils of the morning to where the
cricket sings;
There midnight's all a glimmer, and noon a purple glow,
And evening full of the linnet's wings.

Arise now healthily, ahead forever—the
Marquis Innisfree.

He opened his eyes, expecting to see faeries and golden arches, but this sight was no less splendid. Out from the ramble of boulders came a team of horseman—and not any horsemen.

"The neath!" Aeron shouted and then patted himself down for any signs of blood.

Did he miss?

Boone threw down one of his crossbows and yanked on his horse's neck rein to turn toward the ramble.

Lamark barrel-rolled into Goth and caught hold of his hammer behind her.

As Aeron walked in Boone's direction, he side-stepped the bolt—suspended in midair, as if frozen in time. But it wasn't a bolt at all. It was a scorpidion. Boone had been firing scorpidions!

The scorpidion fell to the ground. Pinching each of its three tails, Aeron picked it up and shuffled three paces to his left to the discarded crossbow. Discreetly, he scooped up the weapon and awkwardly reloaded the scorpidion.

A cackling howl came from the center of the neath charge.

"It's Yeats!" shouted Paloma.

Aeron shielded his eyes. Two people were on the lead horse—Yeats and another clinging to his waist. When that person let out another "AR AR AROOO" Aeron knew right away who it was, and why the bolt had stopped in midair.

Skylo!

From the ground, Goth whistled and her athon charged for the seven neath riders whose beautiful white armor, height, and leafy green bandanas had them looking like woodland gods.

The rider to Yeats's right brought a sword down toward a leaping athon but missed the mark. The snarling beast wrapped its teeth around the man's wrist, sending him toppling from his saddle. Blood streaked his white armor, and it made his weaponless strikes on the athon appear all the more fearsome. Filthy and soiled, he rose and stomped, killing the mongrel, only to move onto the next.

"Viru," shouted Boone with urgency.

Viru leapt onto the athon from behind. The animal let out a blood-thirsty snap of the jaws as Manu remounted too. They rode toward one another. Like a man chopping trees, Viru swung the long sword sideways with all his might. As Manu shirked the cut away, the scythe fractured like ice on the surface of water. One more strike and Manu would be dead.

All of the sudden, the scythe ignited in a blueish hue. Its metal glowed as brightly as morning, energy rippling like the tides. He had Skylo to thank for the Aeros.

Smooth as spring satin, Manu loped closer.

"It's over, Viru. Yield," said Manu, a touch out of breath. "Yield or I'll show you the true meaning of Deathsword."

Viru's voice came back dense and stoic. "Wrong."

Whispering something beneath his breath, Viru raised his long sword with two hands. His shoulders towered as the sword rushed down with all the man's power. Manu blocked without difficulty. Yet, even Skylo's Aeros were no match for Viru's might. The scythe's metal disintegrated into an ashy cloud. All that remained in Manu's hands was black dust.

"Praeth Vee-roo!" Boone's shrill voice came from behind them.

Viru wheeled the athon around. Five neath riders were seconds away. He took a deep breath and stabbed his sword with two hands straight into the air. Then, with a voice like thunder, he sang an Aero.

"Astriolos."

Viru's flameflower lodged like a gemstone into the hilt of his sword. Then it surged up to the tip of the blade and conversed with the clouds. No sooner had it coursed down through the man's blood and muscle than an Aero erupted out from him in a silver plume of force that burned through the air in boulders of energy.

Then, the five neath riders were gone, decomposed and scattered as ash in the wind. Even the athon between Viru's legs turned to cinders.

One neath remained. Yeats hovered over a now-unconscious Skylo whose flameflower had protected them both.

Distraught at the sight of her dead athon, Goth had remounted her horse. The gruesome glower in her eyes was like a mother playing witness to the torture of her children.

In an attempt to unseat the Irkal, Lamark seized her bridle and yanked on the leather. She jabbed her short sword backward beneath her armpit. The jagged Irkallan metal tore into Lamark's fleshy breastbone near where his neck and shoulder met. He fell to the ground as blood gushed out in a hot rush. The arid aerth drank it with joy.

Goth took off in the direction of her slain athon. Scattered on the ground, the remnants of dead neath burned. Their ashes rose to form a cloud floating fifty feet in the sky above them.

"We gottem beat," said Boone. "Let's get your bloody treasure, take the girl, and get on your horse before *Draviño* strands us on this island."

With slow, metered movements, Viru held the cross of the hilt up to his face and raised his white, gloveless hand to hover at its side. With his fingers curled to a claw, Viru drew his hand infinitesimally further from the sword, as if pulling on the flameflower inside it.

When the flaring black object seeped out from the sword, the blade's purple veins disappeared and the sword ceased to pulse. The flameflower looked more muted and less ominous than before.

Seeing one final opportunity, the weaponless Manu lunged his horse straight for Viru, but the horse skidded to a halt upon realizing Manu's intention to bowl them over. So, when the red-eyed athon snarled, Manu's horse launched its rider from the saddle. Manu went crashing to the hard aerth but rose without dallying even though he was clearly in pain.

While Viru remained distracted by the flameflower, Manu dashed over to the lorry where Paloma was doing her best to clear the black ink from its vital parts.

"Oh, no you don't," Boone scowled. He turned the crossbow back toward the lorry and took aim.

Aeron held Boone's second crossbow clumsily. He looked at Boone, to Viru, and then back to Boone.

Trust your instincts.

Skylo's voice echoed in Aeron's head. As much as he wanted to save his friends, Aeron tore his eyes away from Boone and focused the bow on Viru. Once Viru had fully extracted the flameflower, it would mean the end of them all.

Aeron took a deep breath and clenched the trigger. With a thwip, the scorpidion went sailing through the air and lodged itself directly into Viru's shoulder blade. For a second, the man had no reaction.

Then his lips moved noiselessly and the scorpidion jerked free from his flesh. No sooner had the bolt stabbed into Viru's back than it came sailing back toward Aeron, as if time had gone in reverse.

As it was about to strike him, Aeron recalled what he had read in the Journal.

A scorpidion's sting is painless, but it's venom stays with you forever.

A numbness struck across Aeron's belly where the scorpidion entered. His arms went limp and legs wobbled as he fell to his knees.

How?

Facing the field of dead athon and the cloud of ash, Viru raised both hands as if he were on top of the world.

"Athonus anastasis."

Viru's voice came—deep, dauntless, and hypnotic, as if from the aerth itself.

A gentle wind shawled Aeron's shoulders. Eyes screaming at their lids to close, he fell into an endless bin of darkness. But he pried them open.

He had to see.

Beneath a sky darkening with the sharp hues of sunset, Viru stood like a god.

Behind him the cloud of dust was gone, and all seven athon were alive once more.

CHAPTER 36

NO HEROES
RETURN HOME

Gouts of black poison caked the inside of the lorry, and the inky blot covering the passenger seat burned Paloma's skin. She sat nervously in the back seat as the athon rose from the ground.

They look younger and nastier than before. Have the neath gone... inside them?

Through the rear of the lorry, the sun was setting over the mountains with shadows growing on the hardpan. Lamark carried Aeron over his uninjured shoulder, and Skylo lay draped crossways behind Yeats's saddle. Boone and Goth galloped toward the lorry as Manu sprinted for his horse. The wrathful athon pelted toward him from the field. Slowly and deliberately, Viru admired his work like a king looking out over his kingdom.

If Paloma stayed put and waited for him to reach the lorry, as Manu instructed, the Last Great Ranger would be no more.

She had to get to him. Aeron had tried and failed. The neath had tried and failed. Even Skylo had tried and failed.

The only hope to save Longleath was Manu. She had to save him, and even as much as she'd grown close to Aeron, she couldn't save him. Unless…

The purador! The Wraeth need purador to survive. Praeth Viru will smell it the moment I uncork the bottle. That will surely draw them off! Yes, it's time to take matters into my own hands. If I can save Manu, distract them long enough for Aeron and the others to escape and get to the ship, Manu will come back to Longleath. Then he can finally train me to become a Ranger.

She crawled over the seat, burning her elbows on black pus smeared across the back of the divider. Hidden beneath the fuel funnel, Paloma dug the blueish bottle of purador out from a sack of sand. When she uncorked the top, oceans of cool air rushed to meet her nose, lips, and skin. Her heart began thumping like mad, and she could almost feel Viru's attention shift to the lorry.

"Fools!" Viru shouted. "The lorry. Get the lorry."

She closed her left eye and peered down the neck of the bottle. Inside could have been the sea itself, flapping with foam. Paloma turned the lorry's nozzle to "open" and dripped a dash of purador inside.

She heard a low purring noise, as if it was beckoning for more, but then the singed front left door jamb reintegrated itself until it was whole once again.

She dripped another splash in and the purring became louder.

"Come on, girl," said Paloma, rubbing the lorry's dash with desperation. "Give me something."

With a wrenching sound, in between old wood and bending metal, the lorry lurched into motion.

"That's it. That's it!" shouted Paloma, draining the bottle halfway into the lorry.

She felt both tiny and powerful seated in Manu's huge driver's seat. Gripping the wheel, she turned the lorry one hundred and eighty degrees. Still shattered and caked with black, the front windshield was near useless. She hunched over to see through one of the holes.

Paloma zoomed passed Lamark, Aeron, Yeats, and Skylo and headed straight to the gritted fangs of the athon about to descend onto Manu.

"Do not stop!" he shouted.

The first athon leapt, but Manu thrust it off to the side with barred arms. Too quickly, a second athon connected with his right rib, knocking him to the ground. A third athon, larger than the other two and with the mane of a lion skulked in slowly—the alpha.

With its teeth showing, eyes focused, and head tilted mutinously low, the athon stooped three feet above Manu's face.

But Paloma was close now, and she only saw one option.

"Sorry, girl," said Paloma. The lorry gave a hallow wailing sound as she jammed forward on the thrust.

A huge blow hit the lorry, and she felt as if an immense weight had been thrown onto her. She closed her eyes as the front windshield exploded and a waterfall of black shards peppered her face and chest.

The lorry skidded, kicking up clouds of clay, but Paloma straightened the lorry and continued. She checked over her shoulder to see if Manu had escaped. Something panged loudly against the lorry. One of Boone's scorpidion bolts was wriggling in the lorry's metal.

Paloma turned back as hot wind blasted against her cheeks. Boone's hackneyed curses fell away to the distance.

The damp smell of the storm returned, and a gritty taste of chalk lined her teeth. She hadn't noticed if Manu was dead or alive, but he wasn't coming with her anyway. Now, the most important thing was catching the last ship back to Longleath. If she wanted any chance, there was no turning back.

I'm fine. I'm most certainly fine. I wouldn't be thinking this otherwise…

The lorry sped down a roadless straightaway to the left of the boulders from where the neath valiantly sprung forth for their final battle.

"Paloma, ease up," said a disfigured voice, chopped by the wind. "Now."

Oh mercy, am I going to deal with the Wilder's ghost in my head?

The lorry tipped down toward the right side. In an attempt to see if the back wheel had broken, Paloma leaned to the right. It seemed fine. Then the sound of a tumbling barrel clambered from the cargo. When she turned around, Manu's bloodied face glugged moshrum straight from the spout.

The lorry crashed over a sapling tree, jarring Paloma back to the wheel.

"Manu! You beautiful drunkard," said Paloma. "How in the gods…"

"Go left!" he shouted, struggling to climb through the rear window.

Paloma made a hard turn. Soon after, the lorry scampered off the hardpan and onto the Grey Road. Peaks of Elevana City showed over the hill ahead.

"Hooked my belt to the jockey box after you rammed into the beast," said Manu, who seemed to have given up on the rear entrance. "Real question is how you got her moving again."

Paloma hesitated for a second before holding up the blue purador bottle.

Manu said nothing for a few moments. Elevana's greens were returning on either side of the road, but detritus and debris made the road nearly unrecognizable.

Paloma slowed to avoid a string of abandoned lorries.

"They'll be after us," said Manu.

"Who?"

As they rolled slowly, Paloma heard the distant barks of athon. "The athon, for one."

"Will the others make it to the grove before nightfall?" She leaned forward and looked at the sky. The shell was smaller than ever, surrounded in every direction by clouds.

Will we?

"Eyes!" Manu shouted.

At the last second, Paloma swerved around a fallen tree. Manu fell to his knees in the cargo-trunk.

"Sorry," said Paloma, her eyes now fixed to the road.

More and more lorries blocked the way. Over the once bright blue walls, graffiti was scattered over a mural. Though it once read *Our Heroes Return Home*, the "Our" had been sprayed with an "X" and replaced with the word "No." She was beginning to feel the same. No Heroes Return Home, as the graffiti message said.

Beneath the words, the mural of a seven-sided star was further vandalized. Each point had once held a great Ranger's name on it, including "Manu the Wilder." But now each was laced with the letters I-R-K-A-L-L-A.

"These people have never known order. Have they?" asked Paloma. "True order, I mean, not tyranny."

"They've been exiled from their countries or have fled in disgrace. So the lawlessness of Irkalla seems like freedom. Anarchy, yes, but freedom."

"Even though everyone knows Irkalla supports the Wraeth?" said Paloma. "What do the Wraeth even want? What is Viru after?"

"Do you recall," Manu asked, "what happened to the Kingdom of Termara eight hundred years ago? Termara had united the world behind the pursuit of knowledge. But the Wraeth too were smart. They split the head of the world from its body. They set fire to the mind of primankind, and Termara burned. Now the effort continues, poisoning the Tree of Knowledge. If this is done, mindless chaos will ensue. The four rifts will fight one another. They will forget about the Wraeth prowling about. The Wraeth will first separate the four rifts by war. Then they will do so by land and sea. Primen thrive in unity. They die in discord and disconnection."

"What do you mean by land and sea?"

They passed the open door of an empty restaurant filled with picnic tables and wood-paneled beige walls. They cruised slowly enough to see each table had pairs of identical maroon and grey ceramic mugs, carved with palm trees. Before they rolled on, she could see center pieces that rested on the table tops. Large statues of hands, which seemed to have once been holding a centerpiece or a bottle, had now been looted.

"It all goes back to Termara, Paloma. They used the same sword Viru had. The Deathsword. They called on the sea with some kind of Dark Aeros. Then Termara broke from the coast and became an island. Soon after, the country died altogether.

"And that is what the Wraeth want—the end of you and me. With us gone, they will control the world, and every living being that calls Aerth home. Birds will die and bats will survive. Dogs will be replaced by snakes. Thousand-mile tunnels will be dug so the Wraeth need never see the sun. In their hands, Aerth will die. All they want is be the last ones to see the sun go down."

The road turned another corner and Paloma kept a steady pace.

One building past the graffiti was the nicest building she'd seen on the outskirts. Its doors and windows were painted sunflower yellow with brilliant white trim. A middle-aged woman leaned against the doorway with foreboding eyes. Above the door was a mosaic of small blue tiles, depicting two fishermen beneath five windmills perched on the river and a sky heavy with a palace of clouds. It too was outlined by a customary floral pattern and framed by more white trim.

The rear door jerked open and Manu tumbled into the back seat.

"Boone and Goth won't have given up so easily. Stay sharp and we'll get to the dock," said Manu.

"Then what happens?"

A small orange-haired dog scampered across the door of the building, stopping on a large turquoise doorway with steel bolts. Eyes sullen, the stray watched them as rain shot down onto the hexagonal-tiled walkway.

"We sneak aboard."

CHAPTER 37

THE GREAT BEAST
OF FATE

*A*bsolutely blinding!

Between thumps of blood throbbing in his skull, Aeron recalled a passage he'd read from one of the Mason scientists.

Polyouras Scorpidiones: The three-tailed species of scorpidion famous for its use in sedative weaponry. The scorpidion's venom has been said to remain in the priman blood stream for life, though not neath nor Irkal.

Though the scorpidion's sting wasn't painful, being jock-eyed up and down on horseback was torture.

"Give me some 'elp, boy!" Lamark's voice came from directly above him. Aeron blinked his eyes open and tilted his head back. His hair brushed Lamark's belly, and he saw the underside of the man's scruffy neck.

"Where…" said Aeron groggily, "are we?"

"Yer with me on a 'orse," said Lamark. "Now 'ang onto the saddle's 'orn nice 'n' good."

"He is awake? Wonderful," said a man's voice from the right side.

Aeron tried to look at him, but all he saw was a sickening blur of green rushing past.

"Barely. Seems to be driftin' in 'n' out." Lamark's chest vibrated on Aeron's back as he spoke. Aeron closed his eyes and tuned into the sounds around him—a symphony of croaking tree frogs, the clattering of hooves on the hilly aerth, and the soft tinkle of a hummingbird, which must have been following them.

Unless...

"Yeats?"

"I am here, Aeron," Yeats said.

"Have we," Aeron panted, "escaped?"

"Fer now," Lamark replied.

"How?"

"The others were sent after Manu and the girl in the lorry," said Yeats. "They believe your Grapple to be inside. Now try to rest, Aeron. We're getting help for you."

"North!" Aeron shouted himself into a fit of coughs. "We must... North!"

"Settle yerself," said Lamark.

Aeron's knees shook. If he had the Grapple, he could heal himself again. And Viru was too smart. He would soon figure out where it was.

"Skylo?" Aeron asked with distress in his gut.

"Here," said Yeats. "Here and sleeping. You'll both be healed soon."

The time that passed while Aeron drifted out of consciousness may have been minutes or mere seconds.

"Yeats," said Aeron.

"Yes, my son?"

"Your arm..." he said. "I'm sorry."

"Sorry?" Yeats said with surprise. "My arm is fine. Because of you."

"Am I going to die?" asked Aeron.

"In the words of yer friend Skylo," said Lamark. "'Not yet.'"

"Crack of mooorning!" the woman's voice crashed into Aeron's ears.

A column of dim light fell through a circular skylight. Shielding his eyes, Aeron scanned the room. The grotto was no bigger than Elevana's main square and had a large pool at its center. On the rightmost edge of the pool, Yeats and Lamark were arguing. Between them Skylo lay on a high table.

"You no worries for Master Skylo, Aerno," she said, mispronouncing his name. "You safe, he safe, me takes great care to heal Aerno's every hair."

"It's Aeron," he continued, sitting up higher. "Who are you? Where are we? Why am I so cold?"

Aeron looked down at his stomach for the first time. The way the scorpidion had melted into his skin reminded him of the gash on his side after he'd used the Grapple.

"Me knows you." The mousy woman's hair changed from violet to a reddish silver. "Me knows you, Aerno Mason! Me knows many things. Like how to help the scorpidion sting." She brushed the place on his belly where he'd been struck. "And where your stone be!"

"The Grapple," Aeron said, leaning forward. "You know where to find it?"

"Oh yes," said Corie. "But your Grapple found me."

"So you have it! And who is 'me,' anyway?" Aeron asked.

"Aerno Mason! You is Aerno Mason! Do we needs another dip in the lagoon?"

"I know *I* am Aeron Mason, but who are you? And why's my vest sopping wet?"

"You had a nice bath. Lagoon speed up time. Now your body stronger."

"I don't feel saved. I feel like death."

"So you've met her too?" Corie chirped.

Whatever kind of sprig this lady has been smoking, keep me away.

"You no remembers me." The woman was old but she was bouncy as a rabbit. "No, no, no! Why would anybody remember me? Nobody remembers stupid old Corie."

"We've only just met!" said Aeron as he stood up. Though far more aware now, he still struggled to make sense of the strange place. Statues of primen, nymphs, and faeries danced precariously atop ledges and unstable stones. A large tower of boulders sat piled on the other side of the pool. Vines grew down from the cenote to the floor of the cave-lagoon.

"No, Aeron," she echoed, "as we said, me knows you..."

"Look," Aeron began, picking up a crumpled paper-leaf from the ground and unfolding it lengthwise. "I have to get back to the grove. We needed to be at the northern coast before dusk when the shell disappears and *Te Draviño* returns... Hang on, did you say it's morning?"

The storm doesn't sound bad yet. Maybe I can get there quickly on horse and come back here with the Grapple to save Skylo. Without him and Manu, I will never get to the Tree. And without the Tree, the Mason Line will die in infamy.

"Marky!" Corie shouted across the Grotto. "Marky, Aerno ask me if it's morning!"

"Yer awake," said Lamark. "Good. Now Miss Crazy needs to wake up Skylo, pronto."

"Skylo need time," she said. "Time Skylo need. Now, hands in the lagoon please. One dip more, Angel's Lagoon demands."

Aeron leaned over the pool. The reflection made his hands look even larger than they already were. He submerged them in the crisp, clear water. A rinsing sensation spread through him, as if his every tissue were rinsing beneath his skin. "So it's not morning?" Aeron asked, feeling fresh and sharp.

"No, Aeron," said Yeats, holding the charm of his necklace between two fingers. He leaned over Skylo and motioned in figure eights. "A sliver of sun remains."

"Then I still have time," said Aeron. "Lamark and I can go to the grove and come back here for Skylo."

"No, Aerno Mason," said Corie. "The Grapple can't come here. Not heartfruit either. Lagoon no allow it!"

Aeron looked down at the paper. It was the leaf Lamark had given him in the Blue Bat after he'd found the heartfruit and the grove. All a waste. He'd lost the Grapple and dusk was upon them.

Corie sang the words in an easy tune. That beautiful, sonorous, rhythmic voice…

"As it Soars, it Sears
The Skylo Sky-low:
be where you seek.
Grapple's Grapple,
The Inn is free
Beyond the brick blue teak."

While she sang, Aeron recalled a dream, or maybe a memory, or some mixture of the two. A young Aeron played beneath a table with a white-draped cloth. No one could see in, and no one could see out. But he could hear the singing.

Aeron tried to shake his head but that unbalanced him. A rippling chill plunged down his spine. With his feet rooted into the soft sands, he stood for a moment with his eyes closed. He saw the Map of the Reddheart in Lamark's hands.

Aeron jogged over to the place where Yeats and Lamark stood with Corie skipping beside him.

"Gimme that," said Aeron, snatching the map away from Lamark.

"Not sure it even works," said Lamark.

"It works. You'll see—"

The storm had filled over the map like thick smoke. The shell had shrunk to the size of a pin, and there was no line. Only a red and yellow glowing pin.

"Ye see what I mean," said Lamark. "How there's no line telling me where to get what I want. I know what I want. Heartfruit and my Waevy. But it says we're already there. How could we already be there in a cave? I'd 've noticed a heartfruit grove on the other side of the tunnel. But it says we're already there."

"Maybe…" Aeron trailed off, turning to Corie. "Corie. Is the tunnel the only way in and out of this place?"

"Another," she said, shaking her head and holding her elbow like an embarrassed child. "In disguise."

"Where, Corie?" asked Aeron.

She looked away toward a fallen pillar of limestone. Her hair turned from ruddy silver to bone white.

"Where!" Aeron put a hand on her tiny shoulder.

"The bad place," Corie said, her eyes darting high and to the left. "The place where everybody dies." She met Aeron's gaze. "Oh, that great beast of fate—not even Corie can save them." She looked down to the ground. "No matter how hard she cries."

Aeron turned to his right and looked up. At the top of a stack of boulders sat a round door with two brass latches.

The second exit.

CHAPTER 38

THE WASTELAND

Paloma eased the lorry to a stop. Separating them from the port were two hundred yards of primen. Men and women carried haversacks on their heads filled to the brim with child slaves pulling carriages through knee-high water.

"There must be thousands of them…" said Paloma. "They all expect to get on that ship?"

Smaller cargo ships in the port bobbed and weaved in the storm-chopped current but not the marinaer. Like all marinaers, it was originally made to be a massive cargo ship. Its black hull was so large that even the nasty drifts of *Draviño* wouldn't shake her. Three flagpoles struck high in various places across the deck, each a different banner thrashing in the storm's wind. The three banners—Elevana, the Western Rift, and Longleath—clung to their masts for dear life. In the center of the marinaer were three huge chimney-like tubes the ship used for generating power from the air.

Manu shook his head. "None of these folk will board." He pointed to the front. There, the flooding was lesser and people could stand upright. Above them all were two large white signs with red lettering stating: Ship Full—Ship Departing.

As the last blades of sun disappeared, the marinaer hummed and each chimney glowed gently around the rims. The ship let out a huge, chest-shaking horn, indicating departure. Then came the sound of desperate primen splashing in the water.

"They're jumping in!" said Paloma.

"Yes," said Manu touching Paloma's shoulder. "Now come. I know a better way."

They got out of the lorry, walked away from the dock, and headed back toward the flooded city. As they passed the lorry, Manu fished Aeron's haversack from the back, slung it over his shoulder, and gave the vehicle one loving pat. "You did good, girl," he said and turned toward the less-flooded alley to the right. His boots splashed through water on cobblestone as he broke into a limping jog. Paloma followed close behind, still holding the bottle of purador.

The air in the alley tasted like death. Every nerve in her body said to get away from the place. Manu turned back for a second and must have seen the doubt in her eyes. "We're almost there."

Side by side were two storefronts, one of which had been ravaged in part by the storm and in part by heathen looters. Manu approached the door of the intact building.

"The Blue Rose," Paloma read the bright blue sign with gold, wreathed lettering aloud. The door to the one on the left looked weak, like a wet piece of paper from *Draviño's* rains. It was pale yellow with two red-trimmed rectangles around the number "263" in silver door work. The paint looked only a few weeks old and Paloma recognized the strokes of a talented painter. Without even trying the handle, Manu tore the door away from its turquoise frame with such ease she wondered if she could have done the same.

They stepped into an exquisitely designed room that was dark but bloomed with greens, navies, and purples from hundreds of bioluminescent plants and jars filled with fluorescent concoctions.

"What is this place?" asked Paloma, touching the petals of a rare flower, which she recognized from the vizier's gardens in Longleath. The air tasted damp but pure and infinitely refreshing as if it were filled with pure oxygen.

"The Blue Rose belongs to Lamark's wife, Waeve." Manu's voice came from further down. His silhouette glowed purple against the wall from nearby plants.

"And why are we here?" Paloma stepped closer to him at the far wall. He was pulling out drawers on a whim.

"Your only hope to get off this island," he said as a drawer fell to the floor. Glass vials scattered across the floorboards. "*Root of Adaloo*. I know she has it somewhere. Hush and help me—"

He yanked a knob on the main desk. Instead of opening, the entire table wobbled. He gripped the flat-top with one hand and wrenched on the drawer with the other. Wood snapped inside the desk and it flew open. A pungent aroma spread through the air.

"I knew it," he said, holding up a paper bag. "Adaloo."

"It looks empty," said Paloma.

Manu shook his head and held it closer. She took it and felt a few knobby daubs inside.

"Do not open it yet," he said and turned back toward the door, "and take utmost care. There is little, but still enough to sneak aboard the ship." For a moment, he paused and looked cross-eyed at a note on the table. "We must hurry now. They'll have cleared away the fools who jumped in. We only have minutes left." Paloma caught a whiff of lavender as they passed through the door and back into the seaweed-smelling air.

On the opposite wall, two murals buttressed a rusting cage door, which read "no entry." The left was salmon pink but had a powder blue frame and lettering that read "Elevana" in word-art. The painting on the other side was blue with "The Wasteland" written in red lettering that looked like droplets of honey.

This time Paloma led the way down the alley. She dashed down the straight away littered with broken shipping crates and splintered wood until reaching the quick left-right-left that spilled out into the port.

"They're about to pull the bridge!" shouted Paloma. She could barely hear herself amid the manic hollering of the crowd.

"This way," Manu said, following a thin, slightly elevated road out of the flooding but toward the water. It was filled with abandoned bicycles and lorries and ran parallel to the rectangular mass crowded around the dock at the front and center.

"Grab one!" Paloma shouted to Manu as she picked up a brown bicycle from the ground with a black seat and pedals on either side of the front wheel.

Manu continued on foot as she sped past him and reached the final chain-link railing before the ocean. From up close, the marinaer was even more massive. Standing at the front left corner of the square, sea-spray kissed her cheeks. She turned to face the dock, but at least fifty yards and three hundred primen separated her from it.

"Open it," Manu said, coming to a stop beside her.

Paloma looked down at the bag.

"Open it and swallow one," he commanded. "Now!"

She tucked the purador into her armpit and tore a corner of the bag. Inside felt like a few small marbles. She shook one into her palm. It was pink and brown and ginger shaped. She swallowed it without chewing and a warm and spicy aftertaste tickled her throat.

"Now what?"

"Take my arm," Manu said, "And for the great god Cedre's sake, do not let go."

When she locked her elbow into his, Manu charged like a bull through the crowd along the front side of the square. Though they parted the crowd like a chopper at sea, Paloma nearly tripped a handful of times on crying children and various sheaves of junk.

A woman hissed, and a child whined loudly. A pair of men cursed and glared with scathing eyes, but all of them were directed at Manu, rather than her. Halfway through the crowd and fifty yards from the dock, Manu paused.

"Give me one," he said.

She lifted the bag up from her left side. The bag looked as though it floated in the air.

What in the hell! I can feel my hand, but it's gone!

Manu held an open palm to her, and shaking, Paloma turned her hand to drop one of the root-like pieces into his.

He popped the tiny pinkish root into his mouth.

"*Adaloo* is Orangu for invisibility," he said. "Now come on."

As he shoved further forward, the passing came easier. Paloma realized that, to others, the purador must have been floating through the air. She wrapped it inside the bag which had held their Adaloo.

Still odd, but not purador at least...

When she looked up, her heart fell to the depths of the ocean. Not an arm's length from the bridge was a scaly man with a sunburnt overcoat and matching hat mounted on a sad-looking chestnut colored horse. Beside him was the dusky Irkal woman.

"Look!" Paloma shouted. "Next to the bridge."

"No choice," he said, continuing to barrel forward.

At this point Manu was a phantom bulldozer, shoving men and women every which way until reaching the boarding platform.

"I don't give a hoot," Boone howled at the sailor. "Nothing's going to deter me from getting on this boat. Now move aside."

Mounted above the crowd, Boone whipped open his jacket and yanked the crossbow from the strap on his side. He pointed the bow at the sailor with his jacket hanging open. Paloma caught sight of a familiar shade of orange leather peeking from the man's breast pocket.

But the sailor refused to let them board. Two other sailors stepped forward, but neither had a horse.

"Come on," Manu whispered, releasing her elbow.

Her heart throbbing, Paloma slipped between the men and onto the wooden boarding bridge.

"Boone!" Goth shouted from behind. "Look there, on the bridge!"

Had she seen the bag with the purador?

She dared not call out to Manu, nor turn around until halfway across the connector. Gripping the rail with one hand, Paloma turned her back to the boat and tucked the bottle into her waistband. Fifty yards away, Boone pointed his crossbow directly at the sailor and cursed.

The rain was coming down hard in gusty sheets. As she looked back from the port, overlooking all of Elevana, the city was a dark, flooded wasteland. The ominous clouds completed the desolateness of not only the town but the people pleading to board.

Frantically, the man pressed down on the lever and the footbridge jerked violently. Paloma fell on her tailbone. With a bounce, she turned over onto hands and knees. She wheeled around. At least twenty yards still separated her from the ship's deck. She had no hope of making it, even if she ran. Wood swayed and tremored with the wind. Paloma closed her eyes and hung onto the floorboards for dear life as the footbridge moved.

CHAPTER 39

THE DOOR

◇◇◇◇◇

"Here, you takes this, Aeron," Corie held out a small vial made of beechwood. She closed his hand around it with her own. Her skin was warm and soft as old leather, and she shook her head with a crushed look. "Please takes it. You needs purador."

"I feel quite good. Your lagoon…"

"Trust Corie," she said. "You may not feels it… but the scorpidion is there."

Aeron and Yeats connected for a beat, and the neath man gave a nod. Aeron's fingers closed around Corie's vial.

Lamark cradled Skylo in his arm like an infant.

"You go now, Aeron. Yes, now is the time, Aeron, and the time is now." Corie sang softly. "Go there. To the place, to your starting where…" She removed her hand from his. "There you find him. In groves of heartfruit teak. Up there, resting in the air, the Grapple you seek."

"Thank you, Corie," Aeron said with a subtle bow. "And thank you too, Yeats. I hope our paths meet again."

"The Masons have always been friends to the neath…" said Yeats stroking his necklace with one hand. "I trust they always will."

"Storm's only gettin' worse…" Lamark chimed in and turned toward the cairn. "Let's go, lad."

Aeron trotted ahead, wrapping around the edge of the pool until reaching the stack of stones and boulders. The cairn had a clear path for climbing, and Aeron leapt with light feet from rock to rock. Toward the top, his foot skidded atop a puddle of moisture, and the stone went tumbling.

"Look out!" Aeron shouted, turning back for the first time.

Lamark looked up but too late. The stone crushed into his injured shoulder. "*Yaawww*," Lamark let out a riotous howl. Somewhere below he heard thin wisps of Corie's laughter.

"Watch what yer doin'," Lamark said through clenched teeth. "Could've killed yer Skylo."

"An accident," Aeron said turning back to make the final ascent. "Just think about all the heartfruit you'll have in a few minutes. That should numb the pain…"

Lamark grumbled and gripped the rocks.

The stack's ascent thinned and Aeron pulled himself with a bearish crawl onto a flat surface. Up here, the walls were thick and vivid with green sprouts. He gripped his feet to the ground and curtained three hanging branches aside.

"Cripes, boy," Lamark wheezed, as he reached the flat. "To think, I was a climber once…"

"Here," said Aeron, approaching the door. It had the stripes of teak wood, though older and starved for sun, with a tiny door at the bottom for Corie's use. "I'll hold down the latches and you push."

Lamark placed Skylo down to the side on a bed of soft soapstone. The man could have been dead, Aeron thought, if not for his chest's infinitesimal rise and fall.

The brass latches were cold and unpolished and slid on a jagged track. Looming over Aeron, Lamark pressed his good arm against the wood and wedged his other fingers in between the door's gap for grip.

"Floor's slick," he said.

He pressed hard, hiding winces of pain with his feet sliding backward on the slick stone until the door eked open an inch.

Then the singing began.

"I hear it!" Aeron shouted. "Come on!"

Lamark continued to pull, but the door was stubborn, moving only inches. Louder came the familiar sound of Eurovean chanting. Butterfly wings beat against the walls of his stomach.

"One more thrust, Lamark, the Merchant of Herraz— for Waeve!"

"*Graaah.*" Lamark yanked so mightily the door flung open and cracked against the wall behind. Sandy trickles of dust fell into the cave.

Ahead of them a sheer cliff dropped a hundred feet into the ocean.

"We'll 'ave to scale the side…" said Lamark, tucking Skylo over his shoulder.

Aeron leaned his head out the door.

Dark blue, almost grey, the sea crushed together with the clouds as if Aerth and the haevens were one, extending into eternity.

To the left, a ledge stuck out from the wall. Aeron could fit his whole foot, but Lamark would have only room for his toes.

Aeron stepped one shoe onto the ledge to test it. It held decently strong for climbing. But the rain…

"Maybe you should leave him here," said Aeron. "Once I get the Grapple, we can come back for him."

"No can do," said Lamark gravely. "Ye remember what Corie said. Once we leave, the lagoon will not let us back in. 'n' I must admit somethin' to ye…"

Lamark paused and looked to his right shoulder, as if checking to make sure Skylo was still unconscious.

"Old man said somethin' like this would 'appen. Made me promise on Waeve's soul that we'd never leave 'im behind. 'The Aeros will keep me safe,' old man said."

"He meant in the battle, Lamark!" Aeron cried. "I'm certain of it. He never would have expected to be unconscious and carried by you."

"I am not so sure 'n' I won't be trading my Waeve's soul fer this old smoke's." Lamark gestured ahead. "Let's go, before *Draviño* begins for real—the tsunamis."

A moment of total dejection passed over Aeron, but the look on Lamark's face erased it—stolid, strong, and resolute. Corie had done masterful work on his shoulder. Aeron nodded and turned for the door. The Grapple called to him.

The moment he passed through the open door, the humming had filled his chest as if he were chanting.

He found the first nut-shaped handhold. Then a second. He stepped out onto the slope. Heavy and bold, the wild winds blew Aeron's hair. The last rim of sun on the horizon slipped away.

He took the first five steps gingerly. Another five or so steps and he came to the turn of a ledge, which Aeron expected to be safer.

Making sure to keep a hand attached to the wall, Aeron approached the ledge. As he suspected, one swing around the rock and he would be on flat ground. He recognized it immediately—those unforgettable peeks of silvery-gold. The grove.

He turned back around to find Lamark edging out onto the ledge. He had slung Skylo over his good shoulder and leaned his head to that side to assure the old man stayed there. Much larger than Aeron, Lamark needed only two steps to reach him.

Then the rain began, slow and thin.

Skylo slipped off his shoulder—one inch, two inches, a foot—down his arm. Lamark's eyes flared wide. He throttled his handhold with the wounded arm and jerked up with his forearm to catch Skylo in his elbow. It worked, but Lamark's arm was slick. Skylo slid forward as a slug would if it had lost its stick.

Aeron pressed his own hand against Lamark's rooted hand. Skylo fell from Lamark's elbow. Aeron closed his eyes. Chanting sounds and the taste of a dark, cold ocean breeze swept against his cheeks. He cracked one eye and then the other.

Lamark had Skylo in the bucket of his upturned hand. He gestured forward with his head. The wall was slick now from rain. Aeron turned back around, twisted his right leg around the turn of the ledge, and scurried to the safety of the flat.

He turned back around and dropped to his hands and knees. Gripping the ledge, Aeron peered over at three hundred feet of air above the thick layer of sea smoke. Then he turned to the side and saw Lamark's fingers, right foot, and Skylo, now back on the man's right shoulder.

The rain dumped harder. Lamark's hands quivered against the slick rock. They had no more time for measured movements, so Lamark took a leap of faith. Right hand still pressed to the cliff, Lamark spun sharply over his left shoulder as if throwing a vicious left kick and frogged himself toward Aeron with a firm right leg. The move was brilliant and never could have failed.

Catching Skylo sailing through the air, Lamark landed them both safely on the ledge. The man gave a victorious warrior's roar. Still facing the sea, Aeron noticed the door to Angel's Lagoon close with a violent snap.

No wonder it wouldn't budge... the door's a living tree, grown sideways.

The stem of a great tree stuck out from Corie's door, hooking upward toward the sky like a J. It had fewer leafy branches than a normal heartfruit teak and held one heartfruit and one heartfruit alone—the one Aeron sought.

When Aeron faced Lamark, an unnaturally intense wave of wind smashed against Aeron's back. He grasped frantically at Lamark's leg. The singing had turned to shrill, screechy whines.

Then a flourish of wind came from directly above followed by Skylo's body. The man seemed to fall in slow motion. Aeron could have sworn he saw the man's eyes spring open for a moment. As Skylo plummeted through the air, Aeron waited for some masterful burst of Aeros to swoop in and save him... but nothing happened, and the sea smoke reached out to swallow him whole.

"*Nooo!*" Aeron cried, his heart splitting into a thousand fragments as the Sage disappear into the misty oblivion below.

Abrupt as it came, the unnaturally hard wind fell away.

That was no regular wind. If Lamark could scale the cliff and still hang onto Skylo, a gust would have had no chance. No. It was an Aero. Which means...

Aeron stood and saw Lamark's triumphal grin disintegrate into fear. The man's lips were clear. "Go back..." he said without looking down at Aeron. "The door."

The screeches grew deafening, and Aeron turned one hundred and eighty degrees.

Before the pristine array of heartfruit teak trees, beneath interleaved crowns of shimmering heartfruit, above thousands of straggler daisies, and between chimneys of hammering rain, a burnt face, broad shoulders, and barrel chest of a dark figure stared up at the Grapple…

CHAPTER 40

THE LONG DUSK

◇◇◇◇◇◇

Now far enough into the ocean to see all of Elevana, Paloma had an unbroken view of *Draviño*. Standing at the port side of the ship, she understood why people spoke of the storm as if it were a living, breathing being.

From end to end it, it stretched across Elevana. Thick clouds, blustery rains, and even a tornado struck over the country. The sight cast a dire feeling over Elevana.

To the right, by nascent tornado, a pin of golden-blue light beamed like a lighthouse inside a thick barrel of clouds. It shone through the tornado with dreamlike skirts of light.

She realized then why Elevanos were so afraid of *Te Draviño*. All storms cause destruction, but *Draviño* had a mind of its own. This storm had one intention: the destruction of Elevana.

Despite its immensity, Paloma could barely move around the ship without bumping into another person. And despite its congestion, the ship was quiet and maudlin.

Above the stormy seas, the deck rocked and lurched. A few people nearby were sick over the edges. More watched *Draviño* devouring their home with cloudy tendrils.

"Look!" someone shouted from the stairs to the second deck. "It's a yacht!"

Paloma clung to the railing and leaned over.

"They're going the wrong way," responded another.

In the distance, a ship sailed in the opposite direction, toward the storm.

"Look at the flag!" a third voice chimed in. The nearby woman had binoculars. "It's the Merchant of Herraz!"

At once, everything connected. Manu's disappearance at the moment of boarding, the splash that followed, and now the ship that belonged to his friend.

"Pardon," said Paloma sweetly, "would you mind if I had a look?"

"Of course, dear," said the woman, handing over the binoculars.

Paloma held the damp leather with one hand, still clutching the railing, and pressed the lenses to her eyes. On the quarter deck of the yacht she saw the broad shoulders, rippling back, and whipping khaki jacket of her friend, Manu the Wilder.

Suddenly, a horrid feeling curdled in her belly, like abandoning a friend at his sickest moment. As if, yet again, she was running from one set of problems in exchange for another.

For once in my life, I want to feel certain about something. Not like a chicken with its head cut off. I thought bringing the Ranger back would do that. Now he's gone too.

Hands on the bannister, Paloma looked down. On the warped sea-green floor rested a copy of *The Longleath Pulse*. The purchase date read three days prior. She stooped and retrieved it from beneath the lifesaver on the rail.

Snapping the pages flat, the air squeezed from her chest.

In all her days of winning Cannaroo tournaments, she had never made the front page of *The Pulse.*

But there she was, standing next to Aeron and that broken-down lorry from when they had first met.

MURRAVILLOW GONE WILD

She backpedaled and knocked into a large plump woman standing with a fat haversack.

"Pardon me," she said, groping the armrest of her seat.

In a shocking turn of events, Ms. Paloma Murravillow, best known as the Orion on the "Longleath Blaze," has been reported with none other than the last remaining Mason in the exile country of Elevana.

It comes as no surprise to find Mr. Aeron Mason in such a place, but why Ms. Murravillow? Some have theorized that Ms. Murravillow, nearing the age to enter her business, has grown nervous.

Of course, there is immense pressure in such a business. At the time of writing The Longleath Trading Company, founded by Beck Murravillow, is the largest business of any kind in the Western Rift.

When questioned, Beck refused to comment on the matter, thus raising further concerns as to how much the man knows of his daughter's whereabouts.

Yet we now know that the well-endowed Ms. Murravillow is sauntering across an island of outlaws with a known fugitive. It needs no reminding that Mr. Mason recently escaped from Longleath Prison. Young Mason was charged less than a year ago with conspiracy to murder his grandfather, Mendel Mason, and sister.

*Why commit such a terrible crime? Evidence suggests
that Mr. Mason had learned of a dark secret in his family and hoped to snuff the rumor out.*

*Fortunately for Longleath high-society, The Pulse's very
own Oake Murravillow, Ms. Murravillow's uncle, broke
that story. (You can re-read or listen to MENDEL MASON:
SCIENTIST, POET, THIEF, on leaf E4 of this edition.)*

Only two paragraphs remained on the page, but Paloma
struggled to focus her eyes. She pulled her knees in and
hugged her chest. Resting her feet on the base of the chair,
she rolled the newsleaf into a tube and held the opening to
her ear.

The ticky-tack voice of the article's author, Chestter
Crump, finished reading the article to her.

*Little can be said to damage the reputation of the Mur-
ravillow Line and their contribution to Longleath. But
where is the line drawn?*

*So often we treat those who do not deserve it with royal
admiration. Ms. Murravillow may represent this great
city on the Cannaroo pitch, but she is certainly not rep-
resenting it today.*

*In these years of the Long Peace, we give too much lee-
way. Though Ms. Murravillow has officially committed
no crimes, I expect the investigation of Aeron Mason
and his accomplices. It is both shocking and disturbing
to think that a boy of twelve is capable of escaping
Longleath's prison—further proof that Mr. Mason's age
is deceiving.*

*Now, as whispers of the Long Dusk have all in the city
worried, the Longleath Council is rumored to have
begun making preparations for dark times.*

Should we, the Longleath people, not do the same?

*As dangerous times approach, we cannot forget that
the Second Rift War was started by a rogue Mason.
An example must be made of the duplicitous Ms.
Murravillow.*

*And we should hope that history has no interest
in repetition.*

She let the newsleaf unfold and fall to the waves. But
Crump's voice echoed in her head.

*Long Dusk? Accomplice? Duplicitous? Dolts like this are
the reason for the vizier's search. The city needs a strong leader
for whatever lies ahead. Instead, people listen to garbage from
Chestter Crump.*

Paloma looked out over the sea and the sky beyond, wondering if she were a fool to return home empty-handed.

CHAPTER 41

THE HEAD AND
THE HEART

"Throach! Ye fool," said Lamark. "Thought the sedimoctid got the best of ye. Yeats'll be glad to see 'is son's still alive."

Lamark looked up from Aeron, wondering why the boy seemed to have gone all-the-sudden deaf.

"Yeats's son, I am no longer," said Throach. With purple burns up and down the right side of his face, Yeats's farm-hand no longer looked so young.

Lamark dared not look down and draw attention to Aeron; but he hoped the boy had taken heed to his advice. Instead, he gestured toward the heartfruit grove. Night had all but come and the heartfruit grove twinkled with the sweetness of summer.

"Surprised to see ye here without—" Lamark broke off. A loud snap came from the grove and one whole teak tree came crashing down to the aerth.

"You were right to think me dead," said Throach, turning to the grove and showing only the scarred side of his face.

"The last thing I remember was boiling black pus searing my face, eyes, and hands."

Lamark felt a brief flush of air around his ankles—Aeron using Throach's distraction, he hoped. Then the young man turned back to Lamark and continued.

"When I woke, he was there, and the pain was gone. A man who takes death and turns it into life is a true father. My father is in the grove right now harvesting more heartfruit than he has ever seen. Enough for every man still in the Aerohive, he says. Enough to build an army. An army I'm to lead. Think of it! A boy orphaned by the Huntress, taken up by the Wraeth. With Praeth Viru's guidance, I will rid the Aerth of the primen germ."

"But ye forget, Throach," said Lamark, "that ye are primen too."

A flicker of lightning illuminated the cliff. Lamark's reddish hair, weathered frame, and stout body looked like a shadow compared to Throach's young, broad frame.

"I have no knowledge of my parents," he said. "But one of them had Orangu blood. Like you, Lamark."

The nip of a hungry wind cut at Lamark's face like the one that had jarred Skylo, poor fellow, from his shoulder. The gust tasted hot and steamy, as if the breath of the grove itself.

Just keep 'im distracted fer a few moments longer 'n' Aeron'll slip back through Corie's small door. Then I can—

"Tell me," said Throach, gesturing with his hands. "You once had quite the fleet of ships. Did you not? Even a few marinaers for bigger cargo. They say the second biggest armada—behind Beck Murravillow's Longleath Trading Company. You could have that again. You could command the ships yourself. Admiral Lamark Bronta, Merchant of Herraz—what a ring that has…"

"So that's what the Wraeth 'ave in mind then?" said Lamark. "Take the free world by force, tear it apart, and get rid of all primen?"

"Not only primen," said Throach. "Everything that lives and breathes. Animals, plants, primen. It's the same view the Huntress had. The world is pure chaos. Too much is out of our control. But the Wraeth believe in reductionism. Less is more! Less is order! All we need is air and heartfruit."

"Ye forget," said Lamark, "that the 'untress also believed there be some great gent in the sky who'd see their primen sacrifices as good deeds and give birth to 'em once more in a better Aerth. Who's lookin' out for the Wraeth?"

"That's it exactly," said Throach, throwing his hands wide and turning back to the grove.

Lamark turned over his shoulder. Twenty yards higher on the cliff, the tree struck out and up from Corie's door. At first, Aeron was nowhere to be seen. But then something moved on the tree.

Past the midway point on the tree, Aeron stood on one of the long hanging branches. Like a herdsman's whip, the foothold snapped and Aeron leapt upward, catching hold of the next branch with two arms.

At the top of the tree, light radiated like a star. Aeron's gaze was fixed upon it. The Grapple.

"What do you see, Lamark?" asked Throach.

Lamark's heart froze for fear as he turned back to the grove. If Aeron was spotted before reaching the Grapple, Viru would come and destroy them in an instant.

"Don't you see there is nothing else? This life is all there is and all that matters. So eat all the heartfruit and drink all the purador and know as many women as we can! If I wanted anything else, I would not even be a man."

The sweet scent of an opened heartfruit wafted from the grove.

"I see," Lamark began, considering what to say so as not to give himself away. "I see two men, 'n' an entire people with a twisted sense o' what's true. In a past life, maybe I would agree with ye. But fifty years ago I met my Waevy, 'n' she showed me that—man to woman, east to west, neath to Orangu—being together is king."

"*Waeve,*" said Throach, "I look forward to knowing her too."

Lamark lunged forward, drilling into Throach's solid abdomen. Arms entangled, the two crushed hard down to the ground. Bone clapped against bone. Throach drove an elbow between Lamark's legs, and Lamark smashed a bloody fist to his temple in return.

They rolled once, twice, three times over. A chill air gusted from below, reminding them they must be at the edge of the cliff.

Somehow, Throach ended up on top with Lamark's neck in his hands. He pressed his thumbs hard into Lamark's throat and thrust the man's head hard against the aerth. A slap of thunder enveloped them with an instant of light. Throach's face was demonic. Then, Lamark caught his hand on a rock and drilled it into Throach's left ribs.

Throach recoiled and threw two clenched fists straight down. Lamark rolled left and then twisted back and launched a foot into Throach's gut. The man doubled back to his knees, stunned. Lamark seized the rock and lunged.

Now Lamark's knee pinned Throach to the ground. Swatting away a desperate punch, Lamark reared back. His left fist crashed downward into Throach's ribs again.

Throach's muscles tightened beneath Lamark's knee. He gripped Throach's face with his free hand and pressed it back. Throach's eyes gaped, seeing how close they were to the abyss.

Lamark yanked the stone behind his head. He slammed one more blow to the rock. A large chunk hit Throach's temple as an intense thrust of wind erupted from behind, causing him to lose the rock. Tumbling over Throach, he drilled his fists into the ground. Straddled over Throach, he felt the man's wheezy gasps.

The wind died. From the right, a tree gave out a curdling groan. Lamark turned. Endless, unbroken clouds stretched from the sea to the moon. The mist had thickened, but a trim of moonshine illuminated the tree. And it was breaking.

"Lamark!" Aeron shouted, hugging a branch near the top. The world became eerily quiet. The tree moaned once more, this time loudly.

He dashed the twenty yards over to the tree and, without hesitation, vaulted through the air toward the trunk while rain cut sideways against his face in hard pellets.

Lamark crashed against the trunk right where the wood had begun to split a third of the way up.

Wooden splinters pierced his skin and something warm dripped down his legs.

Like a bandage, Lamark squeezed the wood with all his might to keep it from splitting. He looked up to Aeron, and the boy held the Grapple in his hand at the top of the tree. His eyes were closed and he seemed to be saying something.

The wind picked up and Lamark felt the force of his arms beginning to wane. But even as the blood drained from his wounds, Lamark clenched his arms and legs tightly like a belt keeping the tree together. It helped to imagine the tree was his wife.

At the thought of her, remorse ripped through him.

Promised 'er I'd be back for dinner. I'm sorry, Waevy.

A chill passed down Lamark's spine. A few feet away at the edge of the cliff loomed the dark, lithe, leathery figure with one gloved hand. He looked stronger even than when crushing the neath.

Viru held up his white hand. From the heartfruit, the black flameflower exuded an immense energy. The Wraeth's lips moved, but Lamark heard no words. Instead, thousands of shimmering purple and black particles, like a swarm of bees, rushed toward him.

A cosmic heat, hotter even than sun on the hardpan, spread over his body. The blaze roared into his shoulder, causing it to sizzle and stiffen. Next pins of heat attacked his thick upper arm and crystallized like a figurine. Then his elbow followed, frozen like the handle of a pitcher. The Aero crashed into his every fiber, paralyzing as it went.

Inch by inch, the heat spread up and down his body until he was nothing more than a crystal statue.

The head and the heart went last. Lamark thought of his wife as his last fiber turned to glass.

Waeve.

CHAPTER 42

THE SIÑADO

"You *demon!*" Aeron shouted.

Viru now stood beside him, and Throach smiled, his face burnt and bloody. Both stood on the edge of the cliff.

Below, Lamark was frozen, icy, and shiny. His whole body was now the same orange as his hair but made of crystal.

Aeron's only chance was Manu. He would hang on as long as possible and hope the Last Great Ranger would throw Throach and Viru off the cliff.

"It's over…" said Throach. "Come down and… join us…"

"I won't!" Aeron reached up for the last branch. He grabbed the Grapple and held it in his fingers.

"Finish him then!" screamed Throach, with maybe a hint of fright.

Viru remained steady as the flaps of his black suit lashed with the wind. He hadn't moved a muscle but simply watched what Aeron intended to do…

All of the sudden, the sky above him became frigid while the air below still felt hot like a boiling ocean.

From the corner of his eye, he spotted a deep, dense, and towering cloud descending from somewhere behind him.

The world felt shaky and unstable. Even the air smelled dry and of the ocean all at once. Aeron clenched the tree trunk even tighter, resting his feet on a sturdy branch.

The wind became so strong it felt like a great beast breathing down his neck. He didn't dare turn around. Looking away from Viru for even an instant felt foolish.

Draviño's winds sped up, tearing at his back with immense force. Aeron remembered something he'd read in the Journal about "cumulonimbus clouds" and "an unstable atmosphere."

The look on Throach's face, the roiling winds, and waters like the sound of a train crashing through buildings all confirmed Aeron's suspicion.

Tornado.

In his hand, the Grapple beamed a fluorescent blue. The tiny swirl at its center made more sense now.

All he could do was hold on for dear life. He held on and prayed the storm would strike those two deviants off the cliff. Unless…

Did Viru call the tornado? No, nature cannot be controlled in this way. Can it?

Aeron felt doomed and even worse for Lamark. He was remembering the moment his granddad and sister died as he clung to that branch tighter than a snake. He fell then, and he would fall now.

Aeron's thoughts sharpened.

Never in my life have I ever wanted so badly to know the Aero strong enough to stop this man so I can set sail for the tree. They'll help me right the wrongs done to my family and stop Wraeths like this beast before they ruin this beautiful world.

Then do it! Someone shouted from inside his head.

A lightning bug of light, no bigger than a blueberry and glinting with purples and indigos, floated up from below and hovered next to the Grapple. Hyacinth!

Skylo?

"Say the words!" whispered the voice "The runes written in your Journal..."

He recalled the swirling rune that had cropped up all over the island. Suddenly, the word came to him, like the voice of wind.

"Say it now!"

On the cliff, Viru stretched his arms high and wide. He looked like a man on top of the world, ready to destroy it.

Throach smirked, waiting for Viru's next move.

"Aeron," screamed the voice in his head, *"sing the Aero."*

But he had no idea what to say. He felt hopeless, sick, and disappointed all at once.

The voice that came was Viru's. "Megist—" But as Viru's slow, metered chant began, the words came in a rush to Aeron. Without taking a breath, they emanated from his lungs, as if they sang themselves.

"—Megisto Anemo!"

At once, the Grapple felt like it had been suctioned to Aeron's fingers. In the middle of the cyclone, the air, debris, and rains crashed in every direction, but everything slipped around Aeron like oil and water.

An immense force coursed through him like he was the tornado itself. All he needed was the Grapple to set it free.

Aeron angled the Grapple forward an inch but nothing happened. He held it to his lips and tried commanding the tornado forward, but again nothing.

Then he focused every ounce of his attention on Viru and on his own breath. Like Granddad had taught him to do in tough times, he breathed in deeply and evenly.

Viru was hard to look at, but Aeron's gaze remained steady. Viru's image became blurred as the tornado moved forward.

"Praeth Viru..." Throach bleated. "Do something!"

Viru said nothing, but in a flash, a black and purple arc swished over them like a waterfall.

Aeron gritted his teeth. The strain on him was at the same time painful and magnificent. He aimed his thoughts like an arrow as the vortex consumed them.

After a few seconds, the thrill of it all disappeared.

The regular tornado passed further back on the cliff toward the grove. With the Mossy Mountain high and far in the distance, the whole scene was deadly and eerily beautiful.

And there stood Viru and Throach, unharmed, beneath their Aeroshield.

There was nothing left to do. The tornado had failed.

"We can always do more..." the voice of poor Master Skylo came again. "Together!"

Hyacinth moved closer and closer to the Grapple. Aeron wondered what might happen if they touched when Hyacinth slipped straight through the outer wall of the Grapple. Nothing happened at all.

The flameflower became smaller, like a bird flying toward the sun. For the first time, it occurred to Aeron that there was a sense of distance inside the Grapple.

Skylo's flameflower, no bigger than a pencil-tip now, stopped beside the Grapple's core, which was blue, yellow, and shaped like the sun.

He had harnessed a tornado, but the rune had called for something greater.

What if...

Aeron thought of the old legend.

Not a tornado... a siñado. The tornado on its side.

Aeron worked up every little bit of strength he had left. This time he belted the words loudly and for all to hear.

"*Megisto anemo...*" he sang "*Paranta!*"

In a rapid flourish, the tornado became all the more violent. Its color turned from dim grey to black as it flipped onto its side like a fallen tree.

As if the whirling had not already been powerful, the winds thrashed at least twice as fast. Aeron focused his eyes hard, like an archer prepared to loose an arrow. He breathed in for five full seconds, paused, and exhaled for five full seconds.

The barreling, tearing, chomping beast rolled faster toward Viru and Throach. This time, Aeron did not divert his gaze for even a second. Every last inch of breath would crash down on them. He had no other chance.

The siñado approached them, but Viru looked unafraid. Throach seemed vicious with fear.

"Let go, m'boy!" said the voice. "*You must let go.*"

No! Aeron thought. *Only the perfect Aero can destroy this man! I must focus every bit of energy I have, even if it kills me...*

"Wrong, Aeron! Only nature is perfect," said the voice. "You must let go."

Aeron shook his head with tears in his eyes.

Last time someone said that, Aeron thought, *Granddad and Vella died. I won't. I can't.*

He clung to the tree harder than he imagined himself capable as his fingers screamed with fatigue and desperation. Even the crystal-Lamark cracked against such a powerful force.

The siñado passed the final few feet. As it crushed down on Viru and Throach, the shield vanished, and Aeron felt an unfathomable wave of relief.

Then the siñado continued forward... right toward him.

"You cannot control it, Aeron," said the voice in his head.

I can...

He refocused his eyes and breath and gave in to one vast bout of effort. He thought so hard his mind could have crumbled into thousands of pieces.

It had destroyed the heartfruit grove and Praeth Viru, but it would not kill him.

The siñado barreled over the cliff, straight for him. The wind was so strong and the tree so wet that Aeron slipped, but it didn't matter.

Lamark's crystallized body shattered. The teak tree, with Aeron clutching it, went falling... falling... falling... toward the churning waters.

Shearing winds pressed against his belly and legs. His cheeks cooled as he passed through a thin, misty cloud. As he passed through the sea smoke, a tingle of heat on his fingers reminded him about the Grapple.

Rather than splintering his each and every atom against the hard crack of water, Aeron felt the kiss of pillows on his cheeks as if the ocean had opened up and accepted him as its own.

CHAPTER 43

WAVING GOODBYE

◇◇◇◇◇◇

Head resting on the door, Waeve scraped at its flaking yellow paint. The number three was tilted sideways so she straightened it. She took a deep breath and stepped back.

Draviño ended, as always, with an abrupt lurch. The Blue Bat was pillaged and looted dry. Her store, The Blue Rose, needed little more than a new coat of paint.

She'd spent that week cloistered in their home, waiting day and night for Lamark to return. He never did. Instead, she was left with his gritty voice in her head.

"You stay 'ere, Waevy. It'll be nice—a stay-at-'ome 'oliday. We're going nowhere till Draviño kicks the bucket. Not even the store. I'll be back fer supper."

All week Waeve waited by their window, as she had for her mother as a little girl. Day after day, the raucous winds, fires, and walloping hail continued until finally it stopped. Her mother never returned from the war; nor did Lamark's bowling belly come rumbling through her doors.

But *Draviño* was over. Buildings lay in ruin, thousands of primen were dead, and debris lay scattered in every nook and cranny.

She inserted her brass key with a pink tassel and turned, but it was already unlocked.

Her heart froze behind a flash of hope.

Of course! My Marky must have hidden here knowing my plants would keep him safe and nobody would come looting.

She called her store a "closed chain plantery." This meant each and every plant had a purpose for the survival of every other plant. The pungent fumes of one Scarmanagia may feed the little tree above it, which gave oxygen to every other plant, which could then grow and add their own bits to nature's chain of wisdom.

"Marky!" she called, walking through two clusters of plants organized by color and size. A clatter came from the store room in the back. "Lamark!" she cried in a crisscross of fear and excitement.

"Clean. Well-stocked. Fragrant," said a voice that was not Lamark's. "One might never know the country around us is destroyed."

She heard three heavy footsteps from thick work boots as a burly woman with silvery-blond hair toppling from an egg-shaped head appeared from the back room.

"Who?" Waeve stammered and retreated a step. "Who are you?"

"I have never seen such an exotic collection," said the woman. "You are quite the plantress..."

"Please." Waeve squirmed. "Whatever you want... I want no trouble."

"And why do you assume I bring trouble?" asked the woman, touching the leaves of a hanging plig fern. The plant leaned away from her touch, as if her skin were a poison.

"Because you're..."

"Yes," said the woman. "I was born in Irkalla, raised in Irkalla, and *kill* for Irkalla. But you, Madame Bronta, are no target of mine."

Waeve's hair stood on edge.

This Irkal knows things. Maybe she knows about my Marky…

"Then what is it you want, miss—"

"You may call me Goth."

"What is it you want, Miss Goth? I have herbals, oils, salves, powders, teas, even some—"

"I require Dreamroot… among other things."

"Dreamroot?" asked Waeve curling her brow. "I'm not sure I've ever heard of dreamroot. What does it do? Maybe I could interest you in—"

"You do have Dreamroot," the way Goth said the sentence sounded like one eerie word. "Hidden back there in your vault."

Vault?

"Now you will tell me where the rest is," said Goth, plucking a yellow strawberry from the plant on the desk.

Waeve approached the desk and took a seat in the chair. She reached to open one of the drawers and found it had been reorganized, though certainly not by this woman.

"Ah!" Waeve said, pretending to have realized her mistake. "I see the confusion. Our stores mention more how much Dreamroot can be *made* from that little one you have there. Not how much we have."

Goth grumbled and narrowed her eyes.

"After all," said Waeve. "How much of such a valuable substance do you think we could have?

"Fine," said Goth. "But I'll be having a second look around. There are other things I need anyway. Things we cannot acquire in the north."

"Isn't that enough?" Waeve bluffed. "The Dreamroot, I mean. Silly me has never had the courage to try it. But you are brave. I'm sure you've—"

"Yes," Goth interrupted. "I have drunk tea of Dreamroot—in that dream I found my traitor father and killed him. When I woke, he was dead. My dream became reality... but this Dreamroot is not for me. So I need more."

"Welcome to have a look," said Waeve tapping a foot. "And I'll help you with anything else you may need."

"If you expect payment," said Goth, admiring a jar that held a silver-rimmed pine cone suspended in some kind of glowing liquid, "you will receive none."

"I prefer information anyway," said Waeve.

Goth ran two ringed fingers between the bridge of her nose and her eye, trying to hide a tear.

"Oh," sighed Waeve. "What is it?"

"Your mate, and his brother..." Goth turned away.

Lamark only has a sister... unless it's...

"The Ranger killed my twin," Goth said, now stoic again. She yanked at a leaf of the indoor tree. "Murdered in cold blood and stole his horse... you owe me a debt."

"You must be mistaken," said Waeve. "My Marky swore he'd never fight again!"

"Damn right he won't," said Goth with a violent sneer.

Waeve rose from her desk and approached the row of plants where Goth stood. "Please, ma'am," Waeve said, "Please tell me where my Marky is. Is he safe?"

"As safe as my brother," said Goth.

Waeve's confused frustration boiled. The plants in the room stood straighter and the room had grown hot. "What are you saying?"

"I'm saying," said Goth, "that your *Marky* is safe as any dead man I know. And I've made sure all of Elevana knows it."

Waeve's chest pains ignited, and she fumbled for her medicine. The small jar shattered to the ground. Breath short and heavy, she rummaged through her oils. Waeve knocked three jars on their sides before finding the bluish Hydragon mineral she needed.

Her hand trembled violently, spilling a third of the bottle before landing one drop on her tongue.

Her pulse slowed as numbness ricocheted through her bloodstream. She leaned up against the window and blinked away tears.

It can't be true.

She watched blood-red and white blossoms swish over the dusty ground. A yellow-billed bird trilled, perched atop the wall across the street. Two boys stood below it, painting on the walls where the street artists always worked.

One of them, a short boy with a black cap and sandals, stepped back to admire their work.

The background used to be sky blue, but now it was black. On it was the most handsome face she had ever seen.

Beneath it he'd written:

THE MERCHANT OF HERRAZ

The letters were wiry and written in orange—the same color as Lamark's hair.

Painted on the wall to the left was:

NEIA ALASTOS—REST EASY

CHAPTER 44

OLD ARCHES STATION

◇◇◇◇◇◇

The orange moon was setting across the sky from the rising sun.

From above, the barrel man called something down to the captain about a straight shot to port.

The captain caught the message and relayed it to the crowd. "Welcome to Oriendo!" the woman shouted. "And the city of Longleath."

A wave of cheers buzzed around the deck as every passenger craned over the starboard rail for a glimpse.

On the blueberry backdrop, Longleath was radiant. As they slowed, the bow ceased to rise and fall.

"Is that the Arbor Skyline?" asked a girl to Paloma's left.

"It must be," said her friend, pointing. "And look! that must be where they play Cannaroo!"

The view from the deck caught the skyline and everything beneath it in a seraphic golden hue. The lorries, the fruiters, the scramblers, the palace, even the distant stadium appeared like a relic of paradise.

Coming to Longleath for the first time must be a shock. Buildings grown from wood and silver, lorries with no drivers, signs for free food markets… all thanks to Epiphysics. There is no city more natural than this one. But once these primen get to know Longleath, and it gets to know them, they'll see that it too is cracked and rotting and weaker than ever.

The cheers died down and the quiet rustling of the sea returned.

Only a small sliver of water lay before them. Gentle and calm, it sparkled with orange flickers of sun and moon. The tide leaned against the land gently without any crests or foam. Lightly penciled clouds rose over the hills beyond the morning-stroked city.

Her nose tingled at the smell that millions of primen make in living.

The marinaer ship, usually filled with cargo, made its final turn and the crewman locked it into port with chains. Only two other marinaers were docked, but neither had any signs of life. The bioluminescent-rimmed chimneys dimmed and their ship came to a standstill.

A pit fell in Paloma's chest. The Longleath port was clean and orderly, lit only by the low hallowed light from a few watchtowers. Compared to the chaotic bee-swirl of Port Elevana, Paloma found it hard to believe the two places were only five days apart.

She stayed on the rail, watching thousands of primen filing frantically out into the port square. The controlled chaos of it reminded her of something Lamark, of all people, had said in the abandoned church.

"True, *Te Draviño* is a harsh mistress, but the foolish men make it evil. Panic turns primen into sheep. There's no thinkin'. No reasonin.' No order. Nobody listens. But it's beautiful and natural and easy here. This be the Elevana bargain, and it keeps the leaders away. Ye 'ave that in the north, so go back there. A colony without a queen be a colony diseased."

At once, she felt a striking truth. Longleath was no different. Where there was order, people were eager to follow. But primen became headless in the absence of a true leader.

And I've failed to bring back the one the city needed.

A nightjar alighted on the railing nearby. She used to love playing with them when she was a girl. Black and with slick feathers, each nightjar's head was some kind of intricate pattern, like a butterfly's wings.

This one had a brown beak and bright grey circles around a pair of juddering blue eyes. The sight of it made Paloma sick. She felt as if she had walked in on a conversation she was not meant to hear—old friends spreading rumors about her.

"Best get going, miss," said a young sailor from behind. "Bridges are closed today. You'll have to take the tunnel…"

Paloma shuddered. Nothing sounded worse than the dark tunnels of the Longleath tube right now.

"All of the bridges?" she asked.

"Indeed, ma'am," he said, "some kind-of drilling, I'd wager."

The young man nodded and turned back to cleaning the deck. On the back of his uniform was a crest she had seen every day for all of her days—an oak tree with feathers instead of leaves.

HOUSE MURRAVILLOW: PATIENCE IS THE SHIELD

The ship must have been lent by Longleath Trading Company.

Oh, Father… always the statesman. Lending boats for refugees is why I love you.

Thoughts of his company stirred up a flurry of neatly buried questions. He'd been red-face-furious as she walked out the door, and she wondered what kind of expression would be waiting on her return. How long could they talk before topics turned to Cannaroo, and why "Longleath needed her around"?

She gave one last wistful look at the ship and stepped out onto the cross-bridge. Though Longleath was radiant as ever, disgust mixed with her fear, leaving a taste of bile in the back of her throat. Whirring lorries buzzed as primen awoke and went on their way.

Paloma had not even set foot on the port island where all ships debarked when the throngs of guilt and anxiety began.

I forgot that a place can make you feel so terrible with so much as a single breath of its air.

She stepped down from the pass onto the concrete. The port island had only a few buildings and served as a point of entry to the rest of the city. The port islands had been established when the Irkals were driven out one hundred and fifty years before and the city was renamed Longleath.

At least three huge Paladin patrolled the port square clad in their regal white uniforms.

"They only let the sharpest knives into the Paladin," a stodgy man informed his wife, bowing his bald head to the Paladin as he passed. "Smartest, strongest, most capable."

Paloma followed behind the man and woman as the crowd funneled past the ticketing house and a not-yet-open market.

"This tunnel will take us to the trains," he said. "From there we could go anywhere."

Two Paladin were posted at the mouth of the tunnel, one of them holding his helmet against his hip. As they passed, the stodgy man bowed to the young, bald, helmet-less

Paladin. The young man bowed his chiseled, bald head at them. Above a spotless breastplate, the man's face was handsome and had an air of fairness, despite the scar around his left eye.

The way down to the tunnel snaked back and forth like a ball run. At first, the lightseeds were small and gave off a dainty light. She was thinking about the lightseeds in the secret passage beneath Billburry's Haberdashery when a large sign caught her attention. Three dashing Paladin glowed in front of a shady black background.

TO BECOME A LEADER,
ONE MUST FIND A LEADER TO FOLLOW

"You'd think they would find a better way for us," said the man, "seeing as our homes are destroyed."

"No," his wife shook her head. "We are refugees, from a refugee island. If you are surprised, you're more of a fool than I thought."

Paloma's hand slid along the rail. The stone left an imprint of winter on her. Above, the lightseeds had grown as the ceiling opened ever higher. It always amazed her that primen had been able to find and repurpose such massive underground systems, even if the renovation and rail-laying had taken one hundred years.

"Tell me again where your sister lives in Stokelyn," said the man to his wife. They passed a closed-down stairwell, which led somewhere that Longleath really didn't want her to go, given the Paladin standing beside the tape. A hint of fresh air mingled with the dankness of the tube as she passed the stairwell.

The mention of Stokelyn sent Paloma thinking about her family once more and her father's disdain that she still chose to live there. "In the filth."

"Cleaner down here than I'd—" the woman cut herself off. A canvas tent had been pitched atop the tracks beside a flimsy old bed with red and yellow stains.

After a few minutes walking in the low light, Paloma spotted another offshoot ahead to the right. Her father had made her promise to avoid the tubes as much as possible, but if memory served, they were walking beneath the station and had another half-mile before reaching the gate.

As they approached, the stairwell became more obvious, though danker and more dubious than the prior.

It was somber and quiet in this darker part of the tunnel, and all she could hear were footsteps and a few whispering children.

Nearing from behind came the sound of scurrying feet that were too small to be a priman and too bold to be a rodent.

They've got stray dogs down here now?

A woman's hand nudged Paloma to the side and the pattering continued past her. Now beneath one of the larger lightseeds, Paloma caught sight of its hairy back. It was, without question, a priman, but the tiniest she had ever seen, and with shiny bronze hair. The shadowy figure bounced over the rail and padded toward the stairwell.

No Paladin?

This time the sweet scent of freshly baked doughbeans leaked down from above.

A man bumped her from behind, nearly knocking her over. She stopped walking and, on instinct, felt with one hand for her coinpouch—which she had lost on the Grey Road after first meeting Aeron.

A light wind swished by her ankles. Something scurried past. As it did, the purador slipped like soap through her distracted fingers.

Paloma groped out with both hands, but the tiny, bronze haired priman dashed off.

The tiny thief scampered beneath the tape without needing to crouch and, using both hands and feet, took to the stairs.

Where's she going? And how did she...

Rapidly, she replayed the scene in her head.

Distraction, misdirection, all a good thief needs.

Taking to a sprint, Paloma hurdled the bannister, a fallen trash bin, and the tape marked "no entry." She climbed the stairs two at a time and emerged in a dungeon-like room that smelled of rancid potatoes. Even the floor was slick and felt filmy with blood, mucus, or worse.

At the end of the room, a pair of double doors were rimmed with light. A rat squealed and knocked an old mop to the floor. She slid across the room and edged the door open a crack.

Old Arches Station, zooming with the buzz of busy primen. No one appeared to be watching, so she slipped through the door and out into the bright lights of Old Arches. Straight ahead were five long rail rattlers, all still boarding but the nearest one. To her left was the gate, hosting a long line of dispirited primen who'd come pouring in from the docks.

On the wall behind them started the great arch for which this station was named. It was one of the first grown buildings in Longleath, they said, and one of the best feats of Epiphysics to date. She traced the sleek wooden bend for its duration until culminating to her right.

There she is!

The mousy priman leapt onto one of the open gangways between two black and yellow cars.

"All clear!" called the conductor, his head poking out the window. He gave the metal an encouraging pat and all ten wheels on the carriage in front of her trundled to the right. Her eyes darted frantically in every direction.

At first she walked alongside, staying at pace with the conductor.

Relax. I can find out where this one's headed and take the next rattler. But what if she's gone by then?

"Sir," Paloma called. "What direction are you headed?"

"This rail rattler heads westerly," he tipped his cap as the rail rattler picked up speed. "To the end of Oriendo!"

West.

Her head shot arrows of reason, one after another.

What's a half bottle of purador to a Murravillow? She probably won't even know what it is. And if so, who cares that some little thief lives a few extra years?

But Paloma's gut yanked at her every fiber.

Follow her. The Longleath Council wouldn't listen, even if you had the purador. That's no proof. Forget working with Father. Go west. Find Manu, the leader you need. He will teach you to be a Ranger. Go.

She sprinted alongside the moving rattler. Only two cars remained to her left. The first passed by, and the gangway was closed.

The final car was the observation. It had wide windows and was painted a deep shade of yellow, like the late evening sun.

The cars were picking up speed, and Paloma had one chance to leap for the back-most platform.

She staggered her feet and, with a well-timed leap, latched on to one of the railings. Puling herself over the ledge, she gave a huge sigh of relief. Now on the car, all she needed was to track down the thief.

Such a strange one won't be hard to find.

As they slipped out the rattler door and away from Old Arches, Paloma heard shouts come from the station. How could she not have been seen?

Well, I probably earned the front page of The Pulse *again...*

She turned and slid open the door to the platform. Inside was the most jam-packed rattler Paloma had ever seen.

The thief could be anywhere.

CHAPTER 45

THE SAILS OF SOLITUDE

All Aeron felt was deep and rhythmic drumming. Between thumps, the world hung black, silent, and empty. He may have spent a minute, a month, or a millennium floating in the empty void.

A distant, muffled voice came from directly above the drumming, like a god. The drum felt tribal, as if inside him.

From nowhere, a massive wave, the size of ten sailboats, crashed toward his place in the void.

"Aeron."

Aeron woke with a gasp and sat bolt upright, drenched. Manu stood over him, holding an upturned bucket.

"Finally," said Manu. "Have a nice sleep?"

Aeron coughed and wrung water from the cut of his shirt before rising to test his balance.

A ship?

They seemed not to be moving. He held on to the rail and oriented himself to the bright grey morning. In every direction he saw an unbroken expanse of sea.

"I'm…" Aeron said, "not dead…"

"No," agreed Manu, tossing a dry rag at Aeron.

"And Skylo?"

"Unconscious, below."

"And…" Aeron began timidly, knowing already the answer. "Lamark?"

Manu turned toward the bulwarks and shook his head solemnly. "Everything I know about boats," he said, "I owe to him. Including this ship. Bless him for letting us use it."

"I'm sorry," said Aeron and looked down at the surf breaking against the hull. Everything he knew about boats, he owed to books.

"My only real friend," said Manu. "But life continues."

A simple sadness permeated the air.

"How long has it been?" Aeron asked. "And how did I survive that fall?"

"Seven days."

A week? And we haven't reached Oriendo?

"Your Murravillow friend drives a lorry well. We arrived at the port in time, but barely. I'll let her tell you the story, someday. After securing her board, I entered the water. From the port, it was a decent swim to where Lamark had the ship anchored. But from there it was quick. I arrived in time to see Skylo fall through. One moment there was only mist. Everywhere I looked. Mist," said Manu. "Then something happened above—a sound like the sky breaking open. A few moments later, the ship shook and something thudded below. There he was. Not long after, so were you. Grapple and all."

Aeron's eyes blew open. He made a quick turn, and as the boat lurched, he nearly lost his footing.

"Easy," said Manu. "Find your feet first."

Aeron hurried atop the chestnut brown deck toward the checkerboard hatch. He bent and found it too heavy to lift. With a second try and a deeper squat, he flung open the latch and stepped onto the top stair of the entrance below.

"Skylo?" Aeron called below, descending slowly. The ship lurched again and Aeron stumbled forward, catching himself on the rail near the lower deck.

The light was low. Natural light seeped through old satin curtains pulled over a set of four rectangular windows at the back of the cabin.

Aeron was remembering a drawing from one of the books he'd read on sea commerce in mandatory school. It was the interior of a yacht, bright with red velvet lining, furniture, and treasures from across the rifts. An ornate candelabra hung from the ceiling. Toward the back was a large captain's table, which held a large book and a pot of ink.

"Manu," Aeron called upward. "What's the name of this ship?"

"*Winflow*," Manu's voice came from above.

Winflow... it's the same...

But instead of a book and exotic ornaments, the table held a tired old man. Aeron passed a small door that led to the kitchen-galley and approached the table.

Though the Sage might have been as old as some of Aerth's great trees, his frailty made him appear more a memory than a man. Aeron touched the back of his hand to Skylo's forehead. He was ice cold, but still his chest rose and fell like an old water mill.

Behind Skylo, in a dusty chair with engravings up and down its frame, rested Aeron's haversack. He approached it and found three remaining heartfruit.

As the stern dipped lower, Aeron stumbled again. He threw back the curtains to find the windows caked and dusty, only sitting a few feet above the water.

"Manu..." Aeron called again. "What are you doing?"

"Eased the halyard tension," he shouted. "Trying to raise the bow, maybe catch a bit of wind."

So that's why we're still at sea. No wind…

As the ship evened, a peculiar sound rolled across the floorboards, like a marble on the move.

A shine of light peeked forward from a less than comfortable-looking couch…

The Grapple!

He pounced like a cat and caught the Grapple before it could roll away again.

The stone looked and felt different than before—colder than he remembered, more translucent, and with cloudier blues and oranges. The tiny flame at its center still revolved but was obscured by haze. A chill rippled from his heels up to his shoulders.

Aeron placed the stone onto the palm of a hand-shaped wooden jewelry holder. Staring it down, he considered trying the Aero that had healed Yeats. A draft of icy air emptied into the room and a second wave of coldness shivered from his elbows to ankles.

Nearby, Hyacinth floated in the center of a plain storage jar. The bottom was filled with an inch of water and reflected its light, but the flameflower's lilacs and indigos had shrunk to the size of a pea.

It's like they're angry or sick or both… retreating the way a depressed priman would, only making things worse.

"Ggrrrahh" Manu rumbled through the hatch. "How can we beat them there if there's no wind…"

Them?

Aeron turned back to Skylo. In a neat pile next to his head was the Map of the Reddheart. Aeron took off the string and laid it flat on the couch. He sat on the crunchy cushion and allowed the map to materialize.

At first the ink appeared on the paper, but it didn't stop there. It built up and up until the map had taken center on the Huntrian Sea between Elevana and the huge country of Oriendo to the north.

Elevana could fit one hundred times in Oriendo…

He touched a hand to the map where their yacht lay. The water was cool and felt like gelatin. Only ten miles separated them from the mouth of the Northerly River, but according to the map, they hadn't moved more than a mile. The current must have been pushing them in a circle.

"Map's no use," said Manu, startling him from behind, "when you are marooned at sea." To fit inside the cabin, he had to hunch his neck like he had water in one ear.

"How long has it been?" Aeron asked.

"Three days," said Manu. "Like the current knew we were getting close and put a stop to it."

"The Wraeth?" Aeron asked.

"If you ask me," said Manu, directing his eyes to Skylo, "we should be worried about the Irkalla instead. The Wraeth are…" he trailed off and picked up one of the books on the shelf behind them. *The Bat, the Bee, and the Boomerang: Tomorrow's Tales from Long Ago.* "A faery tale."

"How can you say that!" Aeron's jaw unlocked from its hinges. "You fought Viru. You've been ranging half your life."

"Indeed I have. And it is why one hundred million Irkals worry me more than one Wraeth… this book has a tale of mine, you know. Slaying the Huntress. I will add one more chapter before death. The End of Irkalla, they will call it. But this time it will be easier. Once I get to the Tree, they will come right to me."

"You think," Aeron's brow furled, "you alone can beat an entire species?"

Manu shook his head and turned over his right shoulder for the larger map on the wall, the one that showed all of Aerth. He held one finger on Irkalla and one on the Reddwood Citadel, where the Tree of Knowledge lived. Then he traced them both back in the center toward one another.

"See where they meet?"

"Longleath..." Aeron gasped.

"Your Oriendo brothers fight the battle. I end the war," he brushed some dust off his jacket. "People will only remember how it ended. With me."

"What's happened to you?" Aeron asked, baffled. "What's happened to Emmanwell Everett, the Last Great Ranger? Or were all those valiant stories just you swooping in at the end to take credit?"

"Too quick a tongue for a boy so young," he continued, "you and the girl both. Watch it."

A quick tongue...

"Say that again!" Aeron shouted and jumped off the couch.

"I said, you and Paloma'd better watch—"

"She does have a quick tongue. Doesn't she?" Aeron laughed, bolting for the kitchen. It was small and barren, but the chute was where he'd read about it the year before.

"About that..." said Manu from the other room while Aeron was busy unscrewing the latching lid. He came, hunched over, to the door of the galley. "I must tell you something."

Paying little attention to him, Aeron squeezed past Manu and out the door. He felt the chill of the Grapple reach out to him as he passed it and the unconscious Skylo.

Still don't know what to do about you. But I know how to get us moving...

He plucked one of the final three heartfruit form his haversack. The deck rocked diagonally backward, responding to Manu's weight.

"Tell me what you are doing," said Manu. "We need to save those. If we don't move, those will be our only food supply…"

"No, listen," Aeron said. "I've read about this ship. Sometime during Herraz—I mean Lamark's—voyage to the south, he paid to have *Winflow* converted to a partial marinaer…"

"Lamark never mentioned it."

"Probably because he knew you don't believe in Aeros and Epiphysics and the Wraeth…" Aeron reached a hand into the funnel to make sure it was open. Inside was cold and had a breath to it.

A good sign—she's still alive.

"So you're telling me," Manu said, "because marinaers run on heartfruit, this little yacht won't need any wind? I have my doubts."

"It worked on the lorry the day I met Paloma," said Aeron. "It's going to work now."

"I need to tell you something about your friend Paloma, Aeron."

"One second," he said, holding the heartfruit directly over the chute, eyes closed tightly. The ship lurched and Aeron lost hold of the heartfruit, straight down the chute.

For a few brief moments, nothing happened. Aeron wheeled out of the galley and over to the scummy back windows.

"Aeron," said Manu, approaching the captain's table. "I'm trying to tell you who is responsible for all the rumors against you and the Masons."

Aeron turned his back to the window. His eyes were wide, like an animal being hunted.

For a beat, there was no sound.

"Paloma?" Aeron asked in shock. He moved to speak again, but the emotion had cut his grasp on language.

The ship jolted. Aeron fell back into the chair with his haversack.

"We're moving..." said Manu with amazement. He approached the cabin windows. "By gods. You were right. We'll make the mouth before nightfall and the Tree before you know it. Good work—"

"How do you know it was her?" Aeron asked, running a hand through his hair.

Manu gestured his head toward the man on the table.

"Skylo?"

Manu nodded.

Betrayal coursed through Aeron's veins.

"Tell me from the beginning," said Aeron. "I need to know it all."

Manu's eyes changed from shock to confusion, and he seemed to be looking past Aeron.

"What?" Aeron scowled. "You brought it up. Don't change the subject."

Manu wiped one of the windows with the curtain.

"Come on," Manu said, heading toward the companionway. "There's someone out there..."

CHAPTER 46

MUSICAL THIEVES

"Excuse me," said Paloma to a kind-looking older gentle-man. "Have you seen a small priman with bronze hair?"

"Bronze hair?" the man scoffed. "One might think you were searching for the Kingdom of Termara…"

"Sorry," Paloma passed through the gangway connector. On the beige wall to her right a rectangular window streamed with pins of water.

It was evening, and prairie stretched as far as the eye could see. A layer of clouds cast the whole meadowland in a grey hue. She had never been to Palmaria before, but she expected much of the country to look this way—flat land, emmer wheat, and farms.

She slid open the door and found the next cart dead silent. The sleeper.

Only two cars left. Could she have gotten off? Or maybe she saw me and hid.

Toeing quietly through the cabin, she examined each bed—a young couple, a young pair of twins, a mother and her infant. Paloma squinted at the final bed in the cart. Sub-merged by sheets, the figure matched the thief in size.

Impulsively, she yanked the coverings back.

"Hey!" A young girl, about Paloma's age, shot up in bed. "Do you mind?" She yanked the covers back and lowered her blindfolds.

Paloma entered the final cart, thinking how foolish this whole idea had been and planning her way back to Longleath. She turned to the car's first cabin and gripped the brass handle.

Startled, she bit her lip as a mixture of rage and satisfaction flooded her cheeks. Staring at a sheet of music, a tiny woman hugged a small yellow instrument case against her chest, as a child might a toy.

She slid the door open and it clicked in place.

"*You...*" Paloma growled, her head tilted angrily low as she stepped into the cabin. "You stole my—"

Oh mercy. Look at the hair. It's purple. The thief had silver hair.

"No need," said the woman. "No need to be angry. Plenty of space in the cabin. Join us! We were about to make music."

We were?

The woman had an odd way of speaking, but Paloma needed to think. She plopped down across from the woman. She pulled on both ends of the tube and it turned into quite a nice flute. The woman gripped it, closed her eyes, and played. Any and all suspicions Paloma had went out the door.

The song was penetrating and bright with a semblance of poetry to it. Paloma stared out the window. The sky had gone almost entirely dark, but she made out a large body of water extending to the right with a large town before it.

Her father told her she'd been born to travel. Born outside Eurovea in the Central Rift, daughter of the "the man who shrank the world" as the first to do business between all four rifts, this was the furthest west she had been.

Yellow grass, trees, open roads—the world rolled by like a rolling carnival. She watched and listened to the woman's sweet music, accepting that when she returned, Longleath would see a different Paloma Murravillow. Her father would slot her into the business and, soon enough, she would be dealing crops on marinaers all around the world. Ranging could wait.

The music stopped. When Paloma turned back from the window, a bronze lock of hair rested on the seat, and the woman had disappeared.

CHAPTER 47

THE RIVER OF LIGHT

◇◇◇◇◇◇

"Is he breathing?" Aeron asked, kneeling beside the man covered with seaweed.

Manu crouched low and placed three fingers to the man's neck. "He has a pulse, but it's weak."

Aeron cleared the seaweed and flung it overboard. The man was old and bald save for a long pony tail.

"He's from Indoshina," said Manu. "The facial hair."

Though sodden, the man had the customary wispy beard and mustache of the northern country.

"Dangerous?" Aeron asked. Indoshina had been controlled by Irkalla for a century.

Manu shook his head. "Indoshinese hate Irkalla more than you'd expect. Irkals rule by fear."

"What's this?" Aeron asked, pointing to a pin on the man's drenched robes.

"Interesting…" said Manu.

Aeron waited for a response.

"I have no idea."

Reading the signs was a key part of being a Ranger, Aeron knew. If the sea-shelled wasp with no stinger was a mystery to Manu, the man's symbol must be a secret one.

Manu pulled the wet cloak off the man as Aeron rose and looked out for a moment.

Though the sun had been gone for hours, this part of Aerth was never cool, and the humidity made Aeron's breath heavy and labored.

"Manu," Aeron began, "could this be… a trap?"

"It could," said Manu, "but I think not."

"You said yourself that Indoshina is in league with Irkalla…"

"Yes. That is why the Wraeth Prince is no fool. If he set a trap, it would be with…"

"With who?" Aeron turned back to Manu and clicked on a lamp attached to the mast. The man was thin and gaunt but had a mosaic of tattoos across his arms, shoulders, and upper body.

"Someone you would never suspect," Manu said and took a step toward the lower deck. He stopped next to Aeron.

"Like a girl from Longleath."

A javelin of pain crushed into his mind.

No. Meeting Paloma was sheer randomness. It can't be true.

Manu put his enormous hand on Aeron's shoulder.

"Or you…" Aeron pulled away and faced the water once more.

Aeron could hear the smile in Manu's words. "Good," he said, "you're learning…"

Moonlight shined through a thin film of mist. The first peek of land revealed itself in a dark haze.

From the distance, the bluff appeared more like a high and rocky gorge.

Aeron turned back and knelt beside the unconscious man. He traced a finger on the edges of an exquisitely detailed fenix tattooed on the man's upper arm. He stirred in a subtle response to Aeron's touch.

Everything is connected, Skylo said. This man must have come to us for a reason. Maybe he knows the truth.

"Move aside," said Manu from behind.

Aeron shimmied toward the man's legs and saw Manu held a canteen in each hand.

"Hold his mouth open."

He pulled on the stranger's old, cold, bristly chin with two fingers, exposing a scalloped set of yellow teeth.

Manu tilted the canteen forward and a slow, molasses-like drizzle oozed onto the man's tongue. The aerthy, animal aroma sent chill sent through Aeron.

Moshrum.

Manu removed the first canteen and poured the second in a slightly quicker drizzle. Water. After a few seconds, he placed them both to the ground.

"What do we do now?" asked Aeron.

"Wait."

Aeron examined a second, vaguer tattoo. It resembled one he had seen before in the Journal.

The Journal! Why didn't I think of that before? There will be something about the wasp crest, and maybe for Skylo…

Aeron felt his breast pocket. No Journal. He wheeled around and bounded for the companionway. Still open, he took the loud steps two at a time but slowed down after remembering his fall.

The cabin was lit in the strangest hue Aeron had ever seen—a rainbow of blues and violets and saffron yellows. Aeron turned on a lamp so the Grapple and Hyacinth were not the only sources of light.

On the couch, the map seemed to be showing something new, but Aeron's priority was finding the Journal.

He turned the galley over, yanking open every drawer and cabinet. Next he tried the couches, removing every cushion and furniture covering. He moved to the desk and the storage compartments. *Winflow* was like a relic, lost in time. The Journal was meant for a ship like this one, but it never appeared.

"No!" Aeron growled, "No! Nooo!" Sitting on the uncomfortable couch, his blood boiling, Aeron cupped his head in his hands. A terrible, oppressive feeling of despair filled him from stomach to crown. He wept, grasping for breath and devoid of hope.

This is the end. I've lost the Journal, Skylo is dying, my family name is in ruins, and I've made an enemy of the darkest man I've laid eyes on. An archivist without his Journal is no archivist at all. Granddad would be humiliated to know me.

A stack of groans floated down the stairs. Aeron swallowed his tears but didn't bother to look up.

"Manu," Aeron croaked, "I've lost the Journal, Manu. I'm nothing without it."

A soft, smallish hand met the round of his back, too small to be Manu's.

Aeron looked up. The old drifter stood next to him, looking down with gentle green eyes. Aeron recoiled with shock, and the man backed a step away. Aeron tried to make eye contact, but the man's body was mesmerizing.

"Your tattoos," Aeron began, "they're... alive."

One of the older tattoos had a large bird twirling around a lonesome mountain with a temple at its peak. Another beside it showed the face of a crying tiger.

The man nodded once.

"Who are you?" asked Aeron.

The man made no reply but pointed to one of the words on his wrist.

"Qing," Aeron read aloud as the man pointed to his own chest. "Your name is Qing. Where have you come from, Qing?"

The man pointed again to one of the tattoos, this time on his shoulder joint.

Then, Aeron felt a lurch and one of the decorative jars toppled over on its shelf.

We're moving. Fast.

"Manu!" Aeron called above. Qing cringed.

"You have sensitive ears," Aeron said. "Me too."

Qing gripped Aeron's head with two hands. At first Aeron tensed, but then he allowed the Indoshinese man to examine his left ear—the one his father had damaged before he could remember.

He let go of Aeron and wiped what teary residue remained on Aeron's cheeks.

"Can you speak?" Aeron asked. Qing shook his head and then turned to Skylo and put a hand on the old man's head.

Aeron bit his lip. "Do you know Master Skylo?"

Qing shook his head and pointed a finger to his own heart. Then, with his other hand he tapped his head and nodded.

"So you, Qing, have not met Skylo but your... order has?"

Qing nodded once and turned toward the kitchen galley. He flicked on the burner and crouched low to the barrel beside the sink. He touched a finger to the spout and then to his lips. From the barrel, he filled the cast iron pot halfway. Moshrum. He placed it on the stove to heat.

He opened the cabinet and rummaged through piles of spices, herbs, and oils, but he poured nothing into the pot.

"What are you looking for?" Aeron asked.

Qing looked back at him as if he were a fool.

Right. He can't answer that.

Qing touched two fingers to his nose and then gestured around the room. *He smells what he needs but can't find it...*

Aeron stepped closer and opened the cabinet beneath the sink. The man's brow raised and he tilted his head. He leaned his cattish whiskers closer to Aeron and then pulled backward.

Qing pointed his middle and index finger at Aeron.

The boy's right hand palmed his chest and eyes swelled for fear.

"Me?"

Qing shook his head and mimed pulling something out of the place where a breast pocket would have been.

Aeron reached two fingers into his vest and pulled out...

The vial from Corie!

Qing held out his hand. Aeron hesitated, but then Grand-dad's words rang in his head.

There comes a point when you must choose who to trust... Maybe I was too quick and too desperate with Paloma, but I know better now. Trust with watchful eyes.

He handed the vial over to Qing. The man uncorked the vial and smelled it. His eyes rolled back a bit, lusting in the rich, aerthy smell of purador. For a moment, Aeron thought Qing might drink it, but then, rather than pouring the purador into the moshrum, he dropped in the whole vial.

He turned the stove off and put on the lid. If he was making what Aeron thought, the purador would take several hours to steep.

"Aeron." Manu's voice came booming through the hatch above. "Come above."

He and Qing made brief eye contact and the Indoshinese man bowed. Aeron returned the gesture and took to the stairs. Halfway up he turned around. Qing was lighting a candle near Skylo's bed and then picked up a small stringed instrument from the corner of the room.

Aeron turned back and climbed the final two stairs.

"Close the latch," said Manu.

Aeron looked at him quizzically but did so.

On either side of them were steep, towering walls of orange rock. Though night, the river refracted moonlight in a way that made everything visible. Ahead lay one hundred yards of water and a bend around the gorge. The air tasted chalky, something like the hardpan.

"Are we already in the Rizon Canyons?" Aeron asked.

Manu held a rolled maroon scroll to his ear, listening to a message.

"Yes," he replied. "Deep in the River of Light. With heart-fruit, *Winflow* is the fastest ship in the Western Rift. Now read this."

Manu held out the still-rolled scroll. He unstrung it and handed it to Aeron, who read the message scrawled in a neat, compact hand.

You must come at once. The Tree has given the signs. She is afraid that someone is coming for her, and faster than you. It is your duty, Manu. We need you straight away, at any cost.

Aeron heard the sound of wings above. A messenger hawk was perched on one of the cross-beams.

Manu gripped the wheel. "Write this down," said Manu, gesturing at the writing station on a stand nearby. "I will arrive by tomorrow eve. The boy and his guide sometime later. E.E."

"What?" Aeron put down the quill. "We're going together, Manu. How is that possible…"

"Not for long, Aeron Mason."

CHAPTER 48

THE CITY-GIRL BLUES

◇◇◇◇◇◇

Paloma rubbed a brutal crook from her neck. Sleeping upright in a cabin with frustration in her bones, she'd awoken feeling worse than terrible.

"Gather your things," the conductor called to no one in particular, passing through handcar number four. "Only stop till the Northerlies." He passed into number five and repeated. "Gather your things…"

All through the night, no one else had entered her cabin, thank haevens. More space for her sorrows.

Paloma stretched her arms and slid the door to the side. She stepped out into the soft shade of light streaming through the evening blinds.

"Uh, excuse me," came a cranky voice from behind.

Paloma stepped to the side to let a brown luggage cart, so large it almost seemed to be pushing itself, pass down the hall. One of the wheels caught her toe, but Paloma remembered her manners and bit her tongue behind a gracious smile. She recognized the girl rolling the trunk from the night before.

"Hey…" Paloma said. "Sorry, I should apologize…"

"For what?" the girl, about Paloma's age, huffed and trundled her bags over the uneven car connector.

"Last night when I... woke you up," said Paloma. "In the sleeper."

"Hmm," the girl mumbled and pushed once more. "Must've been out like a light. Don't recall."

"Can I ask you a question?"

"Just did," the girl said and brushed her bangs to the side, "but I'll allow it."

"You haven't seen a kind of mousy old lady on board. Have you?"

"The fast kind or slow kind?" the girl asked.

Paloma thought this a strange question but knew exactly what she meant.

"Fast," said Paloma.

"Chews like a cow? Or happens to play music?"

"Yes!"

If her suspicions were correct, the thieving woman had been wearing a wig. That's why Paloma had missed the woman with the flute.

"Yes... what?" the girl said with an annoyed look.

"She played the flute."

"Right," she said, "I know that broad. She was in car six last time I checked. Weird lady, or drunk. I'm going that way. I'll point out her cabin."

Paloma stepped into the gangway. The window had no blinds and Paloma saw that morning was waking over a scrubby river town with ramshackle buildings and grey-green pine and oak trees.

They passed into car number five. The left were two floors of cabins while the windows on the right remained covered.

We must be halfway to the Northerlies or more... Will be a long ride back east.

"So what brought you out here anyway," she asked without turning to Paloma, "and why the city-girl blues on your face?"

"Why do you assume I'm from the city?" Paloma asked, slightly annoyed.

"Hair, body, way you speak and act," said the girl. "Pretty obvious you are garbage."

Paloma's voice rose. "Excu—"

"A joke," the girl turned over her shoulder, hair covering her eyes, and gave a thin grin. "I used to live in the city. Good things there too—museums, food, primen from all over. But once I went west…"

One of the wheels jammed in the gap between car six and the connector. Paloma pressed her shoulder into the side of the cart.

"One, two, three," Paloma counted, "lift!"

The cart tumbled forward and clanged against the silver wall of the vestibule. A chorus of grumbling complaints came from the next car.

"Thanks," said the girl, wiping a bead of sweat from her forehead. She was smaller and wider than Paloma but thin. "Your friend should be in the next one. Try the third or fourth cabin. Best of luck."

Paloma nodded and passed into the next car. As they slowed to a halt, Paloma planned how to seize the woman, take back the purador, and get off the train in the brief few minutes they would be stopped.

The train jerked to a standstill. At least half the doors opened on the left side and a gang of primen emptied out into the hall. Paloma weaved around a kind middle-aged woman with dark hair, a group of three children carrying school trunks, a young man with a large box for tools or carpentry, and an older man with glasses and a newsleaf.

"Get out of the way, miss," the older man grumbled. Paloma stepped into the cabin for a moment and allowed him to pass.

When I'm a Ranger, jerks like him will be grateful I'm around to keep them safe. He'll step aside and let me pass...

From what sounded like the next cabin came a thin layer of flute music.

She slipped out into the hall once more. With the prick of time creeping down her neck, Paloma yanked on the next cabin door. Empty. She darted back into the hall, nearly toppling over a young boy, and into the next. No one. Again and again, no mousy old woman.

The last door in car number six lay closed. A glimmer of hope fluttered through Paloma's stomach. Pulling it aside, Paloma heard the conductor's voice from outside. "Next stop, Northerly Neck!"

The feeling died like flowers buried in snow. She stepped into yet another empty cabin and gave a deep, defeated sigh. Her foot reached back and, in a fit of anger, kicked against the hard-wooden sideboard.

"Hello!" came a spritely shout from behind her. "What's the matter, dearie?"

Paloma wheeled around. Standing in the doorway was her thief.

"You!" Paloma barked and lunged forward.

"Meee!" the woman sang, darting nimbly to the right beneath Paloma's grasp.

Paloma faced her up. Standing atop one of the benches, the tiny woman's streaky hair was no longer bronze, nor purple, but a strong shade of beige.

"Who are you!" Paloma demanded, taking one intimidating step forward.

The woman looked less than concerned. She jumped across to the other bench and landed on her backside with a grin.

"Me?" said the woman. "Me has been known by the name of Corie!"

CHAPTER 49

THE LANGUAGE OF LIFE

Below deck on the *Winflow*, Aeron sat on a three-legged stool beside Master Skylo. Every so often, Qing rose from a cross-legged seat and checked on the mixture.

"Still not ready?" Aeron asked. Qing shook his head and returned to the corner. This time, he picked up a wooden mandolin before sitting back down. He held the body of the stringed instrument to his ear and plucked a pair of notes. The flicker of delight on his face made Aeron smile.

All of the sudden, he had a visceral urge to write in the Journal. He reached a hand to his heart. The empty fabric swam shame through his veins.

He took up a half-torn leaf of paper and an old stylus from a side table. Pressing pen to paper, the weight and texture of the quill felt like pure disloyalty.

First Granddad, now Yeats, Lamark, Skylo, and even the Journal—everyone and everything I love winds up lost, dead, or destroyed.

He paused. Qing's song, soft and melodic, had been written by Aeron's father, Loo.

I could be at Lyceum right now, reading and learning about the successful decisions of past men. But that's not learning. Success gives the illusion of learning. I chose to live because to live is to fail, to fail is to learn, and to learn is to grow. The men and women won their battles and kingdoms by jumping onto the horse, falling flat on their faces, and getting up for another go.

I did not ask to be a Mason, nor an archivist, but this is the soil I was planted in. And now my family is in danger of dying in disgrace without even its book to keep the memory.

Should I be ashamed to have done it all? To have hurt so many people and caused so much damage?

No. I feel for the ones I've harmed, but there are greater powers in play. I've felt the Aeros, seen what they can do. I may be raw and untrained, but this journey has taught me that the language of the world lives out in it, not in its ink.

The music stopped for a moment. Qing rose, carrying the mandolin with him, and resumed the gentle song. He drifted around the room like a leaf in the wind, pulling on strings and creating an aura of a past time. The man entered the galley but continued to play.

Aeron put down the pen and sang a verse.

Little do we know
The way things flow and flow
Trapped by rivers all around
Only in Old Orifornia, my heart's abound.

Skylo's eyes sprung open. He looked as if he had seen into the jaws of a lion, tremulous with fear but awake.

"Skylo!" Aeron shouted and danced a jig. "Qing! Look! Skylo's—" When he turned back, his mentor had fallen back to shallow sleep.

Qing poked his head out back into the main cabin and then returned into the galley. The music stopped, replaced by the clang of iron on iron.

Aeron jumped to clear papers and notebooks from the brass side table. Qing placed the pot down and removed the lid with a damp rag. Steam billowed from the top like a singing tea kettle. Inside, the mixture fizzed and bubbled like rising yeast. It reached the brim and resettled in stillness, midway filling in the pot.

"Is that…" Aeron said, marveling at the silver, inky liquid streaked with wisps of blue. "Adamasor?"

Qing nodded and stuck a brass ladle into the liquid. It smelled like midnight on a mountain.

"Incredible," Aeron said, "as the story goes, the Kingdom of Termara used Adamasor to bring back the twin fenixes."

The spoon came back limp, like a dead flower, and empty. They tried others: made from iron, copper, even silver. All refused to hold the Adamasor.

Qing looked for quite some time at the tattoo on his right arm.

They move…

The tattoo changed from an old woodland into the unmistakable coast of Elevana. Qing furled his brow in concentration.

Aeron backed away from the pot for a second. A sudden flash of insight had him at the corner chair by his haversack. He picked a heartfruit from inside and returned to the pot.

They made eye contact and Aeron let go. For a few moments nothing happened, but then the heartfruit seemed to be draining from within, as if the pulp were being sucked through a hole.

At the end, all that remained was a shell-shaped cup of heartfruit's skin floating on the surface. Inside was a small pool of silver liquid.

Though the steam bit his hand, Aeron plucked the edge of the skin with two fingers. It remained cool. Aeron reached back in, dipping the skin for a bigger dose, then removed the it from the pot.

Qing opened Skylo's lips by the cheeks and, with nervous hands, Aeron trickled drops of hot silver between them.

Nothing changed. If anything, Skylo's chest rose and fell even less. Then Qing gestured for the pot and over toward the top of the cabinet where the flameflower and the Grapple rested.

Hyacinth needs Adamasor too...

Aeron scooped the heartfruit skin once more and, walking slowly so as not to spill, paused at the flameflower inside its jar. He trickled in the silver mixture. From inside the jar came a thin, exultant sigh, strumming the air like the mandolin.

The muscles around Skylo's eyelids strained—up and down, up and down. He drew up and, gathering his senses, threw a frantic glance around the room, clenching a fist of sheets on the table.

"Master Skylo," Aeron said and placed a hand on the bone of Skylo's tense right shoulder. "All is well."

"Where?" Skylo said in a rapid, labored voice. "Where is he?"

"Viru? He is gone," said Aeron. "You must hear how I—"

"A siñado," Skylo interrupted, trying to rouse. Aeron slowed down his movements.

"Yes," said Aeron, "But how did you know…"

Skylo said nothing. Still rising, he gestured toward the side table where Hyacinth and the Grapple beamed more healthily.

"It… told you?" Aeron said. "But you were unconscious…"

"My dear boy," Skylo said, "you know so little of the Aeros." He balanced himself, palms pressed to the table on either side of his hips. "My flameflower and I are one. So long as it is alive, I am Sage. And so long as I am alive…"

Qing stepped forward, holding another cup full of Adamasor.

"I see the Onomasts received my hawk," Skylo said with a gracious nod. He took the cup with two hands and tipped it between his lips. The man shivered but seemed to be improving with every second.

"You sent for Qing?"

"Ono is his title. Ono Qing," Skylo corrected. "And yes, yes I did. You need him to enter the Reddwood Citadel, where the Tree is. The Monomast, their leader, owes me a favor."

"But he was nearly dead when we found him," said Aeron. "Why?"

"Trust, my son," said Skylo. "That all of this was a part of the plan. Now where's my cane?"

Plan? So he and Manu anticipated all of this and never told me? How can I trust when everything is a deception…

"Below!" Manu's words shot through the hatch. "We've reached the river's split."

"Excellent," Skylo said with increased vigor.

Passing by with a woodstone walking stick, Qing nodded with encouragement and patted Aeron's arm. The two of them helped Skylo to his feet, and he leaned heavily on the stick with two hands. As they walked, he spoke.

"What do you know of the Onomasts, Aeron Mason?"

"Very little," said Aeron. As they stepped passed Hyacinth, the flameflower floated from its jar and over to Skylo. "I've only read the name. In the Journal."

"And your Journal failed to tell you that the Onomasts are the original wordsmiths? They have made every word you and I know. Onomasts go further than a vow of silence—to enter their order, each priman pledges their voice box to the Monomast, their king, who speaks for all. Once mute, an Onomast's mind is shared with all others in the order. One is all."

Two steps further and they reached the stairs. Skylo took the first step slowly but then found a more natural pace. Aeron and Qing remained by each elbow.

"I…" said Aeron, voice partway choked. "I lost the Journal. It must have been stolen at some point during the battle."

At once, Skylo paused and whipped his face to Aeron. "This," he said forcefully, "is *kindu…*"

Aeron recognized the Orangu accent but had never heard the word before.

"Danger," said Skylo, as if reading his thoughts. "Your Journal, 'The Mason Grimoire,' in Wraeth hands is…" he trailed off.

"I don't think it's with a Wraeth," said Aeron.

"And why's that?"

"The map," Aeron replied, lending Skylo a hand up the final stair. "It is pointing toward Longleath."

"Interesting," Skylo said, nodding slowly. "Very interesting…"

"Master Skylo," Aeron began timidly. "You don't think it could have been Paloma. Do you?"

"Well would you look at that," said Manu. If Aeron didn't know better, he might have thought there was a bit of cheer in the man's voice. "Good to see you alive, old man."

Manu finished tying the mainsail to keep the ship from moving. Straight ahead, the river was split in two. To the ship's left, the water was crested with white and seemed to rush fast and downward, cutting over itself in rapid flourishes and too narrow for the *Winflow*. In the middle lay a thin, craggy clay cliff with grubby pine trees and long dead brush. To the right was a slow river that looked out over a dip in the land. A dusty town weaved into the canvas of greyish trees and scrubland.

"This," Manu continued, "is where we depart."

"Who?" Aeron asked.

"Fortunately, Master Skylo is awake. I do his plans no justice. He will explain."

Aeron turned to Skylo. "Where's Manu going?"

The man had three fingers to his lips, pensive. "To the same place you are," he said. "Only a different way."

"That makes no sense!" Aeron cried. "Why would we split up when someone like Viru could be chasing us?"

"How did you know that?" Skylo hissed. The fractiousness in his voice frightened Aeron.

I didn't...

"This is why Manu must go," said Skylo. "Praeth Viru is closer than you think. He cannot find you and Emmanwell together. And he cannot be the first to reach the Tree. This is vital, Aeron, and why you must split."

Tufts of silence filled the air between claps of water. Signs of town life floated in the water toward them—driftwood, a bit of rope, an old parka.

"I don't understand," said Aeron.

Skylo nodded to Manu and the man went below.

"Thoughts are like hummingbirds, Aeron. If you cage them, the birds may live, but will be unhappy. If you give them too much space, they will buzz about happily but selfishly. If, however, you teach even one to build its own nest, the plants around it will start to flower. On rare occasions, it is better not to think."

Qing stepped forward and pointed to the sun.

"What good is a wordsmith who can't speak?" Aeron grumbled in frustration.

"More use than a wordsmith who can, my boy. Now enough of that. I need you to trust the plan, Aeron. Like life, it is constantly changing, but I don't do the changing. The Aeros do."

Manu stepped out from the companionway, holding Aeron's haversack. He placed it at the boy's side as a pool of frustration and anger roiled inside him.

Qing stepped forward wearing a simple smile, like a man prepared for holiday.

"I'm sorry," Aeron said, pressing his hands to the rail. "I never should have dragged any of you into this. Not any of you, not Paloma, not Lamark."

"No," said Manu. Aeron turned toward the man over his left shoulder. "We dragged you."

The words melted like ice into the gentle late-summer breeze.

"I must get to the Tree," said Manu. "If I fail, and the Tree dies, my life's work will be for naught. Legacy is like an oak.

It takes hundreds of years to grow but only one moment to die." He stepped over to the bow of the large yacht. Attached to either side were two small greenish waka canoes with tall tails like a scorpidion's.

"I have spent too much time," Manu continued, "dealing with your problems." He unhooked one and it splashed to the water on either side of the *Winflow*. "Only I can save the Tree. And you are too young. You would be a burden to me."

Anger flushed through Aeron's cheeks.

"A Sage and an Onomast..." said Manu. "These are better teachers for you, Aeron Mason. They are your type of primen." He dropped his jacket over the edge into the canoe. "Farewell."

Before Aeron could reply, the Ranger dove over the banister.

Aeron rushed to the ship's port side. Hanging over the left fork, the early afternoon sky was hot and crisp with slight hints of autumn. Though the canoe could carry several primen, it sank heavily as Manu climbed over the edge. Without turning back to even wave, he took the oars and rowed.

"Now," said Skylo. "There are further matters to attend."

Aeron backed away from the baluster and sat on the hardwood floor. He stretched his restless legs out, shaking his head.

"It's all so backward!" Aeron complained. "Every time I think things are going right, it turns out I was utterly wrong."

"Not wrong, Aeron," said Skylo, "but certainly not right."

Skylo took the helm while Qing rejigged the mast to catch some wind. Skylo spun the wheel far to the right. On the spot, the ship veered eastward. The Sage pressed on the wooden lever to the right of the wheel and the ship began moving down the right fork.

On either side, the trees thinned as they made the minor descent. The first house, a ramshackle place made of water-stained clapboard and thin metal, stuck out from above a small creek. Soon after, more houses cropped up, all of similar quality but made from whatever they could find.

Aeron rose from the deck and made his way to the rear of the ship.

"Settled down. Have we?" Skylo asked as Aeron rose over the final two steps.

Aeron sighed. "I guess." He gestured his open palms upward. "There's no use in being angry at what I can't control."

"Indeed," said Skylo. "Now listen carefully, as I may have no other time to explain this."

Aeron faced him head on, a tinge nervous.

"I am sorry things have gone this way, Aeron. I have yet to tell you a great many things. The truth about your parents. The death of your granddad and sister. Your damaged ear. The Journal. Why the Grapple, after a thousand years, has chosen you…

But you will soon be at the Tree. So I must warn you that true learning only comes from experience. They are the best teachers in all of Aerth and will try to keep you enticed by lures of more and more learning. But they know nothing of the True Aero."

"The True Aero?" Aeron replied.

"Imagine, Aeron, that a man goes to the forest to gather a moss that grows only on the rarest tree and returns with a bundle of branches instead, thinking he found what he needed. Would he not be a fool, satisfied with an armful of sticks rather than what was required? This is the recurring story of life. We follow a path that leads us away from old age, sickness, death, misery, suffering, and so on. The moment we gain ground, we become satisfied with the progress and relax in pride. Your teachers are not immune.

The Aeros you have sung thus far on your journey are a bundle of branches. But in order to *grow,* you must find the True Aero."

"But what is it? Is it priman nature? Why are we so restless and confused and always wanting to collect things?"

"You've seen bits of it already in your life's misfortunes. So keep asking questions, my son. Ask and, over time, you will move closer to it."

"Do you know it?" Aeron asked.

"No." Skylo grinned. "But I have learned the lore of the ocean from a sailor. I have learned empathy for suffering from a healer. I have learned frugality from a poor man. I have learned bliss from children playing on the prairie. I have learned of connection from a forest. I have learned of love from a woman who deserved more credit than she believed. I have learned to control my body from a great Ranger, and my mind from his Sage. I have learned honor from a great judge of criminals. I have learned generosity from a priestess in the Northern Rift. And I have learned wisdom from a poet singing songs of lost times in the Southern Rift."

"All from your experiences…" said Aeron.

The river widened and a cove opened to the right. Scads of mangy fishing boats and canoes filled the dock. None could compare to *Winflow.*

"Indeed," said Skylo and turned the toward the dock closest to the center. "Living people, dying trees, even evil—there is learning in everything we see and hear.

"And that's why I cannot come with you, Aeron Mason. I too have more to learn. And you have much to learn without me."

"What?" Aeron cried. "We need you, Skylo. The Tree needs you."

"This is not part of the plan," Skylo shook his head. "I am to sail back down the River of Light until I reach the open ocean. Far away business needs tending in another Rift."

"First Manu, now you…" Aeron shook his head, gritting his teeth.

They landed in front of a brick building, which appeared to be the sturdiest in town and had a yellow post-sign hanging from the roof.

It read, "Next Departure: Three Minutes."

"And another Rift!" Aeron cried. "What if I need you? What if we fail and Viru beats us to the Reddwood City, the Tree of Knowledge?"

"Ono Qing will guide you and give more counsel than you expect," Skylo began. "But, in the end, this is now a journey of your own. Remember what you have learned, Aeron Mason. Listen to the Grapple, and you will succeed…"

Skylo let go of the wheel and barely used his cane down the stairs, his step near to normal. The Sage lifted Aeron's haversack with his stick and removed something thin and square from inside while Qing stepped off the ship and onto the dock.

A horn blared from nearby. From where it came, a crowd splintered in various directions on either side of the brick building.

"Though the seas, plains, and mountains will separate us, we will forever be companions on the *way*. Do you remember what I said to you the first day we met in your cell in Longleath?"

"Life is nature's language," Aeron recalled. "And nature is the language of life."

"Never forget that, Aeron," said Skylo. "Oh and, Aeron… don't be too mad at your friend, Murravillow. She knows as little as you do."

CHAPTER 50

THE COLOR OF NIGHT

"Well, Miss Corie," Paloma said and slid the door closed, "I'd like an explanation why you're stealing from me."

Arms crossed, flute resting on a faux-velvet, Corie's jaw unhinged with a vacant grin.

"I've caught you white-handed," Paloma said. "Why are you so happy?"

"Because, because!" Pink streaks grew into the woman's long hair. "We've come to the best part, that's my because!"

"Your hair..." said a baffled Paloma, "it's not a wig. It changes..."

"Everything changes!" shouted Corie, uncrossing her arms. She tossed the half-full bottle of purador up and down with one hand. "Including me and you."

"Give me that!" Paloma groped forward. But, as she did, Corie gave an acrobatic flip, like a cricket, straight over Paloma and onto the opposite bench.

As Paloma wheeled left, the horn blared and the train lurched into motion.

"Now departing, Northerly Neck," called the conductor. "Last stop before Orifornia."

Paloma fell backward from momentum while Corie, staring out the window, clapped, as if still a giddy young girl.

"You've chosen the best time!" Corie squealed. "The best time to flee."

"I didn't flee," Paloma grumbled. "I came after you..."

"When the sun is lower than you, clouds and the sky bleed orange and blue."

Corie reached up and pressed the window open a crack with her thumb and forefingers. Paloma's nose tickled with a smoky alpine smell.

"Corie," said Paloma, picking up the old woman's flute from by her right thigh. "How about a song?"

Takes two hands to play the flute...

The woman placed the purador in between two cushions and accepted the instrument.

Her song began like slow and gentle trickling water. As the notes went on, the tune grew louder and more tense, yet it still maintained an air of natural tranquility to it.

Corie paused for a breath without removing the instrument from her lips, and Paloma pretended to be interested as the Rizon Canyons were melting from clay into shapeless marshes of musty green weeds and oily pools of dour waters. Stalks of grass and reeds stood like frozen scarecrows, not dead but not alive either beneath rolling fogs, which tasted greasy and bitter.

The train angled for the slow incline. As they ascended, Paloma glimpsed a tall mountain, which stabbed like a silver minaret through strips of clouds. It amazed her how close the clouds looked. Some were thin and wispy like peach fuzz on Skylo's head while others were thick and billowing and begging to be walked on.

Corie resumed with a darker and more tense melody, which seemed to match the late afternoon mist now surrounding the train.

The woman's eyes drifted closed, as a musician's might, and Paloma inched to the edge of her seat. Natural light all but disappeared from inside the train, and the lamps had yet to be lit.

A nearby cabin door slid open.

"Get out!"

Even with Corie's playing, the shout was clear but muffled behind their own closed door. Paloma leaned toward the door and pressed the lock down firmly.

A chill leaked through the open window. The hall, lit in a subdued candle-like orange hue, held two shadowy figures. Paloma's hair pricked at its ends. Two pairs of feet shuffled past beyond their curtained door. The smaller of the two shapes cupped its mouth and whispered to the other.

Do they sense the purador?

Corie's song had grown somber but filled with a high tenor.

The two figures backpedaled and the somewhat larger of the two reached a skinny hand at the door handle.

Click… Click. Click. Click.

A flurry of terrible thoughts sailed between Paloma's ears. The smaller of the two held something bright and hot to the door.

The bolt jostled loose. Corie's song picked up pace and grew brighter as the cabin illuminated with natural white light. A pure blanket of white masked the window. A momentary hole peeked through the clouds to light up the rolling green hills, pools of water, and a distant broken canyon, all miniature as a diorama.

"Corie…" Paloma gasped. "Are we… flying?"

Corie put the flute down as the door slid open.

In the doorway stood an old northerner, pony-tailed with wispy facial hair, and whose every visible bit of skin was striped with tattoos.

"Paloma?"

A more familiar face stepped out from behind the old man's beige robes.

"Aeron!" Paloma cried. "I thought—"

"Corieeeeeeeee," Corie called, laughing to herself.

"And Corie!" shouted Aeron. "Well this is… an unexpected turn."

"Hang on, you two know each other?" Paloma asked, pointing at Corie and Aeron. "No, never mind. Aeron, look. I don't know what you've been told or heard or read since I left, but—"

"What in the…" Aeron shouted, wide-eyed with his hands behind his back.

"Aeron," said Paloma, "you have every right to be angry, but please," Paloma begged, "let me explain."

"But those are clouds! And the mountains, they look… Qing, see there? It's Skylo's ship. He's already moving south."

Qing? Aeron's traveling with an Indoshinese…

"Aeron," Paloma began.

"Stop, Paloma," said Aeron. He pulled his hands from behind his back. The room grew instantly brilliant. Light glimmered against Corie's and Qing's eyes. The Grapple was bluer and more splendid than she had ever seen it.

"You got it…" said Paloma. "Aeron, I am so… proud."

"Me too." A deep, dirty, debaucherous voice punted cheer from the cabin.

All of a sudden, the memory of fresh citrus ran up her spine. Then, his face appeared like a shabbily mended dinner plate. It was glued together with some mixture of clotted blood at the jags. A broad-shouldered, dark-eyed man-boy stepped through the open door—the same boy from Yeats's farm.

The train struck back through the clouds and rattled from turbulence.

"Good to see my friends again," he said.

"Throach?" said Aeron. "Haeven's fury... you never die."

Throach stepped into the cabin. He slid the door closed without turning back, scanned the room, and made sure to show the long spikes protruding from the knuckles of his brass gloves.

Aeron and Paloma both retreated a step, but Qing held his ground.

"And who are you?" Throach asked.

Qing said nothing. The tattoo on his neck-shoulder area seemed to be moving.

"I asked you a question."

Throach threw a mutilating punch straight for Qing. The man ducked with unbelievable quickness and jabbed four straight fingers between Throach's ribs, but Qing's fingers met something hard and crunched with his own force. He jerked his hand back, shaking it with pain.

"Ahh, I see" Throach said with a grin. "Your body guard is a twisted old man."

The train swooped down, up, and then down again, now twisting more actively around the smaller mountains.

Paloma fell backward and grasped onto the ledge. Her heart pounded, imagining the way Throach had bloodied Yeats and nearly destroyed his arm. She could still feel icy lewdness of his finger running down her spine. She wanted more than anything to pounce on Throach and claw at his dark, disgusting eyes until he begged for mercy, but the urge abated as the conductor banged on a door down the hall.

"Now arriving, Demon's Edge. Next stop, Orifornia Flats." The cabin fell silent as a faint orange glow of dusk echoed across the range.

Demon's Edge... if the stories are true, Demon's Edge is part of a mountain, and a short ascent to the Reddwood Citadel.

One mountain stood higher than the rest, though all formed a bowl shape holding a wide pool of green water. A colossal cloud obscured how high the mountain struck. The train seemed to be heading for a large log cabin, which rested on a flat part of the bowl.

"Oh good," said Throach. "We've arrived. I will be taking your little trinket now, Aeron."

"Go away, *Throach*," Paloma hissed, as if his name were fecal.

"Mmm," Throach hummed and straightened his soiled trousers. "Your trinket... and the girl." He stepped forward, writhing with malice.

Paloma backed away a step and readied herself.

Not without a fight...

Throach shoved Qing to the side like a ragdoll as Aeron and Paloma made eye contact. No Aero would save them. The barrel-chested young man reached forward and latched his stocky fingers onto Paloma's wrist. She had no space to dodge as he yanked her toward him.

In that instant everything seemed to move in slow motion—everything except the music.

"Grraaaahh," Throach screamed. "My eyes! My eyes!" His fingers slipped from Paloma's wrist and jammed over his eyes, rubbing madly. "What is this? What have you done?"

"Quicks, we go! Quicks!" said Corie, standing on the corner seat.

Throach rumbled toward her, creating an opening on the right side of the cabin for Paloma, Aeron, and Qing to slip out into the hall.

"This way," Aeron said. At the end of the car, his body was drenched in natural light, which poured in from the exit beside him.

"Now departing!" called a voice from the platform.

Qing slipped down the hall and followed Aeron out the door to the right.

With a metallic screech, the car jerked into movement and something hard clattered to the floor inside the cabin.

The purador!

She lunged. But, a split second before, Corie whizzed between Throach's legs, scooped up the glass bottle, and was out the door.

Paloma slammed the door closed and turned to the right as Corie disappeared down the steps. Paloma bolted after her.

A short ten yards remained of the platform. Paloma could feel the train readying itself for a slow incline.

Jump! It's that or spend the next hours with Throach.

Facing to the exit, she took a step back. Pounding fists took over her eardrums. Or was that her racing heart?

Paloma vaulted forward and landed at the end of the woodstone platform with a hard roll. The world spun, and the sky turned upside down. All pounding fell away, and in rushed the color of night.

CHAPTER 51

A DUTY UNFULFILLED

Even the art in Lera's home in the Reddwood was the same as the day they named her Queen Vizier of Orifornia.

"I refuse to see him," said Lera, standing afront her large, floor-to-ceiling window.

"But, my vizier," said her guard, Charrals, "you sent for him. We need the Wilder to protect the Tree."

"He left us in our most vulnerable moment, and now he has returned expecting my praise?" Lera asked rhetorically. "No, he will do his duty."

"My vizier," said Charrals, "if I may…"

"You know you may, Charrals."

Lera gave a shy smile and took off her modest royal cloak. In red, brown, and gold, it blended with the reddwood chair beneath it. She removed three rare, antique books written in old Orangu and took a seat in the chair with ornate carvings.

"It is unwise to kick one's own guard-dog," he said, placing his helmet down on the table. "Swallow your pride and humor the man. You two have known each other for so many years, after all."

Lera sighed. "Oh, Charrals." She looked out from the manor on the mountain. It was the second highest place in the Reddwood Citadel, apart from the tree itself. She loved the way the Citadel and the villages below seemed to float above the clouds. "Fine, fine. Send for him."

"Madame," said Charrals, "he is already in the antechamber."

Lera picked up her cup of sprig tea from the side table. Holding the drink warmed her cold hands.

"Very well," she said and turned back to the window.

Charrals left the room. A few distant mumbles came from behind the closed door before it opened again.

"Madame Lera," said the unforgettable voice of Manu.

"Hello, Manu," said Lera, maintaining her gaze on the mighty Orifornia Highlands where everything grew tall, green, and healthy.

A few seconds passed as Lera sipped her tea.

"I was sorry to hear about your friend," she said. "Brutish, impractical man, but he righted at the end."

"Lamark was a good man," said Manu.

"Good men don't exist," said Lera. "Only great and terrible." She paused and turned around to face him. He was soiled with sweat and desperately needed a bath. "Which one will you be?"

A piercing moment of hatred flashed before his eyes, but then he relaxed. He sat down at the couera-table and ran his hands on the smooth wooden rings. Manu no longer looked like Manu the Wilder, the Last Great Ranger, but a withering corpse propped upright.

"We both know what comes next," he said, pouring himself a cup of tea from the woodstone kettle.

"And we both know it is your duty to be outside those walls. To protect us from whatever comes next."

"*Duty*," Manu scoffed. "What do you know of *duty?* You've never served a day in your life."

I am serving my duty right now, you fool.

"I know you pledged your life to the Tree fifty years ago and have abandoned it for the last fifteen." Lera spoke slowly, her gaze trained and unblinking on Manu slouched in his seat. "I know you had greatness in you once but have lost sight of your purpose."

"You should be more polite," said Manu, "when asking someone to protect the seat of your power."

"I am not interested in *power*. The Tree of Knowledge is *power*. *I* mean nothing. I am merely a woman steering the ship. What matters is the ship itself, what's aboard."

"And what's aboard then?"

"You know that answer, Manu," said Lera. "Inside the Tree is every bit of knowledge ever uncovered on Aerth. You know that all teaching, learning, and wisdom are derived from inside. You know that while a woman writes a book in Longleath, it is likewise being written inside the Tree of Knowledge."

Manu sighed, finished his sprig tea, and rose from the chair. He placed both arms wide on the couera-table and hung his head between his shoulders.

"Do you know why I left?" asked Manu. "Why I became so angry with this place and the Tree?"

I have wondered for all these years...

"I swore myself to the Tree for a woman. She was priman. No neath blood like you and I have. It hurt to see her age so fast. Skylo explained that I could save her. The ones at the Tree could save her if I pledged myself to protect it."

He paused, almost weeping.

"But they were wrong," he pounded a fist on the table. "You all are always wrong. Your guesses take a thousand years before becoming reality. But she did not have a thousand years. She had ten. And I never said goodbye."

Lera rose from her seat and put a gentle hand on Manu's powerful back. The tension in it relaxed as if his spine were a rope given more slack.

"And I did so for thirty-five years…" Manu said and pulled away from her. "Protect you and your small fortress city on a mountain along with your fanatics."

Lera turned back to the window. On the other side of the house the sight would have been the brown trunk of the Great Tree. But this view was more interesting to her. It looked straight out along the edge of the world. To the right, beneath the clouds, was the endless sea and horizon. To the left, the Reddwood Citadel, the Orifornia villages, and all the rest of Oriendo.

"Until fifteen years ago," said Manu, "when she died. That was the day I gave up hope. I realized the Tree and all your Aeros are less powerful than they present themselves to be. The only thing in control of me is me. And the same goes for all of us."

"Death can make us jaded," said Lera. "Or it can forge a true hero."

The silent iceberg of dusk was creeping in. From the end of the horizon, a pantheon of pinks and oranges were strewn across the dying blue sky. The trees on the ridge were topped with orange and yellow crowns.

"So I will ask again," Lera began without turning around. "Which one will you be?"

Lera waited in a dense silence for an answer. She heard heavy footsteps behind her and the opening of the door.

She turned around and he paused, his back to her, holding the door open with his right hand. He turned over his right shoulder and spoke.

"You're on your own."

CHAPTER 52

THE WALL OF FLAMES

Aeron rushed toward Paloma on the platform. With a gust of wind, the last car blazed past them. Corie was already at Paloma's side. She had a deep cut above her left eye where it had cracked against the platform, but the still-capped purador rested beside them both.

"Use the purador!" shouted Aeron.

Corie shook her head. "No need. No need."

"But she hit her head hard…"

"Sing, sing," said Corie. "You sing now."

He bit his lip and then began the first song that came to mind—the one Corie had been playing when he and Qing entered the cabin.

Some will grow

Corie picked up her flute and played once more.

Some will grow
while others sail the skies.

Some will grow
while others sail the skies.
In search for keys,

Some will grow
while others sail the skies.
In search for keys,
the Orangu know:

Some will grow
while others sail the skies.
In search for keys,
the Orangu know:
on Demon's Edge, she dies.

"Watch the ledge," Corie chimed in. "Watch the ledge at Demon's Edge!"

"Oh mercy, that's where we are?" Paloma asked, fluttering her eyes. "Are the stories true then?" She sat up and rubbed her temple. "The first Huntress and the first Wraeth were born here?"

"Truer than true," Corie said and placed the purador vial on Paloma's cut. She shivered at its touch.

"And no one enters without a guide who's been inside before?" Aeron asked.

Qing nodded.

"Even through the bag, it's frigid!"

"Good, good," said Corie. "Your hands hold it there."

"And it's as hard to cross as they say?" asked Aeron.

"It was," said Corie. "Before you city people built flying trains."

"So…" said Aeron. "Why don't more people come here to the Reddwood then?"

Corie shrugged and pointed below to a vast expanse of simple villages dotting here and there in between hills on a long, green plateau. "Most primen love to dream but are scared."

"Scared?"

"Exactly!" Corie squeaked. "For them, looking up and thinking about Reddwood is enough. More than enough! No risk in dreams! Better to stay at home and pretend to know."

How could someone prefer a thought to a reality? I'll never understand some people… maybe that's why I never fit in.

"Well then," Paloma said, easing to her feet. "Shall we?"

Her words echoed in his head as the faint red circle in the sky leaked lower on the horizon.

"Are you sure?" asked Aeron, looking at Qing for support. "That was quite a fall."

"I've taken far worse in Cannaroo," said Paloma. "We're too close to slow down now… and I find it hard to believe we've seen the last of Throach."

At that, Corie pursed her lips and nodded. Though she said nothing, Aeron could hear the thought loud and clear. "Ohh, me likes this one…"

"Glad to see you two are getting on," Aeron smiled, turned toward the large brick building, and walked.

As they passed the rail station, Corie took the lead. She slipped beneath one of the railings, which led onto a lower ramp meant for luggage. Qing followed closely behind her and Aeron ducked the bar, dropping a few feet onto the stone and nearly twisting his ankle.

"Careful," Aeron said as Paloma hurdled high over the rail. Even with the scrapes and the purador pressed to her eye, she made a far more graceful landing.

"Which way, Corie?"

As far as he'd seen, Corie was the ask-forgiveness-not-permission type. She skipped toward the next ascent and disappeared into a thick blanket of fog.

Aeron followed and found her waiting where the climb had been split into a steep path made from old mill stones to the right and a simple grassy trail heading to the left.

"Fast," Corie asked. "Or slow?"

Paloma rolled her eyes. "Fast!"

"Careful, careful," sang Corie, scampering to the right over the outlook made from millstone and sheetrock. "Always watch out for the fast!"

The stones were slick from the mist and the way forward looked no less perilous.

"Are we sure," Aeron chimed in, "that this is the better way?"

Qing patted Aeron on the back and passed him on the right. His arm had the tattoo of an immense tree, half-living and half-dead, rife with moving birds.

"No trees?" Paloma asked. "I thought they would be everywhere in the Reddwood."

"You wait, dearie," said Corie, leading through the middle arch of an aqueduct—a craggy limestone arch with a twist of tall thickets beneath it. The mist lightened for a beat, revealing the way beyond the aqueduct to be a skinny zigzag shimmying up the side of the mountain.

"Corie," said Paloma from behind the old woman. "Are we lost?"

"You bet, you bet!" Corie sang with one of her little dances.

"What!" Paloma groaned from in front of Qing. "This is a bad time and a worse place to be lost."

"If only Skylo were here…" Aeron sighed.

"So he's gone then?" Paloma asked. "Manu I could understand. He's hard to pin down. But I would never expect Skylo to leave when the times are toughest."

"Skylo will come back. I know it. But Manu-Saunter-Wilder-whatever he wants to call himself is more selfish than the stories say. Maybe it's a part of becoming such a legend…" said Aeron, hoping otherwise.

He paused to catch his breath and let the rest of the group continue ahead. He knelt for a moment in the viridian green ankle-deep grass. He fished the final heartfruit from his haversack and pressed both hands hard to make the first crack in the shell.

"Aeron?" Paloma's disembodied voice came through the mist.

"I'm coming," Aeron called forward and picked up the pace.

The climb had lasted an hour thus far, and Aeron's strength was low. Still, he closed the gap in a few strides as the steepness evened out.

"Unfar, we are," said Corie. "Unfar from the trees!"

Paloma slowed up and let Qing pass on her left.

"Aeron," Paloma whispered. "Are you sure you trust Skylo?"

The question surprised him. "Of course," he said. "He saved me from Longleath Prison, and on the river…"

As the incline lessened, Paloma kept walking at his pace. As they went, Aeron made a second effort to break the heartfruit open. It cracked on his third try and he handed a sliver to Paloma. She accepted with a thankful nod.

"Why do you ask?" Aeron asked, lifting a slice to his lips.

"Me smells heartfruit…" interrupted a foggy Corie ahead. Aeron broke off four more slivers and gave two to Qing and Corie each.

Even from one piece of heartfruit, Aeron felt his muscles fill out and shoulders pull back. His breathing became deeper, and his vision grew sharp.

"It's seems too… convenient," continued Paloma. Qing cocked his head with curiosity.

"Hang on," Aeron asked and pushed past her. "Do you smell that?"

The road had leveled now and gone from zagging to straight. It reminded Aeron of the millstones from below—well-ordered but unchanged for thousands of years. He went a few steps further and the prickly scent of ash grew.

"Are we still lost?" Paloma asked from behind.

When Aeron made another few paces, a thin colonnade of pine trees now lined the road on both sides.

"We are!" Corie's shrill voice carried through the mist like a ripple in water. "Only the lost are found!"

Aeron wheeled around. He and Qing were face to face, and he saw madness in the Onomast's eyes, as if he were someone else. He seemed to be looking straight through him toward the gate.

Aeron recalled something he had read about Onomasts losing their power around the Tree—maybe this was that, not the doing of some evil.

Aeron turned back toward the trail. The smell was unmistakable now, and the world far ahead had a murky orange tint to it.

Fire!

Aeron shoved the last piece of heartfruit into his mouth and flung the skin to the side. Adrenaline coursing through his veins, he sprinted the final hundred meters toward the source.

The path had been all pine or aspen, but the trees ahead struck ten times as high and were, at first sight, hard to believe. Massive, wide, and sporting an air of majesty, these wooden giants were refusing the flames. Their burls ballooned out as barriers above the flames.

Something sizzled like boiling water at the foot of the wall.

Aeron continued closer. The trees were lined in a long row, which extended far out to his left and right.

"More water!" a voice shouted from one of the most charred trees.

A splash of water doused the flames to the right, but only for a moment. Then they rekindled and began attacking the massive wall.

Frantic shouts continued from various places above as Aeron continued forward. The heat stung his eyes and cheeks. Pops of sparking aerth made the voices hard to hear.

From the ground up, the trees were all conjoined, forming a strong wooden wall of interconnected pillars like a log-cabin turned to the side. The higher they rose, the more the trees separated, as they would in a forest. It was the most magnificent piece of Epiphysics he had ever seen.

"Aeron!" distant voices called from behind.

"Here!" Aeron called. "Come quick."

It seems like people are on the wall. There must be a walkway where the trees begin to split, and the guards are dumping water...

The flames leapt up and scorched the sign that arched over the gate door and read: *The Reddwood Citadel.*

On either side of the door, the wooden wall stretched into hazy oblivion.

Footsteps pattered behind him, and Aeron whipped around to find Paloma and Corie.

"The wall is made of Reddwoods..." Paloma said with wide eyes. "Living Reddwoods!"

"And it's on fire..." Aeron replied.

The flames were hot and red, but every so often a flare of purple or black would leap out from them as the wall and the blaze took up arms against one another.

The first had spread. Behind them, pine trees and aspens careened to the aerth. A hose of fire struck the door, seeming to come from a place separate from the rest of the flames. The door had blackened but remained strong.

"What's your friend doing?" Paloma asked, pointing over Aeron's left shoulder.

Qing was walking, slowly and mindlessly, toward what seemed like the source of the hose of fire.

A gust of wind kicked up for a moment and blew a hole through the haze.

Qing stood motionlessly directly in front of the city's oaken gate.

"The door!" shouted Paloma.

"The Citadel opens only to those it knows," said Corie.

The enormous, scarred door unhinged.

"Come on!" Aeron shouted, "it's our chance in. We have to get to the Tree before it is poisoned."

The trio broke forward with scalding air beat against their cheeks. Branches and tree trunks broke in every direction as they weaved around a fallen fir, leapt over three small pines, and narrowly avoided a rain of flaming needles.

They heard a crack as a towering aspen uprooted from the ground to their left. It groaned, crashing toward the aerth.

All of a sudden, a figure smashed into his left side, causing them to roll several feet to the right. The tree's trunk slammed exactly where they had been, and now its leafy crown stung his skin. Woozy and disoriented, he rose from beneath a blanket of leaves and twigs. The haversack was pinned beneath a huge branch.

Only one thing in there matters...

He tore the sack open and retrieved the Grapple, and his savior rose from beneath the green and yellow leaves. Paloma.

Face scraped and cut above her eye bleeding, Paloma was pointing and seemed to be shouting desperately, but Aeron heard only the ambiguous ringing of silence.

Aeron squinted through the smoke. The ringing fell away, replaced by whipping flames and their victims groaning, snapping, crashing to the aerth.

"Qing!" cried Paloma.

Aeron cupped his eyes. The fires were too bright and smoke too thick. Reds and oranges and vicious yellows surrounded them. But one thing was certain. The door, the Citadel's great oaken gate, which had protected it since time immemorial, was open. Two shadowy figures walked through. Behind them, the door rumbled closed.

CHAPTER 53

A TASTE OF PURADOR

"Nooo!" Aeron's scream careened across the evening haze. The door's gigantic locks snapped into place with a thunk-clang, and Paloma's lungs tightened from too much smoke. She knew they had to get out fast or suffocate.

"Come on," she said rasping and grasped Aeron by the arm. "We've got to get away from the flames."

"It's over," Aeron said, slipping away from her. "Qing was our ticket inside."

"But Corie's been inside," asked Paloma. "Hasn't she?"

Aeron's eyes pulled wide.

A corridor of millstone ran flamelessly to the right, wrapping around and paralleling the city walls. Corie was scampering over the hot stones.

"Corie!" Paloma shouted toward her.

"Follow meeee!" The woman's words punched through the groans and crackling as only a soprano's could.

"This woman has lost the plot…" said Paloma.

"But she's our only chance."

The air quivered with heat, and the stones were peppered with charred leaves and windfall. The corridor was twenty yards wide and the stones did nothing to subdue the heat.

As they ran, beads of sweat formed and dried the skin on her forehead.

Trees ran alongside the path, aspen on one side and pine on the other. Each one was like a giant candle wick. Nearer to the ground, the flames were purple and almost invisible. Higher up the trunk, orange flames flailed in errant directions, as if something inside were trying to escape.

Paloma's lips chapped and the taste of charred pine needles filled her mouth. She tried to swallow, but her tongue was an arid hardpan.

Suddenly, Corie veered left, straight toward the flames! She timed it perfectly with a gust of wind, and the fires jumped aside as if the mountain were trying to blow out those two candles. She disappeared between them through the pillar of open air, and the flames went back to normal.

They paused and exchanged a glance.

Did she do that? How are we expected to—

The flames skipped wide again, as they had before. Then, a wind struck a gap through them.

She waited for the subtle impression of wind on her back and lunged toward the fire as Corie had done. The wind pressed at her back as she ran-leapt-rolled through the column of open air and continued for several steps until her feet sank into something unexpected.

Mud?

Somehow, the air was damp and vegetal. Corie heaved against a small boulder, far too big for her to move on her own.

"I can't do it!" Aeron called from the other side.

She turned back to the flames.

"Come, miss," said Corie from behind, closer to the wall of Reddwoods, which was not yet on fire.

"You can, Aeron. Corie and I are here. Wait for a bit of wind and…" Three heartbeats passed. A slow breeze rapped against the tree candles like a door knocker. The breeze became a wind. "Jump!"

The flames parted. Terror mixed with exhilaration as Aeron vaulted through the gap. For a beat, he almost grinned.

"Your vest!" Paloma shouted. The tails of his vest were singed and budding with fire.

"Here now!" shouted Corie. "Here now!"

Aeron bolted past Paloma like a bird with a flaming tail, straight for Corie.

"Water!" Corie shouted.

At once Paloma understood. She followed Aeron and arrived as they slid the rock off to the side.

"In," Corie shouted, pointing to a hole in the ground. She did not have to tell Aeron twice.

He dove straight into the pit. The water sizzled as he splashed in ten feet below. Corie followed right behind him.

Smoke billowed in every direction. Paloma took as deep a breath as her lungs would allow and plunged into the dark, oddly warm waters.

They were completely submerged in a small tunnel, and the only light emanated from the Grapple in Aeron's left hand. The waterway was fresh and empty save for the roots along the walls. Paloma stretched her hand up and felt the roof of the waterway.

No air.

Corie swam up to Aeron, pointing to their right. Though the channel was small, it could have extended in darkness for eternity.

They paddled right. After a short time, Paloma's lungs constricted and panic murmured in her ear. Aeron. Corie.

Roots. Two rocks. Her eyes darted in every direction. Hands. Floor. Roof. Blackness.

Corie grabbed Aeron and pitched her free hand up and to the left where the tunnel seemed to split off. Paloma followed fast on his tail. Five yards in, he paused and held up the Grapple. Light bounced back at him in the worst way.

Dead end.

His face shone complete hopeless fear, sad realization, and a streak of anger.

He jabbed the Grapple against the wall in frustration once, twice, three times.

Paloma was growing faint as her suffocation began turning to quiet and painless tiredness.

Aeron jabbed one final time as Paloma's eyes drifted closed and the water became gentle and cool. Death welcomed her with open arms.

She felt those arms as if they were as real as her father's. They gripped her shoulders, pulled her through the water, and lifted her from suffering. Death became not a thing, but a place—a soft, warm patch of aerth that smelled like morning dew where no one would bother her.

But then something that felt like the sun pressed against her chest as something that sounded like the wind whispered in her ear. A face hovered over her, soft and comforting. It looked like the moon.

"*Anudato Euthanasis! Anudato,*" it came again. "*Euthanasis.*"

The world rushed back in. A window streamed with light above her, accompanied by a damp mid-wood aroma and a boy's voice.

"Paloma!" Aeron shouted. "Paloma, we made it!"

A violent fit of coughs sputtered water from her lungs. She curled into the fetal position for a moment, and something hard pressed into her side. She palmed the ground with her left hand and heaved herself up. She would have fallen if not for Aeron, who helped her to a seat.

"Where's—" Paloma croaked. Speaking was too painful.

"Shh," Aeron hushed her. "Corie? She swam away in the other direction. Seemed to have other plans. As usual." She was looking all around the room. By the shape, it had once been a barn but now held statues of all kinds—marble busts of bearded men, wooden totems of athon and fenix, and star-shaped decorations made from limestone. They were scattered inside stables, atop spare tables, and all around a large vat, which smelled of heartwine.

The walls were smooth and furnished with more care than any old barn. She focused on one of the star-shaped limestones above the door. It was large with mint green workings and, at its center, she saw the same swirling rune they had seen all over Elevana.

"We've made it, Paloma," Aeron said gesturing around with excitement. "And this is probably some famous sculptor's storage closet…"

"Look," said Paloma, pointing to the rune.

While Aeron squinted to see, Paloma tucked her feet closed and pressed up against a small granite fountain with seaglass fish resting inside. Too weak, she fell back to the ground.

"A good omen," said Aeron. "Do you still have it?" Aeron asked. "The purador?"

She reached into her pocket. It was still wrapped in its disguise—the bag of Adaloo from the Blue Rose, Lamark's wife's herb shop. She removed it from her pocket and held it directly into the Grapple light.

"We have to hurry, and I can't do this alone," said Aeron. "Take some. A small sip. That should help."

But everyone has warned against drinking this. For one reason or another, purador must have some negative side effect to it. Or is it simply too rare to waste on a young primen girl like me...

"Paloma, I need you. The Tree needs you. Manu," Aeron continued, "we all need you."

"Hands trembling, she uncorked the bottle. Eucalyptus, lemon, and a touch of something entirely foreign penetrated deep inside her nostrils and made her nose wriggle. She took a deep breath.

Oh mercy...

She pressed the glass to her lips and threw her head back like a dirty old pirate. The liquid was cool, a bit thick, and tasted better than anything that had ever crossed her lips. Sweeter than honey, icco beans, and heartfruit all together.

The room was no longer dim but bright as morning. Her limbs were not tired but strong and fresh. Her jaw and face relaxed, but her mind was firing and alert. It felt as if she had woken up from a long nap, eaten an excellent meal, and heard the most beautiful song known to man all at once.

"How do you feel?" Aeron asked.

"Remember that tree that almost fell on us?" Paloma asked.

Aeron nodded.

"The opposite of that. I feel like... like..." she grasped for the nonexistent right word.

"Don't bother," Aeron said. "Words kill the charm." He turned and pushed the barn door a crack open. The coast was clear, but somehow, Paloma already knew that. And she knew exactly where to go. Aeron pressed his shoulder and swung the door open.

A hazy orange evening threaded out across a row of leafy, exquisite houses made from woodstone, and over a small hill stood the outline of the most massive thing she had ever seen.

Then the words came to her.

...Like I could live forever.

CHAPTER 54

THE TREE OF KNOWLEDGE

◇◇◇◇◇◇

The air outside the barn smelled like burning books. Paloma stepped ahead and looked in both directions. Normally, they might have spied the Tree, but visibility was low behind the smoke. Another home went up in flames, and Aeron felt a bloom of heat on his cheeks.

Was this what it was like the day Termara fell?

"Which way?" Aeron asked.

"To the right," said Paloma, pointing opposite the row of houses. "I can feel it."

"Hold on," said Aeron. "Maybe the map will help."

He pulled the Reddheart Map from his vest pocket. Its rough oldness reminded him of Skylo. He unfolded it part way and the Reddwood Citadel appeared. The red line pointed toward the sea, which was opposite the fires, and directly to the tree.

Yes! This is what I want. Finally. I know clearly that I want to save the Tree and learn the Aeros.

"You're right," said Aeron. "Let's go."

Paloma broke into a run and Aeron followed a few paces behind. The road was well-kept gravel and had no signs of lorry use. Countless seedlings bunched in litters, but she saw no parent tree, only a dirt road and some lowly undergrowth.

"Look," Paloma called, standing near the crest of the hill. The perimeter of a shadow poked out in the distance like a pointed mountain peak. As Aeron passed higher on the hill, he heard the subtle ocean waves and realized this was no mountain. On the hilltop a few steps ahead, pure awe blinked from Paloma's eyes. "The Tree…"

No haze could hide such a magnificent sight. Aeron squinted through the chrismal dusk.

"I thought the treescrapers in Longleath were tall…" said Aeron.

Though they stood on a hill, the Tree, buttressed by a background of sky and sea, struck high as a small mountain. From below, with nothing but a background of dark blue, the crown seemed no larger than that of any other Reddwood guarding the gates. A cloud, streaked with the orange by the now setting sun, rolled in from the sea. Even the large, gassy pillow was only a third of its size.

Down its immense trunk were few branches and only the occasional knob, but each one had smatters of life. Primen lived on the enormous branches with clay lichen roofing and adobe brick homes. A handful of buildings rose alongside these communities on the Tree of Knowledge, each branch with its own unique neighborhoods.

"Are those… houses?" asked Paloma.

"I think so," said Aeron. "Primen made, that's for sure."

A gust of sea breeze refreshed Aeron's ruddy cheeks. The Grapple tickled his fingers and made him grin. The stone surged with color, all emanating from its tiny heart center.

His head felt light, airy, and clear, and a cathedral of wonder bathed Aeron in its natural bells. He could have admired the Tree for a lifetime, as so many did, from a distance.

"One leaf must be enough paper for all the schools in Longleath," said Paloma. "Do you think they turn orange in the autumn?"

"Yes," said Aeron, recalling what Manu had said. "No one is allowed in once the leaves change."

A harsh whip-crack twanged from a building in town behind them. For a moment, Aeron turned back toward it and contemplated going back where they'd come for help. The air was so haze-orange he could have been peering into the guts of a furnace that used a city for fuel.

"Someone's down there," said Paloma, pulling at his arm.

Beneath the Tree, way down on the ground, a few unfathomably small primen were tied at the foot of the Tree. Compared to the red-barked-behemoth striking through the sky, they could have been mere ants.

In front of them, a cone-shaped plot of aerth stretched between the burly pair of roots and the hill on which they stood. A stirring dustiness, thick as a field of burnt straw, suffocated the air. Aeron tried to swallow, but his throat had gone raw.

The city can be rebuilt, but what if that was Viru back at the wall, and he's able to control Qing? The Tree is in grave danger, and it cannot be rebuilt.

"We've got to go," Aeron said. Paloma agreed and, swiping sweat from her arms, began down the zigzagging slope. It was mossy but with enough rock and dirt to ensure good footing. His foot dug into the place where aerth and stone met. He skipped behind Paloma, stone after stone, in the same way, following closely at Paloma's heels. They loped down the hillside without a hitch, knees absorbing each step like youthful springs.

Halfway to the bottom, the ants grew to the size of candles.

It can't be…

Aeron gawked at the three figures tied with spidery-white ropes. The leftmost was tiny and had long, bright orange hair. The middle was a man in beige robes and bald save for a long pony tail. The furthest was a brawny man with hair to his shoulders and a khaki jacket.

"He's got them all, Paloma," said Aeron. "Corie, Qing, and Manu. They—"

As he spoke, Aeron's foot crunched through a false bit of land near a table-sized rock. His ankle sank into a ditch of moss, dead wood, and wheelmites. A momentary pain seared Aeron's right foot but it was too late. A yelp escaped from his lips.

Paloma ducked at once and helped him out of the crumbled moss.

He rose with the help of the stone table. It seemed tall enough to have concealed them from any viewers below. Paloma poked her head out to the sight and, in no time, jerked back into hiding.

An unmistakable voice, deep like the uttering of a horn, echoed over the hill, "I can smell you."

"How's your ankle?" Paloma asked with no fear on her face, her eyes still rippling with purador.

"I'm fine," he said. "But… what are we going to do? Viru knows we're here."

"Maybe," she said, "but maybe not. What if you continue and distract him while I go around to the left? I managed to sneak up on Manu and get your Grapple, maybe I can do so on Praeth Viru. It's not a good plan, but we have no time.

I would go, but I'm afraid of what he's capable of if he gets this…" Paloma held up purador and pulled the wrapping down a few inches. It swished side to side, silent as honey. Something nut-sized fell from the bag.

Her brow and jaw flickered wide with surprise. She knelt and scooped up a tiny, pinkish root from the moss.

"Adaloo, Aeron!"

He had never heard the word before, but it reminded him of the word for *disappear* in Orangu.

"This is going to work," Paloma said with certainty. "But we have to go. Now."

Aeron nodded. "Good luck, Palo," he said as she slunk through the understory behind her.

Alone behind the rock, the in and out movement of Aeron's chest grew choppy as the storm filled into his mind. From the smoke, the sky held colors in daggers of orange and crimson. The angry crash of tumbling water came from the far side of the hill where Reddwood Falls was spitting its steaming water miles down into the sea.

Five counts breathing in, five counts breathing out.

Granddad taught his actors to take deep breaths before taking the stage to help with nerves. Sucking in as much of the burning air as he could, Aeron rose from behind the rock.

"Leave them alone," he called, puffing himself out widely as his simple frame could manage.

The dark figure stood motionless, wrapped in a shadowy, cloud-like wolf-grey cloak. His wide stance and the pull of his shoulders oozed confidence.

Aeron made the first move, bursting through brambles and low grass all the way down the last fifty yards of the hill. With every step, the Tree swelled in immensity, as did Viru. The Tree's two above-ground roots were as big as two-story houses. Those roots melded flush into the aerth and must have stretched deep into the mountain as if they were its spine.

Viru's smoky cloak diffused out over the ground, like death had dawned a wedding dress, giving him the illusion of floating. Each arm of the Wraeth Prince matched Aeron's entire body in size.

Aeron's stomach felt as if it were about tear open.

Standing a few yards from Aeron's tied-down friends, Viru waited for him to descend.

Now lower, Aeron realized why Viru had chosen this spot. In the legends, the first ever Orangu was born here, where the Sky-Tree unfurled its roots at the end of the world.

Viru's back faced his captives and the root. He stepped a short way forward in Aeron's direction. Twenty yards to Viru's left stood an old woodstone sign vined with leaves shaped like arrowheads, which rose from the vantage point. Distant waves and falling waters reverberated over its millstone platform claiming: *The End of the World.*

If I can distract him long enough, maybe Paloma can free the others... but then what?

"You should be more afraid," the muffled words came from behind the man's smoky cloak, "boy." The last one was clearer than morning dew.

"Use it," called Corie, wriggling like a mad animal against the binds. "Use your Aero!"

Aeron held up the Grapple, and it already felt like part of his hand. It beamed fluorescent blue, at once cooling his body as if ice spread through his veins. At first a subtle force pumped with it all through him. Then, the force inside him swelled faster, spreading strong and sharp, like a rumor.

The world fell more silent than the space between sleep and death. His jaws bolted together as if carrying the *Winflow* on his shoulders. A lacerating wind whipped in like hot glass from the end of the world.

Channeling the siñado memory, Aeron angled the Grapple forward an inch and opened his mouth wide.

"*Megisto!*" Aeron cried the Orangu word. "*Anemo!*"

Nothing happened.

He held it to his lips and sang the Aero louder and more beautifully than ever before. But again nothing, and Viru's lack of surprise hurt all the more.

He focused every pin of attention he had on the slithery man and breathed in for a count of five.

One.

A shaft pried the smoke above to each side, sending glints of warm twilight over Aeron's cheeks.

Two.

The shards of wind fell into place, tickling his back like a shadow.

Three.

Viru tilted his smoke-masked head two inches to the side, reminiscent of a curious wolf but angrier and more vile.

Four.

Bodiless footprints sank into the soft ground behind Viru, one by one.

Paloma's… invisible?

All of a sudden, he lost his attentional spotlight and everything the Aero had built up. The smoke returned, the wind dissipated into a stale bed of air, and Viru's concern twisted back into vainglory.

The footsteps continued forward toward the party on the wall.

"You fool," Manu's words rushed in to break the silence.

"Yes," agreed Viru, "but he is still young." Viru slowly turned to Manu in smug candor and said, "What does that say of you?"

The dark man returned his gaze to Aeron.

"Serve," the Wraeth commanded and whipped his hands out widely so his arms and legs made an X shape. The smoke-cloak wisped away, leaving behind a man whose muscles rippled beneath a tight skin of leather. "Or die."

The Wraeth reached his marble-white hand to his left hip, where a small sheath resided, and yanked out the silver hilt with no blade.

"No," said Manu. "I will," he shook his head with childish fear. "I will serve."

He means it! Who is more pathetic, him or me...

"You will," said Viru, looking away from Aeron for a moment. "Won't you?"

Aeron slid a few paces to his left, nearer to the lookout and his friends. The rushing hiss of the falls to their left, cascading hundreds of meters below, covered his footsteps.

"But I have interest in the boy," continued Viru.

Aeron froze in place, still facing Viru.

Where are you, Palo?

Viru removed the strap on his shoulder and knelt beside his grey and silver quiver on the ground. From it, he pulled one large rhombus-shaped shard of glass with slanted edges on the broadside. He wedged the black glass into a slit in the Deathsword's guard and twisted. It locked with a familiar click.

"Why me," Aeron pleaded. "I'm scrawny. I can't fight. I'm not well traveled, and I've no neath blood..."

"Yes," Viru said from low in his throat. "This is why."

As he pulled the second shard from the case, Aeron caught a scent... eucalyptus, lemon, honey.

That's the Purador. This is my chance. While she's distracting him. A chance to prove to the world I'm no thief nor murderer nor runt. If I can get the last shard, I'll toss it over the ledge and he'll have no Deathsword. With no Deathsword, he has no way of poisoning the Tree. Even if I die, I'll have saved the Tree. The last Mason, the last archivist, a hero.

Viru paused. The hood of smoke rippled where his nose might have been. Aeron's heart skipped. The second shard locked into place like an old key.

Now!

Aeron lunged forward as the man turned forty-five degrees away from him, revealing a straight shot for Aeron to grab the quiver. One hand cradling the Grapple, he pitched forward, his free hand outstretched. The black cloud around the man's feet made it less than visible. Aeron missed the case but snagged his fingers on underside of the strap.

He bent low, readying to bolt off to the right. Eyes fixed on the cliff, Aeron's back knee released and he sprung away like a rabbit, clenching the strap for dear life.

He stopped a few yards from the sign and wiped sweat from his brow with the Grapple hand. The flames must have spread, for every second grew hotter than the last.

In his right hand he held only a severed strap. No quiver. No shard.

Viru's black boot rested on top of the case. He must have cut the strap as Aeron fled, or stepped on it before Aeron had even gotten there. He knelt and removed the final shard from the quiver. The blade sparked mutinously as it locked in place.

"Let them free," said Aeron with exasperation. "I am yours. Leave them be."

Though Viru said nothing, Aeron had the odd feeling the man was smiling. With a two-handed grip, he slashed the blade left, right, and then straight down into the soil, black and purple flameflower now orbiting the blade and still working to weld it together.

Aeron stepped toward Viru. Far behind him, a door had appeared at the tip of the triangular plot of land, at the foot of the Tree where the two roots came together.

The entrance… help must be on the way.

"Give me the stone," Viru demanded. "Prove your allegiance."

"I can't," Aeron said, shaking his head vigorously. "I need it to be of any use to you."

"Give it," Viru said, taking a step closer. The Deathsword was complete. Its blade, wide as his legs, belted out a subtle yet harrowing purple light from handle to point. "And I will spare you."

"No," shouted Corie. "No! No! No! Lies. Lies!"

"Give." Viru pulled the sword from the ground. "It." He closed the distance toward Aeron at the end of the world. "Now."

"*No!*" Aeron shouted.

"A fool, indeed," said Viru. "Like your grandfather and all Masons." His fingers tightened around the sword. Flames threatened from over the hill to their right. The man's leather flickered a terrible shade of orange. He could have been forged from in a live volcano, his body of pure obsidian.

All of a sudden, a familiar voice wired through Aeron's head.

You must trust yourself, my boy, your instincts, said Skylo. *Never rely on others coming to your aid. Trust, Aeron. Trust the will of the Aeros above your own. Remember—everything is one, and one is everything.*

Viru closed the distance, now only two sword lengths away. He held his gloved palm out, face up. The man's presence was ice cold, even in this heat. "Save your friends."

"Nooo!" shouted Manu.

"Tricks!" Corie echoed. "Tricks!"

Aeron took one long look at the Grapple's beautiful pulsation, its beating heart, and held it forth. His head screamed in alarm, but Aeron's gut told him to hand it over, as Skylo would.

He dropped it into Viru's hand. At once, an agonizing scream careened through Aeron's ears, screeching out from the Grapple itself. Aeron thrust his hands over his ears to blunt the noise.

"Yes," Viru boomed, pointing the Deathsword victoriously toward the sky in one hand, the Grapple stretched up in the other. "*I am the mountain!*"

He dropped the Grapple from over his head and it landed on a patch of grass in the soft aerth. His free hand gripped the sword's pommel and he turned the weapon over so the blade pointed down. Its dark blade moved so fast it disappeared from side-on.

When Aeron removed his hands from his ears, a song, deep and harrowing, rose from the aerth and jutted through the sound of cascading waters.

The Ode to Irkalla.

"Me people!" Corie was writhing beneath her binds. "Me people."

"Now watch," said Viru. "Watch my flames begin to burn the Tree, my hands destroy your Grapple, and my sword poison your people's only hope to survive."

He motioned violently with his gloved hand and the flameflower swelled to the size of his head. His hand was the hand of some gruesome storyteller spinning webs of death around the seat of history. From that hand, a hose of flames, so hot they were nearly invisible, thrust in an arc toward the tree.

It seemed like a particularly vulgar pleasure to Viru, to see the flames striking against the left root, where Qing, Manu, and Corie once had been tied.

Aeron made to lunge for the Grapple once more, but Skylo's voice returned.

No, my boy. Do not force it. You must trust the Aeros.

Aeron fell to his knees as his eyes and head filled with pressure. Fire was snaking up the Tree's veins. He had lost. His family would forever be branded with his never-ending failures. A tear of utter failure fled his eye and evaporated on his cheek. Then Viru struck.

The blade, wrapped in its flameflower glow, slashed downward. Fiber by fiber it slaughtered the darkened evening air, leaving behind a trail of purple light. The Deathsword's point connected with the top of the Grapple. A burst of color and shadow erupted, as if the two objects were fighting. For five counts, all light was sucked inward like the vacuum following an exploded star.

From the eruption, an expansive bloom of energy rippled out in every direction. Viru fell backward to the ground. Aeron doubled over and grabbed hold of a root beside the escarpment. The Tree itself shook as if struck by an aerthquake. The blue energy pressed hard down on every inch of flame until it had no oxygen to breathe. Even the largest blazes, which had snaked high up the Tree, were shrouded with blue. At once, the energy collapsed inward and snuffed out the flames like water.

The Deathsword fell into shards that clattered to the ground. Viru's flameflower shrank to smaller than a pin, a neon dot of nothingness. Unscathed, the Grapple glowed softly, white, and simple, and a wave rippled out of it over each shard.

One by one, they turned from sable black crystal into a living, breathing nightjar. The first had a purple stripe down its back and blue eyes. The second was smaller with a gold strip and gold eyes. The final had no stripe and no eyes but seemed ferociously intelligent. One by one, each flew off, flapping toward the sea.

"*You!*" Viru rumbled, rising and making sense of what was happening. "You *will* die, alongside your Tree." He squeezed the empty hilt so tightly a stream of blood fell from his white hand. Then he tucked the hilt away as he lunged forward like a black leopard.

He soared through the air straight for Aeron. Aeron closed his eyes, awaiting death.

All of the sudden, footsteps thundered from the left. A huge shape soared through the air, intercepting Viru in midair.

Manu!

The Ranger's large shoulder barreled into Viru's exposed waist. Aeron rolled further to the left to avoid them. He turned back only to see Viru having pinned Manu to the ground, inches in front of the ledge. His fist thrashed down once, twice, but Manu caught the third by Viru's wrist.

"*Graaah*," Manu growled. Viru's fist opened into a spidery white hand, trying to writhe free from Manu's grip.

But Viru was too strong and too nimble. His arm jabbed harder and Manu's grip splayed out wider. The tree branches shook with their weight. Viru's open hand pressed hard into Manu's face, so hard his thumb pressed Manu's jaw open wide. Not a smart move. Manu bit down, but Viru pulled away, giving Manu enough freedom to throw a fist at Viru's head. The Wraeth Prince dodged and Manu's hand swished through smoke.

They traded blows as Viru cracked his gloved fist into Manu's cheek. Manu growled and jabbed at Viru's ribs while Viru cocked back to strike. Beads of blood flew from Viru's thorned glove as his fist crashed down again. Manu grasped a flat rock by his hip and blocked the jaggy punch, causing the rock to split in two. Brilliant. Now Manu had a weapon.

Manu regripped the rock, sharp end out. The blood and bruising from Viru's glove made Manu's grin scabrous. He thrust the rock at Viru's heart. Though Viru wore no armor, only leather and a hood of smoke, he allowed the blow. Then the unthinkable happened. The rock connected with his shoulder, but it crumbled. No blood followed, and only a button-sized hole appeared in Viru's leather revealing untarnished white skin.

Viru throttled Manu's throat and the Wraeth's fist flashed through the air. Manu recoiled, but the strike landed square to his temple. *Move, Manu, move.* His nose absorbed the next two blows, then another crashed into his temple again. Manu's eyes glossed over with delirium.

Viru grasped the red cloth necklace Manu always wore. With two hands, Viru twisted it tightly like a noose and yanked. Manu's mouth opened wide, gasping for air. Manu's cheeks reddened and then deepened to purple.

He reached out for Aeron, and Aeron rose from his knees to charge at Viru. He had a straight shot, plus the element of surprise. From nowhere, an invisible forearm crushed into Aeron's chest causing Aeron to fall back in shock.

Paloma?

All of a sudden, the scent of honey came once again. Floating beside the pinned Viru was the bottle of purador. It tipped straight into Manu's mouth.

The man's eyes flared an even truer shade of sandy green than ever before, and his limp body filled with oxygenated power. He pressed his feet into the ground, his knees high, and grabbed Viru by the shoulders. Without a moment of hesitation, the Ranger hugged the Wraeth Prince close to his heart.

What are you doing, Manu? Crush him!

Manu had the thin grin of victory on his face. In a lithe flourish, he thrust his feet hard into the ground.

Praeth Virusyrus, Wraeth Prince of the Harroes, went flying off the end of the world.

And the Last Great Ranger went with him.

"*Manu!*" Paloma and Aeron cried in unison. Aeron scrambled over to the ledge. Out from a craggy hole in the side of the mountain, Reddwood Falls spat icy water straight down the cliff toward the sea, as it always had.

Twisting in midair like a spinning jenny, fighting until the last moment, Manu jabbed a hard fist into Viru's face. The hood disappeared, revealing the top of a bald, ivory white scalp with scales and a scorpion's tail striking out from its center.

The waterfall's cold steam reached up for its first victims in a thousand years. Two figures fell through the mist like droplets dissolving into the sea, still struggling with one another.

"He saved us," said Aeron, still leaning over the edge with amazement. "After all that talk... Manu saved us."

"No, Aeron," said Paloma, slowly becoming more visible. "You saved us. You trusted yourself in a way I never could have. You let darkness and light have their dance. And the Tree lives."

"But the city is burned," said Aeron, "and the Tree... it will never let me in after all the damage I've caused. Unless..."

The Grapple! Maybe I can use the Grapple to heal with water like I did with Yeats and my side.

He knelt beside the stone but it seemed to have been absorbed partway by the aerth and wouldn't budge.

"No, Aeron," said Paloma, now visible again. A glimmer radiated from the dark pink horizon around her dark skin and delicate features. "I think that was the Tree's final test for you—giving up something so powerful and trusting that the will of the Aeros would run their course."

Aeron clawed at the aerth around it but came back with nothing but dirty fingernails.

"It's your time, Aeron," said Corie, pointing toward the door. "The time is yours."

Qing placed a hand on Aeron's shoulder. He pointed a finger over toward the Tree. The tattoo of it on his arm was growing green leaves where it had once been poisoned, and a large bird circled around the crown, teeming with life.

The Tree's great door slid open from all directions, like slices of pie.

His thoughts melded with one another into a muzzy pool emotion. These were the first friends—real friends—of his life, and now he had to leave them. Pain skipped with the beat of his heart like a skipping stone.

"Thank you," he said. "All of you. I never deserved your help, but you gave it anyway."

The Grapple shrank, inch by inch, into the ground. Qing reached into his robe and pulled out something palm sized wrapped in a leaf. The paper had two words in thin, spidery script.

For Aeron.

He recognized Skylo's hand at once and bowed to Qing.

"We'll meet again soon," Paloma said, hugging Aeron as he turned to face her.

"And you'll be a Ranger when we do," said Aeron with certainty.

"No," said Paloma, shaking her head, "but you will be a Sage."

Only the topmost rim of the Grapple showed now, still glowing a faint white.

He began turning toward the tree but paused halfway and reached into his vest pocket. He unfolded the corner flaps of the Reddheart Map. It had only one red pinpoint marked, and it was right beside him. The Tree.

"Here," he said, handing the map to Paloma. "Take it. You always know exactly what you want. I admire that. It'll serve you well."

"Aeron…" said Paloma, "I can't accept this. Skylo gave it to—"

"And now I'm giving it to you," Aeron said and closed her hands around it. "When you get back to Longleath, see if you can track down the Journal. I'm afraid of what could happen with all that history in the wrong hands."

He turned before she could refuse and made for his destiny.

Approaching the tree, thin sheets of music—viola, mandolin, organ, and harmgiano—rang through the slowly closing door. The door, carved into the Tree's foot, could have fit ten Aerons stacked tall.

He paused beneath the doorway. To his right stood a lone thicket of spathodia. The last blade of sun shined as if a spotlight on the plant's red blossoms. The door frame held a familiar etching, a poem. He read only the last few lines.

Close the door.
Find the end of truth,
Hanging in the
A
i
r

Aeron stepped through the threshold, away from his past and toward who he was meant to become.

Inside the Tree smelled as a freshly printed book would, lying patiently on a picnic blanket thrown over a bed of summer grass.

Step by step passing through the entrance, Aeron's eyes adjusted. At the end of the hall, an orange lamplight poured in from the opening. He stepped out of the vestibule and into the vastest hall he had ever laid eyes upon. It stretched a mile above, like a cathedral, with every inch lined with books and art. Its awesome power hushed the music, and all Aeron could hear was his heart beating against the grandest of wonders.

EPILOGUE

◇◇◇◇◇◇

"You have no idea what's coming, do you?" the Queen Vizier had said before asking Paloma to stay in the citadel. Paloma was in no hurry to get home. Having given her an apartment in the Redd House, adorned with many flowers and furniture of rich mahogany, Paloma expected the Vizier Lera to pay her a visit.

Two nights passed after the "infiltration," and Paloma found herself in the vizier's gardens after a long day of walking the city. A half-painted easel stood in front of a wide row of hanging fuchsia, patchy bunches of blue heliopsis, crimson-yellow lillycocks, and more white flickerflower.

Today, I will consult the Reddheart Map and be off. No excuses. The old Paloma would be too afraid to see what she wants. But I am not.

She put the flat brush down into the tray and took up a smaller round brush in a cup of water beside it. After squeezing away the excess water, she dipped the brush into a small puddle of creamy white paint and raised it to finish the last building in the town square. A handful of short, wispy strokes and the corner was complete. She backed off to look at the part-burned Reddwood Citadel on her canvas.

The stories depicted the Reddwood Citadel as old and protected from time—the ever-growing woodstone, the locally formed brick and adobe, the cream white schoolhouses and paint shops and cafes. Everything in the Reddwood was believed to be idyllic, but the truth was quite different.

"You show things as they *are*," said a thick female voice from behind her. "Not how they *ought* to be."

Paloma put down the brush and turned back to face her.

"Vizier Lera," said Paloma with a bow. "I appreciate your kind words."

"I only say what is true," said Lera, adjusting her gold spectacles with her forefinger and thumb. "The space between summer and harvest is such a wonderful season." Lera cupped a flickerflower between her middle fingers. "Shall we walk?"

"I would quite like that," said Paloma. "My vizier."

Hands cupped behind her, Vizier Lera nodded and turned back around toward the gates. Paloma left the painting as it was and followed closely behind.

The round-faced woman strolled as if she had all the time in the world.

"May I ask a question, my vizier?" asked Paloma

"Yes," said Lera, nodding to an older guard who was resting on a wooden bench in the walkway. "As many as you would like."

"So much of the city burned, even places nearby," said Paloma. "Why not here?"

"The simple answer," said Lera, "is to look around you. You will see no trees, though we are in the Reddwood Citadel. The same is true of the hill leading to the Great Tree. To protect it."

"And the less simple answer?" said Paloma, as they approached the gate. Two men swung each of the reddwood doors wide open. The gravel walk stopped crunching beneath her feet as Paloma stepped out onto polished cobblestone.

Paloma loved the morning bustle of the Reddwood already. It reminded her of Longleath, had the city existed a thousand years ago. The busy street quieted as Lera stepped out followed by a wisp of ocean mist. The teasing Georgias on Lera's modest dress changed from red to a more muted yellow, exuding the humility in her mood.

Someone applauded from the right followed by another from straight ahead, and far to the left. Soon, the entire street was filled with cheering men, women, and children. Lera smiled graciously and stepped aside, facing Paloma.

"Do they always cheer for you?" Paloma asked as Lera bowed to the crowd and turned back to the left to continue their walk.

"They're not cheering for me," said Lera. "They're cheering for you."

At once Paloma felt thousands of eyes on her. "Me?"

"You saved their city," said Lera, waving to the owner of a small artisan shop—an old and dark-skinned man of the mountain with long hair and a vaunted array of infinitely colored buckskins. Then she waved to his wife, a woman with a white lace cap whose dress was a kaleidoscope of color. "And these are some of the smartest people on aerth. They know you went above and beyond. If the Tree were to die…"

A young boy streaked in front of them, racing over the cobblestone toward a rubber eggball. It rolled to a stop beneath a newly assembled street-stage, which held a group of old rail-men dressed in musical garb, smoking cigars and stringing their mandolins and horns.

"So would he," Lera gestured her head for the boy, "and all of them." She waved toward the musicians.

"It wasn't me," Paloma denied, taking off her cap. "Aeron did everything. I was a coward."

Lera shook her head. "My least favorite part of Longleath," she said, "is that its women always give their credit away."

Paloma passed the next minutes of busy road in silence. As they passed down the road, the morning became sleepier and more restful. They passed an artist's den filled with paintings of the Southern Rift with all of its brushes and endless pools of colorful paints. Lanterns swung from an Indoshinese inkwagon filled with every kind of writing stylus imaginable. The sweet scent of freshly baked bread reminded her of Pillee Hazel. Cream white cottages fringed with burnt roofs and decks were wedged between shops selling costumes, dresses, and wigs from tribes in the Long Sands.

Every cross street had the name of some famous actor or writer or country. Larkwood, Groome's Square, Jackova Street, Adobe's Den, Lefty Meadows, the Twisty Fern. The names echoed the slow pace of Reddwood life and its spice of culture.

"This city may be small," said Lera, "but its people all have different styles and habits—the dirty ones, the noisy ones, the sweet ones, the strange ones, the artistic ones. And you should see it during Bloom's feast, when the night ignites with jugglers tossing fire and piano music dances through the streets, as do its people. Luxuriating together, men and women of all ages and kinds and creeds."

The road ahead became a hill, and the sounds of life were replaced by the ocean. These last houses on the road were charred, and their shudders hung crooked from warping.

"But our city has its darkness too," Lera said, stopping to acknowledge a house that could have been beautiful, had it been free of its putrid smell and crumbled columns. A bust of an old man, charred by fire, stuck out on the porch.

They ascended the same hill she and Aeron had ascended two days before.

"These are not houses. They are people. And these people now must start over. There are at least a thousand of them. Yet..." Lera trailed off. The woman's face was stoic, but her eyes rested on the ground several feet ahead. She rubbed a hand over her mouth and continued to walk. "Yet I am not sad.

"For thousands of years, the Great Tree has been rescuing women and men, boys and girls. Think of what you saw—the salons, the sculpture gardens, the book stores, the cafes filled with elegance. Every inch of growth begins here, in the Great Sky-Tree, the Libraery, The Tree of Knowledge, whatever it is you choose to call it. And we, me included, need hardship to grow. Without it, we would be too simple to understand."

Understand what?

Paloma waited for her to continue, but the stocky woman was breathing heavier now as the slope inclined. The crown of the Tree, blanketed by clouds from the marine layer, appeared over the hill. After some time had passed, they neared the peak of the hill and Paloma bit her tongue no longer.

"Without it, we would be too simple to know... what?"

"If *we* were simple enough to understand ourselves, we would be too simple to understand," said Lera, reaching the crest. "That's why we have the Tree." Lera faced up the Tree and looked upon it as if for the first time. "Aerth's greatest gift."

Reddish, like cinnamon bark, the Tree struck hard against the bright blue morning. Where Viru's flames had scarred it, the tree now budded with green moss, aerth's natural bandage. The foot of the tree was calm and eerily empty. The loopy tangle of Viru's spidery white ropes still lay in a lump beside the left root where she had cut her friends free.

Paloma took a deep breath. A pair of stones sat beside the "end of the world." One of them was beige and turned jade by moss. Even from afar it reminded her of Manu, and the thought of him tumbling over the edge to certain death dizzied her.

Far above, a small group of primen crowded like bees on the short branch where Aeron had pointed out the houses. As the air resounded with a mixture of morning warblers and ocean mist, she wondered if Aeron was one of them.

"Ms. Murravillow," said Lera, stealing back Paloma's attention. "I would like you to stay here. An athlete, an artist, a friend with a heart of true courage and loyalty—I see great potential in you. My sister, Corie, agrees. We see the things Longleath overlooks."

Sister? Stay here—in this mythical place where it feels like holiday forever? How could I refuse a queen?

"I…" stammered Paloma, "I'm not sure what to say."

The flap of wings resounded from far above, like a drum suspended in the sky. At the midpoint of the Tree, the fenix glided circles around the Tree. The memory of their time at the church in the hardpan, with Lamark and Manu, whispered to her.

Manu always knew what he wanted and what was right. At this moment in my life, staying here is wrong.

"That's most kind of you, Madame Vizier," said Paloma. "But I think my city needs me… only they don't know it yet."

A gentle wind brought a quick aroma of sprig tea from town.

"More than you know, my dear," sighed Lera. "More than you know."

A soft fluttering zipped around Paloma's left fingers. She lifted her hand and a large bumble bee whizzed away.

"I have faith you will have other chances to learn from me, and I from you," said the vizier, brushing a lock of hair from her forehead. "What will you do next?"

"Well," said Paloma, "I think it's about time I go back to the place that knows me as nothing more than an athlete with a rich father. As far as which road... we'll have to find out."

"It seems your mind is made," said Lera, flicking a small stone with her foot. It tumbled down the hill right past the point where Aeron's foot broke through the moss. "But I will offer you one little piece of counsel. Do with it what you wish."

The woman closed her eyes for a moment and held her face high in the sun.

"Whether we are aware," she said, opening her eyes, "we all believe we can control the journey of our lives. But this life is all one beautiful, elaborate trick of Aerth. The difference is only a fool refuses to listen."

Paloma bowed her head. "Your counsel falls on fertile ground, my vizier. Thank you."

Lera turned away from the Tree. She reached into her pocket and pulled out a leaf-kerchief to wipe away a solitary tear.

"Vizier Lera," Paloma began.

"Please," interrupted the woman, "enough with the formalities. We care little for them in the Reddwood."

Paloma nodded. "How many Masons have entered the Tree, Miss Lera? And how did Aeron know the Grapple would save the Tree?"

"As far as the second question," Lera began, "I expect the Aeros themselves to be responsible. You see, so often we try to control our fate, but we are far more powerless than we like to believe. Something told him not to give up, but to give in, and he did. Call it instinct, call it luck, but at the Great Tree, we call it the Aeros."

"Could he have read it in the Journal?" asked Paloma. "From one of his ancestors who have also entered the Tree?"

"No, my dear," said Lera, "for the Tree has never, in all its years, known a Mason. Until now. And not a moment too late, for time is running out, my child. Soon, the Wraeth will be strong enough to leave the north. They will descend upon the four rifts until every man, woman, and child is disconnected or dead. If they win, this vibrant, living, uncontrollable, endlessly creative Aerth will change shape, and then it will die.

"The world needs help, I believe, to see it with new eyes. But I do not know how, nor does Master Skylo, nor any elder in the Tree. Only an archivist and a Sage can learn to speak the language of the Aerth. And now we have one."

A chill rippled down her spine.

"Maybe I should stay then," said Paloma. "To be here when Aeron is ready."

"No," said Lera with as gentle a smile as she could muster. "You have your own curves in the sky."

Paloma understood. There were battles to be won in Longleath, and getting home before the Bloom's Feast, the Harvest holiday, would be no easy feat.

Paloma pulled out the Reddheart Map and unfolded its weathered pages with care. Lera looked on with great interest.

A bright red line streaked all the way across Orifornia back to Longleath.

Lera said, "This map, and Ono Qing, will guide you through Oriendo, to the great one called Ruella. Then to the Shaman, and finally your home."

"Could it..." Paloma began, "help me track down something small?"

"I should think so," Lera replied. "If you want it enough..."

"Aeron gave me this map," said Paloma, "and in exchange I have to track something down for him."

"Well," said Lera, "if it has anything to do with Praeth Viru, I'd rather not know. For now."

Paloma grinned.

It most certainly does.

"Should you need help, seek out a man named Arkwright."

"How will I find him?"

"Given your... profession... he shouldn't be hard to find."

"Thank you, Lera," said Paloma. "I hope one day to repay the kindness."

"You will," said Lera, beginning the descent back to town. "What will you do first after returning home?" asked the vizier.

"First, I'll see my family," said Paloma turning back one final time, for one final look. "Then... well, you know, the last few years I've come to hate Cannaroo for some reason. But I think I'm going to have a ball out on the pitch this season..."

Paloma breathed in a marvelous gulp of mountain air and turned back one final time, wondering how many books Aeron was reading inside the Tree of Knowledge.

ACKNOWLEDGMENTS

◇◇◇◇◇◇

If you've come this far, you'll know that I believe that each and every inkling of our lives is connected—every event that's happened, every dream we've had, every person we've met. The list of people whom deserve acknowledging could go on forever, so I'll do my best, but apologize in advance to those who I've omitted. I still appreciate you.

First off, I cannot thank each and every one of the Streich *mishpacha*. Mom, Dad, Matt, Bryan, Ashley, Cooper, Lindsey, Dean, Holden, Neil, Lisa, Puck, Fran, Jake, Jon, Jessie, and Evelyn. The Dakiches, Rings, and Sterns. You've all supported and put up with me over the years—without your support, this book would not exist.

Starting at the roots of the tree, I want to acknowledge the 02818, my hometown and community. Every one of my teachers, coaches, and administrators in the East Greenwich school's system—I thank you for creating a challenging but inclusive environment for growth.

I could fill a whole book with the amazing friends and teammates of my early life, but there are a few I want to thank outright. David K. Casey, Brendan Higgins, Ryan DePasquale, Sam Podbelski, Nick Rossetti, Bradley Van

Fechtmann, Jonny Lamendola, Max Palmer, Kevin Mason, Jason Light, Kellie Mason, Timothy Graul, Ethan Zink, Scott Cullinane, Mitch Maloof, Marcus Caron, Emma Tesler, Ryan Barnes, John Drumm, Carter Bates, Andi Gladstone, Sam Covington, Julia Elson, Holly Macdonald, A.J. O'Connell, Davis Settipane, Alex Christie, Jake Dellagrotta, Divya Mahadevan, Natalie Wong, Gwen Luvara, Leticia Luz, Skylar LeBlanc, Kerri Whelan, Julia Waicberg, Leah Shoer, Anna Palmer, Juliana Walsh, Roxanne Comito, McCaffrey Cooney, and Keri Pallister.

Also to Chris Spock, Chad Verdi, Chris Gemma, John Macnie, Sam Toolson, Nick Migliori, Kyle Palmer, Alex Cleary, David Hopkins, Jack Trutza, Ryan Gavin, Colin Bernier, Patrick Lavan, Peter Hunziker, Jake Moss, Kyle Matus, Nolan Cooney, Fabien Nascimento, Matt Cruise, Jack Payette, Tyler Amaral, Matthew Sgrignari, Chris Sgrignari, Jason Harlam, Alex White, Paul Andreson, Jack Feeney, Brett Estes, and Andrew Miner.

Likewise, to all my friends from the college years at Nova, in Madrid, at Georgetown. To name only a few: James Nirappel, Brady Galen, Dylan Faulkner, Tom Clemente, Christopher Lee, Daniel Roman, Connor Peterson, Patty-Jane Geller, Marshall Huggins, Violaine Jacques, Gajan Vivek, Carter White, Mike Hilyard, Maria Muñoz de Fernando, Claudia Múgica Soto, Hugo Vidal Ochoa, Miguel Saez Poveda, Patrick Browne, and Anderson De Andrade.

Now I pause to single out a pair of Georgetown professors who shirked the conventional and encouraged Nandini, Alex, and me to co-write our first novella. I thank you, Maureen Corrigan and Barbara Feinman Todd, for your warmth and for setting the wheel in motion.

A similar thanks to Cal Newport, Ani Flys Junquera, Dr. Maghan Keita, Dr. Earl Bader, and many other professors at Nova and Georgetown, as well as to Dean Chester Gillis for a book recommendation and his kindness when I most needed it.

There are always the people you meet "in the wild"—not in school, on teams, nor in other institutions. As it so happens, they happen to be some of the people I most appreciate and admire. Thank you Daniel Breyer, Danielle Strachman, Patrick McGinnis, Sonia Hunt, Bryan Talebi, Peter Crane, William O'Herron, Kim Emerson, Leon David Wilkinson, Peter Keller, Jim Brown, Corky Logue, Jazmine Sausameda, Tod Moore, Brendan McKenna, Christopher Schroeder, Rory Gale, Matt Krenik, Alex Smith, Jeremiah Steinert, Rachael Bird, Keith Amidon, Dom Centorino, Adam Friedman, Randy Horn, Niki Gastinel, Chris Johnson, Molly Colvin, Matt Oakley, Josephine Pond, James Medina, Mark Etem, Andrew Grosser, Luke Kim, Wendy Salome, Conor McAnally, Nate Newman, Joseph Sunde, Scott Buckstaff, William Siegel, Greg Buckner, Emily Rowley, Adrianna Polit, Jordan Gross, Callen Turnbull, Gita Abhiraman, and Dr. Selena Bartlett.

Plus too many to count from the Next Gen community like Paul McNeal, Malekai Mischke, Artem Koker, Andrew Frawley, David Kobrosky, Nick Staib, Dan Schneider, Alaina Warburton, and of course Dylan, Justin, and Rachel.

Now I would be remiss not to mention a few people who feel like extended family. Beth, Jeff, Adam, and Elissa Salk, Pam Noble, Beth and Kevin Hopkins, Jane and Mike Litner, Trevor Toolson, Peter and the Borowsky's, Kevin Malloy, Michelle and Chad Verdi, Rosemary Miner, Wendy S. Buckler, Tom and Kim Spock, Janice and Joe Cooney, Mark and Sue Cruise, Kevin C. Malloy, Julie and Mike Gemma, and Mark and Pam Macnie.

I also want to thank David Vargas Racero, Hitesh Patel, Carolina Cioara, Tara Kabatoff, Patrick Huang, and Vish Kumar for their business mentorship.

Three years ago I mentioned a 250,000-word manuscript to Eric Koester. Without Eric, Brian Bies, Haley Newlin, Michael Bailey, Amanda Brown, Mackenzie Finklea, Gjorji Pejkovski, Josip Perić, Stephanie McKibben, and everyone at New Degree Press, this story might never have seen the light of day.

Books, like trees, outlive us all.

Thank you all for the support. If we've met, you helped mine grow.